.J. Tata

ion. Names, characters, places and incidents are prod-
magination or are used fictitiously and should not be
resemblance to actual events, locales, organizations or
l, is entirely coincidental.

LLC (USA).
g.com

alog Number 2009928924

2-09-6

rry Rostant
J. Tremblay
y J. Tremblay
ott

o at: www.ajtata.com.

10 9 8 7 6 5 4 3 2 1

A

This is a work of fict
ucts of the author's i
construed as real. Any
persons, living or dead

Variance Publishing
1610 South Pine St.
Cabot, AR 72023,
(501) 843-BOOK

Published by Variance
www.variancepublishin

Library of Congress Ca

ISBN: 1-935142-09-7
ISBN-13: 978-1-93514

Cover Illustration by La
Jacket Design by Stanley
Interior layout by Stanle
Map by Jackie McDerm

Visit A.J. Tata on the we

To my parents Bob and Jerri Tata,
who taught me to always care.

ACKNOWLEDGEMENTS

I have to start out by thanking the awesome Variance Publishing team, especially Tim Schulte, Jeremy Robinson, Shane Thomson, and Stanley Tremblay. They are a first class group that works tirelessly to get it right. Shane, as my editor, did a superb job of working through both the content and the line edits. He made *Rogue Threat* a better book, plain and simple. Stan steadily promotes all things Variance and is a huge help in the public relations department. Tim is the best friend and publisher an author could ask for.

As usual, I appreciate the technical expertise of Rick "The Gun Guy" Kutka, who ensures this officer employs his weapons systems properly.

I also want to thank the team at Ascot Media. Trish Stevens and Rodney Foster have worked around the clock to get the word out. As many of you know, I dedicated 100% of my royalties to the USO Metro DC Hospital Services Fund. Trish and her team helped drive that total royalty donation to the USO to nearly $30,000.

Elaine Rogers and her dedicated Metro-DC USO team deserve all of our thanks every day for what they do for our soldiers, sailors, airmen, and Marines. It continues to be my privilege to donate all of the royalties from Sudden Threat, hard cover and paperback, to this great organization.

As always, thanks to Amanda for helping my dream come true.

Rogue Threat holds a special place in my author's library. I enjoyed developing the characters beyond Sudden Threat and introducing Peyton O'Hara, the lithe Irish-American tough girl. This story began back in 2003 when I asked myself, "What happened to the weapons of mass destruction in Iraq?"

I surprised myself with my own answer, "Does anyone really care?"

ROGUE THREAT

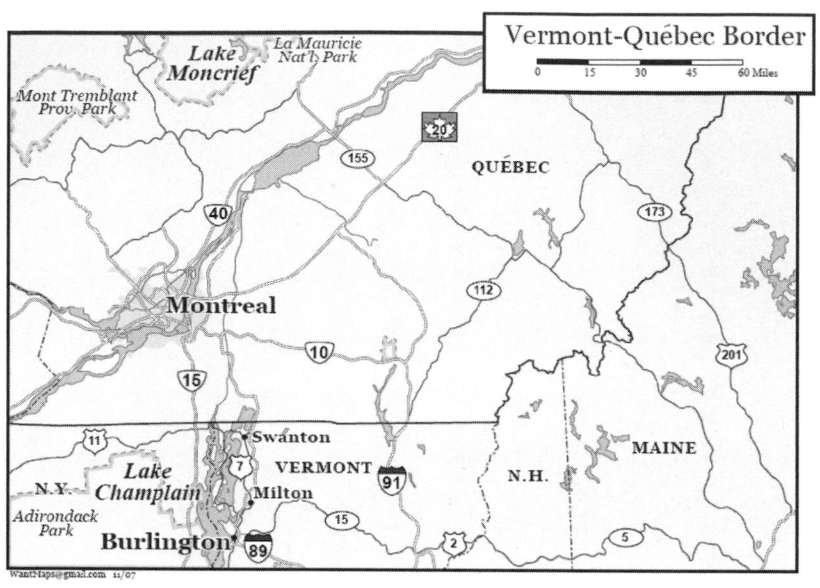
Vermont-Québec Border
0 15 30 45 60 Miles
Lake Moncrief
La Mauricie Nat'l. Park
Mont Tremblant Prov. Park
20
155
QUÉBEC
40
173
112
Montreal
10
201
15
11
Swanton
7
VERMONT
91
MAINE
N.H.
N.Y.
Lake Champlain
Milton
Adirondack Park
15
Burlington
89
2
5
WantMaps@gmail.com 11/07

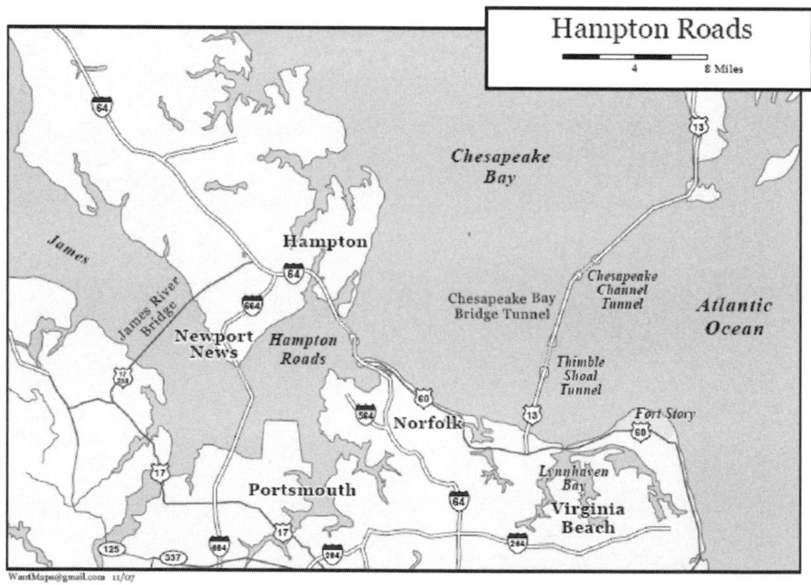
Hampton Roads
4 8 Miles
64
13
Chesapeake Bay
James
Hampton
64
James River Bridge
664
Chesapeake Channel Tunnel
Chesapeake Bay Bridge Tunnel
Atlantic Ocean
Newport News
Hampton Roads
Thimble Shoal Tunnel
60
564
Norfolk
13
Fort Story
60
Lynnhaven Bay
17
Portsmouth
64
Virginia Beach
17
125
337
664
264
264
WantMaps@gmail.com 11/07

PROLOGUE

IRAQ, FEBRUARY 27, 1991, DESERT STORM

Jacques Ballantine snatched his AK-47 rifle from the desert floor and raced toward his command vehicle, stumbling as the artillery volley shook the ground beneath his feet. A funnel of sand blew into the sky, already darkened from hundreds of oil-well fires that Saddam had ordered set the day before.

"Henri," Jacques stammered, approaching the back of the drab olive vehicle filled with radios. "Are you okay?"

Henri Ballantine pulled a crewman's helmet from his head and leaned out of the small hatch of the Russian-built armored vehicle. His face showed the strain of weeks of U.S.-led Allied bombing of their defensive positions.

"Fine," Henri said. "Orders?" The two brothers spoke in English to keep their subordinates from eavesdropping.

"We fight," Jacques said. "We stand and fight."

Jacques' younger brother stared at him a moment and then nodded.

"Hand me my backpack," Jacques ordered, motioning with his left hand while holding his rifle in his right.

Henri looked at him briefly and then turned toward the inside of the small command center. A moment later, Henri's hand reappeared through the hatch of the track with a dusty rucksack about the size of a high school kid's book bag.

"This," Jacques said, taking the bag and shaking it, "this will set us free."

Henri looked at him with doubting eyes, the cackle of machine-gun fire emphasizing his skepticism.

"The enemy is just over the ridge. What good will this bag do?" Henri challenged.

"This will save us, brother. Trust me," Jacques said.

"I have always trusted you . . ."

Machine-gun fire danced at Jacques' feet as he turned toward the American line advancing upon them. "Give the order to counterattack. Now!" he shouted and dashed the fifty meters to his T-72 tank, where he saw his driver's eyes wide with fear.

Jacques Ballantine commanded the Tawalkana division of Saddam Hussein's Republican Guard. Childhood friends of Hussein's, the Ballantine brothers had moved with their parents to France when they were adolescents. Their original names, Beqir and Aliwan, had given way to their mother's hope for a new life. In the suburbs of Lyon, they had lived a simple life. Then the two boys left home and returned to Tikrit, where they reestablished loyalties with their childhood friend. When Saddam had decided to attack Kuwait, his loyal and trusted friends received high-level assignments in his elite Republican Guard tank corps.

Jacques scrambled inside his tank, chased by the loud report of American M-1 Abrams tank rounds whistling overhead.

"Launch the counterattack," he shouted into the radio handset. "Attack! Attack!"

Popping his head through the turret, he looked over the long bore of the tube. His driver had positioned the tank perfectly in a low spot so that only the main gun was visible as it stretched along at ground level.

"Counterattack is on the way," Henri reported to his brother over the command radio net.

Jacques could picture his younger brother sitting in the command vehicle, peering through the periscope, wondering what would happen next. The Americans would surely overwhelm them, but they had always seemed to find a way to survive.

"I'm getting reports our infantry is surrendering, Jacques."

Jacques Ballantine stared into the dark horizon, the sounds of war buzzing around him like a burst beehive. He could not surrender. Ever. Grabbing his AK-47, he radioed his brother, saying, "Meet me in the wadi to our front." Then he jumped from the turret of his tank to the desert sand.

He ran toward cover, watching as twelve of his T-72 Soviet-produced tanks raced from their hidden positions and began to suppress the American M-1s and M-2 Bradley Fighting Vehicles. The long bores of the T-72s awkwardly hung over the chassis of the tanks, spitting flame and causing the entire tank to heave upward at every shot. The counterattack accounted for stopping four enemy vehicles before Jacques noticed a larger formation moving to their flank.

The air filled with the incessant chatter of coaxial machine guns and the loud report of tank main-gun rounds breaking the sound barrier as they sought out their targets.

Crouching in the wadi, Jacques turned and began firing at an American infantry column that had flanked his position. He saw the American soldiers rushing for a few seconds and then hitting the ground, never allowing him to get a decent shot.

Jacques looked over his shoulder as a sabot round crashed into the hull of his tank just a few meters behind him, causing the turret to pop off and spin like a top on the sand. The fireball reached out and licked his face, a demon from hell saying, "Come with me."

Not yet, he thought.

Jacques shouted to the men of his unit, now beginning to run from their tanks as they watched the others explode in bright orange fireballs all around them.

Jacques turned to look for Henri and shouted, "With me, men! Fight with me!"

Suddenly someone was on top of him, wrestling him to the ground. "Cease fire!" an officer shouted, holding a 9mm Beretta to Jacques' head.

Out of the corner of his eye, Jacques saw Henri rushing over the hill. It took the man less than a second to fire two rounds into Henri's face, killing him. Jacques watched his younger brother's face explode as if someone had placed a stick of dynamite into his mouth.

Pumped with adrenaline, Jacques moaned, "No!"

He twisted free from his assailant's grip and attempted to escape, but the man butt-stroked him with the pistol, making everything seem like it was moving in slow motion. And before he knew it, the soldier had flex-cuffed him, and he was being carted away in the back of an American command post vehicle.

As Jacques bounced in the back of the dusty personnel carrier he felt a knife cut away his backpack. Turning to look, he watched the American paw his way through the contents and then zip the bag closed before placing it near the radio mounts on the other side of the cabin. Jacques watched him pick up the radio handset and give crisp, clear orders to his men. Then he heard the call to higher headquarters.

"We have captured the Tawalkana commander, General Jacques Ballantine," he said.

How do they know who I am? Ballantine strained to see the young officer's nametag. He was wearing a sand-colored battle dress uniform. The officer hooked the handset onto a piece of cord hanging from the top of the inside of the crew compartment and turned toward his prisoner.

Ballantine sat dazed as a medic applied ointment to the cut on his head. The medic's skilled hands worked diligently on the laceration the pistol had left on his forehead, applying bandages the best he could in the rumbling track.

"Speak English?" the lieutenant asked.

Ballantine nodded.

"We're taking you to headquarters."

Ballantine saw the lieutenant's jaw tighten and flex. His green eyes radiated from a face coated with sand and dust as he leaned over to offer water. That's when Ballantine saw the name.

Garrett. Lieutenant Garrett.

As Garrett's face grew closer, Ballantine saw a scar that hadn't healed properly, cutting across the man's chin. It almost looked like a cleft, but ran horizontal to the ground. He stared at it.

"Brother shot me. Accident. Here, drink some water." Garrett reached out to his prisoner with a canteen cup. "We need you healthy."

Ballantine gave him a hard stare through his narrow, dusty eyes.

"You killed my brother."

Garrett held his gaze for a few seconds, but it seemed like an hour. They bounced in the loud track. Metal clanked everywhere. The radio hummed a loud static buzz, pierced by rapid spot reports from scouts. Despite the noise, both men sensed silence.

Lieutenant Zachary Garrett was thinking about the time his brother, Matt, and he had been hunting. Their dog Ranger was about fifty feet in front, pointing with one leg at an old corn field. Five quail jumped and flew directly at them. Matt swung his shotgun, firing twice by reflex. A pellet from the second shot nicked Zachary. Zachary, older by three years, resisted the urge to punch his little brother. Instead, he worked him hard in the fields with the horses and cattle. He was close to his brother, and Zachary wondered at that moment how he would feel if this man had just killed him. He lowered his eyes.

The moment was not lost on Ballantine.

Garrett held out a cup of water for Ballantine, spilling half of it as the vehicle lurched. He pulled on his crewman's helmet and climbed into the turret, leaving a young soldier to stand guard over the captive.

Jacques Ballantine listened as the lieutenant returned to his command role and delivered concise orders. *Professional*, he thought.

Exhausted, Ballantine's mind spiraled toward sleep. He watched endless replays of Lieutenant Garrett shooting his brother in the face. Henri was dead. His insurance policy was in the hands of his captor, its significance unrealized, for now. Secret deals for secret weapons were captured in a few conspiratorial conversations, and he was certain they would be useful with the right interrogator. He was glad he had done his homework. The seeds of a plan to use these insidious weapons came to him. The Americans had no idea of what had transpired or what was to come.

In his drifting mind, Garrett's quick-drawing pistol never stopped firing. To stop the noise in his head, Ballantine made a promise to himself: kill Lieutenant Garrett, kill his brother . . .

And then retrieve his backpack.

PART 1:
SEEDS OF REVENGE
(TWELVE YEARS LATER)

CHAPTER 1

APRIL 2003, FRIDAY EVENING, 1700 HOURS, LOUDOUN COUNTY, VIRGINIA

Matt Garrett stood and stretched, physical scars sending waves of pain through his body. He looked at the fading blue sky from the deck of his Loudoun County home, perhaps seeking a nod, guidance—anything really—from his dead brother Zachary.

A paramilitary operative with the CIA, Matt had been wounded in the same fight in the Philippines last year, where his brother was killed. Coincidence, mostly, but the fact remained that Zachary was dead, and Matt had almost died.

He lowered his head and stared at his backyard, the terrain gently sloping away from his one-story brick rambler. Thoughts of Zachary had dominated him over the past year and had stymied his recovery. He knew he needed to move on, but he refused to let go.

Matt thought fondly of Zachary's graduation from West Point, his brother's service in Desert Storm, his agonizing decision to leave the service and work the family farm in the mid-nineties, and then, after the 9/11 attacks, his firm resolve to get into the fight. Which he had done.

Which had gotten him killed.

"If only he had stayed on the farm," Matt muttered.

It was nearly six p.m., and despite Matt's near-paralytic state regarding Zachary, he did sense an uncertain stir of change in the wind. Perhaps that was what kept him hanging on. The towering pine trees in his back yard bowed with the breeze, and Matt closed his eyes, trying to understand everything that had transpired.

Operation Iraqi Freedom had kicked off and was an apparent success so far, but he had his doubts. With all the fanfare over Iraq, he couldn't help but pick at the open scab of his failure to kill al Qaeda senior leadership when he had had the shot. Now the opportunity was lost forever. True, high-ranking officials had denied his kill chain, and a JDAM bomb had struck closer to his team than to the al Qaeda leadership, but he still blamed himself. That failure, coupled with his brother's death and Matt's own physical wounds, were enough to make him doubt himself. And in his business, there was no margin for doubt—no second guessing.

Since when did you start following orders, Garrett? Should have stayed, taken the shot.

He shook his head and looked to his left, where a small hill rose above the stream. There was nothing but forest for about three miles. The April evening was filled with the hum of spring in the Virginia countryside. Through the pine thickets Matt saw budding dogwoods and darting squirrels. The temperature hovered in that optimistically comfortable range where he would begin to wear T-shirts and shorts when relaxing at his home. He stared at the pieces of a fading blue sky that shone through the pine tips to the rear of his property. Then he looked down at his batting cage.

Matt walked down the deck steps, grabbed a Pete Rose 34-inch bat, and stepped into the rectangular mesh netting. He liked the thin handle and the wide barrel of the bat. Even if Charlie Hustle had been banned from baseball, it was still the best bat in the sport. Matt flipped a switch on a small post, and the machine hummed to life. Some people meditated, Matt figured; he hit baseballs.

Absently, he wondered if he entered the cage to duel with himself. Whether it was post traumatic stress or prolonged grieving, Matt was in persistent internal conflict. Sometimes he had gnawing at him the urge to get in his old Porsche, fill the gas tank, and drive dark, dangerous roads at high speeds.

Other times he stepped into the batting cage.

His angst was no different, he figured, than the way some of his soldier buddies who were suffering post traumatic stress might wake up screaming, grab for their elusory weapon in the middle of the night, and move through the house, methodically clearing each room, calling "One up" to invisible partners, buddies who had been killed right next to them in combat.

Matt needed to fill that emptiness left by Zach's absence and burn his adrenaline. The grief welled inside him, he repressed it, and then it reappeared somewhere else like a magician's trick. One moment it was an obvious thought; the next it was a repressed memory. Post traumatic stress was tricky that way. The repressed memory went latent, seemingly forgotten, only to surge forward at the least expected time, manifesting itself as a spontaneous action, sometimes benign, often not. Only on intense reflection or therapy could the sufferer follow the byzantine trail back to the original mournful feeling.

So today, instead of a suicidal drag race in the Porsche, Matt stared down 95-mph fastballs moving with enough velocity to kill him. No helmet. That was part of the risk, the game. This way, at least, his edginess was more predictable, like Russian roulette. Which bullet, which fastball, might hit him? He never knew when one tire might catch the stitches and spit at him a left-handed curve ball hard and fast directly at his temple. Just as bad as a bullet. Maybe worse. He would see it coming. Would he duck?

Or smile and stand there, ready to join his brother?

The first ball blew past him before he could even think about swinging. With each successive pitch, his cut migrated toward what it once was. He had been an above-.300 collegiate batsman. Soon he was hitting a few frozen ropes back at the machine, which was protected by a wire mesh fence. The calm evening rang resolutely with the distinct crack of the wooden 34 against the quiet hum of the pitching machine's spinning tires.

Matt focused, and he tried to forget about Zachary's death. The War on Terror had claimed many casualties. The fact that Zachary had survived, even thrived, during Operation Desert Storm, only to succumb to a small-scale action in the Philippines, would forever confound Matt.

As he rifled balls into the far netting, his mind drifted to a few men that he politely referred to as *those bastards*, the upper-echelon Rolling Stones groupies who conspired to start a war in the Philippines simply to avert another war in Iraq.

A fastball came whipping at him, and there was Bart Rathburn, killed by Abu Sayyaf rebels. Swing. Crack. Rathburn, who had been an assistant secretary of defense using the pseudonym Keith Richards, was gone into the back of the net.

The tires then spit him a slider, low and away: Taiku Takishi, a Japanese businessman turned rogue, also known as Charlie Watts. Smooth swing. Solid wood. Takishi, who led the Japanese invasion of the Philippines, was gone into right field.

Another pitch knuckled straight at him. He swung defensively and swatted away the face of Secretary of Defense Robert Stone. Stone, using the nom de guerre Mick Jagger, orchestrated the entire conspiracy. Following Stone's knuckleball was a 98-mph fastball that blew past him.

Ronnie Wood.

Though not located in the year since his disappearance, CIA director Frank Lantini, Matt was convinced, played the ever elusive Ronnie Wood.

Every time I was close, he moved me.

But there were other possibilities, Matt knew. His mind briefly churned, visualizing these Beltway heroes who pulled the marionette strings of so many great Americans, using them as the fodder that they were. A bolt of anger shot through Matt when he realized that it was only those with whom you served that you could trust to be on your flank, to help you in a time of crisis. That notion brought his mind reeling back to Zachary.

Why couldn't I save him?

Like the baseballs punching into the far end of the net, Matt's angst over Zachary's death was tightly confined in his thoughts by a web of guilt and remorse.

The injuries to his body—the gunshots to the abdomen and shoulder and the bayonet slice across the forearm that screamed with every swing—had mostly healed. And with each pitch and swing Matt focused his mind on the task at hand, hitting the baseball, the action removing just a bit of the pain, working out physical and emotional scars. *Just keep swinging*, he told himself. *Stay in the game.*

"Keep your elbow up."

Matt turned toward the voice just enough to move his body into the path of one of those 95-mph fastballs—bb's, aspirin tablets, rockets, as he used to call them—whipping in high and inside. It struck him squarely on the left shoulder.

"Son of a . . ." Matt took a quick knee and pressed the stop button.

A woman came running toward him. "I am so sorry."

"Aw, man." Another pitch rifled above his head punching with a demonic thud into the back of tarp. "Go get some ice out of the freezer. Back door's open." The machine spit a final ball that landed about halfway toward Matt, the rawhide rolling next to his knee.

Gotta go easy in there, Matt thought to himself. Adrenaline dumped, he shook his head. Truthfully, he had been pushing the envelope in his rehab in an attempt to get back into the fight.

Matt pulled up his shirt-sleeve and noticed a welt was already forming.

It took a minute to register that he had no idea who he had just sent into his house. An attractive woman returned with a towel filled with ice. She was wearing a blue pants suit with a white blouse. A string of lapis beads circling her neck made Matt think back to Afghanistan, where lapis was mined extensively.

"Who are you?" he asked through gritted teeth as she put the ice on his shoulder.

"Name's Peyton O'Hara." She showed him a badge. "The vice president of the United States requires your services, Mr. Garrett."

"So he sent you?"

"It seems your phone is—"

"I shut the phone off." Matt looked down at the welt on his shoulder.

"As I was saying, I work with the vice president. He needs your help."

Matt grabbed the towel and took a step back, registering the concern on the young woman's face. She was a natural redhead with hazel eyes and a nice figure. Setting the towel on the deck rail, he pulled off his shirt, catching her eyes glancing at his muscular frame. At six foot two, he was considerably taller than she. Though he had been recovering from wounds, he had also been lifting and running almost every day. Her quick glance confirmed in his mind that he was, perhaps, in the best physical condition of his life. He reapplied the ice to the bruise.

"What happened?" She pointed at his forearm.

"Hunting accident."

"I see." Peyton looked at him suspiciously. She took in his green eyes and light brown hair, strangely glad the vice president had asked her to come find this enigma. "And there?" She pointed at his stomach where a large scar that looked like a grotesque blossoming flower had healed, revealing minor lumps of skin that never reformed in exactly the right place.

"Appendectomy," Matt said, stone-faced.

"Must have been one hell of a huge appendix," she smiled.

"What are you? A hooker or something? Blake Sessoms send you here?" Matt asked. "Like those strippers dressed as cops?"

Blake was Matt's closest childhood friend, save Zachary.

"Funny," Peyton said.

Matt looked down at the welt on his shoulder.

"Another lump for the collection?" she quipped, following his eyes to the rising lump on Matt's upper arm. "Adds some symmetry don't you think?"

Ignoring her comment, he sat in a two-dollar lawn chair he had picked up from K-Mart a few weeks earlier. It was either that or five hundred dollars for deck furniture that was not as comfortable.

"So what's Hellerman want?" Matt's voice was flat.

"He wants you to come over to his Middleburg mansion. That's where his alternate command post is now and where he's set up a special task force on terrorism. He wants you to be a part of that. He's talked to Houghton at CIA, who said you're available. With the Iraq war going well, he is making sure we're watching our six on other extremists."

Matt stared at her a moment. He had been out of action since being wounded and was now being considered by the president to serve as a special assistant to the CIA director. He figured Houghton would never say no to the president or vice president after his recent confirmation as Lantini's replacement at CIA. Matt was on a leave of absence from his position with his unit and figured Houghton thought this might be the best way to ease him back into the fight. But Matt was part mercenary and part intelligence analyst and had never participated in a special task force—other than raiding some dirtbag's hideout to kill him.

"And he wants me to ask you about your work on the Predator project," she mentioned, almost as an afterthought.

Matt calmly looked to his left and then his right, and then turned his head toward her and leveled his eyes on hers.

"Predators? What are those?" Matt asked.

She stepped toward him.

"Everyone knows about the former administration's technology transfers to China, Mr. Garrett. What I'm telling you is that we may have some new information, and we don't have much time to sort it out. We're five miles from civilization, and if it will make you feel better, we can whisper, but we really need to know what you saw in China."

Matt had spent two months touring China as a photojournalist, trying to find eighteen AWOL unmanned aerial vehicles (UAVs) that were not so much missed for their aerodynamics as they were for their payload capabilities. The leads had taken him to the Philippines, where he got caught up in the insurgency that had wounded him and killed his brother.

"Sounds like you should speak to somebody who knows what you're talking about. Maybe the Rolling Stones? You a groupie?" *Those bastards.* "This is a dead end." *Literally, it was for Zachary,* he thought with a wince.

She stared at him with piercing eyes. She was a cross between Julianne Moore and a Fox News anchorwoman whose name he had forgotten. She crossed her arms and looked away, thinking. Matt saw her eyes fixate on the batting cage then return to his abdominal scar. Then she looked at him with a satisfied countenance, appearing to have figured something out.

"Well, the vice president thinks you know something you're not telling us," she said.

"You're right." Matt considered her comment. "The Predators are a hockey team in Nashville, right?" He placed the towel on the deck, stood and walked over to the railing of the deck and leaned back, towering over her by at least eight inches.

She pursed her lips and said, "Funny." She showed him her National Security Agency badge again, which he agreed looked authentic enough. Then she pulled out her Top Secret White House Basement Operations Center pass.

"Impressive."

"Need my shoe size?" she asked.

Matt smirked. "Screw the vice president." Then, "Sorry, if that's in your job description, you know."

Peyton stared at him and smiled. "They told me you could be an ass. I just didn't expect it to surface so quickly."

Matt considered her a moment. He figured her mental calculations had been to determine which course to choose: sympathetic to his loss and injuries or hard-nosed negotiator completing an assigned task? Her selection of the firm approach caused him to gain a measure of respect for her. He didn't want her sympathy.

"Who cares? I put everything in the report, and nobody believed it. We couldn't get jack past the political appointees. If you're truly working with Hellerman, then you know the Stones conspiracy set us back light years."

"I know that was a difficult time for you—"

"Difficult?" Matt asked, incredulous. "You have no idea what you're talking about, lady."

Matt picked up his baseball bat and tossed it from hand to hand, working off his anger and frustration. Who was this person interrupting his sanctuary, his ritual?

Peyton eyed the bat. He figured that she had read his dossier and knew about his mandatory shrink visits. The psychiatrist said he had a hair-trigger temper. *Good, make her think*, Matt thought.

"This is important, Matt. You know my credentials," Peyton said, keeping an eye on the bat.

"So we discuss top secret, compartmented information on my back deck? Here's a clue. Check out a warehouse in Mindanao in the Philippines. I went there, got shot, and then came home. You know the rest."

"Well, actually, I knew what you just said, but something doesn't add up."

"What's that?" He was mildly interested but tiring quickly. He had baseballs to hit. With another month of convalescent leave on his docket before his return to Langley, he needed to sort out a few more things. Unscrew his head. On that note, he flipped the bat against the deck railing, walked into the house and grabbed two Budweisers from the refrigerator. He handed one to Peyton by the top. She knew the trick and turned the bottle while he held his vice grip on the cap. With a slight sound of gas escaping they opened the bottle, and she took a sip. He popped his open with the same hand and drank half the beer in one tilt.

"Let's just say we're concerned about the location of those Predators, based upon some intercepts we've received." She looked away as she spoke, holding her amber bottle chest high.

"Oh, I get it. I share top secret information with you, and you share bullshit with me. Seems fair," he fumed, his temper edging to the surface. He took another long pull on the Bud.

"Listen, we've got traffic that says the Chinese might try to use those Predators against Taiwan, but it's not clear yet."

"Okay. But I've told you everything I know. I tracked them to China and Mindanao by studying shipping logs, going to the ports, bribing dirt poor dockworkers, and even shooting a couple of people. I suggest you do the same," he said.

"Did you ever see any of the Predators?" she asked, ignoring his rebuff.

"It's all in the report, Peyton."

"If it was all in the report, Matt, I wouldn't be here."

They held their beer bottles in front of themselves as if they were ready to fence, Matt's tilting toward her, hers toward him.

They exchanged long, hard stares. The obnoxious ringing of Peyton's cell phone interrupted the painful silence. She answered it, "Peyton," and listened a moment before handing it to Matt.

"Matt, this is the vice president. I need you to meet me at Dulles Airport in an hour. VIP gate. Bring a suitcase. Tell Peyton to come along too. I'll be waiting." Then the line went dead.

"What's this all about?" he asked, handing the phone back to her.

"Beats me, but we should probably get moving."

The cool spring breeze snapped past them both. Truthfully, today he could not care less what the man wanted.

"Whatever. I'll see you there," he said as Peyton bounced down the steps. He casually followed her, a guard ushering an unwanted visitor to the exit. He stopped at the corner of his brick rambler and watched as she mounted a Ducati Street Fighter.

"Don't be late, Matt Garrett."

She shook her hair, donned the helmet, and turned the ignition. The bike roared to life. She punched the gear box and rolled away.

"Bizarre," Matt muttered and then strolled inside his house.

CHAPTER 2

DULLES AIRPORT, NORTHERN VIRGINIA

Matt yanked his "go-bag" from beneath his bed, which he always kept ready and within arm's reach as he slept. He checked the Baby Glock and ensured he had four magazines of 9mm ammunition, two with full-metal-jacket rounds and two with hollow point. He opened his Duane Dieter Spec Ops knife with a quick flip of his wrist, then pressed the detent button to collapse the blade. Handling his weapons made him wonder just where the hell Lantini might be . . .

He then quickly stuffed a variety of clothing and toiletries in the small duffel. A few minutes later, he jumped in the fifteen-year-old Porsche 944 he had purchased from the same junk yard in which he had found the pitching machine. He ran the "black bullet" wide open, quickly covering the short distance to the airport.

Pressing speed dial on his cell phone, he listened as Blake Sessoms, his childhood best friend, answered.

"This is Blake."

"Blake, Matt here."

"Hey, wildman. Long time."

"Got a few things to talk about, but don't have much time right now." He paused, then continued. "It has been tough without Zach around."

"I miss him, too," Blake said. "It's been a year . . . a tough year, brother."

The two friends let a moment pass over the crackling cell phone airwaves.

"Roger that," Matt whispered.

"Going anywhere you can tell me?" Blake asked.

"I'm not sure what's happening, but wanted to let you know I am heading out of town. We'll catch up later."

"Sure thing, bro."

"Are you going to be around in the next few days?"

"Yeah."

"I'll call you."

The two friends hung up. Matt reflected briefly that it had been months since he had spoken to Blake, with whom he used to chat a few times a week. They had grown up together in the Blue Ridge, playing baseball and fishing, and they had both started college at the University of Virginia. Matt opted for a career in the Agency; Blake chose a path that eventually led him to Virginia Beach and a small fortune.

Downshifting into the arrivals/departures fork in the road leading to the airport terminals, Matt saw the sign for the VIP gate and followed the arrows until he was stopped at a closed chain-link gate in a remote area about a half mile from the main terminal. The gate opened as he slowed.

Pulling through the opening, he saw the shiny, black scalp of Alvin Jessup, the vice president's lead Secret Service agent.

"Hey, Alvin," he said, rolling down his window. Jessup, a hulking man dressed in a black overcoat, looked every bit the former collegiate fullback. He walked up to Matt's window with a dour face.

"Finally coming out of your hole, Garrett?" Jessup asked.

"Just following orders, Alvin."

"Well, you just keep on following orders and move along before all my money falls out of my pockets and into yours."

"Was that the last time I saw you?" Matt said.

"Uh huh." Alvin nodded. "Ain't playing poker with you anymore, that's for damn sure. Whoever heard of giving all the money to a homeless shelter, anyway?"

"Didn't feel right keeping your life's savings," Matt said. "What's going on?"

"Not sure, but the man's been on the phone with Fort Bragg a lot."

"Okay, Alvin, let me get in here and see what's happening."

"All right, my friend. There's another land mine over there, so watch out." Jessup motioned with a turn of his head to the airplane.

Matt drove through the open gate and steered toward a U.S. Air Force Gulfstream parked about a hundred meters away. He stopped next to a car that was parked against the chain-link fence. He could see the vice president's armored Suburban next to the airplane.

Matt stepped from his Porsche and walked to the steps of the Gulfstream, wondering what Jessup could have meant. *A land mine?* He saw the vice president walking down the small step ladder from the jet.

Then he saw the land mine: Meredith Morris, her blond hair bouncing off her shoulders as she followed the vice president down the jet stairway.

My Virginian, Matt wanted to say, but he didn't dare utter those words. Still, he waited for Meredith to lift her eyes and notice him. Though he knew he should look away, it was impossible. He could not deny the flutter in his chest. As recently as four months ago she had been his fiancée.

"Matt," Vice President Hellerman said, "join me for a few seconds, son."

Hellerman was motioning Matt into the back seat of his Suburban for a private chat.

"Yes, sir," Matt said without moving his eyes from Meredith's face. She looked up at him as she reached the tarmac, lifted her face slowly, and smiled. His heart leapt, but his mind locked tighter than a vault door.

"Hi, Matt," she said. "Good to see you."

"Meredith," he said.

The vice president's hand pulled at his shoulder, breaking the spell. He slid into the Suburban, watching as Meredith climbed into the back seat on the opposite side. Interesting that she would be with the vice president, Matt thought. She worked for the national security adviser, Yves Gerald.

Matt had taken the time to grab a sport coat and pulled it over the black Underarmor shirt that looked painted onto his muscular frame. He wore khaki cargo pants and lightweight, brown Belleview boots. Not a typically snappy dresser, Matt figured the blazer concealed his weapon relatively well.

"Matt, glad you could make it," Hellerman said, closing the door of his vehicle. "We've got some leads on a terrorist named Ballantine, a former Iraqi general."

Matt paused, thinking.

"I know the name." There was no escaping Zach's death, Matt thought. He remembered talking to him after he had returned from Desert Storm back in 1991. The detail with which Zach had described the fight that led to the capture of Ballantine was incredible. Zach, the best storyteller Matt knew, had painted such a clear picture that Matt had long savored the pride he felt for his older brother in securing what might have been the most prized capture of Operation Desert Storm.

"Yes, Ballantine," Hellerman continued. "I thought you might recognize the name. We think he's established a fishing guide service up in Quebec and that he uses a lightweight float plane to ferry supplies—deadly attack materials—into the United States. He may even be part of a supply chain that funneled the WMD's out of Iraq."

Matt considered what the vice president was saying. He remembered that Hellerman, while serving as an assistant secretary of state, had answered the call to duty during the First Gulf War by way of volunteering to be activated from his reserve status as a military intelligence officer. Given Hellerman's experience Matt placed some credence in his analysis.

"My team in Middleburg is running our own operation with limited support," Hellerman said. "We had a CIA agent have a small world moment with this guy when he was on leave doing some muskie fishing in Canada. Seems Ballantine opened this small enterprise a few years back and called it Moncrief Fishing Company. Flies a Sherpa into a small airport outside Burlington, Vermont, where he picks up his customers and, we suspect, a few other things."

"We got anybody working this?" Matt asked. His mind continued to drift back to the day Zach had returned from Desert Storm. Their small hometown just north of Charlottesville, Virginia, had thrown Zachary a huge welcome home party. After the festivities, Matt and Zachary, both in their early twenties then, had sat by the river that framed their property.

They drank a six pack of Budweiser while Zachary discussed the details of capturing Ballantine and then delivering him to military intelligence for interrogation. As the laundry bag full of beer, anchored to a rock next to Matt, shifted with the subtle currents of the river, Zach conveyed his belief that Ballantine had been released in a prisoner exchange. And when the Americans didn't find him in Iraq after the seizure of Baghdad in Gulf War II, the intelligence community dismissed his absence in favor of rounding up their vaunted deck of playing cards.

Matt was intrigued by Hellerman's assessment. Ballantine was more dangerous than either Hussein or bin Laden, because he not only had means, motive, and the courage of his convictions, but he was on nobody's screen.

Hellerman stared at Matt a minute and said, "Yes, we're about to get an agent in. Canada doesn't want us making a mess up there, but they also don't want to get involved."

"Screw a bunch of Canadians. Anybody I know?"

"There aren't many you don't know, but you know I can't answer that, Matt."

"Right. So what am I doing here?"

"I want you to head down to Joint Special Forces Command at Fort Bragg and talk to some of the special ops command down there. You'll be a presidential envoy. You know all those guys anyway," Hellerman said.

"Presidential envoy?" Matt chuckled. "I'll get laughed out of there. Now, maybe if I'm part of a take-down team . . . they'll believe *that*."

Matt's thoughts trailed off as his mind reeled with the possibilities. As an operator in the most elite counterterrorist outfit in the CIA, he was already visualizing the enemy situation. Then, as it always did, his mind spun back to that day in December 2001 when he had had his sniper rifle, his target in his sights, his team, and about a thousand airplanes overhead, all wanting to drop a bomb on bin Laden and claim victory, backing him up. But before he could pull the trigger on a clear shot, they shut him down. "Kill chain denied. Say again, kill chain denied. Return to base."

Matt looked at Hellerman, letting his thoughts play out on his face.

"I know what you're thinking, Matt, but I'm one of the good guys here. And I'm bringing you in on this thing to get you back into the action. That's what you want, right? While you can't go on the eventual raid, you can work with me on this thing in my command post. Advise me.

"Anyway, with your injuries you'd be no good to anyone. Plus, the president would have my ass if I sent you on a tactical mission when he wants you preparing for this job advising the director."

"I'd prefer to go after Ballantine." Matt's voice was stone cold.

"I've talked to the president and Director Houghton already, and they both want you on this mission," Hellerman continued.

Matt waited a moment with his eyes fixed on the vice president, then spoke. "I'm an operator, sir. That's what I do."

"I know you're an operator. Hell, the entire world knows you're an operator, and that's part of the problem. Everyone knows you. Anyway, you'll be representing the president. The Department of Homeland Security is barely even an agency; it's just some people looking for office space. You know how to wade into the middle of chaos and sort it out."

"That I do," Matt said. "What do you want me to talk to them about?"

Matt had never turned down an interesting assignment in his life, and now was not the time to start. If terrorists were coming after the country again, he wanted in on the hunt. He had made his case, so now he would just see where the situation led him.

Hellerman smiled. "Look at their plan. It's called Maple Thunder. Then see what they've got on the missing Predators while you're at it."

Matt stared at Hellerman, wondering why there was so much interest in the Predators all of a sudden.

Ignoring his thought, Matt said, "Right. So my mission is to get down to Bragg and be a spy for you. Is that it?"

"Exactly. Here's a satellite phone. Keep in touch. I'll be at Middleburg, which, of course, is top secret. And tell Peyton everything you know about those Predators, too. That's at least as important as Ballantine." Hellerman handed Matt a small, black object, and Matt promptly put in his shirt pocket.

"One thing," Matt said, returning to his personal albatross.

"What's that?"

"No Rolling Stones. No Fox and Diamond-type antics. No bullshit, right?"

"We've cleaned that mess up, Matt," Hellerman said. "President Davis understands your sacrifice and appreciates your service."

"Then why does Stone still have a job as secretary of defense?" Matt's voice was like granite. "And where the hell is Lantini? You telling me you guys can't find a former CIA director?"

"I've got nothing to do with Lantini, Matt. Get over yourself. We've got a war going on in Iraq. We need as little turbulence as possible after last year's nightmare in the Philippines, so the president decided to keep Stone in place, keep the momentum going."

Matt looked at Hellerman and then Meredith.

"I made a promise to Stone," Matt said, "that if he ever came after me because of what I know, *I* would know about it. And then I would execute what I believe you people term 'preemptive actions.' I know you and Stone are close, but I need you to look me in the eye, with Meredith as our witness, and swear to me that this is a legitimate mission, directed by the president of the United States."

Matt kept his cold gaze locked onto Hellerman's gray eyes, which never fluttered.

"I know you're not making a threat against the secretary of defense, which would be illegal, so I'll ignore that last comment about 'preemptive actions.'"

Matt shrugged and ran his hand along his blazer, beneath which his Glock was holstered.

"This is legit, Matt. We're trying to get you back in the game. This is the first step," Hellerman said. "Trust me."

"You had me until you said, 'Trust me.' I don't trust many these days," Matt said, his eyes shifting to Meredith, who looked away. "Produce Lantini, Ronnie Wood, for me, and then maybe we can build some trust."

Hellerman stared at Matt a moment and said, "I don't think we'll be seeing anymore of Ronnie Wood or the Rolling Stones. Only a select few know about that, so let's just leave it be."

Matt shook his head, then looked at Meredith. There was something about her countenance that rang hollow, sort of a vacuous gaze.

"Then don't trust me. Trust your instincts. I'm giving you a jet to fly to Fort Bragg. You can't be in Iraq right now, where all of the action is, and I know it's killing you."

That much was true, Matt thought, returning to Hellerman.

"Okay. If you're getting me back into the game, then *I'm* game." Matt said.

"Good," Hellerman said, leaning back, shaking his head, as if to move on to other pressing issues. "Maybe one day this country will wake up," Hellerman added under his breath as Matt was opening the door.

Matt stopped and looked over his shoulder at him, catching the sour look on the vice president's face. *What is he talking about?*

"Excuse me, sir?"

Hellerman looked at Matt. "Just talking to myself. Damn people in this country are so complacent. Take everything for granted. Not even two years removed from Nine-eleven, and we're back to our old ways—political infighting, stupid debates about the Iraq war—and everyone's so consumed with themselves. No sacrifice, except the military." Hellerman stopped a moment and then looked at Matt.

"You know, the other day I was at Fort Bragg talking to a soldier who told me, 'Sir, the military's at war; the country's at the mall.' Pretty insightful."

Matt shrugged. Privates usually had a pretty good perspective on life, he thought. Rang true. Still, he kept his mouth shut as he watched the smoke clear off the vice president for a moment and then turned toward the Gulfstream.

"You ever read Rostow?" Hellerman's question caught Matt off guard.

"Maybe once," Matt said, lifting his duffel bag, and looking over his shoulder.

"Think about the term *secular spiritual stagnation*. Then we'll talk."

Matt nodded, barely interested, then leaned back into the Suburban and said to Meredith, "Nice to see you. You look good." It was all he could allow himself.

He saw a brief flash of the woman he had once known. It was a moment of recognition in her face. He didn't know if her eyes were wistful . . . or pleading. He knew full well, though, that heady politics had vaulted her into a new circle that, perhaps, she had been gunning for all along. Or maybe she was operating in a realm for which she was unprepared. Either way, she had broken off the engagement four months earlier and had become aloof. Not fully understanding what had happened between them hurt the most. The moment was an awkward one—the vice president between them. Matt felt the pluck of a banjo string in his heart and then did the only thing he could do. He turned and walked up the steps.

He ducked as he entered the small airplane and nodded to the two Air Force officers who would fly him to Fort Bragg. One was blond with blue eyes and looked like he had just graduated from the academy the day before. He wore lieutenant's bars. The other was a bit older, more ethnic-looking, and with eyes staring at his cockpit instruments, focused on his preflight routine. He was a captain, and Matt presumed, in charge of the flight. He noticed a cell phone sitting in the pilot's lap and a Bluetooth headset in his ear like some Star Trek device.

As Matt turned into the small, eight-seat cabin, he was greeted with another surprise.

"How's the arm, slugger?"

"I'll live," Matt said with a shrug, standing next to Peyton's seat, duffel in hand.

"The vice president asked me to accompany you. I couldn't get out of it."

Matt surmised that she didn't seem too disappointed.

"Well, name's Matt Garrett," he said, sticking a large hand out and giving hers a quick shake. "Don't think I ever formally introduced myself."

She looked at him briefly and squeezed his hand. "Peyton O'Hara."

"Nice grip," he said, offering her a polite smile.

He walked to the back of the small airplane, sat down, put his duffel in the seat next to him, patted the weapon beneath his jacket, leaned back, and shut his eyes.

CHAPTER 3

Matt had fallen asleep during takeoff. He was awakened by what he thought was turbulence but was actually Peyton O'Hara dumping his feet off of the facing leather chair so that she could sit down across from him.

"While I've flown helicopters before, I get bored stiff riding in the back of these things, so let's talk," she said.

"Helicopters?" he asked, motioning to the seat across from his.

She stared at him as the Air Force flight attendant offered them drinks. Peyton chose apple juice. Matt asked for scotch.

"Previous life. Army Blackhawk pilot," she said. "Flew with the 101st Airborne, got bored after Iraq version 1.0, and decided to work in DC."

He held up his Jack and Coke. Doing quick mental calculations, Matt decided Peyton was in her early thirties—his age. "Thanks for your service."

He tipped his glass in her direction, and she gave hers a perfunctory wiggle that passed as a toast.

"Something's up with those Predators, Matt. We really need to figure this one out."

"Well, if they're in Canada with Ballantine, then things are already serious. That puts Boston and New York within range."

"But how would they get the satellite capability to monitor and steer the Predator?" she asked.

"I'm sure they've got it. That was part of the campaign-cash-for-technology swap that went on a few years ago."

"How do you know?" Peyton asked.

"I just know," he said quietly, staring at her. Changing the subject, he said, "So, what's your story? Blackhawk pilot. Ducati Street Fighter."

"I went to Harvard undergrad, and then, after my pilot stint in the Army, Georgetown for graduate school. I was president of my class. I come from an old Irish family, complete with the politics and the temperament," she warned.

"Right," he said. "That explains the helicopters and motorcycles."

Peyton shrugged. "They require no more explanation than the armament you have in your go bag."

Matt shrugged back at her and remained silent.

The plane carved its way above the snowcapped Blue Ridge Mountains, hurtling south toward Fort Bragg, North Carolina.

He put his empty drink down and ordered another as the military flight attendant moved past them. When the drink arrived, Matt studied the stewardess. She was attractive in a rural sort of way. Her blue Air Force uniform was a bit too tight in some areas, making it obvious that she worked out. She was average height but looked as if she might make a good second baseman on a softball team. Probably from somewhere in the Midwest.

"Thank you," Matt said to the orderly. He took a sip of his drink, and lifting his eyes over his cup, saw Peyton examining him closely. "What?"

"Don't I know you from somewhere?"

"You're kidding me."

"Maybe something on the television?" Peyton asked.

"Not likely." Matt studied Peyton. She was wearing a white silk shirt that blended with her porcelain skin. Her strawberry-blond hair was disheveled in an intentional manner, and a constellation of freckles jumbled up either side of her nose. "So tell me, what was all that stuff Hellerman was saying about Rostow and secular spiritual stagnation?"

"Fine. Quid pro quo. I tell you about Hellerman's Rebuild America program, and you tell me about the Philippines."

Matt shifted in his seat. He didn't want to go down this road. *Not now, not with a stranger,* he thought to himself.

"You are the famous Matt Garrett that got into a big fight in the Philippines, right?"

Matt nodded. "Perhaps. Hard to tell who anyone is nowadays."

"I'll ignore the philosophy and just dive right in. Hellerman created a special, compartmentalized task force called Rebuild America. He actually got the idea for the name before Nine-eleven. He had been working on the concept for a while."

"What's Rostow got to do with that? His sixth stage?"

"Exactly." Peyton pointed a finger at Matt as if to award him a gold star. "Rostow, as you seem to know, studied societal development and labeled his stages, starting with the *traditional society*. You know . . . the primitive, tribal, subsistence-farmer types. Then there is *preconditions for takeoff, takeoff, drive to maturity*, and *high mass consumption*."

Matt looked at Peyton's pearl necklace. "Sounds like he got the last one right, anyway. So?"

Peyton ignored the comment and continued ticking the list off, using her fingers.

"So, he spoke primarily in economic terms. His thesis basically argued that we had moved over a couple of centuries from farmers to industrialized mass producers and consumers. His point, at the end, was that he couldn't see the future, but since we were in the high mass consumption stage, where people could buy and spend at will, he predicted a people that felt less beholden to society and their government yet deeply selfish. Rostow argued, and Hellerman agrees, that our wealth would insulate us from the sacrifices of those who have gone before us. The principles that have made the United States great—freedom, liberty, and capitalism—could ultimately create a cocoon for those not involved in the tough, day-to-day fight to preserve those very principles. What do I care what's happening overseas, for example, as long as I can buy my Xbox? Combine that with an all-volunteer military, and there's no shared sacrifice. The people simply live in oblivion while our troops get after it. In the sixth stage, the nation's spirit diminishes. The flame flickers."

"No argument here. What's Hellerman doing with all that?"

"He's trying to bridge that gap. He hired a bunch of smart people to talk this through and develop a plan to 'rebuild America.'" Peyton used her hands to form quote marks when she said the last two words of her sentence.

"And Meredith is one of those smart people, along with you?"

"Meredith, yes; me, no. I'm on loan for a year through the White House Fellows program. I'm really a lawyer."

"Great," Matt groaned

"Oh, be original," Peyton said cheerily. "Anyway, it's your turn."

Matt brushed off his cargo pants and rubbed his neck against the soft collar of his T-shirt.

"I was in the Philippines once. That's all."

"That's all? I know a little bit, what Hellerman told me, but not much."

"What did Hellerman tell you?"

"Like I said, not much."

"Don't really want to talk about it," he said, taking a sip of his drink and looking through the dark oval window.

"You promised." She smiled.

After a long pull on his second drink, he set the plastic cup on the table. He turned and stared out of the window. He could see the roads and buildings of some anonymous city spread 30,000 feet beneath him in a bizarre pattern of yellow and white dots. He knew that once he began talking about Bart Rathburn, alias Keith Richards, he wouldn't be able to stop. But he forged ahead anyway.

He hadn't really talked to anybody about his Philippine experience except Meredith, and not that much with her. He had talked to absolutely no one about Meredith. Usually he would talk to Blake Sessoms or his sister, Karen. He had become a recluse and found it too burdensome to even begin to discuss the deep emotions with which he was wrestling. Maybe one short conversation with a stranger wouldn't hurt. But he knew that it would be difficult keeping it to just one. Everything was so complex, connected: The Rolling Stones, Zachary, Meredith, Fox and Diamond, and his past life as a paramilitary operator, his new career, whatever that might be. And Lantini, *that bastard . . .*

Focusing on the city below him, Matt began. "It's complicated. Last spring in the Philippines I find Chuck Ramsey's A-team, all shot up, and a Japanese weapons factory. Then I hop on a floatplane to Palau, where I meet Meredith and Rathburn. From there I get sucked back to Manila, where Rathburn and his cronies try to get me killed while they start their insurgency in the Philippines.

"Anyway, I was unaware until the end that Rathburn was dirty. So when we get captured, he blows my cover directly before he gets killed and we escape. Then I go back in for Rathburn and we bury him while a CNN correspondent films it."

Matt could feel Peyton's gaze. He focused on nothing in particular. His thoughts were spinning wildly back to a time that he had left hidden in the recesses of his mind.

Peyton snapped her fingers. "His satellite hookup was working." She spoke with a sense of wonderment. In her mind's eye she replayed the CNN broadcast of Matt's eulogy for Rathburn. Barefoot's camera panned away and zoomed in on the brutal execution of an unarmed Filipino civilian by a Japanese soldier. That video had been the trigger for the president to authorize the use of American conventional combat forces in the Philippines.

"We were on the run for days." Matt's voice was monotonous, recalling the events as mere facts, devoid of any emotion. It had to be that way. "They finally caught up with us—Barefoot, Sturgeon, and me. Jack got shot in the femur. Barefoot took a few hits in his right arm. I killed a rebel soldier with my knife and took his gun. We held for four hours before I got hit in the stomach. Hence the 'appendectomy.' We were surrounded."

"How'd you survive?" Peyton asked.

"Zachary, my brother, was an infantry company commander stationed in Hawaii. His unit was on a mission in the Philippines and got caught in the rebellion. I had no idea he was there. Zach's guys were attacking the enemy we were fending off when they found us, when Zach found me. The last thing I remember is my brother holding me and someone on the radio calling in a medical evacuation for me."

"He saved your life."

"That's true. But then he goes and gets killed two days later in the final battle. I should have been there." Matt's voice was nearly a whisper. The sky outside of the airplane was dark. Small groups of white and yellow dots slid beneath the fuselage. Matt's heart churned inside his chest. Zach would never be back. And why did he just expose his primary vulnerability to this stranger?

She watched him and thought about reaching across and touching his arm, but resisted.

"Zach's body was so mangled they wouldn't even let us view it before the funeral," he said.

Peyton let a few minutes pass in silence, the heavy roar of the jet engine droning.

"You blame yourself for Zachary's death. But he died doing what he loved to do."

"That doesn't make it any easier, Peyton."

"Think of all the lives he saved."

"Think of the one I didn't."

Matt left it at that.

CHAPTER 4

Peyton had excused herself to the lavatory, and Matt had just closed his eyes when he awoke to an unusual sound in the cockpit. It was a thud of sorts—not a normal airplane sound. He knew that much.

He heard something else come from the forward VIP cabin, where Peyton had originally been sitting. It was a rustling sound followed by some gurgling.

Never a nervous flyer, Matt rubbed his face and craned his neck to look toward the cockpit.

"What the—!" he said, getting to his feet.

The flight steward was crawling slowly toward him, her throat slit and blood gushing onto the floor. He heard a noise behind him and instinctively turned to defend himself.

"What's going on?" Peyton said with a curious smile. And then she saw the woman on the floor and froze.

"We've got a problem in the cockpit," Matt said, running to the steward. She reached out to him.

Matt bent down and grabbed her hand as he felt the airplane bank sharply to the right. Holding onto the armrest of a leather chair, he knelt down.

"What happened?" he whispered to her.

"Pilot . . ." Her voice was weak, and blood aspirated in a fine spray onto him as she attempted to speak.

That was all she could say before her head fell to the floor. Matt felt for her pulse and knew she was dead as he eyed the long trail of blood she had left in the aisle.

Peyton watched Matt, covering her mouth with her hand.

Matt pulled the steward to the side, placed a blanket over her, and said, "She's dead. Nothing we can do for her. My guess is that the young pilot in there is dead also. I think we've got a terrorist operative flying this plane."

"How is that possible?"

Matt looked at her. "Wake up, Peyton. Hellerman set us up."

Matt pulled his Baby Glock from his hip holster and flipped off the safety.

"That's bullshit," Peyton said. "I know Hellerman."

"Pull your head out of your fourth point of contact, lady."

Peyton ignored Matt's paratrooper reference to her rear end. "What are you doing?"

"I'm going to kill the pilot, and then you're going to fly this thing." Matt's voice was calm as he turned toward the cockpit. Then he stopped and turned around.

In his pistol were full-metal-jacket bullets. He ejected the magazine and the chambered round and dug out a magazine of hollow points from his kit bag. He didn't know their altitude, but considered that hollow-point rounds might serve them better in an airplane because they would flatten on impact, penetrating less than FMJs. Sliding the magazine into the weapon, he turned back toward the cockpit, walking carefully through the cabin door and into the VIP suite. He paused to look at the blood trail the steward had left, starting at the cockpit door. He noticed splatter marks along the communications panel to the right and thought she must have been standing there when she was attacked.

While only a small tragedy in the large scheme of things, it was not lost on Matt that some family who had lived clean and right had just lost their daughter to a brutal fate.

He felt along the cabin door and could see a small bit of what looked like white putty jammed along the door latch.

He inspected the entire door and made a plan, to which he gave a ten percent chance of success.

“Matt, I don’t do fixed wing,” Peyton whispered.

Matt looked at her briefly and turned back to the door. “Well, you’re going to have to figure it out,” he said.

CHAPTER 5

The airplane hurtled through the sky, Matt and Peyton feeling the power of the engines pushing them toward an uncertain destination. Where were they going? Matt wondered. Were they merely extra payload on this guided missile, or was it something more? He wasn't going to wait to find out.

As he heard the flaps of the jet begin to lower, he looked at Peyton.

She was seated with her back against the steps of the airplane, her knees drawn to her chest. Her slender arms were wrapped around her legs, her face pressed against her knees. Matt's impression was that she was deep in thought—not scared, but pensive. He wrote it off to her way of dealing with stress.

"Ready?" he asked.

"For what?" she replied.

"Just follow my lead."

"What are you doing?"

He knelt next to the communications panel, which ran perpendicular to the cockpit door.

"Garrett?"

Matt could sense the airplane losing altitude, and rather clumsily at that. He used his Leatherman to remove the four screws holding the communications panel. He lifted the two-foot-by-two-foot panel, exposing a deep cavity of circuit boards and switches designed to route ultra-high frequency and satellite communications around the world, and carefully placed it on the floor.

Another two minutes of work with the pocket tool and Matt removed another panel, this one loaded with circuit boards and wiring. Then he removed the hook connectors of the wiring harness for the satellite communications panel before going to work on the ultra-high frequency panel, disabling the pilot's ability to talk to anyone outside of the airplane.

"We're getting lower to the ground," Peyton whispered. "The landing gear just lowered, I think."

"I heard it, thanks." Matt's voice echoed from inside the cabinet, his body now half inside as he worked on the forward panel. The Leatherman was beginning to slip on the worn grooves of the screws, yet it was working.

He carefully removed the final panel and navigated its path through the opening to avoid contact with any of the communications gear. His retrieval was silent.

As Matt reentered the cavity, he could see the back of the pilot's head. The man was wearing the standard headphones, which had helped mask Matt's maneuvers thus far. He looked to the left and saw the lieutenant lying back in his chair, his throat cut like the steward's, his head hanging limply, as if it might fall and roll onto the floor at any moment. Matt's inspection confirmed that there was some sort of device placed against the door, though it did not seem to be as dangerous as he had first thought. Matt knew his explosives, and this was no more than a few ounces of C-4. Still, it could do plenty of damage to the small aircraft.

He felt a tugging on his leg and withdrew through the cavity.

"We're getting low. I think I saw airfield lights," Peyton said.

"Okay, time to move," Matt said.

Matt leaned back in, squinted at the panel, and saw that the autopilot light was on. With that information, he lifted his pistol and shot the pilot in the back of the head once. He aimed so that the bullet would enter low in the back of the skull and have to travel through the entire length of the brain, hopefully not exiting the cranium with enough force to crack the windscreen.

The pilot's head jerked once, blood spraying forward against the starboard side of the windshield. The bullet clearly exited, but the integrity of the glass seemed intact.

Retracting himself, he said, "Let's move."

He went to work on the door hinges, using his Leatherman to back out the screws from the two brass facings.

"Stay behind me," Matt said. "I'll get you into the pilot's seat."

"I told you I don't know the first thing about this aircraft," she said.

Matt lifted the door off the hinges, causing a loud explosion that knocked him into the communications cavity and sent Peyton tumbling down the center aisle.

Though stunned, Matt quickly moved forward into the cockpit. The pilot was slumped against the instrument panel, dead.

Looking at the dead terrorist's face, Matt felt his own satisfaction. It had been a while. The kill felt good, as if perhaps he had avenged a small portion of Zachary's death.

Matt looked back for Peyton.

"Come on," he said. "You've got to fly this thing."

No response.

He looked out of the pilot's windscreen and could see the nose of the airplane aimed directly at a tiny strip of lit asphalt. Looking down at the instrument panel, he noticed the autopilot indicator lit up in orange.

"Peyton!" he shouted.

He pulled the dead lieutenant out of the left pilot's seat and dumped the body into the aisle.

"Peyton, we've got to—" He was cut short by surprise as he turned and found her lying unconscious on the floor.

Geez, he thought. The steward, the lieutenant, Peyton, and the terrorist pilot were all incapacitated, and he was in an airplane a thousand feet off the ground.

"Come on, Peyton, wake up. I can't fly this plane," Matt said, lightly slapping her face. He felt her neck and got a faint pulse. From the marks on her face, he guessed she had caught a significant portion of the blast. She was bleeding from somewhere on her head as well.

Realizing she was not going to respond in time, Matt moved Peyton into a passenger seat and buckled her in. Then he moved quickly into the lieutenant's cockpit seat and watched as the plane rocked against the wind and approached the lighted runway.

They were less than a half mile from the small runway, yet he had no clue as to where they might be. He presumed somewhere north. *Canada perhaps?* He looked at the controls and felt helpless. He could improvise quite a bit, but felt that right now he could do more harm than good.

The runway looked no bigger than a toothpick, and the small jet wobbled as it lowered toward its narrow target.

Heavy turbulence rocked the plane, jostling the pilot's lifeless body forward onto the yoke, pushing the jet over into a steep dive. The violent shudder and abrupt pitch downward threw Matt's stomach into his throat. He instinctively grabbed the controls and tried to manipulate them, but the dead weight of the pilot's body worked against him.

Matt grabbed him by the shirt and jerked him down between the seats, freeing the yoke to respond to his command. A calm female voice began a surreal mantra. "Terrain. Terrain. Pull up. Pull up." Matt pulled back hard on the controls, leveling the aircraft out of its steep dive. Just as he thought he had bought a moment's reprieve, the soothing voice was replaced by a shrill buzzer that seemed to increase in volume and intensity as he lost airspeed.

"C'mon, man," he muttered in frustration. He grappled with the controls, cast a quick glance over his shoulder, willing Peyton to step forward and say, "Just push that button."

Turning back, he stared intently at the flashing lights on the instrument panel and then grasped the throttle and pushed forward, not sure how the aircraft would respond. The engines' whine dissipated and Matt felt the hollow sensation of weightlessness.

The jet yawed to the right and steadily fell toward the toothpick, which now, in the ambient light of the airfield, actually looked the size of a decent country road. Matt knew the plane was going to crash. There was no doubt about it. He vaguely recalled Peyton telling him that landing gear had lowered before he shot the pilot. It occurred to him that he was fodder in the nose cone of an unguided missile destined to plow unceremoniously into the asphalt and break apart wherever the hell he was. And he was curiously reminded of the old adage that all landings are controlled crashes.

Nothing controlled about this crash, he thought.

It all happened very fast. The wings tilted port, then starboard. Bright lights and warnings came alive in the cockpit. The now-familiar, automated female voice warned him of fast-approaching terrain. "Pull up. Pull up." Matt brought the nose up and lined it up with the runway before he lost sight of it and the evening sky filled the windscreen. He was testing the response of the rudder pedals when he felt the aircraft pound into the ground, the landing gear absorbing much of the impact before rebounding him aloft.

Matt observed that he had at least hit part of the runway. Whether that was a good thing or not remained to be seen. He frantically switched ON buttons to OFF, pulled back on the throttle, and felt the airplane smack the ground again—hard this time—belly-flopping on the blacktop.

His neck snapped back, and the last thing he remembered was thinking, *I should have told her about the UAVs.*

CHAPTER 6

1800 HOURS, FRIDAY
LAKE MONCRIEF, QUEBEC PROVINCE, CANADA,

Jacques Ballantine landed his lightweight Sherpa with ease along the rocky bank of Lake Moncrief, Quebec Province, Canada. Stepping from the aircraft, he absently touched his fingers to the scar above his eye. A crisp north wind stung the wound that would never heal. The smell of jet fuel in his nostrils reminded him of the oil wells burning twelve long years ago and further fueled his sense of purpose.

The scar also reminded him of his purpose today, so many years removed from the fury that was the mother of all battles. He had not aged well since his capture in Iraq and the loss of his brother. With every thought of Henri he could feel the burning in his eyes, black onyx that faintly concealed his endless desire for revenge. While Jacques had been unable to secure his insurance policy before Garrett had blended anonymously back to his combat outfit, he was fortunate to have been funneled to the right interrogator in Riyadh. Simply the idea of what might be in the backpack had been powerful enough to motivate his questioner into negotiating for his release. Jacques' part of the deal was now coming due, his interrogator having lived up to his end of the bargain. Jacques was more than happy to fulfill his obligation.

Ballantine stared into the Canadian evening sun as it dipped into the horizon. To the north he could see the oxbow lake that had been his home for the last two years.

He found his way along a small trail, past a clearing on his left, and entered the forest. Picking his way through the undergrowth and towering fir trees, he found the dilapidated shaft. Rotten four-by-fours crisscrossed the entrance to a cave. Years of rain and sun and insect infestation had worn the wood to its core. He carefully stepped through the weeds and stooped below the fallen logs into complete darkness.

Jacques laid his AK-47 against the timber and pulled open a small wooden door that gave way to an unusual series of lights and sounds that contrasted sharply with the serenity of the countryside.

Inside the mineshaft, Ballantine found his staff and the communications systems with which he would lead the war against America. The Central Committee was calling this Phase Two. The first phase had been the 9/11 attacks. Now was the time the Central Committee would best be able to achieve its goals, catching the Western world leaning hard in the wrong direction, the United States and Great Britain having committed hundreds of thousands of troops to the attack on Iraq in March. *Off balance* was how he had described it to the others.

"Virginia, are we ready?" he said to an attractive black woman standing near several muted television screens flickering a variety of images.

"The Central Committee in Panama City has delivered its message," she said, handing him a printed e-mail.

Jacques looked at the piece of paper. His anonymous Yahoo! e-mail account had worked just fine. His exchanges with the committee had allowed them to plan their attack as if it were a wedding. He was the groom, coordinating with all of his groomsmen around the country for a wedding that was to take place tonight.

"Congratulations on your long-awaited marriage," the note from the North Korean read. "We hope to see you at six p.m. tonight. We are sure it will be a wonderful affair."

It was innocuous and direct. Of the billions of e-mails sent every day, this one would surely not raise any suspicion.

"Jacques, it's time," Virginia said, handing him a satellite phone. "We do this. We pick up Matt Garrett and retrieve your rucksack. And we're done."

He stared at her, remembering why their love affair had ended. He had tried to love her, and maybe did, but the sorrow he carried with him since his brother's death had turned to hate—to poison—melting any positive emotions he would experience. A former American military intelligence officer, she was a traitor to her country. Although that was cause enough for him to be smitten with her, she also had an elegance that he could not resist.

He took the Qualcomm satellite phone from her hand, his fingers lightly brushing hers.

"I wanted to kill Matt Garrett while Zachary Garrett watched," he said, blankly staring past her at the television screens. "I can still see that man killing my brother every day. It never leaves me."

"Zachary Garrett is dead," Virginia said. "Someone else took care of that for us."

"That was *my* mission," he spat. Then he forced a half-smile. "But it is done."

She paused. "Did you ever think that we would be able to get all of the weapons out of Iraq and to their destinations?"

"I always believed it was possible." Ballantine saw that the Americans had fallen for everything. Saddam's last stand would go down as a strangely reversed Trojan horse. Instead of offering a gift, Saddam lured the Americans into his own country after Ballantine and the others had positioned his WMDs elsewhere. *Brilliant*, he thought.

He turned toward his executive officer and said, "Chasteen, are all cells ready to go?"

A burly, blond Canadian parolee from the Quebec province, his head almost touching the low-hanging beams in the command center mineshaft, Chasteen had proven crucial to helping Ballantine get his ersatz fishing guide service up and running two years earlier. Since then, the Sherpa had been invaluable in running supplies across the Canadian border into a small airfield in Vermont.

"Yeah, boss. They're set. All met their reporting windows this morning," Chasteen said. All of the groomsmen had notified the best man that they were attending the wedding.

Ballantine felt the cool air of the damp mine shaft crawl across his skin. He turned and walked toward the center of the room. A few of the other staff members were monitoring radios and satellite communications. This was a state-of-the-art command and control center.

"Okay, team," Ballantine said, "today it begins. This is Phase Two."

They nodded.

Ballantine pressed the green button on the phone and transmitted.

CHAPTER 7

CHARLOTTE, NORTH CAROLINA

Groomsman No. 1 felt the weight of his cell phone in his pocket as it vibrated against his leg. Opening it just outside the Charlotte Sting locker room in the coliseum, he said, "Hello?"

"What does the attendance look like tonight?"

"Looks like a full house," the groomsman replied.

"The groom appreciates the tickets."

"Anytime," he said into the small handset.

The groomsman flipped the phone shut, took a deep breath, and moved toward the first concession stand.

The benefactor of one of the most controversial presidential pardons ever, Groomsman No. 1 had been released fourteen years early from a mandatory, no-parole, sixteen-year prison sentence at San Quentin. He had been caught by DEA and FBI agents, operating the largest cocaine ring in the Southwest. His father had laundered and funneled his drug money into massive political payoffs that wound their way up the channel, resulting in said pardon.

It had been nearly seven years, and the groomsman had been a model citizen, obeying the speed limit, paying his taxes, avoiding the gangs and cartels—except for being caught within Jorge Cartagena's long reach.

Cartagena, baron of the infamous drug cartel in Colombia, was a key player in the Central Committee. He was leveraging the fact that when Groomsman No. 1 had gone to jail, he was nearly one million dollars in debt to the organization. Supply chain problems. Cartagena gave the groomsman one option, which was to get a job in North Carolina as a concession manager.

The groomsman wiped the sweat from his forehead, reasonably confident he could get away with what he was about to do. Hell, if his father was able to bribe the president of the United States, well, then, that added a whole new perspective to things.

The groomsman was dressed in his typical work attire: an old Hornet's No. 12 shirt, baggy, black dungarees, and Nike high tops. He kept his hair cropped close to his glistening black scalp and wore black wraparound sunglasses.

He walked up the ramp to his first concession stand, which he found stacked with lines twenty-deep. Each concessionaire was doling out popcorn, hotdogs, and beer. Keg beer fed through taps, each keg containing forty gallons of beer. Five hundred such kegs, thirty of which the groomsman had personally delivered in his coliseum work truck early that morning, were emptied by thirsty fans every game. He had driven right through security, tipping his hat at the attendant he had known for five years.

Cartagena had put the groomsman in touch with the keg supplier, an oily-looking man who nervously stacked and secured the kegs inside the extended Chevy van sporting a large, teal and indigo Sting symbol on a white background. "Most are loaded with a hundred pounds of explosives. Three contain enough VX nerve gas to kill the first responders. Should kill just about everybody," the supplier said. "Be careful, bud. Watch those speed bumps. Oh, and make sure you keep the remote with you, or nothing will work," Cartagena's contact added, handing him a box of remote-controlled fuses as if it were a box of doughnuts.

Groomsman No. 1 had driven the short way from the link-up point at no more than twenty-five miles an hour, palms sweating the entire way. He off-loaded the kegs one at a time and used a modified golf cart to move them in pairs to each of the fifteen concession stands. He tucked these special kegs into the back of the storage coolers so that that they would be the last to be used.

He inserted the fuses and armed them, only needing the radio-frequency-delivered code to start the clock ticking toward a simultaneous explosion of 3,000 pounds of explosives, all conveniently stowed beneath the upper bleachers and near the support columns of the arena.

He whistled as he walked toward the first concession stand and pressed the small, black remote control that looked similar to the average television handset. He then negotiated his way past the assembled crowd, opened the stanchion, and nudged his way through the concessionaires into the storage locker.

"Hey, baby," the sound of a voice startled him, "good to see you." Charlene Pierce worked the concession nearest the best courtside seats because she was attractive. She had smiled her way into the position where she now waits on the wealthy patrons that would occasionally wander out and mix with the commoners.

"Hey, Charlene. Good to see you too," the groomsman said, completing his task. Normally he would have kissed her on the cheek, but he was on a mission, and he knew that he didn't want to be caught in the coliseum when the business went down.

But she didn't let him off the hook. She grabbed his arm, her hand wrapped around his large biceps, and said, "Come here, baby, and give me a big kiss."

"Not now."

"What's wrong, honey?"

"Nothing, baby. Just got lots of checking to do, you know?" But he acquiesced and stopped, spinning around to give her a quick peck on the cheek.

She pressed her body up against his and started to push him into the storage room.

"Maybe we should just check this stuff out together," she said, her long eyelashes fluttering close to his face.

He stared into her large brown eyes, pushing her away. "Baby, let me check you later. Boss man is really upset," he said.

She grabbed his crotch playfully and said, "You my boss man, big guy. Come back and see me."

"Sure thing," he said, giving her another quick peck on the cheek. He thought to himself that he had always wanted to pursue Charlene, even though she was only nineteen. Too bad he would never have the chance.

He found the kegs and leaned over the two in which he was interested. He saw that, indeed, the timer was working: *28:15 . . . 28:14 . . .*

He had wasted precious time with Charlene, but now that he was sure the remote worked, he could cruise past the others and simply press the button. He had calculated fifteen minutes to make the full circle and get outside. He would be pulling onto Interstate 85 about the time the explosives cut the building in half.

As he walked, he heard the announcer's voice bellow over the loudspeaker system. "And we have 12,000 in attendance today. Congratulations on another smashing day of attendance for our own Charlotte Sting!" He dragged the last word along until it was dwarfed by the roar of the crowd.

The groomsman quickly proceeded around the main corridor, pressing the remote as he passed each concession stand, briefly catching a glimpse of the red light flashing, indicating the radio signal had been delivered.

It took him twenty minutes to complete his rounds. He had run into three people who wanted to shoot the breeze with him, and two concessionaires had flagged him down from a distance to complain about one issue or another. He eventually found himself looking from a distance at Charlene, back where he had started his journey. Her eyes caught his and she winked. He waved, then trotted down the ramp toward the locker rooms and out past the security guard to the employee parking lot.

Charlene smiled as she thought about the possibilities. She pulled the beer tap forward, and foam started spitting out at her.

"Time out, time out," she shouted, laughing. Her customer stepped back, smiling. "Gotta get another keg," she said.

Charlene opened the storage-room door and walked to the back of the keg room. As she walked, she made a mental note that she and the keg-man could do a quickie if everyone were really busy out front. She grabbed the dolly at the rear of the storage room, and instead of moving to the front row of kegs, neatly lined two-deep along the cooler wall, she slid the dolly beneath the keg nearest the back.

As she nudged the platform of the dolly underneath and pushed with her hand on the upper lip of the keg, she noticed a small black box with red flashing numbers situated where she would insert the tap in a few seconds. Not understanding either the weight or the black box, she edged the keg back onto the floor and leaned over to inspect it further.

"What the hell is this?" she whispered to herself.

The flashing light read *00:08* . . .

00:07 . . .

00:06 . . .

00:05 . . .

Even her simple, uneducated mind figured it out with about two seconds remaining.

"Oh, my–" she said, backing away.

Groomsman No. 1 was pulling onto I-85 when he heard a dull thud in the background. In his rearview mirror he saw dust pouring out of the coliseum in a large, billowing cloud. Oddly, he felt no guilt. Yet for some unexplained reason, the use of nerve gas seemed unfair to him. He had placed 30-minute time-delay fuses on the VX nerve gas aspirators that would release a fine, toxic spray just as the first responders were arriving to help those unfortunate few who might have survived the blast.

Regardless, it was not a bad day's work. It would be nice to have Cartagena off his ass. The groomsman blended anonymously into society, never to be heard from again.

CHAPTER 8

MINNEAPOLIS, MINNESOTA

Groomsman No. 2 felt the sweat trickle down the base of his spine. He took a deep breath and steadied himself. The basement tunnels of the Mall of America were deathly quiet. The only noise was the water moving along the miles of plumbing and air-conditioning pipes.

He clipped his cell phone to a small wire that ran through one of the ventilation ducts to the roof of Macy's department store. He had installed the wire the previous week in preparation for the "wedding."

The groomsman's job as an inspector working with McGraw Maintenance Systems over the past six months allowed him unlimited access to the maintenance tunnels under the mall. He engineered his route, covering nearly a mile of passageways beneath the huge complex, using the blueprint he had downloaded from the *Architectural Digest* Web site.

Two years earlier, after his release from the Minnesota State Prison at Stillwater, he was contacted by an old Earth Liberation Front buddy, who invited him up to do some muskie fishing. After a week this friend, Chasteen, had sold him on Ballantine's plan. It sounded like a good thing—a second chance. Besides, he had grown tired of spray-painting sport utility vehicles and setting fire to new housing developments, clearly the minor leagues for eco-terrorists. And Chasteen's offer to strike a blow against the largest symbol of capitalism in the Midwest held an additional attraction for him. It would graduate him to the next level.

Moreover, knowing Chasteen like he did, the groomsman understood that once he had been made aware of the plan, he would either accept the invitation onto the team or wind up as mulch around Ballantine's boxwood hedgerow. He preferred option A.

He opened his cell phone as he watched the green flashing light turn red, indicating an incoming call.

"Anything on sale today?" a voice asked.

"Wedding gifts seem to be the item of choice," he responded.

"I'm sure the bride will be impressed."

That's it, the groomsman thought, shutting the phone. *Time to get to work.* He stuffed the phone in his pocket, looked to his right, and armed the first of twenty-nine high-explosive devices placed near structurally important supports. He then moved out like a rat in a sewer to arm the others.

Groomsman No. 2 moved quickly along the tunnel, checking the last few arming switches, making sure the explosives were synchronized to detonate at precisely the same time. Arriving at his destination, he stooped low to avoid some water pipes and then stopped at his last set of explosives.

He worked quickly as he flipped the metal toggle and watched the red numbers begin their countdown.

He had chosen his route so that he would finish arming his last igniter near the restrooms downstairs. This would allow him to exit up the escalator and out through any variety of doors on the main level. He could get in his truck, which he had parked near Macy's, and escape the carnage about three minutes before it occurred.

The groomsman grabbed the metal knob and pulled the gray door open. A burst of light met him as he stepped onto the tile floor of the mall's bottom level.

"Hey, Mister Saunders," a little boy said, smiling as he stepped away from the ladies' room door.

Groomsman No. 2 stopped, nearly tripping over his feet, as he noticed eight-year-old Erik Larsen standing by himself. Quickly regaining his composure, he said, "Hey, Erik, where's your mom?" He had graduated from Braham High School with Erik's mother, Joan. They had dated for a time and remained friends ever since.

"She's in the bathroom with the girls," he said. Erik looked down, and noticing that he had drifted from the spot where his mother had told him to wait, he took two steps back toward the wall and looked up. "Mama told me not to move."

"Then you best stand still."

"Yes, sir."

Saunders wiped his sweaty palms on his tan workpants and then pulled his baseball cap down over his forehead. His eyes shifted left and right, his body telling him he needed to move out, and quickly.

"Tell your mom I said hello," he said.

At that moment, Joan Larsen came tumbling out of the ladies' room with her three other children in tow, all relieved and ready to go shopping.

"Hey, Johnny, what are you doing here?" Joan smiled, happy to see a familiar face so far from home.

"Oh, hey there, Joan. Just doing some window shopping," he said nervously. "Look, I gotta run."

Joan frowned. "Oh. Well, I guess I'll see you around."

"Yeah. Sure."

In all his time walking the maintenance tunnels beneath the mall, Johnny had stayed out of contact with the people above, like a bridge troll who never came out of hiding. He walked over to Joan Larsen and kissed her on the cheek. He rubbed a hand in three-year-old Chelsea's hair.

Chelsea hugged his leg and said, "Bye, Mister Johnny."

"Goodbye, Joan," Johnny said, his eyes beginning to burn. He promptly turned and began running toward the exit, leaving Joan confused. He figured he had about two minutes.

Joan watched as her childhood friend sprinted up the steps and through the Macy's door. She stood a moment, staring into empty space, until Erik said, "What's wrong with Mister Saunders, Mama?"

It took a minute, but in typical fashion, she shrugged it off and gathered up her troops.

"Okay, gang. Where we going first?"

Chelsea started to say, "Camp Snoopy," but the explosion prevented her from ever uttering the words.

Groomsman No. 2 pulled out of the parking garage in his rusted Ford pickup truck, turning his head as he heard the detonations. He knew that those not killed by the explosions would suffer from anthrax poisoning.

His job done, he would never be heard from again.

CHAPTER 9

FRIDAY, DELAWARE RIVER

Groomsman No. 3 waited impatiently, toying with his cell phone. *Did it work? Would they call?* He continued to check the black Motorola StarTac. Sure enough, it was on.

His forty-two-foot Newport sailboat rocked softly in the gentle current of the Delaware River. His left hand rested atop the captain's wheel, his right hand palming the phone. He looked at his mainmast, the sail wrapped tightly around the aluminum pole. The stiff breeze funneling down the valley caused him to huddle against himself, and he wondered whether there were others performing the same tasks this evening, or if he was the lone operator. He guessed the prison network had produced other operators looking for an easy payoff, and perhaps a bit of revenge against the system.

The call needed to come within the next ten minutes for his attack to be successful. After that, the window of opportunity would close for twenty-four hours. And then it would be too late.

The call came.

"Hello," the groomsman said.

"How are the winds today?" a voice asked.

Those were the words he was waiting to hear. "Perfect for a honeymoon sail," he said.

"We'll see you at the wedding."

The groomsman's heart leapt at the thought that he was going to make history. He cranked the engine and maneuvered the sailboat to the middle-support pylon for the Amtrak rail bridge. The track carried the daily Metroliner from Washington, DC, through Philadelphia and Trenton, finishing at New York City's Penn Station.

He had seven minutes.

He lifted a coiled rope and fed it through one of the pulleys and into a rusty piton drilled into the concrete pillar. The bridge maintenance personnel used the pitons to hold their barges against the current when they were making repairs on the bridge trusses. The sailboat adequately secured to three pitons, the groomsman dashed below to the galley and armed the explosives. The red light came on and began its countdown.

He had five minutes.

He took one last look around the galley, where explosives were stacked to the ceiling like boxes in a moving van. *This will be perfect.*

He emerged onto the aft deck and stepped over the taffrail onto the teak platform. He untied the half-hitch in the nylon rope and stepped onto the bobbing Zodiac. He figured there were about three minutes and change remaining.

In the rubber boat he crawled to the outboard motor and pushed the ignition. The motor coughed and spit white smoke at him. Not good. It always started on the first try. He waited a few seconds, trying to be patient, careful not to flood the engine.

Another push on the starter produced more coughing, more smoke.

"Come on . . ."

He was starting to worry. There were five hundred pounds of explosives sitting less than a hundred feet from his rubber boat. He knew who would lose that contest.

The boat merged into the painfully slow current, but it wouldn't carry him beyond the blast radius in time if he didn't get moving. With less than two minutes to go, he heard a faint noise in the distance, and looking up, he saw the train approaching the bridge. *Right on time.*

The groomsman had rehearsed this part many times in his sailboat, dropping anchor about a quarter mile away and just watching, timing the train every night, taking the mean average of the time the train would hit the lead portion of the bridge and calculating his timing from there. The train never varied more than a minute from its scheduled time of 6:07 p.m. Blow up the bridge too soon and the conductor would have the opportunity to stop; too late, of course, and the train would continue safely on to the next stop. Whoever kept the train running on time was doing a good job, the groomsman thought.

Less than a minute now.

Sweat was dripping from his forehead onto the manifold cover of the motor. *Please, God,* he thought, unconscious of the incongruity of his prayer and his objective, as he tried again.

The Evinrude 125 engine roared to life, drowning out the sound of the fast-approaching train.

The groomsman opened the throttle, snapped a 180 in the Zodiac, and aimed his nose south, away from the bridge.

He felt the heat from the explosion lick at the back of his neck, coaxing him to turn around. Groomsman No. 3 watched the fireball arc skyward, highlighting the smoke against its orange brilliance. The pylons crumbled as though they were made of plaster. He held his breath as he watched the middle span of the bridge buckle and then sag, swinging as if on a hinge and dropping toward the base of the northern supports.

He had opened a gap in the bridge by dropping a thirty-foot span into the river. The train was entering the lead edge of the chasm and there was nothing, *nothing*, the conductor could do.

The groomsman slowed for a second to take in the beauty of his work. It was almost an art form. There, against the roar of the fire, screeching metal, and the sputtering of his Evinrude 125, he watched the Metroliner dive into the Delaware River. First the engine and then the passenger cars careened off the severed rail and plunged, almost in slow motion, into the water.

Groomsman No. 3 was certain none of the 530 passengers would survive. He steered his rubber boat silently along the black water, stopping at a boat ramp five miles downstream. He leapt into waist-deep water, holding the boat by a rope. Leaning into the raft, he flipped the timer on another set of explosives, giving him five minutes to get out of the water and into his pre-positioned vehicle.

Pulling away, he watched the small boat explode and burn.

He would never be heard from again.

CHAPTER 10

MIDDLEBURG COMMAND POST

Meredith Morris shook her head in disbelief. *How could this happen?* Less than an hour after Matt and Peyton had lifted off toward Fort Bragg, the call came into the Suburban that Charlotte Coliseum had been brought down with explosives. Then, immediately after the first report, they received the information about the Mall of America in Minnesota and the Amtrak train in New Jersey.

Meredith traveled with the vice president back to the Middleburg command post, where the vice president immediately put his team to work gathering intelligence and monitoring developments and where she had a temporary office in one of the cottages, owing to the increased amount of time she had been spending with the vice president's command team over the last several months. Since 9/11, the administration had divided the government into halves, so that if more attacks came, there would be fully functional primary and alternate command posts.

Hellerman had the domestic security, or Homeland Defense, portfolio while the president focused on the wars in Iraq and Afghanistan.

Since her performance during last year's Japan-Philippine crisis, Meredith had assumed a central role on the vice president's team, even though she technically worked for the national security adviser. Hellerman had asked Meredith's boss, Dave Palmer, to lend her to his detail and straightaway promoted her to senior executive service status, meaning she had the same rank as a general.

She stared out of her office in one of Hellerman's old servant's quarters. She could see acres of rolling countryside and the long airstrip that Hellerman used for aerial commutes to the White House. She sighed as the gravity of the situation settled over her.

She had spent so much time in Middleburg that she decided to appoint her alternate office with Civil War paintings, a Remington bronze statue on the coffee table, and a couple of Peggy Hopper paintings she had purchased on a visit to Hawaii. She figured it was the right mix to demonstrate to her mostly male peers that she had the balls to do her job.

Meredith had lived most of her life near Appomattox, Virginia, and had been unable to escape the magical history of that area. After graduating from Virginia Tech in nearby Blacksburg, she had fought her way into the Pentagon with her political science doctorate. From there, her looks and her brains had both played pivotal roles in securing her present position.

She sat back at her large mahogany desk with a cut-glass top. The desk had come from the vice president's personal collection, she was sure. She flicked on the small green lawyer lamp and opened the top right desk drawer. Three framed pictures of Matt stared at her from inside: two of Matt by himself and one of them both on Skyline Drive in the Blue Ridge Mountains.

Of course, the televisions stayed on CNN and Fox News, with their continuous news tickers scrolling at the bottom: *Metroliner rail down in Trenton, NJ . . . Terrorism suspected . . . Five hundred believed dead . . . Mall of America implodes . . . Thousands believed killed . . . Charlotte Coliseum destroyed . . . 12,000 in attendance . . . Dead and injured tally unknown.*

Meredith shook her head. *All the warnings and inspections and new government offices to prevent this, but somehow we failed.*

"We're still getting information in," a voice said behind her. "We'll have a meeting in thirty minutes in the operations center."

She turned and saw Hellerman poking his head in her door. He had a handsome, tanned face framed by two shocks of gray hair that gave way to natural brown on the top. Perfect, bone-white teeth flashed, even when he wasn't smiling.

She placed the pictures back in the desk and stood.

"I was just reading some of the cables. Have you seen this?" She held up a small manila folder.

"What is it?" Hellerman said, entering the office.

"This Predator thing," she said, "I'm thinking this might be linked somehow. Was Peyton able to get anything else out of Matt?"

For weeks she had been studying the Predator case. Highly classified technology had been given to the Chinese, and now it seemed the military was missing eighteen Predators. *Those things don't just get up and fly away*, Meredith thought. Each of them was concerned that China could migrate the technology to the Iraqis, who could then put them to use in the current conflict. She knew she was treading on thin ice; most of the transfers were suspected to be political paybacks from several years ago.

"I don't know. Let's just hope we can put the genie back in the bottle, as they say," Hellerman said after a moment of thought.

"I think the saying is, 'You *can't* put the genie back in the bottle,'" she quipped.

"Have you seen *this*?" he said with raised eyebrows, changing the topic.

She stepped forward and took the folder from his hand. Someone had placed a Top Secret cover on it. Opening the file, she saw the standard cover disclaimer telling the reader that he or she would be shot at high noon on the White House lawn if he or she ever disclosed the material within to unauthorized personnel, or words to that effect.

Turning the next page, she read the cover, "Operation Maple Thunder."

"Of course, but do I need to read it again?" Meredith asked.

Hellerman sat in a burgundy, high-backed leather chair facing her desk. Meredith sat in its twin across the small table with a bowl of candy in the middle.

"I think Ballantine is behind the bombings today. We have an operative ready to go in alone and snatch him in his hideout in Canada. The Canadians are refusing to cooperate and assure us there's no terrorist operating from their country. So the trick is doing something, but making it look like we did nothing. Our operative is perfect. He has the perfect cover. He can go in and do this thing and if he fails, we have deniability; if he succeeds, we have deniability. Read it," he said pointing down at the folder. "We need to talk to the president shortly."

Meredith opened the file and scanned its contents then placed it in her lap. Her first thoughts were sparked by instinct, but she fought them back in order to formulate an objective report. *Huh*, she thought.

"Sounds like a good idea if we really believe this guy can get close to Ballantine. So, really, what's our deniability?" she asked.

"Complete. In the administration only the president, you, and I know about this. On the back page are the names of two people at Fort Bragg who know: the special operations commander and the doctor who brought him back to life, so to speak. And they are the only ones who know this individual's name."

"When I was looking at this the other day, I wondered whether you were okay with this from a moral point of view," she said.

"What's not to be okay?"

Meredith watched him carefully. He was baiting her. He wanted her to fight him on this one, she could tell.

"For one, the government is taking an individual and giving him a new identity without him knowing who he really is. As you say, *we* don't even know who he is. The legal, moral, and ethical implications reach far beyond what any of us can imagine." She spoke without emotion, no hint of criticism in her voice. She was just playing the role she knew he needed.

"Sure, but if we get close to Ballantine and can stop him before he kills another five thousand people, then we justify it," Hellerman countered.

"First, we don't know that Ballantine did this," she said, pointing at the television. "Second, even if that's true, what happens to our secret killer? We've now programmed him to be someone else. Does he continue in this vein, or do we then try to fix him back the way he was?"

"Too hypothetical, Meredith—"

"I don't think so. Maybe it's too hard, but it's not hypothetical. We have to think about the end state with this guy, assuming he can do this."

Hellerman tapped a finger against his pursed lips. "Your contention is that we are only doing what is expedient now, the future of this one individual be damned."

"It's a position," she said neutrally. She wasn't quite sure what she believed, but everything she had said sounded logical to her. They were both making it up as they went.

"Well, we're told that he has recovered completely from his coma. Colonel Rampert, the special ops commander, and the doctor worked out a rehabilitation regimen for him and they say he's ready."

"What are the possible courses of action?" she asked quietly.

"Simple," he said. "We either execute Operation Maple Thunder, to kill or capture Ballantine, or we don't."

"Yes, sir, but how do we do it?

"Look, in fifteen minutes we need to advise the president about what he should do."

Fifteen minutes, my ass.

"I mean, do we send him up there to fish, or do we parachute him in and let him wander up to the fishing camp—"

"Both options have been considered along with a few others. But ultimately, it's Rampert's call."

"We should know. The president should know, sir." She wrinkled her brow in determination.

"I agree. We can do a video teleconference and save time."

"Let's do it," she said.

Ezekial Jeremiah, a tall, black Naval Academy graduate stuck his head in the door, eyes wide with concern. "Uh, sir, we've . . . we've lost contact with Matt Garrett's airplane."

"What do you mean, 'lost contact'?" snapped Hellerman.

"Exactly that, sir. Transponder went off about thirty minutes ago, and now we have no idea where the plane is. We've lost contact with the pilot and radar is not tracking it. I've contacted the AWACS; they may be able to collect on it from the air," Jeremiah said.

"Where was the airplane's last position?" Hellerman asked.

"Crossing from Pennsylvania, near Williamsport, into New York, heading north."

"New York? Why so far north? Weren't they going to Fort Bragg, in North Carolina?" Meredith asked.

"That's correct."

"Okay, work the AWACS and notify special ops. Meanwhile, I'll call the president so we can get this briefing spun up."

"Yes, sir."

Hellerman walked toward the door then turned.

"I know how you feel about Matt. I hope this isn't as bad as it sounds."

Meredith watched him depart, turned toward the window and swallowed the palpable fear in her throat. *Be strong*, she thought to herself. The tear seeking a lonely path down her cheek was the only outward manifestation of the dread growing inside.

Meredith wiped her face, composed herself, and walked into the buzzing operations center.

CHAPTER 11

VERMONT

Despite his mind-numbing headache, Matt recalled the crash quite vividly. They had dropped like a stone from about a hundred feet. There had been fire and smoke, but he recalled seeing the plane still in one piece. Something must have gone right for him to survive. The landing gear *had* been down, apparently.

Then he remembered the words the man had said, "Ahmad and the woman are dead."

Was Peyton really gone? He looked at his arms and felt his face, as if to determine the severity of the accident via the nature of his injuries. Below his rolled-up sleeves, he saw multiple cuts and abrasions from what he figured was the instinctive reaction of putting his hands in front of his face as the aircraft struck the ground. On his face, he could feel one deep laceration that had etched a diagonal across his forehead. This, he thought, was most likely the source of his concussion. His body ached, but all things considered, he was doing pretty well for just having emerged from an airplane crash.

A rat came sniffing in his direction, and Matt nudged it away with his foot as he was reminded of the cell he shared with Rathburn, Barefoot, and

Sturgeon in the Philippines. He stood slowly, pain leaving his body in the form of a low growl. He was hurt.

Knees popping and back aching, he leaned against the wall and breathed heavily, pulling in as much oxygen as he could in the dirty cavern. The room was dark, though his eyes had adjusted sufficiently to discern shapes. He noticed the faintest hint of artificial light skidding beneath the door and limped the thirty feet or so separating him from it.

Extending his hands before him, he found the edges of the door and worked his way to the door knob, which was a loose piece of brass that felt as though it might come off in his hand if he turned too hard. He twisted the knob slowly and then pulled the door ajar a fraction of an inch. He felt a chain rattle and scrape along a hasp that he could now see affixed between the door and the jamb. A master lock about the size of a gym lock held the chain in place. The chain itself was a heavy gauge.

The faint light originated not directly beyond the door but well down a narrow hallway. Matt could see what appeared to be a lone figure to his right, about a hundred feet away. To his left the hallway appeared to end, with no other doors or windows.

The man at the end of the hallway turned aimlessly in his direction, giving Matt a good look at him. He was about six feet tall and modestly built and was smoking a cigarette.

Matt began to close the door and then stopped.

Walking down the hallway, approaching the guard, were two more people. One was a female and the other a male. His immediate sense was that they were together, but then he realized that it wasn't possible when he noticed that the female was Peyton O'Hara.

She had a small limp and her left arm was in a sling. Must have been a medical checkup, Matt thought, but then why the hell wasn't he receiving any specialized care?

As they approached, the man walking with Peyton stopped and opened a door for her about thirty feet from where Matt stood peering through a paper-thin crack in his door. As Peyton turned into the room, the open door cast a light across her face that let Matt see she had been badly cut across one cheek. Her shirt was blood-soaked and her face, though absent any apparent signs of fear, was weary with pain. Turning, Peyton lifted her head toward Matt's door, and for a brief moment, Matt believed their eyes met. She stumbled as she entered the room, and Matt quietly closed his door.

Peyton was alive, which meant that the disembodied voice he had heard earlier must have been talking about the poor Air Force attendant.

Matt knew from his training that the length of time spent in captivity is inversely proportional to one's likelihood of escaping. The more time his captors had to plan his demise, the more successful they were likely to be. As for the prisoner, all the planning in the world would not make up for a lack of resources to execute an escape plan. The one resource upon which Matt had drawn in the past was the element of surprise. Although a year-long layoff had dimmed his instincts a bit, he already knew what he was going to do.

The door opened and one man led another into the room, each carrying a Browning pump shotgun. Interesting choice. That told him something about his situation. He guessed they were in an area that was not entirely secluded—not public, but not altogether isolated. The shotguns could double as hunting weapons to local onlookers.

"I see you have returned from the dead, Matt Garrett," said the second man, who was clearly in charge. He had a soft, musical voice.

"Either that, or we're all in hell," Matt scowled, his throat raspy. Hearing his own voice after hours of silence confirmed, in a strange way, that he was indeed alive.

"Yes, well, hell for you it may be," the man retorted, drawing near, his shotgun crooked into one arm as if bird hunting.

Matt could see that the other captor, however, was training his Browning directly on his midsection, another indication that these were not amateurs. Shoot for the largest body mass to wound and then kill if necessary. The shooter's principle was to ensure a first-time hit.

Matt watched as the man with the musical voice approached him assuming that Matt was too weak or wounded to be a threat. Truthfully, Matt was acting the part just a bit, like a prizefighter limping along, doing the rope-a-dope, to cajole his opponent into letting down his guard. In his lower periphery, Matt could see that the approaching captor's weapon was hanging loosely along his forearm. The butt of the weapon was pressing upward against his triceps.

"I have someone who is very interested in meeting you, Mister Garrett, but our actions of the last twenty-four hours have jeopardized our ability to travel. We have instructions that now the meeting will not take place," the man said in lilting tones that, when he spoke, made his sentences seem almost poetic.

Matt knew immediately what "Now the meeting will not take place" meant. His captors' instructions were to kill him, plain and simple.

"Someone wants to meet me?" Matt asked, not particularly listening to his own words. His mind was reeling, threading several different scenarios through his own unique process of visualizing the course of action and war-gaming the potential results. Which one was most likely to succeed, most dangerous to him, most dangerous to his opponent, and least obvious?

"*Wanted* to meet you. My instructions are to inform you that his name is General Jacques Ballantine and that he lost his only brother during the invasion of Iraq in 1991. In fact, General Ballantine tells me that your brother, Zachary, murdered him that day."

During that war, Matt was on his first assignment in Northern Iraq, working with the Kurd resistance movement. He had been redeployed shortly before his brother. It was hand-to-hand combat, Zachary had told him. There were no options. Zachary had said he would do it again in the same situation. No regrets. Resulted in a major intelligence find. But the general, for reasons not explained to lowly Lieutenant Zachary Garrett at the time, had been promptly released back to Iraq.

And now, Matt figured, Ballantine was out for revenge on two different levels. First, on a personal level, he wanted to seek justice for his brother's death. Since Ballantine probably knew that Zachary was dead, Matt would likely be the next-best target. Or perhaps the first-best target. Brother for brother. Second, Ballantine could also, through his prism, blame the United States for the loss of his brother and many of the other ills that had befallen Iraq over the last decade. So Hellerman was right, it was Ballantine who might be planning to distribute attacks throughout the United States with a purpose of wreaking havoc, reopening the still too-fresh wounds of 9/11. *Like jujitsu,* Matt thought, *catch us leaning one way and follow up with a well-placed kick to disable us.*

"I see," Matt said. "So he has delegated the dirty task of killing me to you? He wants you to avenge his grudge?"

Once again, Matt's mind was not truly monitoring the words his well-trained brain was formulating and causing his mouth to speak. Every ounce of his analytical power was operating faster, more powerfully than any Intel microchip could ever push a computer hard drive. Scores of chess moves played out, then the board reset, then another option played out, then the board reset, and so on.

There is one last chance, and only one, he surmised.

"A task that I do not mind at all. In fact, it gives me great pleasure to do this," his lead captor said.

Matt noticed as the man began to transfer the shotgun from a carrying position to a firing position that the butt stock was passing beneath the assassin's armpit and would begin to rise toward his chest. Matt had run this possibility through five or six different permutations.

As the butt stock passed the man's armpit, Matt lunged with the quickness and ferocity of a mountain lion, catching both of his captors unawares. As part of his mental algorithm he had calculated the length of the long barrel and how much time it would take for the man with the musical voice to swing it into action. Having hunted fowl with a Browning before, Matt knew that the barrel was maddeningly long and that only skilled and experienced hunters could maneuver it with precision. Most fumbled clumsily with the awkward length. Matt had also noticed that both weapons seemed practically brand new. They were shiny, with a light sheen of oil, and clean, with no marring on the butt stocks.

Without warning, Matt grabbed the long barrel and thrust it sharply upward, catching the man squarely under the jaw, snapping his head back and causing momentary shock. He kicked the stunned captor in the stomach as he ripped the shotgun from his grip, launching him off balance, then instinctively thumbed the safety off and fired into the belly of the man with the musical voice. The shotgun created a thunderous boom. But another boom, not created by Matt's weapon, quickly followed and he felt a searing hot pellet rip through his biceps. Then he quickly fired another round into the skull of the backup man as if he were knocking down two quail that had taken flight at the point of his dog, Ranger.

Matt confirmed what he already knew, that both of his captors were dead, as he moved briskly to the door. He realized that he would be in a race with the guard at the end of the hallway to Peyton's room. Leading with the shotgun barrel, he quickly turned into the long hallway. He picked up the movement of the guard racing toward him, fumbling with his pistol, and Matt squeezed the trigger. The shot stood the guard straight up, splaying his hands into the air as if he had suddenly decided to surrender. The pistol came tumbling toward Matt, involuntarily tossed to him by the forward motion of the guard's arm. Matt secured the pistol and stuffed it in his waistband. Then he snatched another pistol magazine from the guard's belt, shoved it in his pocket, and moved toward Peyton's door, still leading with the shotgun.

He kicked the door open, turning into the room and visually clearing each corner. In the adjacent corner, he saw Peyton cuffed and gagged, eyes wide with fear and pointing behind him and to his right, the only unclear corner. Swiftly, he dropped the shotgun, and with the skill of a ballerina-turned-gymnast, he drew the pistol from his belt and fired three shots as he turned. As Matt's eyes caught up with his shots, he heard the first two slap against the stone wall, but the third made a wet thud. He watched as his would-be attacker slumped to the ground with a widening crimson hole seeping blood from his chest.

Unsure of how many or how soon reinforcements would arrive, he moved quickly toward Peyton, removed her gag, and freed her wrists.

"You okay?" he asked as he worked on a troublesome knot around her ankles.

"Fine, fine," Peyton said. "Where did you learn how to shoot like that? Not that I'm complaining."

"Let's go," he said, grabbing her by the arm.

"Wait!" Peyton insisted as she followed him out of the room. "There's a man in another room. I saw him."

"No time," Matt hissed, handing her the pistol and hustling along the hallway. He stopped at the corner, and leading with the shotgun, spun into the adjacent hall.

"How the hell do you get out of here?" Matt asked.

"Stop here! Stop!" she yelled as they approached a door on the right.

Peyton pushed into the door, but it didn't budge. "Stand back!"

"What are you . . . ?" Matt began to ask but stalled out, observing Peyton draw the pistol, level it just above the door knob, and fire with an unexpectedly fluid and natural motion to disable the lock. She pushed the door open with her foot and rushed into the room, unconcerned with what lay behind the door.

"Where is he?" she shouted.

"Who the hell are you looking for?" Matt said, following her in. Then he saw a man sitting in the corner of the room staring at a small glass, mesmerized and oblivious to their presence.

"Come on! Let's go!" Peyton yelled running toward the man.

He was wearing the kind of white smock used in laboratories. His gray hair was balding and wire-rimmed spectacles framed his eyes. The man wore blue jeans and tennis shoes, making him look a bit like a mad scientist, frizzy hair and all.

Turning his head slowly, the mad scientist looked at Matt, or rather, looked through him. Matt turned to see what he was staring at and took a step back.

Peyton had already stopped and reached her hand out to the man.

"Peyton, let's go!" Matt yelled.

Peyton released the arm of the catatonic scientist, spun on her heels, and ran toward Matt.

"What the hell are all those bees doing in here?" she shouted, darting past him.

In the back of the room, Matt saw hundreds, maybe thousands, of bees, all swarming in basically the same spot, about fifteen feet away. As his adrenaline ebbed, the high-pitched whine of thousands of wings snapping hundreds of times per second created a vibrant hum in the room, like the feeling of a jet engine thrusting just before takeoff.

"I'm not sure I want to find out," he said, moving out of the door, only to be greeted by automatic gunfire. He spun quickly back into the room and waited two counts before he swung the barrel back into the passageway and laid down two suppressive shots. Out of shells, he turned to Peyton. "Trade me," Matt said, motioning to the Glock in Peyton's hand. She handed it to him and accepted the unwieldy shotgun without taking her eyes off the swarm of bees. Matt checked the magazine and shoved it back home. He took a deep breath and asked Peyton, "Where to?"

"To the right and across the hall, that's the way they took me to the doctor," she said.

"Okay, follow me. We're running," Matt said, focused.

He fired three more shots from the pistol to his left and then darted in the direction Peyton had suggested. He found the door open, pushed through it, and burst into the dark night.

CHAPTER 12

JOINT SPECIAL FORCES COMMAND, FORT BRAGG, NORTH CAROLINA

Colonel Jack Rampert, commander of the U.S. Army's elite commando force, put down the phone and looked at Dr. Ted Tedaues.

"Okay, we've got the word."

Tedaues' calculating eyes stared back at him blankly.

"You think he's up to it?" Rampert asked.

"No," Tedaues said. Then he added, "But do we have a choice?"

"*He*'s got no choice," Rampert said, turning toward the window. In silence they stood and watched the man on the treadmill, who was breathing into a spirometer, measuring what turned out to be the incredible volume of his lung capacity. Each steady, forceful breath slammed a small ball to the top of the plastic casing every time he exhaled.

"What is his assignment?" the doctor said.

"You don't want to know."

"Look, our man in there is a human being, and I'm assuming he's got family and friends and all that. It doesn't matter that he doesn't remember who he is."

"Ted, we've been through this. That soldier in there died a year ago," he said, pointing through the one-way glass. "His family has mourned his loss. They've buried him. But now he has the opportunity to do something very important for this country."

"You think he'd do it if he remembered who he was? It's a fair question."

Rampert studied his friend.

"I know he'd do it. That's why I was recruiting him to join our team in special ops."

"I don't like it. But he's as ready as he'll ever be. Really a physical specimen, as a matter of fact. He's been running five-minute miles on the treadmill, benching 320 pounds, and climbing ropes like he's Spiderman. Based on what you've told me, he seems more physically fit than before his 'death,'" Tedaues commented.

"He's a warrior. A natural," Rampert said.

"We've had great improvement, but I'm still concerned," the doctor responded, continuing his prognosis. "Physically, he couldn't be better. But mentally, his mind collects and retains information today as if he were a genius yet he has no apparent memory prior to the incident. I don't know . . . I feel like I'm building Frankenstein in there. And I still don't know his real name. That's not right. I'd like to know that, at least. He's been my patient since you brought him to me in a coma."

The colonel looked at him with dark eyes, no differentiation between the iris and pupil, just stone cold blackness providing windows to the mysterious soul of the most notorious commando in modern U.S. history. Rampert's face was cragged with age and battle scars. A modern day Achilles, Rampert had been cycling through the commando and Special Forces communities since Charlie Beckwith, his mentor, created the secret organization.

As for Tedaues, he had served with Rampert for ten years as the combat surgeon on every big mission they had executed.

"Ted, you're the best combat doc I've ever seen. I'll tell you what you need to know in due time. I've never steered you wrong. Just finish the job." Rampert spoke in the same manner he had given the order to destroy Taliban and al Qaeda fighters.

Jack Rampert's Army combat uniform, too, told the story of the military's premier warrior, with combat infantryman's badges from three different conflicts, three gold stars on his master parachutist wings indicating combat jumps into Panama, Afghanistan, and most recently, the

Philippines, and a right-shoulder combat patch of the Joint Special Forces Command. Rampert's career had been filled with unique missions, all an extension of his Special Forces bona fides. Combat jumps, reconnaissance deep behind enemy lines, and interrogation of high-value enemy prisoners of war all fill his portfolio. He saw the exhaustion and frustration etched on his friend's face.

Tedaues shifted around a bit, kicking at the floor.

"What's the problem?"

"No problem, sir."

"All right, then. He's going to go kill us one bad actor."

"Ballantine?"

Rampert paused, then stood and walked toward the door, which he checked to ensure it was locked.

"That's right. Ballantine." He sighed and then continued. "All right. In Iraq we lost one of our deep black ops guys. He was right next to Hussein, was gonna take him. Somehow he got caught. He was due to rotate back. I was going to put him on the Ballantine mission—"

"I remember."

"They iced him. Strung him up by his thumbs, beat him with a baseball bat, then shot him through the eyes. After that, they dumped him in front of Baghdad International, right in front of the headquarters. They were saying, 'Don't mess with us anymore.'"

"Then we know where Ballantine is?" the doctor asked.

"Yes. He's an Iraqi general from the first Gulf War. He laid low during this go around. Might be connected to what just went down today. Don't know, but we think so. We've got signal intelligence and some imagery suggesting that he is running a fishing guide service out of Canada. We've monitored some intel that says he's been orchestrating something. Now that these attacks have happened, we think he's the one."

"All right. Connect this thing."

"This soldier in here," Rampert said, pointing through the window at the young man on the treadmill. "Damn Canucks refuse to cooperate, won't let us go in there with guns blazing. So we need to do something; we need to send someone. Then why not send someone that we can deny ever existed? This soldier's supposed to be dead. He no longer exists. And with a new name, we can get him in close to Ballantine.

"I lost my best guy. This is the only other soldier I've ever seen who could do what needs to be done, alone. He's a paratrooper, a fighter. He's killed and he's been killed."

Rampert watched Tedaues consider his comments. No doubt, Rampert figured, that the good doctor was thinking that a one-man mission was insane, unheard of, and Rampert needed to allay the concerns of the only man who knew about their resurrected man. Rampert broke his gaze from Tedaues and looked at his protégé thumping on the treadmill at five minutes per mile as though he were on a Sunday walk.

"What about his family, Colonel? You're telling me to go back in there and finish this series of experimental coma-release treatments, which you and I both know could erase what is left of his memory. It's like reformatting your hard drive."

Rampert looked back at Tedaues. "We'll worry about that when the time comes. His family has grieved its loss. Why not let him do this mission and see what happens?"

"What if he has lost his instincts? What if he wants to be an artist when you brief him on this mission? This is like jump-starting a car, Colonel, without knowing where the positive and negative terminal posts are. Cross the wires and we might do something terrible. Then again, just like a broken bone heals stronger than it was before, his memory may suddenly appear in Technicolor before his very eyes."

"To everyone else, he's already dead. I'll take my chances. He's ready now, you said so yourself, and I know this son of a gun. He's the best damn soldier I've seen. He'll be fine. Besides, you've seen him train. You can't tell me you don't see his instincts in what he's doing. It's just his memory—"

"Until he remembers something from his past life in the middle of this mission and he comes unraveled. It's that simple."

"Yes, it is that simple."

Tedaues studied Rampert. The two friends let a long moment pass between them. Rampert had pushed the envelope so many times in his career that, truthfully, this mission seemed rather ordinary to him.

"So the key is that he's expendable, and deniable?" Tedaues asked.

Rampert didn't need to answer. His glare said more than words. Rampert knew that Tedaues and the other unit members were aware of some of his prior questionable activities. He knew what the doctor was asking.

"Ted, just know that he's a soldier, and he can do soldierly things. It's not like we're trying to fix up a civilian here to do these things."

"It's risky," Tedaues said, "and unethical."

The colonel looked at him hard.

"I'll have him ready."

"That's all I'm asking." The colonel unlocked the door, opening it as a dim light flowed into the dark room, then turned his head and looked over his shoulder. "If you're still worried about our boy here, you're welcome to accompany him on his mission when the time comes . . . to keep an eye on him."

"Yeah, right," Tedaues said with a chuckle. "I've been on enough of those. The only cutting I want to do is with this scalpel." The shiny blade glistened in the crease of light.

"Call me in an hour," Rampert said.

He nodded as the colonel departed and turned back toward the treadmill. The patient was on his seventh mile, no slack in his pace. Truly amazing.

He had given a dead man a new life . . . only to send him to his death.

CHAPTER 13

VIDEO TELECONFERENCE

Meredith sat in the video teleconference room of the alternate command post in Middleburg. It was equipped with bright lights, a large plasma screen, and two cameras. The vice president was seated to her left. No one else was in the VTC room with them, though the Pentagon and White House were also connected. Meredith noticed the secretary of defense, Robert Stone, and chairman of the Joint Chiefs, General "Shark" Shepanski, on the Pentagon feed. President Davis and Roger Houghton, the CIA director, were on the White House feed. *Too many people*, she thought.

Colonel Jack Rampert began speaking and talked with a slight country drawl Meredith couldn't exactly place, maybe Arkansas, or Texas. Somewhere in the South, she was sure. Wearing his Army-green uniform, he looked every bit the elite warrior that his reputation purported him to be. His crew-cut hair, rough-hewn face, and lean frame fed the image of his standing as a no-nonsense combat veteran.

The surgeon who had operated on the man they called Boudreaux was seated next to Rampert. Meredith guessed he was in his late thirties, handsome, but he seemed to have a certain hardness that was out of synch with the rest of his character. Perhaps all of these guys were that way. They have killed and have been shot at who knows how many times. It probably took something different to deal with that lifestyle.

"This is Dr. Ted Tedaues," Rampert said. "He's our surgeon, and quite frankly, one of the best all-around doctors in the country. He's jumped into combat from an airplane flying five hundred feet above the ground; he's been on multiple special operations missions that served the vital interests of this nation; over the past year he has helped Boudreaux rehabilitate from combat wounds, and now he is ensuring Boudreaux is ready for Operation Maple Thunder."

Rampert's voice trailed the movement of his lips because the secure satellite delayed transmission of the visual images by a fraction of a second. Meredith watched as Rampert punched a button on a remote, causing a PowerPoint slide to appear on the VTC screen.

"This chart shows our patient's progression over the past eight months. He was in a solid coma for two months," Tedaues explained, pointing at a matrix on the chart. "He first showed signs of recovery in September of last year. His right hand had a muscle spasm, not altogether uncommon for coma patients." He paused and looked at Rampert, then flipped another slide onto the projector. It was a picture of a skeleton with muscle mass.

"But what followed was an immediate contraction of the bicep, here, and an extension of the forearm muscle, here. For two weeks we had no other movement."

Tedaues paused again and Meredith began to wonder where all of this was leading.

"Then we saw a series of similar muscle movements in the opposing arm and in both legs. It was as if the patient was trying to force himself out of the coma. Really quite extraordinary. Naturally we had twenty-four-hour camera coverage of his entire body. In early October the patient lifted his head and opened his eyes."

Another pause and another chart.

"From that point, he was officially conscious and registered a three on a fifteen-point scale that certified neurosurgeons use to classify coma patients. Our patient was different, however, than others that I have worked with and any other that I could find in my research. From the moment he became conscious, he had almost all of his physical capabilities. Only his cognitive abilities lagged behind his ability to move, sit up, and shortly thereafter, walk."

Meredith cocked her head. *Remarkable.*

"This individual, before going into his coma, was an impressive physical specimen. He remains one today. Throughout his dormant stages, his body would go through a series of muscle spasms every day. Over time it appeared as though his subconscious was performing isometrics, stationary exercises. For example, his bicep would tighten for about a minute then relax. Then his forearm would flex, and relax. Most of his major muscle groups got some form of isometrics every day. Craziest thing I've ever seen."

"Who is this person?" Hellerman asked.

Rampert interjected quickly and said, "His name is Winslow Boudreaux. He's from Louisiana. He is a special operations soldier. And he is ready for the mission."

Meredith looked at the vice president, wondering why he would ask that question. Her curiosity was piqued. She turned back toward the VTC screen, looking at the chart and then the doctor. She also wanted to ask what the patient's real name was but knew she would be rebuked. Even at her level, these things were best kept secret. Plausible deniability was a very real fact of life in the national security business and knowing just a bit of Rampert's reputation for risk-taking, Meredith logged a red flag in the back of her mind.

"For the past two months, he has been more physically active than most Olympic athletes," Tedaues said. "Every day he has been running, swimming, jumping from airplanes, lifting weights, and training with weapons."

"Mentally?" Meredith asked.

Tedaues hesitated, looking at Rampert. "Operationally, he's fine. He only lacks a recollection of experiences prior to his coma. But his instincts are formidable. He cannot tell you, for example, his name or phone number prior to his accident, but from the minute he woke up, he has been an expert marksman, just like before."

Meredith sighed and looked down at the table. This was a more complicated problem than she had originally considered.

The door opened, producing a short male dressed in a blue blazer, white shirt, and red tie, with khaki pants. He looked harried, racing toward Hellerman. Ralph Smithers, Meredith noticed. Usually the bearer of bad news.

"Sir, we've got a confirmation. Over five hundred passengers and crew members were killed in the train derailment. We're still working the Charlotte Coliseum and Mall of America, but it's . . . it's bad," he said.

The VTC room fell silent, and Meredith could tell that everyone in the president's situation room and the Joint Operations Center at Fort Bragg had heard Ralph's comment.

"When can he go in?" The president's voice was crisp and sure.

"Sir, he's ready now." Rampert's voice was decisive.

Meredith looked at Hellerman and nodded. He returned her knowing glance. They were about to send Frankenstein to meet Ballantine.

The vice president turned to the video camera with a confident stare. "Mr. President, I recommend we execute Maple Thunder, now."

CHAPTER 14

VERMONT

“This way,” Matt whispered to Peyton.

Looking at her in the moonlight, he could see a hardened edge to her expression. Her eyes darted back and forth, focusing and searching for danger. He grabbed her arm and guided her through a small thicket of woods toward a distant gathering of lights. The air was cool but not frigid. Their adrenaline was sufficient to keep them warm as they raced away from the terrorist camp.

“Any idea where we are?” she whispered, keeping up with him.

“Don’t know, but these fir trees and maples make me think we’re somewhere up north, maybe New England. The airfield was small and remote, so I don’t remember much other than the landing heading on the runway. It was 355 degrees, almost due north. We banked hard after the woman was killed and didn’t turn much on our final approach, so I have to say that we are north of where we started.”

They continued to jog through the forest. After he figured they had run a couple of miles, Matt slowed to a brisk walk, steam pouring from his mouth with every breath.

They continued walking, side by side, along the deserted road. Matt let some silence pass.

"Who was that guy?" Matt asked.

"What guy?"

"The mad scientist you wanted to rescue."

"Oh, him. Don't have any idea." Her diminishing voice seemed elusive to Matt. He gave her a sideways glance.

"He was a prisoner just like us. Why wouldn't we want to save him?"

"Why didn't he come with us?"

It was a cool spring morning. Dense fog was settling into the low ground.

They had come upon a gravel country road running perpendicular to their axis of escape. Peyton had discarded the shotgun while Matt maintained control of the pistol, which had two rounds of ammunition remaining. He had noticed during their escape that Peyton was in superb physical condition. She had been able to keep up with him the entire way, and truthfully, had pushed him early on.

Matt ran his hand along his ribcage, pressing down slightly, feeling the scar tissue and the razor-sharp pain that accompanied the year-old wound.

"Okay?" Peyton asked.

"Fine. Now, answer my question."

"How the hell do I know?" she snapped and left it at that.

They approached an intersection with a two-lane asphalt road with faded yellow stripes down the middle.

"Which way, Kemo Sabe?" Peyton quipped.

Matt looked at his watch: one a.m. Looking up, he stared at the black sky, picking out a quarter moon sitting low along the treetops to his right. He had noticed the moon directly over their heads a couple of hours ago, and so he knew they would be traveling west if they turned to the right.

"We've been heading mostly southeast away from the airfield. Low, flat land to our right. Outline of mountains to our left and front," Matt said, pointing as he spoke. "Lots of hardwoods, probably maple trees. Feels like the Green Mountains in Vermont. I skied Smugglers Notch once, and if that's the case, there are plenty of good trails locals used for smuggling booze from Canada during prohibition. Lots of caves and small towns."

Matt breathed deeply and looked around once more. "Let's keep heading in this direction until dawn," he said. "How are you holding up?"

Peyton had discarded the sling on her arm when they climbed the chain-link fence on the far side of the runway. She seemed okay but Matt could tell she was eating some pain.

"Don't worry about me," Peyton said.

As they made the turn, Matt thought he heard a sound in the brush, maybe a squirrel or another small animal.

He admitted to himself that after nearly a year out of the spy business, his instincts, while still very good, were perhaps a nanosecond behind what they had been in his prime.

He heard another sound. His mind began racing with the possibilities. Sure, it could be a small animal, but it was likely something more dangerous. They were in a remote area at a prominent intersection with one of the roads that led to the airfield. Honestly, they would not be hard to track. At that moment, he derided himself for following a road and not pushing past the gravel and into the rising terrain further east.

"This way!" he said, grabbing Peyton by the arm and yanking her into the long arms of fir trees. The branches slapped them as they bolted.

He heard the first tell-tale sound of a silenced weapon firing in their direction, the bullet missing its mark but snapping a branch above his head.

"What the hell?" Peyton said in a hushed tone.

Two more shots zipped past their heads like angry hornets as they tumbled into the soft undergrowth beneath the fir trees.

"Hurry, they're coming!" Matt spoke through clenched teeth as he pulled Peyton to her feet. They darted deeper into the forest, running with such ferocity that it reminded Matt of the Philippines, where he was chased by a hundred Abu Sayef rebels. His lungs burned as they processed oxygen exponentially faster than normal. His mouth was dry, and he swallowed hard against a tight lump in his throat.

He started angling their route toward the east, which led them to higher, more protected ground. Without breaking stride, they darted across the road and continued another hundred meters into the forest. Then he stopped, and they hid behind two large chunks of granite that formed a *V*, with the crevice giving them a view of the gravel road.

"Quiet," he whispered.

Peyton looked at him and nodded her head. The thought that she was beautiful suddenly popped into his head. He quickly pushed the irrelevant notion into the dark recesses of his mind, where it would die a quick death.

Peyton pointed to his left at the same time he was hearing a slight rustling near the road, then voices. Two men were moving fast but had slowed considerably from their initial pace. The voices were heavily accented.

"Here," one said, pointing at the gravel in the road. "Footprints."

There had been no time to do the old Indian trick of covering their tracks with a tree branch, but Matt's makeshift plan might work anyway.

The pursuers looked up and began moving into the woods. Matt cringed when he noticed one man slip something onto his head.

Night-vision goggles.

He pulled Peyton slowly below the sightline of the granite and pointed at his eyes. Peyton understood.

Matt slipped the pistol from his belt and slowly moved the safety switch to disengage the trigger of the weapon. He could hear the men moving quickly now, almost adjacent to their position.

"Mustaf, wait," one man whispered.

Matt could see that they were no more than ten feet from his position, and now they had noticed the granite formation.

Before they could advance upon his position, Matt lifted his pistol as he ran directly toward them, firing once at the man with the night-vision goggles and then expending his last bullet on him when the first bullet did not find a vital organ.

The second one did.

Matt altered his course toward the remaining pursuer. The dark figure was faintly silhouetted against the black forest and was bringing his weapon into firing position. Matt, out of ammunition, barreled into him, tackling him to the ground. They fell atop a large chunk of granite and rolled together against a tree trunk. They stopped with Matt on top, punching the man in the face, until he caught the motion of the assailant's pistol moving toward him from the ground. Too late. It was up and firing, the loud report ringing in his ears, his shoulder on fire.

He released the man's neck and grabbed at the pistol hand before he could fire another shot, but again he was too late.

The man's pistol hand reeled backward, responding to a sharp kick from

Peyton, who spun and swung her leg down like a guillotine, with her heel crushing the man's windpipe. Matt heard an audible pop, which he initially thought was his attacker's throat. But when he considered the force with which Peyton had chopped downward, he knew she had snapped their pursuer's neck.

Matt looked up to see Peyton moving toward him.

Peyton looked at Matt's arm and then into his eyes. "You're shot."

He placed his hand onto the wound, feeling the familiar, sticky wet of oozing blood. The bullet had grazed him.

"Just a flesh wound. We need to get moving. There'll be more on the way," he said.

Matt stood motionless for a second, listening. He thought he heard something. Not anything on the ground, but something in the air. *What was that? A low hum, maybe? Like the bees?* The noise was gone in an instant, but it got him thinking.

Matt quickly scavenged what he could from the dead attackers—antiquated night-vision goggles, nearly spent weapons, full ammo clips—and blended into the night before others could pursue.

CHAPTER 15

After an hour of darting through a thickening forest and undulating terrain, Matt stopped, looked at Peyton, and said, "Let's take a quick break."

He was breathing hard, smoky wisps of breath looking like locomotive steam escaping from his mouth. They took a knee and Matt inspected the weapons. An AK-47 and a Makarov pistol.

"Old Russian weapons," he said.

"Those guys weren't Russians. They were Arabs," Peyton replied.

They had been on the move for about an hour, continuing on a southeasterly track. They had crossed two gravel roads and one paved road that looked like a county highway. Keeping perpendicular to all means of routine travel, Matt figured he was making pursuit more challenging. Heading downhill, they were bound to eventually find water, and water usually led to population. They stopped on a level piece of ground spotted with tall hardwoods. The lack of ambient light created a pitch-black backdrop for the millions of bright stars dotting the sky like pinpricks.

He tossed the AK-47 aside and pocketed the pistol. Considering something, he stared at the sky, then looked at Peyton.

"I'm still thinking about that other guy. Why you wanted to save him. How you knew he was there." Matt looked at Peyton's eyes.

"I told you, I saw him when they were taking me to the doctor."

"I had a question about that, too. I mean, I was pretty banged up, yet you got first class medical treatment."

Peyton turned away.

"What are you implying?" she whispered under her breath, folding her arms across her chest.

"That you know a hell of a lot more than you're telling me."

"Not true."

"Bullshit," Matt said. He started walking again. They continued on their journey, a bit tired and with no water, no food, and no means of communication.

They crossed a small stream. The cool water felt good on their aching feet, but Matt knew the soaked shoes would make for a tough leg ahead. They drank from the stream, hydrating until they could feel perspiration glistening on their skin.

"We think Ballantine's got something to do with those Predators," she conceded, her voice cutting through the still night.

"Okay, tell me what you know."

"Ballantine's not totally connected to al Qaeda, but he does have ties to Ansar. He began plotting this directly after he was released from prisoner-of-war status at the end of the first Persian Gulf War. We think he built his support in France, organized his efforts in Canada, and then slipped into Lake Moncrief to set up his base."

"I pretty much figured all that out," Matt responded.

"Well, the one thing that Ballantine had, that a terrorist in Afghanistan or Northern Iraq didn't have, was true state sponsorship. Negotiations were going on between Iraq and China, North Korea, Syria, and many others all under the guise of typical state business. Other terrorist organizations didn't have that luxury. Sometimes it's a benefit to be a non-state actor, but sometimes it pays to have 'state' cover."

"Okay."

"When we traded technology to China for campaign cash, it was kind of like sending an e-mail to someone," Peyton said. "They'll get it, but you never know who they might forward it to."

"Okay."

"We have indications that there was communication between China and Iraq prior to Gulf War Two and that one of the reasons Hussein was buying time prior to the battle for Baghdad was so that Ballantine could get set."

"A strategic move on his part. Get our military decisively engaged in Iraq and have a Phase Two ready to go. But this one is on our turf, using our freedoms to conceal his moves," Matt said.

"Exactly."

"But Hussein's not that smart, so he had to have some help. He gets some help from China, maybe, which guides him on how to do this. They set up some cells and come in from the north."

"Makes sense."

"And the dog that never barked?" Matt asked.

Peyton looked at him, knowing exactly what he was talking about.

"WMDs," she said. "There's a suspicion that Ballantine has been moving the chemical and biological weapons out of Iraq, through Syria, and into Quebec."

"Is that what we're dealing with here? The reason we never found anything?" Matt asked.

Peyton looked away and muttered under her breath, "Oh, I hope not."

They walked for another thirty minutes before Matt stopped. "Wait," he said. He looked at the horizon through a growth of small trees, the land angling downward, away from him. "There's some light, barely noticeable," Matt said, pointing.

They maneuvered through more low ground, feeling the scrape of what Matt called wait-a-minute vines against their pant legs until they found a blacktop road. They followed the road from the wood line for another mile, toward the light, and then they saw a sign: SHELDON SPRINGS, VERMONT: POPULATION 2,014.

"Make that 2,016," Matt whispered. Ever cautious, he was glad to be near civilization.

CHAPTER 16

SHELDON SPRINGS, VERMONT

Before they reached the actual town of Sheldon Springs, they found a small farm on the south side of the road. A wood rail fence lined the front of the property and followed a gravel drive to a two-story white house with green shingles. Further to the rear of the property was a red barn that seemed to contrast the purity of the white home.

Matt led Peyton around the outskirts of the property and entered the barn from the rear. Eyes already adjusted to the darkness, he could see a few tractors and other farm equipment. Hundreds of empty baskets—for apple farming, he presumed—were stacked on one side. He saw exactly three milk cows that returned his gaze with the sullen stare that all cows seemed to have.

"Up there," he whispered, pointing at the loft. True to form, there was plenty of hay that would provide at least a bit of comfort for some much-needed sleep.

"We should be rather anonymous up there," Peyton said. "Just don't get any ideas."

It had been a long day and even longer night, and Matt found he was unprepared for her humor. He smiled. She noticed.

"The only idea I have is sleep," he responded, ignoring multiple witty comebacks that instinctively popped into his head.

They climbed the ladder and each found that their adrenaline prevented them from sleeping. Peyton looked across the hay mound at Matt.

"Matt, earlier today you said that your brother knew Ballantine. How did he know him?"

He didn't want to get into the details, but knew that he had to start trusting someone. He might as well start with this good-looking woman he had known less than a day, he figured.

"How does your brother fit into all of this?" she asked.

"Zachary captured Ballantine. And in the process, he killed his brother."

"Do you think Ballantine's out for revenge?" she asked.

"Makes sense. I know how I would feel if I could ever find the man who killed Zachary," he whispered.

Matt stared out of the hayloft. A diminishing moon hung in the frame of the loft like a piece of children's art.

"How would you feel?" she asked.

"Do you have any brothers or sisters?"

"One sister. We're not close," she said, looking away.

"I was close to Zachary. The emotions I have wrestled with since his death have consumed me. Sometimes I just want to kill anyone who might have had anything to do with Zachary's death."

"Do you really think that would make a difference?"

"Nothing else has."

"Seems you have no problem killing people," Peyton said, remembering the last several hours.

Matt turned to look directly into her eyes. "It's not about the killing."

Peyton felt a chill as his eyes locked onto her like a laser. A fine mist escaped his mouth as he breathed the fresh Vermont air.

"Besides, you put your heel through that man's windpipe as if you've done it before," Matt said. "Obviously not your first."

She paused and looked away, stiffening. "Wouldn't you like to know?"

"Actually, yes."

When Peyton didn't respond, Matt let the question go but logged it away in the back of his mind. He had noticed a tough streak since their first encounter, but now he was beginning to believe there was much more to her, a certain nefarious depth that he couldn't quite place.

"Why don't you tell me about those Predators?" she asked.

After a long pause, he responded. "Okay. I know some stuff. You're right. It's probably time to talk about it."

Peyton looked up at him, remaining silent, not wanting to interrupt.

"Roger Webb, another member of my organization, and I worked on this thing together, this Predator project. When we learned that the previous administration had given the go-ahead to release the unmanned aerial vehicle technology—technology that enabled us to arm the Predator with Hellfire missiles and other payloads—to China, we were pissed. We got involved, against CIA orders. Of course, the CIA director was in the president's pocket. Anyway, this technology is very sensitive."

"So . . ." she prodded.

"So I followed some leads from China to the Philippines, where things got pretty ugly."

"How so?"

"Well, in China, the director figured out I was chasing this stuff down and turned Chinese intelligence onto me," Matt said.

"Can you prove that?"

Matt chuckled at her naiveté. "Of course not. It's just one of those things you know. When you're half way across the world with a perfect cover and suddenly you have ten operatives following you, including one American you recognize, you get suspicious."

"I see."

"Anyway, I managed to avoid the Chinese palace guards and find a contact who could give me the information on who had this technology and what they were doing with it."

"Was it just a computer disk, or was it the actual stuff?" Peyton asked.

"It was sixteen or eighteen Predators, which they could probably have built, or at least come close. But the ground control stations that use satellite technology for guidance are the key. That's what I was looking for."

"How did eighteen Predators get away from the United States?"

"Remember that big campaign-cash-for-technology scandal?" Matt asked. "What I found was that, to avoid our satellite tracking, the Chinese had actually built a small test facility on a remote island in the Philippine chain."

"So where are the Predators and these stations now?"

"If I knew that, I wouldn't be here," he admitted. "The question is," he said, staring directly at her, "what do *you* know about these Predators?"

"Only what you tell me," she lied.

"Bullshit."

"The only information I may have," she whispered, "deals with some F-117 stealth fighters that we had shot down over Kosovo and Afghanistan."

"Stealth Predators?"

"Maybe," she said, looking away.

A long moment of silence passed between them. Matt looked skyward, staring at the wide planks in the ceiling of the barn.

"Rumor has it that you had the shot," Peyton said, deflecting the conversation back toward Matt.

"I did. I think about it every day. Haunts me. They denied my kill chain."

"You don't seem like the higher headquarters-approval type of guy," Peyton said.

Matt turned his head toward Peyton, taking in a bit of her beauty, finding solace in that for some reason.

"I should have taken the shot," Matt sighed.

He paused a moment and decided to reverse the conversation toward her.

"Apparently you know all about me. So what about you?"

"Nothing unusual. Just a normal Irish girl born in Boston to overachievers. Went to a small parochial school and then got the hell away from home."

"Ever been to Ireland?" he asked.

She turned her eyes away again.

"Something I said?"

"No. No. Yes, I've been to Ireland. Spent some time there during my college days."

"Some kind of exchange program while you were at Harvard?"

"Yes, exactly. University of Belfast," she said.

"Why did you do that?"

"Wanted to learn everything I could about the issues between Ireland and Britain. It was a fascinating period of my life."

"I'm sure. So what was it like?" he asked.

"I wrote my dissertation on some of the darker factions of the Irish Republican Army. I allowed myself to be blindfolded and taken to places to meet leaders and terrorists. Usually they were hidden from sight, sort of like a confession booth."

"Why did they let you do that? I mean, talk to them?"

"They wanted their point of view to be heard. The press was so biased against them that when they had an opportunity to be heard through a legitimate forum, they took it. Of course, all of that has changed now." She paused. "After Nine-eleven, I mean."

"Weren't you ever concerned that you might be in danger?"

"All of us are in danger every day, Matt."

"True. But you have to admit that hanging out with IRA terrorists back then was on the far end of the scale."

"They are just like you and me, Matt. They have beliefs and hopes and dreams."

"You mean 'were,' right?"

"Say that again?" Peyton asked.

"You said, 'They are just like you and me.'"

"Right, I mean *were*," she said, looking away. "Just like my parents *were* gunned down by British paratroopers in the streets of Belfast."

Matt shifted in the hay toward Peyton, caught off guard by the information. "I'm sorry."

"They were on vacation. Their bodies were shipped home, and I had to bury them. You've buried a brother, so you know what I'm talking about. My sister ran away right after that. She was sixteen. I get an occasional post-card or phone call, but she never stays in one place. And so I've got no family to speak of—only demons, I guess."

"We've all got demons, Peyton."

She paused before responding, unsure why she had shared her most personal information with him. "You asked what I learned. I learned that no one can conquer the human spirit. That no one can oppress the will of a people. I especially learned that no matter how strong or powerful a nation, it has weaknesses that can be attacked. And that's how the IRA operated against Britain."

He had detected a slight accent, and having learned that she had lived in Ireland for a short while, he figured she had picked up a minor inflection in Belfast. He decided to change the subject and lighten the conversation.

"So you're a Ginger, then?"

She paused a moment and smiled, large green eyes blinking at him in the square of moonlight casting through the barn window.

"I'm surprised you know the word for an Irish redhead."

Matt considered her comment a moment and said, "I imagine you're full of surprises as well."

For a moment, the gravity of the situation eluded him. The hijacked Air Force airplane, firefights with extremists, and an arduous escape through rugged terrain were all momentarily set aside by the fleeting, yet all-too-natural, allure of a beautiful woman. The anxiety and worry subsided like an ebbing tide, leaving exposed something he was unprepared to bare.

"Well, get some rest," he sighed, stitching up the moment. "We'll need it."

Matt rested his head against the straw. His mind automatically drifted to a time when he and Zachary were growing up on the farm. Some people were close to their siblings, others weren't. Matt had never understood why families would diverge and lose contact. Perhaps being raised in the Blue Ridge, where neighbors were nice but remote, he and Zach had focused on their family. So much land and space between families created a natural pull inward. Instead of walking across the street to join the stickball game, he roamed the 120 acres with his brother, exploring their own world. Losing Zach had devastated him, but now he felt as if he were pulling out of his nosedive. Hellerman had been right. Shed the self-pity and get back into the game.

Garrett nestled his head further into the straw.

Resting. Uncertain.

Thinking.

He looked through the open barn window at the children's art moon and closed his eyes. Like Jesus appearing in a prayer, Zachary's face hovered above him like an angel as he fell asleep.

PART 2:
BROTHERS IN ARMS

CHAPTER 17

SATURDAY MORNING, 0100 HOURS, MC-130, APPROACHING MONCRIEF LAKE

Major Winslow Boudreaux bounced in the back of the MC-130 Combat Talon as it flew just 100 feet above the ground. The pilots had taken off from Pope Air Force Base in south-central North Carolina, kept a due-east heading until they were fifty miles off the coast, then turned north, keeping at 200 feet above sea level. To the pilots, the ocean was a solid mass, indistinct from the dark horizon. They passed Boston and Halifax, then banked west through Cabot Straight into the Gulf of St. Lawrence. The north shore was the thirty-minute mark. Their instructions were to stay off the civilian radar screens. Half an hour from the objective, they had some climbing to do before they reached the drop altitude at 20,000 feet.

Boudreaux felt the airplane rise suddenly, shooting skyward like a rocket. If they were lucky, they wouldn't stall. Two men had fully briefed him on the mission. They had used maps and photographs. For the past two weeks he had rehearsed this mission and believed he knew every detail. But there were blank spots that sometimes didn't make sense with what they had told him.

He was on a classified mission for his country, which was fine. He was a member of an elite organization, and he could never reveal his identity to anyone, even if captured. Especially if captured. Fair enough.

He was recently wounded in combat and had gone through extensive physical therapy to become fully mission-capable again. Sure, he remembered most of the therapy and had some instincts, some memory of that kind of information, but other things bothered him.

They told him his name was Winslow Boudreaux, that he was from a small town in Louisiana and had been in the army for nearly twelve years. They had shown him pictures of his childhood. They were trying to get him to remember something, anything, from his childhood or even from his recent past. Nothing seemed to work. None of it rang true.

Something about the doctor had bothered him. The man was nice enough but seemed troubled. In his white smock, the doctor often would sit in a wooden chair next to Boudreaux's Spartan bedroom and go through the pictures with him. It was more *educational* than exploratory, it seemed. Endless days of reviewing the same thing, over and over. Boudreaux felt as if the information was being pushed onto him from the outside, as opposed to his delivering any conscious memory from inside his mind.

And so he knew his name was Winslow Boudreaux and that he had a mission to kill someone named Ballantine. He would go do that and then think about these other things.

He watched Colonel Rampert get close to him to inspect his equipment. A spark of memory erupted in his mind like a flashbulb in a dark room, and quickly faded. The man was leaning forward, his tightly buzzed haircut like bristle, his weathered face darkened with streaks of green and black camouflage.

They each squatted to absorb the rapid ascent of the airplane. They had even practiced this part of it in the rehearsal. He remembered that much, but the rest of his memory was like a sieve with large holes. Only the big chunks were captured: his name, his mission, his enemy.

And so Boudreaux was able be forward-thinking, connecting smaller details and using his instincts for guidance. It felt as if the instincts had never left him. He was a soldier, a killer, and a patriot. That much rang true.

He looked at his reflection in the porthole window. Dark hair, longer than it should be, he thought. He didn't know why that thought had come to him. It just seemed that it should be shorter. Strong face with high cheekbones, dark green eyes, almost neon.

Rampert walked him through the mission one more time. "I've checked your parachute for the third time. It's okay. Watch your altimeter and remember to open at eight hundred feet. You should be above the horizon with canopy for only a few seconds. If you're spotted, move to hide site number one, come up on satellite communications, and wait. We have Pave Low helicopters ready to extract you in less than thirty minutes. You've got enough ammunition to hold anybody off for that long. But remember, you've got to be near an open area. We've got a beacon on you so we'll know where you are all the time."

"Yes, sir." Boudreaux nodded.

"You won't be detected, though. You'll get in under the cover of darkness and find your way to Ballantine's camp. If you're compromised there, just kill him as quickly as you can, then fight your way out. The Pave Lows will be able to respond to any trouble you get into. If you're not compromised, move to your link-up site. There, you'll find an old, green john boat with a nine-horsepower motor. There will be two fishing poles and another Satcom radio inside. The radio will be in the live well, so don't put any water in it. Call in at each checkpoint so we know your progress. If you can, try to find the operations center first. You've got the three template locations. It has got to be one of those."

Rampert talked slowly, his eyes locked onto Boudreaux's. The vice president had asked him to guarantee success. He couldn't do that. He never guaranteed anything. Particularly now. He had personally saved this man's life a year ago, and now he was certainly sending him to his death. Rampert remembered being there.

They were hidden in the creek bed watching the enemy file out of their base camp, ready to smash the weak Marine defenses. The weather had prevented any kind of air power, and it looked like the Marines were going to fight without reinforcements. Rampert remembered the enemy artillery opening on friendly positions with the distinct report of the cannon, the nerve-racking whistling, and the deadly explosions.

Out of the wood line from across the field came a deep bellow, reminding him of the rebel yell he had read about. U.S. infantrymen rushed the enemy fighting positions and artillery pieces, firing anti-tank missiles and destroying most. The enemy soldiers turned on the Americans, and their lines merged in a fight more akin to a Civil War battle than the high-tech warfare of late.

Rampert watched an officer and his radio operator come charging from the woods and join the fray. He recognized the man. They had been scouting him as a candidate for the Joint Special Forces Command. He knew the soldier's record; this man was a warrior.

The radio operator was shot in the chest, spinning him backward. The man grabbed his M4 carbine and fired it until it went empty. He pulled his pistol from his holster, shooting it until he was out of ammunition. Pulling his bayonet from its scabbard, he fought hand-to-hand.

The rain was moving to the north in a typical thunderstorm pattern. Rampert was vectoring friendly aircraft into the fight using his high-frequency radio. One minute away. But one minute and the fight might be over. He gave the radio to his assistant team chief, grabbed his M4 carbine, and began to suppress the enemy near the officer. He moved slowly from the creek bed under the cover of a row of bamboo shoots. He changed magazines.

Artillery and mortar shells began to rain upon them. The explosions were deafening, and he thought he could feel his ears bleeding. Wasn't the first time.

He saw the officer take a bullet in the lower abdomen. Then an enemy combatant rammed a bayonet through the officer's shoulder. Rampert shot the enemy soldier from twenty feet. He raced to the officer and slung him into a fireman's carry at the same time that he saw another company of infantry emerge from the creek bed two hundred meters to his south. The diversion gave Rampert enough time to move the wounded officer over a small rise where several American soldiers lay dead or wounded.

He removed the man's uniform and dog tags and then called the team medic to his location. They performed life-saving measures and guided in a Pave Low medevac for the man. Rampert sent the medic with the wounded officer, while he and the rest of his team stayed and fought with the others. A mortar shell landed on one of his best friends, who had been with the team for over ten years, cutting the veteran operator into so many pieces it took them an hour to collect the barely identifiable remains.

Rampert held the dog tags of the decimated operator and the severely wounded conventional-force officer in his hand. Looking down, he said, "Good-bye, Winslow," dropped the shredded shirt and identification tags on his dead friend, and boarded the helicopter.

As he looked at Boudreaux, these unpleasant memories came rushing back to him. *What have I done?* he wondered.

Boudreaux felt the plane level at the drop altitude.

"Ten minutes," Tedaues shouted to Rampert. Tedaues had climbed down from the cockpit and walked toward them. He and Rampert were both wearing B-11 square parachutes used for high-altitude, low-opening (HALO) jumps. Neither Tedaues nor Rampert were jumping, but they wore their parachutes in case they either needed to jump or fell from the airplane while performing jumpmaster duties for Boudreaux. Boudreaux had the same suit but was outfitted with a reserve that would automatically deploy if his altimeter read 600 feet above ground level and his main had not deployed. Rampert decided setting the altimeter was the moral thing to do in case Boudreaux mentally froze on his descent. But 600 feet was not very high.

The three men were standing at thc back of thc aircraft as the ramp began to lower. Boudreaux watched the platform separate itself from the top of the aircraft, making him feel like Jonah in the stomach of the whale. Pitch-black night greeted them as the ramp leveled even with the floor of the aircraft.

"You'll break through a thin layer of clouds at about two thousand feet. After that, you should be able to pick out the drop zone. When you're under canopy, take about five seconds with your night-vision goggles and search for an infrared marker. There should be one at the southeast portion of the drop zone. From there, you'll find the boat."

"I'm ready. I know what you're telling me; you don't have to keep repeating it, sir." Raising his voice above the din of the aircraft, Boudreaux sounded like he was shouting. Rampert and Tedaues looked at each other, a sign of acknowledgment. It was time.

"Good luck," Rampert said.

Boudreaux thrust his arms outward, practicing his flair as he walked onto the ramp. Hindering his movement was a dark green rucksack rigged behind his buttocks. Once his parachute deployed, he would use a twenty-foot nylon line to lower the rucksack beneath him prior to landing. In it he had packed a tactical satellite radio, one hundred and fifty rounds of

5.56mm ammunition for his M4 carbine, six MRE combat rations, two gallons of water in his Camelbak, an assortment of smoke grenades, star clusters and other pyrotechnics, a Berretta 9mm pistol with four magazines of ammunition, and a set of fishing clothes hand-picked by Rampert out of the North Face catalog. He wore an outer tactical vest where the other half of his M4 ammunition was stored in five 30-round magazines.

"One minute!" Rampert shouted. They were jumping on time and azimuth, not really needing to see any reference points. Boudreaux was leaning over the ramp watching the earth pass beneath them. Small dots of light, a few glimmers of moonlight skidding off oxbow lakes. Then he saw a lone car driving from north to south on a road. That road was the one-minute mark. Rampert's call was right. They were on schedule and on target.

"Thirty seconds!"

Boudreaux stood and practiced his flair a final time, stretching his chest muscles, splaying his hands to either side. He looked over his shoulder at Rampert and Tedaues. He flashed them a thumbs-up. Rampert moved toward the ramp, holding both hands forward, fingers spread. Five seconds passed and he dropped his left hand, then counted down with his right. Four, three, two, one.

The green light flashed. Rampert howled, "Go!"

Boudreaux jumped, spreading his body into flair position, catching the wind and riding it into the night. He slipped into the silence not unlike the coma he had emerged from several months earlier. One second ago, he was bouncing in the noisy, manmade machine; the next, he was floating effortlessly in quiet solitude through the thin air, rushing toward the ground.

Seconds passed into perhaps a minute. The wind beat against his chest, the air rushing around his helmet, forcing his head back. He fought to maintain balance against the turbulence. He turned his left wrist inward and glanced at his altimeter: 6,000 feet.

Formations on the ground grew larger. Single lights were now small groups of lights. He could distinguish buildings. He slipped on his night-vision goggles to search for the flashing infrared light that marked his optimal touchdown point, turning the world green. Once-indistinguishable lights were suddenly bright flares. He pivoted his head from left to right. He noticed an area that appeared to be a clearing, but there was no flashing light.

He spun his body 180 degrees and saw another larger clearing. In the back of his mind, he was counting the seconds. Too many had passed. He was plummeting now, probably 2,000 feet, only a few seconds away from having to deploy his main canopy.

One final scan. A blip. Two blips. Could be a flashlight, even a firefly at this height, but he would aim for it. He had to go somewhere.

He lowered the night-vision goggles and stuffed them inside his outer tactical vest. He had to stow his night-vision goggles to prevent damaging them during the opening shock of the parachute. The metal rip cord grip felt cool to his grasp. He looked at the altimeter one final time: 700 feet. Too low.

He yanked hard and listened as the main parachute deployed and snatched him, slowing his descent to a manageable rate.

400 feet.

Deployment had taken three hundred feet. Perfect. He would soon be below the horizon.

He began steering the square toward the spot where he had last seen the flickering light. He raced about three hundred meters, then began to spiral down. The ground was nearby now: tree tops, a lake about a half mile away, then level with the trees, open field, a ditch, some high scrub. He released his rucksack and then yanked down on both steering toggles. He let the ground come up to him as he kept his feet and knees together. The ground smacked him, and he rolled with it. His landing was soft enough for him to stand quickly and roll his parachute, stuffing it into an aviator's kit bag. On one knee, he retrieved the necessary equipment from his ruck.

He snapped his night-vision goggles onto his head harness, screwed the silencer on his M4 carbine, attached his night scope, then chambered a round, putting his weapon into operation—the first priority.

He quickly broke the brush toward the wood line. Instinctively, he walked toward the lake he had seen out of his periphery on his way down. Chest-high ferns swayed in a cool breeze, brushing against his gear. He walked in the green world of the night-vision lens. Pale greens were lighter objects; dark greens and blacks were darker. The ferns and shrubs reached up toward him like the hands of begging children. The trees were about fifty meters to his front.

A sudden brightness raced across his field of view. It appeared to come from his right. He waited. There it was again. Another flash. He lifted his goggles and looked in the direction of the flash. He waited. Nothing. Snapping the goggles back on, he immediately saw the infrared beacon. He walked toward it, secured it, and switched a small button to turn it off. He extracted the small map Rampert had given him, and using his infrared light, he read the instructions.

Two hundred meters, 349 degree azimuth. Hit a small stream, follow it on azimuth of 11 degrees. Equipment at stream and lake intersection. That was it. Simple note. Simple job.

After twenty minutes of walking, he found the boat tied to a tree with pine branches draped across its bow. He found the plug sitting loose and replaced it.

So far, so good. Everything was just like the rehearsal. Nagging at the back of his mind was the fact that, as he descended through the sky, there were flashes of memory, things he couldn't recall outright.

He would deal with that later.

He checked his watch: 0200 hours. He had about five hours until daylight. He wanted to use the night to his advantage. If he could take the shot tonight, he would. The sooner, the better, Rampert had told him. But he needed to find the operations center and shut it down.

All the right things were going through his mind. He was aware, like a panther. He could feel the wind against his skin. He could pick out the different smells: the pine needles, the bream going to bed in the lake shallows. The night sounds were amplified in his ears: a squirrel jumping from branch to branch, an anonymous animal burrowing in the underbrush, the smack of a fish against the water's surface.

Lying in the prone, he tested the AN/PAQ-4C night lasing device using his night-vision goggles. The small device attached to the muzzle of the weapon pulsed an infrared laser to the point of aim. He sighted on a distant shore line, picked out a log rising above the water, steadied his aim, and then lowered the weapon. It seemed okay.

Time to move. He switched the infrared beacon on and placed it in the nook of a branch in an oak sapling. Focusing his night-vision goggles, he depressed the azimuth indicator on his monocle.

Turning until the indicator read 36 degrees, he struck out through the woods in search of Ballantine.

CHAPTER 18

MONCRIEF LAKE, QUEBEC

Ballantine watched the rhythmic motion of her breasts as she slept. The sex had been great, starting in the kitchen and finishing in the bedroom, her black body grinding against his olive skin. They had fallen asleep after two hours of ravishing each other. It was better than a good workout. *Hell, it was a great workout*, he thought. He wished they could do it more often.

But he had other priorities now.

The red numbers of the clock told him it was three in the morning. Ballantine was normally a heavy sleeper, and it wasn't like him to rise before sunrise. But something had told him to wake up—instinct maybe. He leaned on his elbow, watching Virginia. Her soft skin glowed in the moonlight. He had never truly loved any woman. Virginia, though . . . she had beauty, power, and raw sensuality. She acted with a controlled abandon that continued to attract him. Love, he didn't think so. But perhaps.

He had met her shortly after his release from the POW camp in Riyadh. They shipped him back to Baghdad in the back of a five-ton truck, having gained an early release by cutting a deal with his interrogator, an American military officer who ironically was still serving the U.S. government. Ballantine had remained in intermittent, coded contact with the man until recently. Once Ballantine was back in Baghdad, Saddam had given him an award and asked him to stay to remain in command of the Tawalkana. He declined, telling Saddam he wanted to return to Paris to think about his life without Henri. Today, he was satisfied with both his decision and the instructions Saddam had given him since his departure.

As he stared at Virginia's mocha skin, Ballantine recalled meeting her in France. He had resumed his painting and started writing once he returned to Paris. He was on the River Seine doing a watercolor.

He was unhappy with the blue he had put into the river. Too light. He tried to darken it with some browns, but that didn't give him the contrast he wanted with the sandy hue of the ivy-shrouded villas sitting on the bluffs. Frustrated, he stood and walked away from the easel to clear his mind. Pacing across the concrete path that bordered the river, he spotted a young black woman watching him from a bench.

He sensed her following him with her large brown eyes, tracking him as he paced away from his easel, then back toward it. He scratched his head and slowly turned toward her. He was wearing his standard painting garb—an old blue T-shirt with multiple paint stains and olive army pants cut off at mid-thigh. His hair was almost shoulder length at the time, and he had grown a black mustache that drooped down on either side of his mouth. After that terrible moment in the desert, he had altered his appearance to the point that sometimes even he didn't recognize himself in the mirror.

He wasn't sure what she was seeing or thinking, but she was definitely looking. She was dressed in a bright yellow halter top that revealed ample breasts and a taut stomach. A matching hair band held her straight black hair away from her forehead. She was wearing black shorts that, with her legs crossed, showed her slim brown legs all the way up to her buttocks.

He approached her, and as he did, she flashed a large grin of white teeth.

"Hello. Jacques. Jacques Ballantine." He offered his hand in greeting, and she shook it firmly as she stood.

"Virginia. Virginia Winfield." She laughed as she spoke. "I think we both just sounded like James Bond."

He stared into her eyes, realizing she was as tall as he. She had a thin but muscular body, part natural, part honed in the gym.

"You are more beautiful than any of the Bond women," he said, smiling.

"That's quite a compliment. Is painting your profession or your hobby?" They had begun slowly, carelessly walking toward the easel.

"I could either take that as a compliment or as an insult," he said with a smile.

"Either way, you do it quite well."

"What's that? Deflect the question or paint?"

She laughed again, looking at the canvas, then at Ballantine. "Both. But something's not right about the river. Too light, I think, but I see you were going for a contrast between that and the villas."

"Could I offer you dinner tonight? I'll make it at my place. Something simple, a bottle of wine, maybe some pasta?" Ballantine offered.

They ate the pasta, drank the wine, and made love all night.

He reflected on that night and so many others like it over the past six years. She had helped him heal, to both assuage the pain and to develop a plan that would put it all to rest, forever. The fishing camp, the bombs, the germs—the ultimate plan was borne out of discussions late at night after world-record sex. Lying in bed, staring at the ceiling, he thought about killing Matt Garrett to get revenge. It would be easy to find Garrett's house, go there, and kill him. Too easy. Too trite. Not what he wanted.

Zachary Garrett had killed Henri in an epic struggle between two of the world's largest armies. Sure, killing Matt would be part of the solution, but he also blamed America for his loss. In Ballantine's mind, the Americans had no right to be there in the first place. It was a regional issue that could have been solved by regional powers. Kuwait had been stealing oil from Iraq, millions of barrels a day. Kuwait's pampered princes and non-practicing Muslims deserved to be roughed up a bit, as far as Ballantine was concerned.

Tens of thousands of Iraqis had been killed along with Ballantine's brother. He owed it to Saddam, his countrymen, and his brother to exact revenge in whatever measure he could upon those that had led the charge into Iraq. Jacques and Virginia had developed a detailed plan they believed could work. The Central Committee was eager for his participation, but so was someone else. After discussing the matter with Virginia, he determined he could satisfy both entities.

So he reestablished contact with his United States government source (the "someone else") and communicated that he was prepared to honor the debt he had incurred when he was released from the filthy detainment center in Riyadh. The source required two commitments: to have a hand in the plan and to get the last copy of the tape. The Central Committee only required that his actions be timed in concert with theirs and that he synchronize his efforts with the admiral commanding the *Fong Hou*, a Chinese commercial ship with special cargo.

Agreeing to the conditions, Ballantine had begun spiriting small amounts of Ricin, botulism, VX nerve gas, and other lethal weapons of mass destructtion into his fishing guide camp. Moving chemicals and biological agents from Iraq to Syria and onto ships in the Mediterranean had been the easy part. Landing his Sherpa at night along the St. Lawrence River as these ships churned toward their final destinations was more difficult. Yet, in so doing, he was able to rapidly move the supplies. Luckily for Ballantine, the American government was a warm-blooded animal, looking south toward the heat—toward Florida, Texas, California—what the government saw as its porous underbelly.

Very little thought was given to the North. Too cold. Too friendly. No problems. Virginia had said, "Why not just set up a small business in Canada and start going back and forth with your supplies?"

He had agreed; developing the fishing-camp concept gave him a reason to have a plane, which in turn gave him unrestricted access, complete freedom. The Iraqi government had given him half a million dollars for his service. And loyalties ran deep, even in countries that were on the brink of poverty because of international sanctions.

Ballantine had said to Virginia, "I remember the planes coming over Baghdad, dropping bombs, the cruise missiles. The sheer terror of it all. I want to strike the same fear into the hearts of Americans. An unpredictable fear that they feel every day because they don't know *what* is going to happen next, but they know *something* is going to happen."

His mind spun back to the present, fighting off the feeling that someone was watching him. He lit a cigarette and shook the match as he tossed it into the ashtray. Try as he might to discard the notion that eyes were upon him, his instincts were wide awake, screaming at him. He snuffed the cigarette and slid from the bed, reaching between the mattress and the box springs for his Glock. He pulled on some sweatpants, a T-shirt, and running shoes and grabbed a pair of AN-PVS-7B night-vision goggles before quietly padding out of the bedroom into the great room of the cabin. He edged through a sliding glass door onto a small balcony where the lighting was mediocre under the quarter moon.

He held the night-vision goggles to his eyes, turning the world lime green, and scanned the wood line from the lake's edge on his right to the back of the second cabin thirty meters to his left.

The woods were dense, but there was enough moonlight to give him visibility well into the forest. He saw nothing. No deer, no fox. Nothing.

Then he heard a slight rustling in the leaves to his left coming from behind the cabin. He trained goggles on the area, waiting, moving them back and forth. But he still saw nothing. The rustling was so slight it could have even been a mouse. But still, it was there.

Virginia came stealthily onto the balcony, looking instinctively in the opposite direction, covering his flank. "What is it?" she whispered.

He didn't respond initially. "Let's go back inside," he said after a moment. "We have a visitor."

CHAPTER 19

Boudreaux could feel the dew settling on his face. The warm days and cool nights of Quebec in April created temperature extremes that could range forty degrees. A cloud of mist wafted in front of him as he breathed slowly and stared at the fifth cabin through his night-vision goggles.

He had looked into four of the five structures and then moved toward the last cabin, the one closest to the water. He always moved perpendicular to the foundation of the cottage, never parallel, so as to minimize his visual signature. Stepping quietly along the wood line, he slipped up to the back of a cabin, looked in the bedroom window, and then moved to the next one, still not sure whether he was in the right place. His land navigation certainly told him he was. And his global positioning device gave him a precise grid coordinate.

This location was one of the three suspected sites. The first turned out to be a dilapidated stand of buildings that looked as though they had once housed miners. Those small huts weren't near the lake, and he thought he saw some dark spots in his goggles as he scanned the hillside. Caves, maybe. Or old mine shafts. He would check on that location last, as his target folder had indicated that there was a large amount of signals intelligence in that specific area. If he could find Ballantine alone, unguarded, that was best. The assumption was that he was using the mineshafts as a command center and would be heavily guarded accordingly.

This group of cabins was directly on the lake, but they were a good kilometer from the command center location that Rampert had given him. Perhaps it was all one large complex.

He moved from behind a large pine and looked up at the A-frame of the final cabin. There was a large deck outside a sliding glass door and a smaller deck near a large window on the second floor. He guessed that the room by the upper deck was a loft. There was a porch light, but it was not on. He could feel that someone was in the cabin, awake maybe, thinking, maybe sensing that he was out there casing the place.

Boudreaux stepped from the wood line and began to move toward the cabin. He chose a route following a string of shrubs that separated the last two cabins. He did not want to approach from the lake side, where he would be silhouetted against the smooth, glassy water.

He watched the ground to avoid fallen branches or leaves that might make noise. As he did so, he heard an almost imperceptible sound, like something heavy was sliding. He paused for a second before he realized it was a window to his left. The noise was coming from the target building.

Boudreaux quickly crawled through a gap between two bushes, cursing himself when he snapped a branch off a dead boxwood. He held his position and steadied his breathing.

Boudreaux held still, huddling against the thick hedge, hoping whoever was there was just going out for a nightly smoke or enjoying the fresh country air. But he doubted it. He sensed immediately that he was in the right place. And if he was in the right place, whoever it was would probably have some sort of night-vision device. Maybe not the best in the world, but good enough to see with a quarter moon. So he held still and didn't risk a look. Any movement might be noticed.

Boudreaux heard talking. It sounded like a woman's voice, and then he heard the deeper baritone of a man. They were whispering, as if they expected something, some*one* to be out in the shadows. They were on the defensive.

He was in the right place. This was Ballantine's cabin. He felt a surge of adrenaline coupled with a tightening of his stomach.

He experienced another flash, like before. A flash of memory, maybe. The flash was a face matched to words. A sound, actually. He was picking out intonations, bits of words they were saying. Something about "inside," then the sliding of the window. He waited, listening. *Had they seen him?*

And what was the flash? Like a camera snapping a picture in the night, he had a blind spot in his eyes until he could focus again. In the flash, he saw a face, a haggard, worn man, worried about something. *What triggered the flash? The location, the mission, the voice, what?*

Five minutes turned to twenty. The rhythmic croak of a frog kept him company as he slowly shifted his vision 360 degrees, watching, listening. Another fifteen minutes. It was almost four o'clock. Serious fishermen would be waking in an hour or two. He needed to move.

He slowly edged his way back using his hands to push into a reverse low crawl. He got to the edge of the shrubs and scanned the cabins one last time. Seeing no movement, he raised himself to all fours and crawled until he reached the dense undergrowth about fifty meters into the woods. The pines began to envelope him, heightening his sense of security. He began to walk hunched over, increasing his speed until he was deep into the forest.

Boudreaux shifted his attention to his front, expecting that he had been spotted near the cabins and that Ballantine had alerted security. It was the worst case scenario, he knew, but it was how he operated. Plan for the worst and expect it to happen. Now he was sliding through the trees, upright, with his M4 carbine at the ready, the reassuring weight of the 9mm pistol slapping his thigh. His goggles pressed against his face and the thin sapling branches reached out, clawing at him, making light scratching noises.

He spotted the flashing strobe, grabbed it, and shut it off immediately. Moving up the stream about one hundred meters, he found a small rock outcropping he could slide under. He checked his night scope on his M4 and braced it against a small rock.

Boudreaux was ready for whoever might come; he would wait to take down Ballantine. Perhaps he would find the operations center first. He figured the command node was probably in one of the mines or caves that he had seen.

As he rested and recalibrated his next moves, he had another flash, blinding him. There was desert, sand, heat, guns, and a face. What was the face? Was he just seeing the target photos of Ballantine that Rampert had prepared? Or was this something from his memory surfacing from another time and place?

CHAPTER 20

Boudreaux' eyes moved to the sounds of leaves rustling about twenty meters away. During his short rest, his hands never left the butt stock of his M4 carbine. Peering through his scope, he watched two squirrels dart through the brush.

He looked at his watch. It was just past five in the morning; *0500 hours,* he translated. Military time for a military man. More firecrackers were popping now, flashbulbs bursting with photonegative images appearing briefly in their wake and fading just as quickly. *Uniforms, weapons, men shouting, gunfire, a young man with a radio, someone named Slick, palm trees, rice paddies . . .*

Reality. He had been hiding and resting for an hour. It would be another hour before the sun would rise, so he snapped his night-vision goggles onto his headset, then watched a small deer nose its way past him, stop, stare at him with large eyes, then move slowly toward the lake. He could see the lake shore one hundred meters below him. A beautiful calm morning was about to dawn, just like . . . *Just like what? What exactly was it just like?* His hand scraped the dirt. *What is happening?* So far he had been executing his tasks with machine-like precision. "No emotion, no mistakes"—that was what they had told him.

But the darkness and morning tranquility settled over him like it had another time. He vaguely pictured soft, rolling hills that gave way to mountains—gentle ones that rose subtly from the foothills. There was a stream, with rocks. *But where was it?*

He slowly moved from the rock crevice, less than an hour until the sun nosed over the horizon. What the military called "before morning nautical twilight."

Boudreaux picked his way past the stark trunks of the pine trees, sometimes finding more space between the trees than he was comfortable with, increasing his chances of being detected. He listened to the Canadian morning sounds that joined the rhythmic echoes of his breathing. Animals were awakening and so, he figured, was his prey. He counted his paces as he strode, tying a knot in a cord hanging on his equipment for every one hundred meters. He had nine knots so far. He checked his global positioning system, a small on-demand, illuminated watch-like piece of equipment he wore on his left wrist. He was within one hundred meters of the third objective area, according to the data he and Colonel Rampert had preloaded into the system.

He stopped and went down on one knee. His fingers flexed around the grip of his weapon. He had a mental image of his objective. He pictured a small cavern built into the face of a wooded hilltop. He looked up and scanned the higher ground to his front. Through his night-vision goggles he detected a faint shimmer of light, undetectable to the naked eye, sneaking beneath a dark spot in his display.

He moved quietly, one foot over the next; a hunter stalking his prey. He was acutely aware of everything that moved, the slightest twitch of a branch in the wind, the turn of a chipmunk head away from an acorn in its grasp. He was also aware that if he had been detected near Ballantine's cabin that the objective area would be at a heightened alert status, whatever that meant for this particular group. He moved to the west of the lighted area in order to come down on the objective from higher ground.

Echoes of a past too soon forgotten began to ring in his ears.

CHAPTER 21

"We may have a visitor," Ballantine had spat into the phone.

Chasteen placed two guards at the only entrance to the mineshaft that housed their command center. One guard was outside of the entrance in a makeshift fighting position that provided clear observation of any approach. The other guard positioned himself directly inside the mineshaft opening in case the first position was compromised.

Chasteen felt his adrenaline surge. All of the preparation was manifesting itself today. First, the three successful attacks, and now he had received an intruder alert. And this was only the beginning.

He walked slowly along the worn AstroTurf, ducking to avoid the low crossbeams in the shaft. He looked at a series of television screens, all displaying footage of the attacks. Scrolling news bars shouted from beneath the talking heads: *al Qaeda suspected in attacks. . . . Terror strikes U.S. again. . . . U.S. unprepared for attacks. . . . More than 500 confirmed dead in Metroliner crash. . . . Casualties unknown in Minneapolis and Charlotte. . . . Thousands believed dead.*

Two radio operators sat at a small console, monitoring radio transmissions and recording significant events into small laptop computers that fed into large-screen displays the size of big-screen televisions in sports bars.

The interior of the shaft reminded Chasteen of a high school locker room, both in size and smell. With only one ventilation shaft, air circulation was meager at best. He took a deep breath of the stale air and studied the map hanging on the wall. The U.S. map had red stars covering large cities and key chokepoints where specific actions were to take place this week. He noticed the radio operator had placed three green stars on the map. Green was good. It was a go.

He took another deep breath, and the stale air made him think again of the ventilation shaft. *Why did they only have one shaft? And why was it tucked around a corner, out of the normal path of the air circulation? Surely they could cut another hole in here.*

With that thought, he decided to walk outside to check on the guard and get some fresh air.

Boudreaux low-crawled, sliding only a few inches at a time to the top of the hill. Checking his global positioning system, he found that the grid coordinate registered within plus or minus five meters of his third objective.

Sliding his hand forward, he felt metal protruding from the ground. He was concerned it could be a mine, but knew it was probably something less dangerous. He let his fingertips dance gingerly on the protrusion while he slowly turned his head to view the device. With his free hand, he refocused the monocle on his night-vision goggles. What he found was the outline of a metal leg of some type. It appeared to be a base leg, holding something up. He followed the leg upward and saw twigs and leaves covering a round, metal object.

Boudreaux slowly moved his hand and found the other two base legs, then traced his hand around a metal dish. It was a satellite dish, he knew that much.

He was in the right place.

He found the wires connected to the dish and followed them, continuing to low-crawl as he did so. Suddenly the wires dived down through some sort of hole. His goggles detected light skidding up at him. He closed his goggle eye and noticed that the light was barely discernible, noticeable only through the lens of his night-vision device.

Boudreaux removed his knife from its sheath and probed downward, following the path of the wires. His knife struck something that gave, then resisted. He felt it with his hand and determined it was a screen of some type, loosely installed. Removing his Leatherman from its pouch, he opened the pliers function and secured the screen, pulling upward slowly. It gave, and soon he had lifted the screen away from the hole.

His hand retraced the wires and now struck what felt like cloth loosely secured, perhaps to block light. He removed his night-vision goggles, allowing a minute for his right eye to regain its night vision. Once again, he used the pliers to pinch a small piece of the cloth near a corner. He slowly removed the fabric and laid it next to the wire mesh. A dim light, just bright enough for him to see that the tunnel led into a larger area, shone through the hole.

What he saw was a two-foot square cut into the ground that gave way to a larger earthen tunnel. He carefully lowered his body into the hole, feeling secure once his feet found purchase on the firm bottom. He gave himself a minute to adjust to the new sounds around him. There was only one direction to go, so he stepped carefully that way.

His M4 at the ready, Boudreaux turned a corner and saw two men wearing headsets. One man had his head buried in what looked like a notepad, writing something. The other man was staring at one of several televisions lining a wooden shelf directly above them.

To his left, Boudreaux noticed a slight movement produced by a third person. He was dressed in camouflaged fatigues and was holding a pistol. Boudreaux raised his M4 and fired a single shot into his skull.

With mild amusement, Boudreaux noticed how quickly and quietly the man slumped to the floor. He immediately aimed his weapon at the two headset-clad men, one of whom was turning toward the slight noise created by the interior guard. Wasting no time, Boudreaux double-tapped the turning man, then with robotic precision eliminated the remaining target.

That's all they were to him: targets. Rampert had drilled into him time and time again that the enemy was not a living human being but a target, just like the wood and paper targets he practiced with in the Fort Bragg shoot house. See. Shoot. Move. He did so with machine-like accuracy.

He did a quick survey of the area, taking in data such as the five television stations on various news and weather channels, a row of communications equipment, maps of the United States with large red and green stars dotted on certain cities, and a chart. The chart was white poster board with the word *Predator* written at the top, followed by 18/18 and *Fong Hou.* A listing of city names ran down the left side. Realizing he did not have much time, Boudreaux pulled a small radio out of a pouch on his belt. He typed in a code and then a digital message:

Target No. 3. 3 EKIA. 5 SATCOMS. 5 TV. News/weather. Chart—Predator 18/18. *Fong Hou*. EOM.

His message indicated that at the third objective location he had killed in action (KIA) three enemy personnel. Also, he had found five means of satellite communications, five televisions that were indicating news and weather, and a chart bearing the words he had typed.

He had no idea what *Fong Hou* could mean.

After typing EOM, meaning "end of message," Boudreaux scanned the city names, mentally trying to log most, if not all. Then he saw one name than made him stop: Charlottesville, Virginia.

His eyes lifted slowly to the map next to the chart. He saw several stars spotted around Virginia, but one star was distinctly separate from the others. This star was larger and seemed to have been traced many times over, almost obsessively. He walked slowly toward the map, staring at the dot with an inexplicable awe, transfixed. Almost catatonic, oblivious to any danger around him, he nearly pressed his nose to the oversized map tacked onto the support beams.

Represented on the map, the state of Virginia was a large triangular shape about the size of a mailbox. He could see cities, roads, and relief features indicated on the map. He saw the star next to the city of Charlottesville, and then his eyes followed Route 29 north to a small town called Ruckersville. He traced, intuitively, a road to the west to a small town called Stanardsville, which had been highlighted with a yellow felt-tip pen several times.

About the time he heard a noise coming from his left, Boudreaux noticed the word *kill* written next to the circle.

Then it all came back to him.

CHAPTER 22

The sound of a door opening in the dark alcove across the musty mineshaft did not give him time to contemplate the fact that he had suddenly realized his name was not Boudreaux.

He looked away from the map and stared into the dark corner from which the noise had come. He stepped slowly to the side, finding cover behind wood beams next to a plywood shelf that held a row of Internet switching devices.

His heart raced, pounding in his chest like a war drum. His memory had washed over him in a massive wave of recognition, but had left his initial purpose for being in the mineshaft clear, like a rock amidst the current.

The door opened partially and then stopped against something on the floor. He saw that the body of the guard he had just killed was blocking access to the mineshaft. He raised his M4, sighting along the crack between the door and the frame. The outline of a head looked down at the body long enough for "Boudreaux" to fire a shot from his silenced weapon. The head kicked back from the force of the bullet and led the body to the floor.

He kept the weapon sighted along the door, expecting others to come streaming through.

But his expectation was unrealized.

Chasteen tossed his cigarette aside about the time the guard tumbled back toward him.

"Quit screwing around, eh?" Chasteen said, pushing him aside in irritation. The body slumped to the floor. Lifeless. "Sloan?"

Bending down, Chasteen lowered his face toward Sloan and in the dim light noticed the bullet hole squarely in the center of his forehead. Expert shot from an expert marksman. He wondered whether one of the radio operators had killed him or if someone else had infiltrated their hideout.

Chasteen pulled his Glock from its holster and stepped carefully toward the door. Hearing a slight rustling behind him, he stalled.

The cold steel pressed against his neck made him freeze. He started to bring his hands up.

"Visitor," Ballantine whispered in his ear.

"Shit, you scared me," Chasteen said, dropping his hands and sighing in relief. "Sloan is dead. Probably the others in the shaft as well."

Ballantine seethed for a moment, long enough to refocus his mind. *Who was this intruder attempting to disrupt my part of the plan?* He knew that everything else hinged on this phase of the operation.

"You cover the front door. There's only one other way in, the satellite shaft. Did you have that covered?"

Chasteen dropped his head. "Never occurred to me."

Ballantine's heavy gaze fixed on Chasteen, who knew he had made a critical mistake.

Eating his anger, Ballantine immediately went into planning mode. "You stay here and move into the front in about a minute. I'll drop down through the shaft."

"Right."

Ballantine circled around the hill to the small opening where he figured their attacker had entered. The camouflage had been disturbed and the access screen removed. The intruder had entered through this approach.

Lowering himself into the hole, Ballantine kept his eyes focused on the lighted area around the corner. Upon getting his footing, he raised his pistol as he slowly moved to the edge of the wooden support beam to view what was waiting for him inside.

The man who knew his name was not Boudreaux heard the noise from his left, but perhaps a bit too late. He saw the door move again and now had to contend with possible threats from two locations.

The first bullet whipped past his head before he heard the sound of the pistol explode in the cavernous mineshaft. Going low instinctively, he knelt on the floor, finding himself thinking it odd that they would have Astro-Turf inside of this place.

He saw three naked florescent lights suspended from a beam and felt absently for the night-vision goggles hanging around his neck. Remembering he had four full magazines stored in his outer tactical vest, he quickly fired a single shot into each light, shattering the thin glass and bringing on near darkness. The televisions behind him cast a flickering glow across the mineshaft, making it more difficult to detect movement. To remedy that situation, "Boudreaux" snapped off five more rounds, one into each television, leaving him to deal only with the dim liquid crystal displays from the Internet-switching devices and radios.

"Are you here to kill me or all of my equipment?" a voice called out.

"Ballantine?"

"Yes, I'm here," Ballantine said, a faint hint of recognition registering in the back of his mind.

"Then I'm here to kill you."

"Well, I count four bodies already, so I presume you are very good at what you do."

"That's why they sent me. Seems you're a bad man, Mr. Ballantine."

Boudreaux felt the first drop of sweat trickle down his forehead and fall onto the dusty, green grass beneath him. A radio behind him squawked, causing him to turn.

"Signal base, this is Viper. Operations in zone two ready to begin."

A second shot from Ballantine's Glock nicked his shoulder, drawing blood. He winced in pain, disappointed in himself for becoming distracted, losing his focus.

"Did I get you, my friend?" Ballantine asked.

He knew he had been close. But he was taking his time because he was trying to place the voice. He had heard that voice before. *But where?*

"Just a scratch. It pales in comparison to what I've already done to your televisions, not to mention your friends," Boudreaux shouted across the room.

"Who sent you? The Americans? The Canadians? Who?"

"I wish I could remember," Boudreaux quipped, half-jokingly.

Chasteen was moving slowly along the interior wall of the mineshaft perpendicular to Boudreaux's line of sight. Ballantine used two quick strobes of a small flashlight to gain Chasteen's attention, indicating to him to slow down. Ballantine wanted to develop the situation a bit before they killed the intruder. The voice was from a distant past. It was an unpleasant reminder of something, but he wasn't sure what.

"Tell me, what is your name?" Ballantine asked. "Please enlighten me before you dispatch me the way you did my friends here."

Boudreaux thought for a moment, unsure of what to say, primarily because he knew that he had two names. It was an amusing interlude to an increasingly strange situation. He found himself recognizing the voice or inflection, or both, of his primary adversary. There was a slight French accent mixed with the more guttural Arabic tones. He knew there was another attacker inside the mineshaft and figured him to be working the wall, which Boudreaux could not see clearly. But it was the voice and the elusive cockiness of the man who had fired the wounding bullet that intrigued him.

"They call me Boudreaux."

"Well, Boudreaux, you're too late and unwelcome here in my camp. Things have already happened and there is nothing we can do to stop the rest of them now." Ballantine laughed.

"So, then, what's—" Lightning flashed through his mind as a board caught him hard on the head from behind, dropping him into the row of Internet switching devices, unconscious.

"Maybe we should go fishing, eh?" Chasteen said.

Ballantine moved quickly toward the fallen intruder.

"Was getting a bit concerned about you, boss. Thought you might invite this chap in for tea," Chasteen said.

"I know this voice from somewhere." Ballantine's voice was distant, removed.

"Right, that was my next question. So, let's see what we've got here."

Ballantine knelt down, reaching forward with one hand while Chasteen leveled his weapon at the assassin's head. Ballantine slowly rolled the body toward him, noticing the brown hair and strong angular jaw.

Recognition of the man was probably not the most surprising event of Ballantine's life but it was certainly the one in which he felt the most good fortune. Suddenly, everything seemed possible.

"Chasteen, I believe we have struck gold."

"How so?" Chasteen responded, still leveling his weapon at the motionless body.

Ballantine used his hand to lightly brush along the man's strong face, caressing it softly like he might a favored pet. His eyes never strayed from him, as if to reconfirm over and over again that this was indeed who he thought it was.

"As you know, part of our operation here is to kill Matt Garrett," Ballantine said.

"Yes, of course. We have rehearsed that part of the plan many times."

Ballantine turned his head slowly, staring directly into the handsome Chasteen's narrow eyes.

"Do you remember why I want to kill Matt Garrett?"

"Yes, for revenge. His brother killed your only brother. But he was killed, and Matt Garrett was the best remaining target."

"Well, that has changed somewhat," Ballantine remarked, a sliver of a smile growing at the corner of his lip. He turned his head back toward the unconscious body.

Chasteen hesitated, slowly turning his gaze toward Garrett, comprehension creeping into him like an Indian stalking a deer, ever so slowly.

"This can't be Matt Garrett. . . ."

"No. No, Chasteen, this is none other than Captain Zachary Garrett."

Chasteen smiled in recognition of what Ballantine was saying, even if he thought the Arabic man was a bit delusional. He reached down and pulled away Garrett's woodland camouflage-pattern shirt, snapping the ID tags from his chest.

"*Winslow Boudreaux, 713-54-8245. O Positive. Catholic.* Nothing here about Zachary Garrett, boss."

Ballantine looked back at Chasteen, only inches away from him now.

"I don't care what the fake tags say. This is the man who killed Henri." He lifted his face upward, closing his eyes. His voice was a whisper cutting a crease into the silent mineshaft.

"I can see him now, on top of me, pistol in his hand, all in slow motion. Henri coming over the rise toward the wadi. Garrett lifting that pistol, firing it over and over into Henri's face."

Ballantine's voice carried an iciness that spoke to Chasteen, telling him he should trust his boss and keep his mouth shut. Ballantine looked back at Chasteen, emerging from his trance.

"Help me cuff him and get him back to the cabin. Call Virginia and tell her she needs to come to the operations center. Let her know we've got casualties. We need to secure Garrett and then, once he awakens, I will interrogate him. We need to know who sent him."

"Roger."

They rolled Garrett onto his stomach, took a pair of plastic flexible cuffs from Garrett's own gear, and used them to bind his wrists behind his back. Ballantine then swung the unconscious man onto his back.

"Take the Sherpa to Vermont at first light and check on the forward ground control site for the UAVs," Ballantine told Chasteen. "I had planned on doing that, but I need to think about this new development. Swarming operations will commence soon, and I want to make sure we are set."

"No problem." Chasteen was an accomplished bush pilot of many years. He had flown fat-cat loggers into the deep forests to survey future cut areas. "I can be ready in an hour."

Being careful not to step on the bodies littering the mineshaft, they walked into the morning dawn, weapons at the ready in case Garrett was working with a partner or the military had an automatic response cell. Neither appeared to be the case.

As Ballantine's boots crunched into the morning frost, he considered his good fortune and the limitless potential for the new situation.

Yes, just as he knew the pale gray line to the east would be followed by an orange hue licking its way slowly across the terrain, bringing light and warmth, he knew that the cargo he now carried on his shoulders was none other than Captain Zachary Garrett.

Ballantine's heart leapt, surging with love for his brother, Henri. Allah had delivered his prayer.

CHAPTER 23

PACIFIC OCEAN, NORTH OF KIRIBATI ISLAND

Admiral Chi Chen sat in his "captain's chair," watching the large terminal play for him the real-time full-motion video of a Predator unmanned aerial vehicle.

Chen's assistant, Seaman Ling, rapidly moved the mouse of the computer that controlled the launch and connectivity of the Predators. The icons for five UAVs circled on another computer terminal display. Scaled numbers and target indicators showed that each aircraft was flying at 10,000 feet above sea level in roughly parallel orbits, each focused on a different island in this sparsely inhabited chain of atolls.

"See there, Admiral," Ling said, pointing at the screen. Chen stared at one Predator video feed of a small shack on a tiny atoll northwest of Kiribati. As far as they could tell, it was uninhabited; though, they had not done any formal assessment beyond watching the building for half an hour.

"I see. So?"

"Now, watch, Admiral. Bees swarm using pheromones to communicate. The American insect scientist has given us the ability to replicate this communication using 'digital pheromones.'" Ling moved the cursor to a link he had created and labeled SWARM. Once he clicked the SWARM button, he saw four of the icons move in the direction of the master Predator that Ling had manipulated to deliver the swarming command. Unseen to Chen and Ling were millions of digital data packets emanating from the master Predator to the other drones. Soon they could see in the video feed of the master the other four drones circling beneath at 8,000 feet above sea level. They looked like broad-winged seagulls circling above baitfish in the ocean.

"Now watch, Admiral," Ling said. He pushed a button that fired an inert hellfire missile into the shack. Instantly, the other four drones fired similar missiles. Despite the absence of munitions, the shack exploded in a granulated display of dust and wood chips after five cement-filled training rockets slammed into the target.

"Those were not real, correct?" Chen asked.

"Correct. Now watch this," Ling said. Though it was hard to remove his eyes from the billowing smoke cloud rising from where the shack once stood, Chen watched in amazement as Ling entered commands into the computer that caused the master Predator to arc into a nosedive directly at the smoke cloud. The drones followed suit, like synchronized swimmers, all lining up at the exact same attack angles and along the exact same route.

Though Ling pulled the master drone out of its dive in time to keep it airborne and bring it back to the ship, it was clear to Chen that if he had five nuclear bombs rigged on those five Predators, they could overwhelm any air defenses that any nation might have protecting its capital.

And he had 18 of them.

Chen watched Ling perform the maneuvers with the master as the lead aircraft circled and slowed and then landed through the gap in the *Fong Hou*'s bow. A chain lowered the lip of the bow and raised the empty containers on top, no more than a shell, like the maw of a hungry animal. Each drone followed the other onto the improvised runway, caught the steel cable with its improvised tail hook, and was rushed out of sight by a crew of Seaman Ling's counterparts.

Ling looked at Chen, who was still staring at the blank screen.

"Full ahead," Chen said. "We have some time to make up."

CHAPTER 24

SHELDON SPRINGS, VERMONT

Matt rolled slightly and then bolted upright.

The morning sunlight was edging through the cracks in the barn's wooden planks. He had heard a noise down below. It was a metallic screeching sound followed by some dull thuds and a voice. Talking. Someone was talking, but he could only hear one voice.

"How's my Emily Lou this morning?" he heard a female voice say. "Is she ready to feed the family?"

Matt slowly crawled to the edge of the loft and placed a foot on the ladder, turning his back to the young lady who had placed her bucket under a cow and was now working her practiced hands across the udder. Sharp sprays of milk resonating in the bucket masked the sound of his feet lightly descending the wooden ladder from the loft. At the bottom, he moved quietly toward her.

He registered that the sound of the spraying milk had stopped a few seconds earlier as the woman spun off her stool and lifted a .22-caliber Derringer toward him.

"Stop right there!" she barked.

Matt stopped and lifted his hands into the air.

"We slept in your barn last night." Matt took a step back, holding up his hands.

"Don't move," she ordered, pulling a cell phone from her coat pocket. She punched a button and got a walkie-talkie beep. "Dad, we've got trouble in the barn. Bring the boys and the guns."

Matt stood still, arms raised, eyes locked onto hers. She was pretty, he thought, in a fresh, farmgirl sort of way. She had clean skin, a wide mouth, and dark hair pulled back into a ponytail. Her eyes were a deep brown that locked onto him like radar.

"I can explain. My partner and I, she's still up there," he said, pointing. Peyton was actually awake now, looking over the rail of the loft. The woman shifted her pistol up toward Peyton and then back over to Matt.

"While this may not be the smartest thing to say in Vermont, we're with the government," Matt said. "The federal government."

"Right about that. Not too smart," a male voice said over the woman's shoulder. This was a big man, Matt noticed. He was a good foot taller than the woman. His daughter, Matt presumed. A barrel-chested man, the father had an untrimmed beard, wore overalls, and leveled a 12-gauge shotgun at Matt. Looked to Matt like an old Remington 870. Made sense. Good sturdy weapon and Remington had made over 5 million of them, still counting.

"We have no weapons, no wallets, no nothing," Matt said. "All we need to do is make one phone call, and we'll be on our way. When we get our car back, I'll even repay you for the overnight stay."

The father actually seemed to mull this over and then said, "Nope, sounds like bullshit. I'm calling the cops. They'll let you make a phone call."

Matt sensed the man was bluffing. If the farmer was going to call the cops, he would have already done so. He also knew that Vermont residents were infamous for their independent streak and their lack of confidence in government.

"Come on, look at us." Matt motioned with his hand. By now, Peyton had climbed down the ladder and was standing next to him. "We've been on the run all night long, being chased by some really bad people. We found your barn, thought we might be able to get some rest and slip out without being noticed. We should have asked, but we got here about five this morning. We were wiped out. These people have stolen everything we had on us."

"What, you two running drugs?" the farmer asked.

"No, nothing like that," Matt said. "You can check us out. We're good people. All we want is one phone call, and then we'll leave. You can keep all your weapons aimed at us while I make the call and until we are off your property. I know we trespassed, and I know we endangered you by hiding here."

"No danger as long as we've got these," the farmer said, holding up his weapon. "None of these rag heads going to get us."

Matt wasn't sure what the farmer was referring to, but it occurred to him that something terrible had probably happened. The melodic terrorist voice from the prison cell hung in his mind. *The events of the last twenty-four hours.*

"One phone call. Please?" Matt asked.

The man looked at Peyton, then back at him. "You guys look pretty roughed up. Scared my girl here, though. Don't appreciate that."

"I apologize, deeply, sir," Matt said.

"Stephanie, let the man use your cell phone. Toss it over to him. When we get the bill, we'll charge him."

"Thank you," Matt said, catching the phone Stephanie launched at him.

Matt punched in the only number he could remember that might help. He listened as the phone rang and felt awkward as the father-daughter combo stared at him. Out of the corner of his eye, he thought he noticed some movement and then heard a squeak in the rafters. The sound was probably the boards expanding under the heat of the morning sun, Matt figured.

"Hello," said the woman's voice on the other end.

"Meredith, this is Matt."

After a slight pause, she said, "You're alive! Thank God."

Meredith had practically shouted the words, and everyone could hear. The daughter and father looked at one another, keeping their weapons trained on Matt and Peyton.

"Listen—"

"Are the others okay? Peyton, the crew?"

"Peyton's with me, Meredith. The others are not. Listen, I'm on someone else's cell phone right now, and it's not a great situation, so I need you to get us some transport back to your location as quickly as possible."

"Okay, okay," she said. "Where are you? Why is it not a good situation?"

"We're in Sheldon Springs, Vermont . . ."

"I knew it. They were taking you north."

"Right."

"Hang on. I'm bringing up my computer. Is there someone there with you that you can ask if they know where the nearest airport or airfield is?"

Matt moved the phone away from his mouth.

"Is there an airfield near here?"

"Yea, about fifteen miles up the road to the northwest," the father responded. "Route 7 or 89 will get you there."

"Thanks." Then to Meredith, "We're twenty miles. Take us about two or three hours to walk it, probably. Less if we can get a ride."

"I've got it. It's a small airfield to the northeast of Swanton, Vermont."

"Swanton?" He looked at the farmer.

"That's right." The farmer nodded.

"Go there now, and I'll have some of *your* very good friends pick you up," Meredith said.

"Thanks. I really appreciate this."

"It just occurred to me, have you heard about the attacks?" Meredith asked.

"What attacks?"

"Matt, they've struck again. The Charlotte Coliseum, Mall of America, and the Amtrak from D.C. to New York were all destroyed," Meredith said.

Matt was speechless. Peyton watched him and asked, "What?"

He looked at the farmer and his daughter, immediately understanding their reaction to his and Peyton's unannounced presence in their barn.

"More attacks," Matt whispered to Peyton.

"Matt, just stay safe. I thought . . . well, we all thought we'd lost you," Meredith said.

A thought raced through his mind that Meredith had lost him several months ago when she returned the engagement ring, but the heavy reality of more terrorist attacks crushed such insignificant thoughts.

"Thanks. We'll be safe."

He pressed the off button and held the cell phone out to Stephanie, who stepped forward and took it from him.

"Three terrorist attacks—"

Matt heard another noise, a footfall, in the loft and figured it was another family member.

"You got anybody else with you?" the father asked.

"No, but we were being chased," Matt said, quickly.

"Anything to do with all this news about terrorists?" the father asked.

"Maybe. We think so," Matt said, his mind reeling.

"What happened?" Peyton demanded.

The first bullet whipped past Matt's ear and caught the father in the right shoulder, spinning him around, causing the shotgun to bounce on the cement floor like one of those Marine ceremony tricks. It flipped directly into Matt's hands as he dove toward Stephanie, instinctively trying to protect her. Stephanie fired a shot at Matt, missing him with her unsteady hand.

"Damn it, I'm a good guy!" he said through clenched teeth. "Save the bullets for the bad guys." He rolled to his left and lifted the shotgun, drew a bead on the movement in the loft and fired twice.

Peyton had run beneath the loft and was staring upward, pointing.

Matt shouted at Stephanie, "Get out of the barn and go to the house!" He fired two more shots at the loft and then swiftly dragged the father to safety. Matt flipped the man onto the ground outside of the barn, and Stephanie raced over to her father.

"Daddy!" she shouted. Then to Matt, "What have you done!"

"Here, put pressure right here," he said, laying down the shotgun in order to hold a rag to the man's shoulder. "He's going to be okay. We just need to stop the bleeding."

He could see she was crying, but she had followed his directions.

"I'm okay, honey. Just do as he says," her father muttered through clenched teeth.

Matt scooped up the shotgun and peeked around the corner. He saw Peyton holding up the head of a dead man lying on the rafters of the barn.

"Any others?" Matt asked.

"Not that I can tell," Peyton replied, looking down at him.

"Let me see that," Matt said, pointing at a small satellite phone she had retrieved from the body.

Peyton was about to pocket the phone, but Matt took it and pressed redial.

"Check him for other stuff," Matt directed.

"Already done. That's it," she said, pointing at the phone. "And this Russian pistol."

"Is he dead?" came a voice in accented English through the satellite phone. "Vulture still has coverage with his flock, but not for long."

Matt hung up the phone. *Vulture? Have we been followed? A vulture circles looking for dead carcasses. What could it mean?*

"We need to get to that airfield, quickly," Matt said to the dairy man's daughter.

"We've got an extra pickup, take that. The ambulance is on the way for Daddy," she said. "The police will be coming, too. We'll blame this whole thing on him," she said, motioning toward the dead Middle Eastern-looking man. She added, "Sorry I shot you."

"No biggie. You missed," Matt said, then added, "Thanks for the truck."

As they prepared to leave, the daughter tossed Matt her cell phone and handed him a box of shells, saying, "Take these and the shotgun, we've got another in the house."

He checked her father one more time. He was lucid.

"Bin Laden?" the old man said.

"Worse," Matt said.

"Protect us," the Vermont man said, his proud voice raspy.

Matt and Peyton jumped into the 1975 Ford pickup truck and turned onto the road to the Franklin County State Airport.

Garrett was on the move. Adrenaline rushed through his veins, pushing him toward the airfield where he knew more chaos lurked.

"Wade into the middle of the chaos and sort it out," the vice president had said.

He was back in the game.

And at the center of the storm.

CHAPTER 25

MIDDLEBURG

Meredith ran into Hellerman's office, opening the door without knocking.

"Sir, I just spoke to Matt. He and Peyton are alive. I've directed a special ops team to Franklin County Airport in Vermont to pick them up."

She could barely control her excitement. Hellerman spun in his chair and leaned back, putting his hands behind his head as if he were performing a full nelson on himself.

"Well, that's great news, Meredith."

"I can't believe it, actually. He just called out of the blue. He didn't have much time. I think they're being chased."

"Is Rampert involved?" Hellerman asked.

"Yes," she muttered, still catching her breath.

"Let's give it about thirty minutes and then check on their progress. They need to be on standby for the Boudreaux mission in case anything goes bad there. Meanwhile," he said, stepping out from behind his desk, "I need you to look at something."

"Sure. What?" Meredith asked.

"Well, you're not going to like this, but I was looking at this." Hellerman showed her the manila folder in his hand. "You remember the Philippine action?"

She turned and looked at him without speaking, as if to say, *You're kidding, right?*

"Of course, you do," he said with a smirk, realizing there might have been a brighter question to ask her. He motioned for her to sit down in a burgundy leather chair facing his desk.

"This is about the Ballantine mission. Something has me concerned about Rampert's briefing."

"What's that?" Meredith asked, stepping away and truly not wanting to deal with anything but the rescue of Matt and Peyton.

He looked at Meredith and reminded her, "I think we were all over it yesterday asking about the guy's identity. I've been involved in some deep black operations before, but never anything like this, where we've actually taken someone out of a coma and sent them on an operation."

"So what are you thinking?" she asked.

"When Rampert was briefing the president, I just couldn't help but think about the Special Forces operation we had going on down there while Zachary Garrett's infantry company was fighting for their lives."

"What's your point?" she asked, not caring to rehash the painful turf.

"You said you went to Zachary Garrett's funeral, right?" Hellerman asked.

"Yes, sir, I was there. That was back when Matt and I had just started dating." *And everything seemed possible.* "I thought both Matt and Zachary were dead." Meredith's voice diminished to a whisper.

"Yes, I know." Hellerman leveled his eyes at Meredith's. "Did you ever see Zachary Garrett's body? For that matter, did anyone see the body?"

"No, there was no viewing, I think, for obvious reasons."

Where is he going with the question about Zachary? She remembered last year having several detailed discussions with Hellerman about the Garrett family. The vice president seemed oddly intrigued by Zachary's bravery and Matt's courage against what seemed insurmountable odds, both in Desert Storm and in other combat actions, such as the Philippines. Questions about Zachary eventually gave way to detailed questions about Matt.

Meredith's political instincts told her that he was simply investigating Matt's background prior to his nomination as an adviser to the CIA director. Those suspicions had been confirmed when, a few weeks later, the announcement had come.

"You might want to take a look at this," Hellerman said, standing. He looked out of the window at the rolling hills of his property. "I'm going for a walk around the grounds. Be back in about twenty minutes, and I'd like an update on Matt and Peyton."

"Sure," she said, haltingly.

Hellerman gave her the folder as he walked past, his index finger grazing her wrist. Locking eyes with her, he said, "That is absolutely great news." He held her gaze, a tight smile creasing his face.

She dropped her eyes when she saw something slide across Hellerman's iris, like a circling raven effortlessly guarding its lair. She used the moment to look at the file, stand, and then return to her office. Once there, she sat at her desk and tugged on the brass chain to her green lawyer's lamp.

She carefully read the executive summary, which was nicely written yet somehow lacked authenticity. It seemed a bit too . . . what was the word? *Contrived?*

She turned the page to a biography on Winslow Boudreaux. He was born in 1970 in Alexandria, Louisiana, to a farmer and mill worker. Winslow was an exceptional athlete in high school who enlisted in the Army when he turned eighteen years old. After a short time in the 82nd Airborne Division, Boudreaux tried out for and was accepted into the elite commandos at Fort Bragg, North Carolina. From that point, his biography became markedly sketchy.

While Meredith understood that the files of Special Forces soldiers were necessarily pristine, she also knew that, within Special Forces, they kept detailed records on their personnel. This was the special operations file, and it was practically empty. It was almost as if Boudreaux was in the witness protection program. Everything was too neat, too tidy.

She picked up the phone and dialed.

"Louisiana information, may I help you?" an operator asked.

"Yes, I'm looking for a Kendrick and Emily Boudreaux in Alexandria, Louisiana."

After a few seconds, the operator responded, "Here you go, hon."

Meredith scribbled down the number, hung up, and then dialed. After the second ring, a woman's voice said, "Hello?"

"Is this Emily Boudreaux?" Meredith asked.

"Yes it is. May I ask who's speaking, please?"

Meredith listened to the decidedly southern accent, perhaps even a bit Cajun. She seemed like a gracious lady.

"Mrs. Boudreaux, my name is Sally Jones, and I am from the Department of Veterans Affairs. I am researching a case we have not yet closed on your son, Winslow."

Meredith listened to the awkward pause on the opposite end of the phone.

"Ma'am?" Meredith asked.

"Yes, I'm here. I just don't understand why the VA would be calling about my son. He's dead." Her voice was flat, a mixture between sadness and anger.

"I'm so sorry," Meredith said.

"He was killed in the Philippines, the Army said. Wasn't nothing to show for it, though, but some ashes."

"I understand. I'm so sorry for your loss." Meredith wanted to quickly steer away from the present line of discussion out of respect.

"Why were you calling, anyway?" Mrs. Boudreaux asked.

Meredith paused for a moment, thinking, as she thumbed through the bio sketch on Winslow Boudreaux. Her eyes stopped on the second page.

"We've got some belongings from a missing soldier, and I was just curious, what size was your son? Was he a tall man?"

"No, hon. He wasn't a stick over five foot six inches."

"Then these things we've got don't belong to him. I'm so sorry about having to call you and am so grateful for the service your son provided to our country. Thank you."

"No bother. Have a nice day." Her voice trailed off.

Meredith hung up the phone, staring out her window. She shook off the fact that she had just caused more anxiety to a grieving mother. What she had done was necessary. She looked down at the folder.

Winslow Boudreaux/6'2"/205lbs/Brn hair/Grn eyes.

If it wasn't Winslow Boudreaux executing the mission in Canada right now, then she had two questions. First, who *was* in Canada? Second, where was Winslow's body? She felt her skin crawl as she considered the possibilities.

Hellerman's question, that simple question, "Did you see Zachary's body?" was fluttering in her mind, refusing to disappear. The question it begged, the much larger issue, was too big to even consider.

She stood and walked to her window, her mind somehow shifting back to thinking about Matt and all that had happened over the course of the past year. She did love Matt, dearly. But she weighed the effects of her decision to hold off on marriage against her career.

Zachary. She had never met the man but certainly felt as though she knew him after being so close to Matt. She had helped Matt deal with his brother's death. She chased away the thought that Matt's obsession with Zachary's death may have contributed to her decision to hold off on marriage. Then, of course, there was the funeral. Meredith thought to herself, *The funeral that had no viewing—where the body was too badly mangled to show.*

Looking out the window, she could see the treetops along the ridge to the south bending in the light breeze. She thought about Matt, picturing him standing in his back yard, holding the baseball bat over his shoulder, smiling, green eyes boring into her, brown hair matted to his brow, crooked grin flashing white teeth at her.

That was Matt, all six-foot-two of him.

A cold chill shot up her spine like an electrical current.

No, it couldn't be.

Or could it?

CHAPTER 26

FRANKLIN COUNTY, VERMONT

"Where did they attack?" Peyton demanded again. This time, though, no one was shooting at them.

Matt was negotiating a hairpin turn that led them into the valley that made Franklin County Airfield possible. Tumblers were falling into place in his mind. The terrorist pilot he killed. The cell where they were held. The chase to Sheldon Springs. This was personal as much as it was part of some grand enemy strategic plan. Ballantine wanted him, Matt Garrett, in an eye-for-an-eye exchange. Brother for brother.

"Where?" Peyton demanded again.

"Charlotte Coliseum, Mall of America, and an Amtrak train somewhere in New Jersey."

"How is that possible?" Peyton whispered, turning her head to stare blankly out of the window.

Matt looked at Peyton and saw her determined, set jaw, eyes reflecting off the window with concern, perhaps something more.

"Probably more to come."

Peyton continued to stare out of her window. "Last night, when we were talking, I didn't tell you that my sister contacted me just last week," she said. "She came down to D.C. She needed money."

Matt let her continue, sensing there was something more.

"I told her she could stay at my place and gave her two thousand dollars. She left me a message that she was heading back to New York yesterday."

"On Amtrak?" he asked.

"On the Metroliner."

"Here, call her." Matt handed Peyton the phone.

"No, I have no way to get in touch with her."

"Call your house. Maybe she's there."

She turned and looked at him.

Matt pulled the truck over to the side of the road, and they sat in silence a couple of minutes. Like adrenaline masking the pain of an injury, the rapid pace of events had mitigated their ability to fully comprehend what had just transpired. Terrorists had successfully attacked the nation again. Matt knew that, most likely, thousands of people were dead, thousands more were injured and maimed, and there would be almost no family in the nation left untouched by the attacks. He suddenly felt a wave of grief sweep over him. Was *his* family okay, he wondered? What remained of it, anyway, with Zachary and his mother now gone.

"Here, call her now." He offered her the cell phone again.

He saw a coldness glaze over her. She became more distant at his second urging. He thought about how he had been acting the last several months. No one could get close to him. Like a dance, if someone had tried to step closer, he would step back, keeping the distance. He saw the same hardness in Peyton. The last twenty-four hours had been traumatic, so he let it go. Then he saw her look away and mouth a curse word, as if she were scolding herself.

"Fine," he said, rubbing his hands on his pants. He put the truck into gear and nosed onto the country road. "Let's talk about something else. We can regroup as we drive. We might be rushing headlong into something here. Instincts are telling me that."

Peyton looked at him and shrugged as if to say, *Okay, what?*

"First, how the hell could we have missed these attacks?" Matt asked. "I mean, something that takes down the Charlotte Coliseum and the Mall of

America simultaneously with an Amtrak train."

"Maybe it's not so unbelievable today," Peyton said. "It is signature al Qaeda."

"Maybe, but this seems different. I've fought al Qaeda, and this is more sophisticated."

"What are you saying?" Peyton asked.

"I think there's a level of capability and organization here that we haven't seen before. I think this is only the beginning."

"And the second thing?" she asked.

"Bees."

"Like the birds and the bees?"

"Well, birds too, but mostly bees," Matt said. The airfield was in sight, about four miles down the long valley. He picked up Stephanie's cell phone and dialed Meredith's number. "Meredith, I need two things. First, what is Rampert's ETA? Second, I need you to get me information on the leading mind on nanotechnology."

"Rampert will be there in fifteen minutes. The nanotech thing might be a bit tougher. Why do you need that?"

"Just a hunch. Just get me his name and a phone number, ASAP, please."

"Okay, hang on. Let me do a Google search for you."

Matt cocked his head, holding the cell phone to his ear, and listened as he heard Meredith peck away at the computer keys. "Get ready to write this down," he said.

Peyton searched in the truck's dirty glove box for a pen, found one, and prepared to take a note.

However, Peyton's eyes were fixed on the horizon. "That can't be Rampert's plane can it?" she asked.

Matt looked up and saw a small, white Sherpa on approach to the airfield. "That looks like the airplane Hellerman told me Ballantine flies."

Meredith's voice came back on the phone. "Okay, there are two names that keep popping up. One is Martin Fierman. He lives in Atlanta and teaches nanotechnology at Georgia Tech. Big physics background, and then he branched into computers and digits and so forth." She gave him the number.

"And the next?" Matt asked.

"Well, this is different, but his name is Samuel Werthstein. He is described as a leading mind in biotech and nanotech, and has recently branched solely into nanotechnology with an emphasis on using digits to replicate insect behavior."

"Bingo," Matt said.

"Bingo, what?" Meredith asked.

"That's who I'm looking for. Where is he?"

"Well, the Internet has got him listed as being an adjunct at the University of Vermont."

"This starts making more sense by the minute," Matt said, eyeing the Sherpa. They were less than a mile from the runway.

Meredith gave him the phone number, which Matt repeated to Peyton, who dutifully scribbled it down. "He also has an extensive background in entomology—you know, the study of insects."

"Okay, gotta run, here, but one last question," Matt said, negotiating the parking lot and hearing the distinct pop-pop of small arms fire. "Is there a picture of him on any of those Web sites?" Then he motioned to Peyton to reload the shotgun. She needed no instruction as she opened the box of shells and clicked them one at a time into the receiver.

"Of course, I'm looking at one right now. Looks like a typical absent-minded professor, like Albert Einstein."

"Matt, we're taking fire!" Peyton shouted.

He shut the cell off and stuffed it into his shirt pocket, pulling hard on the steering wheel to drive toward a small building that would provide cover.

Machine-gun fire chewed the right front fender of the truck as Peyton dove into Matt's lap, avoiding a spray of bullets that shattered the windows on the passenger side. Without losing control, Matt veered left off the side of the road and into the ditch running alongside.

Matt dove from the truck, pulling Peyton through the driver's-side door, which afforded them the most protection.

"How the hell do these guys know where we are all the time?" Peyton shouted.

They scrambled into a small culvert that gave them cover from the bullets zipping past them like angry hornets. They were safe, for now, but it was a precarious position. All someone needed to do was get onto the second floor of the hangar, and their location would be exposed.

"Bees, that's how," Matt said.

A burst of machine-gun fire spit dirt into their faces.

"We can't stay here for long," he said, pushing Peyton into the dirt. "They know we're here, and it's only a matter of time before they maneuver on us."

They moved farther down the ditch and hunkered down against the fire aimed at them from over one hundred yards away. The shotgun was completely useless.

More bullets gnawed at the top of the road that separated them from the flight-line warehouse.

"Bees? What the hell are you talking about?" Peyton asked.

The cell phone rang. It was Meredith.

"Matt, Rampert's five minutes out with an MC-130. He says it's a small airfield and wants you to mark it for him."

"We're in a firefight here, Meredith," Matt said. "That airplane needs to land quickly and be careful. Tell Rampert there are about five tangos shooting at us from the west side of the large runway hangar. He'll need to get a team into the hangar right away. If he has any kind of escort, they can provide some covering fire."

"No escort right now. Every fighter plane flying right now is protecting critical targets around the country."

The cynic in him registered immediately that he was not considered a critical target. He smiled and said, "Just give him the intel. He'll know what to do. Ballantine's airplane might be in there, too." He hung up.

They continued to take fire, though it was not well aimed.

He rolled over in the dirt and looked at Peyton lying next to him. She was dirty and tired, but he noticed her steely resolve, which had been consistent throughout their ordeal for the last twenty-four hours. She looked at him.

"What?" Peyton asked.

"You seeing anyone?"

"Come again?" she said, looking up into the top of the mound as dirt spilled onto her face from a burst of machine-gun fire.

Matt shrugged and looked away. As always, when under pressure, he saw no point in fretting over that which he could do nothing about until an opportunity presented itself. They were pinned down and surely the bad guys would run out of ammunition, get bored and give up, or advance upon them. Matt was betting on the third option. Until that time, unsure why, he found himself uncharacteristically attracted to this enigma playing army with him.

"What's the plan?" she asked.

"I figured we'd start slowly, you know. Maybe dinner and a movie—"

"I'm talking about—"

A loud explosion interrupted Peyton's protest.

Matt looked at her and said, "Okay, that's the diversion. I figure there are three men providing cover fire for one or two others maneuvering on our position. This shotgun is totally useless until someone gets within fifty yards of me. The warehouse is about three times that. I have four shells in this weapon. I'll use one or two on the attacker or attackers that try to root us out of this hole. That will leave two or three for the enemy in the building. If Rampert gets here, fine. If not . . . well, then, we have to think of something else."

"Ever consider the possibility that there might be more than a few of these crazies out there?" Peyton asked.

"This is suppressive fire intended to keep our heads down so we don't see them moving on our position here. As soon as you hear a large volume of fire, it will mean that the team has reached their assault position and is about to move the final distance across the open ground. Probably from the left, over there near the woods. When you hear the fire from the building stop, that's when you know they are within fifty yards, because they won't risk shooting their own guys." Matt pointed at the north side of the ditch, where he and Peyton could see the tips of a wooded area just above the top lip of their protective ground.

She stared at him for a moment.

"No. Not right now. Not really," she said.

Matt did not seem to register that she was answering his original question about whether she had a boyfriend. Enemy fire picked up intensity with orange tracers whipping overhead.

"Get ready," he said, lifting the shotgun. "As soon as the heavy fire stops, I'm popping up. If I get hit, you grab the shotgun and defend yourself until special ops gets here."

Suddenly he could hear only the echo of automatic gunfire rumbling along the valley floor.

"Screw that," she said, standing with him.

Matt immediately picked up one man moving low, holding an AK-47 at the ready. Matt raised the shotgun, felt two shots zip past his ear, and then dropped the attacker with one shot to the torso.

"Watch out!" Peyton shouted. She spun around and grabbed the AK-47 of another man, who had approached them from the backside. Three shots ripped from the assault rifle, spewing powder and fire into Peyton's face as she pulled him into the ditch, using his forward momentum as an assist.

Matt spun, placed the shotgun on the man's forehead, and noticed Peyton was holding the AK-47. It took every ounce of control he had not to pull the trigger, and perhaps he should have, but he saw Peyton standing atop this enemy combatant, taking deep breaths and staring down at the man with frightened eyes. She wanted to kill him. He could see the bloodlust in her eyes.

"Don't do it," he whispered.

Those eyes darted toward him and then back toward the Middle Eastern man lying in the ditch, staring at both of them.

"Go to hell," she said, lifting the rifle.

"Let me ask him a few questions first," Matt said, lifting his hand and pushing the AK-47 away.

She quickly moved the weapon back and fired a single shot into the man's head, killing him.

"Damn it! What the hell did you do that for?" Matt shouted.

"He tried to kill you. You should be thanking me," she said. "Watch yourself." She pointed her rifle at the grenade in the man's hand.

Matt looked at the dead man, then at his hand. The grenade, pin still intact, was nestled in the palm of his hand reminding him of how a pitcher might grasp the ball for a changeup. He looked up at Peyton, then over the lip of the ditch.

"They're jumping in broad daylight," he muttered.

"What? Who?" Peyton asked.

"Special Ops." Matt lowered his head again, trying to avoid becoming a target for too long. He moved to another portion of the ditch and reemerged. As he peered over the ledge, he saw four square parachutes deploying dangerously low to the ground.

"They're landing on the roof," he said in amazement at the balls of the four paratroopers. While he had done that himself in a previous life, watching it was another thing all together.

He heard four small thumps as the commandos landed on the hangar. Though he could no longer see them, he could visualize their actions. In less than ten minutes, the hangar would be under the control of the special operations forces.

"Let's move. Maybe we'll draw some fire and take some heat off the spec ops while they move," Matt said.

"The least we can do," she muttered sarcastically.

"Let's go," Matt said, leaping from the ditch and dashing toward a small copse of trees to his left. He watched Peyton emerge from their protected space. She was holding the AK-47 and looked like she might have stuffed the grenade in her coat pocket. *Interesting.*

Matt could hear the stray rounds zip through the trees overhead. They had been seen, but clearly the shooters were not aiming their fire.

"Hear that?" she said.

Rapid gunfire was echoing from inside the building. They were short bursts that Matt knew from experience were typical of close-quarters combat. Multiple shots in short succession indicated surprise and defensive actions. The special operations guys would be using silencers for the most part, so he took this as a good sign.

"Let's move now," Matt said, rushing toward the building. This time, there was no fire as they slammed into the side of the hangar, breathing hard.

"Door?"

"Door. I'll go first," Matt said.

They slid along the hangar wall until they reached the gray metal door secured by a small hasp and padlock.

"Watch out," Matt whispered.

He butt-stroked the padlock, which held, but the hasp came swinging free. He kicked the door into the hangar and did a combat roll through the opening, coming to one knee and looking down the shotgun's barrel. He felt Peyton move into the room and go to his left . . . just how an infantry fire team performed the drill.

"Clear right," he said, instinctively.

"Clear left," she responded.

They moved slowly in the darkness of the hangar, letting their eyes adjust.

"Listen," Matt whispered.

It was the sound of a small aircraft engine cranking.

"That's Ballantine's Sherpa. Let's go," Matt said, running to the far side of the hangar only to be pushed back by intense machine-gun fire.

Peyton laid down a base of covering fire, but was unclear where she should be aiming. Matt rolled to the right and felt an explosion push them backward. His first reaction was that it was a thermite grenade. He hoped that he was not fighting with friendly forces but didn't figure they would be down from the upper floors of the hangar yet.

Suddenly the hangar doors flew open. Through the smoke, Matt saw the Sherpa taxiing rapidly along the apron, then lifting off quickly and banking hard to the north.

Running outside, he took two hapless shots at the low-flying aircraft, as if he were shooting quail that had already taken flight beyond his reach. He had done it before and once even got lucky with a long shot.

But not this time.

"You okay?" Peyton asked, jogging up next to him.

"Yeah. That was Ballantine's plane. But we've got to find the special ops before they shoot us."

"Let's check out what they destroyed," she said.

They scrambled to a smoking hulk of scrap metal. The contraption was totally disfigured and nonfunctional. Matt recognized it for what is was immediately.

"No way to tell what that was," Peyton said.

"On the contrary. You've been asking me about this since I met you."

CHAPTER 27

FRANKLIN COUNTY AIRFIELD, VERMONT

Matt was thankful that the link-up with the special operations team had been uneventful. Apparently the four operatives who had jumped in had been briefed that he and Peyton were in the vicinity and possibly armed. Colonel Rampert's MC-130 command and control aircraft had landed, and the special ops commander himself had deplaned to personally inspect the scene.

"Jack Rampert," the colonel said, holding out a large, leathery paw.

"Matt Garrett," he said, shaking the man's hand. "This is Peyton O'Hara."

"Know all about Miss O'Hara here," Rampert said.

Matt raised an eyebrow.

"Sir," Peyton said, shaking his hand.

"Got two wounded men," Rampert said. "The terrorists are dead. I've called the FBI. They're on the scene, blocking the locals from gaining access to this place. I've got another crew coming in to do sensitive site exploitation. We also found one weird, scientist-looking dude in the tunnel network down below."

"Below?" Peyton asked.

"I thought this place felt familiar," Matt said.

"You're telling me this is where we were held?"

"That's right, and that's got to be none other than Dr. Samuel Werthstein," Matt said, pointing at the man two commandos were escorting to the back ramp of the MC-130. Werthstein was walking slowly in his white smock, his gray hair disheveled and his hands flex-cuffed behind his back.

"You know that hero?" Rampert asked Matt derisively. "Bunch of damn bees flying around in there where we found him."

"I know who he is, and depending on what those bees have taught him and what he has given the bad guys, it could be bad news for us real soon."

"Why don't we go talk to him?" Rampert said. "Meanwhile, Peyton, I've got instructions to send you back to Middleburg to debrief the National Command Authority."

"No way. I'm going with you guys," she said.

"Not happening. See that Pave Low helicopter coming in? That's your chariot," Rampert said.

"See you when I get back," Matt said to Peyton. She was standing defiantly, holding her AK-47 as if she were a freedom fighter being told her services were no longer needed.

"This is bullshit," she said. Peyton turned and walked toward the hovering Pave Low, then stopped. Above the din of the aircraft she shouted, "Be careful, Matt Garrett! We need you back alive!"

Rampert and Matt walked to the MC-130 ramp, pushing through the competing prop washes of the Pave Low and the MC-130.

"Got some clothes for you in the aircraft. Gotta ask you a question, Garrett."

"Okay, shoot." Matt stopped at the top of the ramp and looked at Rampert as his radio began chirping. Matt recognized the voice. It was Meredith, evidently calling him from the command center in Middleburg.

"For you," Rampert said, handing him a small Motorola radio.

"Matt?" Meredith asked.

"Yes?"

"Please forgive me for saying this. I know you've got a lot to think about right now, but I just need you to listen to me for a second. Get your mind to a point where you can analyze what I'm about to say without a knee-jerk reaction."

"Don't you think there's a better time and place for this stuff?" Matt said. Through the open ramp of the MC-130, he watched the weakening spring sun begin to touch the New York mountains in the west. The sun was a flaming ball nestling atop the jagged ridge. He looked back at Peyton, who was boarding the helicopter with the assistance of two Air Force loadmasters.

"I'm not talking about us, Matt. I'm talking about Zachary."

"Well," he protested immediately.

"Drop the attitude, and let me finish."

"Okay, you have my undivided attention, Meredith."

"This operator we have in Canada right now, the one we haven't heard from . . ."

"Okay?"

"Well, you remember that Hellerman told you this in the Suburban yesterday before you left, right? Anyway, Rampert briefed us that his name is Winslow Boudreaux. Ever hear of him?"

"One of the operators, right? But I'm not certain."

She paused, then said, "I pulled the file on one Winslow Boudreaux because something didn't seem right when Colonel Rampert briefed us. There was too much mystery."

"What's that got to do with Zachary? Did he know him?" Matt looked at Rampert, who was standing about twenty feet away. Rampert tapped his watch to demonstrate his impatience.

"Matt, we never saw Zachary. We never identified him. I think Winslow Boudreaux or someone else is in a grave in Stanardsville."

Matt let the comment hang in the air for a second, and then Meredith continued.

"And I think Zachary is still alive in Canada. Right now."

Matt dropped his arm to his side, the radio handset almost slipping from his hand. *No way.* Then he considered the old Meredith, who would have only mentioned something of this magnitude for one of two reasons. One, he figured, she thought she was right. Second, she was trying to present him with the opportunity to do something about it. That's the way the old Meredith, the one he loved and had wanted to wed, operated. She gave him the facts as she knew them, and then let him make the decisions.

"Matt, you there?" He could hear her faint voice near his hand.

"Yes, I'm here. I'm trying to give you the benefit of the doubt."

"Thank you."

It was not so much that he did not believe her. Rather, he was unable to accept that the information was true. His analysis of the information was removed from Meredith totally. He considered her speculation without emotion.

About the time he thought he might want to say something, he heard the unmistakable noise of four C-130 propellers racing. He looked at the aircraft and saw Rampert slicing his hand across his throat, indicating he needed Matt to cut off his conversation.

"I've got to go. Rampert's giving me the high sign."

"Matt?"

"Yes," he said, becoming frustrated.

"I do love you. Good luck."

"I . . . I'll talk to you later. Bye."

He tossed the radio back to Rampert and then followed him into the bowels of the MC-130. The loadmaster handed him a pair of earplugs, which he needed, but did little good. As he walked along the nonskid, painted aisle, Matt was reminded of his first five jumps from the U.S. Army Airborne School at Fort Benning, Georgia. Since then, he had made hundreds of jumps, both static line and free fall. Toward the nose of the aircraft was a communications pod that he knew was Rampert's command post.

Along the starboard side of the aircraft were two litters with the two wounded operators. A medic was attending to each. Their wounds appeared serious enough to require intravenous fluids, probably mixed with morphine. Along the port side of the aircraft, Matt saw five body bags stacked like cord wood. The special ops had even secured the two that he and Peyton had killed.

The two other operators were checking their gear and reloading their magazines. One was inspecting his parachute.

Matt sat next to Rampert inside the enclosed communications pod.

"Our operator in Canada has missed two reporting windows," Rampert said. "Our standard operating procedure for that contingency is to do an emergency extraction. We lost the beacon on him about four hours ago, but we believe we know where he is. Because I've got two wounded operators and there is a sense of urgency to this mission, I am jumping in with the two men you see out there preparing. That gives me three. We need a fourth."

Rampert let the invitation hang in the air.

"Who is the operator?" Matt asked, Meredith's conversation fresh in his mind.

"Major Boudreaux," Rampert said.

"You're lying."

His steel gray eyes locked onto Matt's.

"You jumping or not? We don't have much time. It will just be getting dark. We climb to twenty thousand feet over Canadian airspace along the Saint Lawrence River, jump into the breeze, and glide onto the Lake Moncrief landing zone. We find our operator, kill Ballantine, and get extracted by Pave Low helicopter. Afterward, we tell the Canucks what we did. Maybe."

Matt thought for a moment. What did he have to lose? It had been a while since he had done an oxygen-assisted freefall, but it was like riding a bike. Worst that could happen was that he would burn a smoking hole in the Canadian countryside and never be heard from again. *Better than dodging baseballs in my backyard*, Matt thought.

Best that could happen would be that they rescue Boudreaux, or whoever he was, and get Ballantine. It seemed like a pretty good reward for the risk. Already he had been shot at twice, once by a farmer's daughter and once by a terrorist. His fresh wound made the wounds from the Philippines a year ago seem like a century removed. There was still pain in his ribcage and a scar across his forearm, but somehow being able to do something, to go after someone, was helping, both psychologically and physically.

Matt had wallowed in his own self pity for too long. He had mourned Zachary's death and his inability to prevent his loss, despite his proximity at the time. He had convinced himself that he had become a liability to Zachary and had distracted him from his own mission, which ultimately led to his brother's demise.

Irrational?

But now Matt was being given a chance to avenge the loss of his brother. While he knew that he had better odds of getting struck by lightning during a shark attack while celebrating a Power Ball lottery win than of finding his brother in some Canadian fishing hole used as a command post by terrorists, he had to try. *What if?*

"Okay, I'm in."

CHAPTER 28

ABOARD U.S. AIR FORCE MC-130 SPECIAL OPERATIONS COMMAND CENTER

Matt's stomach crawled into his throat at the nearly forgotten feeling of an MC-130 aircraft climbing to altitude faster than it was designed to. Matt leaned back into the red mesh webbing and shut his eyes for a brief moment, visualizing the pilots, frustrated fighter jocks, discussing whether or not to do a barrel roll or a corkscrew. The smell of jet fuel filled his nostrils, and it began to work its magical effect of making him drowsy.

"You say you know this guy?" Rampert interrupted. He was pointing at Dr. Werthstein. Matt rubbed his face and then looked at him. He considered that the doctor could be a body double for Albert Einstein in a biopic.

"No. Don't know him, but know *of* him," Matt said.

"Well, we can't get jack shit out of him. Why don't you try?" Rampert said. "But make it quick. You need to suit up."

"Roger."

Matt slid next to Werthstein, grabbed a K-bar knife from a sheath hanging in the communications pod, and cut Werthstein's flex-cuffs free.

"Thank you," the old man whispered, eyes looking down at the floor and hands rubbing his bruised wrists.

"Why didn't you come with us when we tried to get you out of there?"

Matt asked.

"They would have killed my family. There is no escaping them."

"No escaping who?"

"What have I done? Oh, what have I done?" the doctor whispered, looking away.

"That's what we're trying to establish here. What *have* you done?"

"My family . . . is there any way to protect my family?" The old man was nearly in tears and for the first time made eye contact with Matt.

"Where is your family?"

"They are being held captive in France. We tried telling the French government these people were after me, but because we are Americans they told us to go to hell."

"Who is holding them captive, and where are they?" When the man answered, Matt wrote down the information and handed it to Rampert. "See if you can get some of your buddies to go to this address and secure a woman and three children, ages nine to fifteen."

Rampert looked at Matt, then at the professor. "All right. I'll see what I can do."

Matt walked back to Werthstein, who had witnessed the exchange between Matt and Rampert.

"Now, quid pro quo," Matt said.

"I know, I know. Lord, help me."

"Start with the bees. They communicate, right?"

"Yes, the bees. Very good. The bees communicate throughout the swarm by pheromones. Ants do much the same thing. When bees are out looking for nectar, one scout finds it and he can send pheromone signals back to the swarm, allowing all the drones to mass on that one area. Ants are similar except, of course, they don't fly. They scavenge for food, find what they are looking for, and then mark the trail back and forth between the colony and target area so that all the other ants can simply follow the pheromone trail."

Matt saw Rampert in the background, talking on a telephone, nodding his head. Matt felt the MC-130 shoot upward again, leaving his stomach on the floor.

"Okay, now tell me how that is a bad thing." Matt asked.

"I am the only one who has been able to replicate this activity through nanotechnology, using microscopic chipsets and advanced computing power that isn't even in the experimentation phase at Oak Ridge and Lawrence Livermore. I have written the program that allows entities to communicate by way of dropping 'digital pheromones.'"

"And who has this technology now?"

"Well, me, and those terrorists that kidnapped my family," Werthstein spat.

"Okay, and what have the terrorists done with this technology?"

Werthstein hesitated. Matt could see the strain on his face. Faced with the impossible moral dilemma of watching madmen execute your family or handing over secret and lethal technology to your nation's enemies, no man could predict how he would react until faced with the problem set. This man, Matt believed, was no different. Despite the crushing reality of his situation, he suffered under an incredible burden of guilt. He was given the worst of all choices: a lose-lose situation.

"They made me apply it to a fleet of UAVs. Now they can communicate with one another, flying in the sky for days. How do you think they tracked you?"

"That's exactly what I thought, but how did the UAVs know to track me, Matt Garrett?" Matt said.

"I accessed your files, your medical records from Walter Reed. Really not very secure at all. I uploaded your physical characteristics and some photos of you into the UAV database. The microprocessor on the queen recalculated your dimensions into a data packet it could transmit to the drones. The drones then took turns following you in the sky, all from different directions, all for short duration so as to avoid detection. It's all biometrics. Really quite simple to do today."

Matt stared at Werthstein, speechless.

"This was a passive activity though, Mr. Garrett. I believe what they have in mind is not passive."

"Go on," Matt said. "Tell me, how many UAVs do they have? What kind are they?"

"They never gave me the number. They just flew me to a couple of different places—blindfolded, of course—and made me input the code into the ground control stations, the queens. Any one queen can communicate and direct a limitless number of UAVs. I loaded four machines, but I'm not certain if they were all ground control stations. They wouldn't tell me what type of UAVs they are, but my belief is that they are Predators. They may have also exported the data over the web, but I can't be sure."

"Why do you think they are Predators?" It was all coming together now. Iraq, or some rogue terrorist supporter, would not have the satellite or bandwidth capability to put a bunch of Predators in the sky and let them roam around the countryside. However, when he thought about countries like China and North Korea, he could visualize the satellite capability and a cartel of sorts with the capacity to do precisely what Dr. Werthstein feared.

"I believe they are Predators because they had to give me the weight, wing span, and so forth so that I could write the code properly."

"What's the worst that can happen?" Matt asked.

"The worst that could happen?" Werthstein paused. "Thirty, forty Predators roaming the skies, all programmed with one target for redundancy or many programmed with several targets. Once one Predator sees its target, it will communicate instantly to the rest of the swarm, just like the bees, and move to the target area. Only, these Predators will be armed, and I believe they will be armed with nuclear weapons."

"Ten minutes, Garrett. Got to get ready," Rampert shouted.

Matt sat back, stunned, staring at Werthstein.

"Normal air defenses will expend all of their ammunition, destroying some of the Predators, yes, but because they can swarm, the redundancy will defeat even the best defenses."

"What are their targets?" Matt asked.

"They made me program about fifty different targets: people, places, ground transportation hubs such as ports, as well as nuclear power plants and electrical switching grids. There are many others. They made me put the targets into a central database. Now all they have to do is use a computer mouse to click and drag a specific target to a UAV icon on the computer screen and the queen will automatically program that specific UAV for that specific target. Even if the target is moving, like a convoy, the drones can follow, mass, and destroy the target."

"Using the digital pheromones?"

"Precisely. That's how they followed you."

"How do you stop it? Kill the queen? Destroy the colony?"

"If you kill the queen, the drones can act independently, sending the digital pheromones to one another. They have a survival instinct. If you don't kill the queen, she programs the drones to attack one, some, or all of the fifty targets I loaded."

"Let's go!" Rampert shouted.

Werthstein paused for a moment, then looked Matt in the eyes.

"Will God forgive me?"

Matt continued to look at Werthstein, unable to remove his eyes from the man who might have rigged the terrorists with the ultimate weapon. The enemy could find what it wanted, mass on the target, and destroy.

"Perhaps—as soon as we kill these bastards," Matt said, standing.

Matt walked to and leaned over a small computer terminal that was hooked up to the satellite antennae atop the MC-130. He typed a quick e-mail and sent it to the one person in the world he felt he could trust right now.

Stepping back, he took a deep breath, slipped into his parachute, and walked toward Rampert, who quickly inspected him and handed him an M4 carbine. Matt tucked the weapon inside his parachute waistband. He donned the helmet and oxygen mask, took a couple of deep breaths, and exhaled heavily.

"Ready?" Rampert asked through the microphone in the helmet.

"We need to talk about Werthstein when we get back," Matt said.

Rampert gave him a thumbs-up.

"One minute!" came the jump master's voice over the loudspeaker.

Matt watched as the jump master crawled along the lowered ramp. He could feel the cold air rushing into the back of the MC-130 Combat Talon. How many times had he done this as an operative for the Agency? he asked himself. He had lost count.

Matt watched the light turn green.

"Go!"

Then he was tumbling into the pitch black night with Colonel Jack Rampert and his two men.

Matt's mind was processing about as much as the human brain could handle: terrorists on U.S. soil, nuclear Predators that fly and communicate like insects, and the remote possibility that his dead brother was alive.

Truly, Zachary's fate was all that mattered to him as the cold Canadian night air buffeted him.

CHAPTER 29

MONCRIEF LAKE, QUEBEC

It was the image of Jacques Ballantine's face hovering directly above his own that brought Zachary Garrett/Winslow Boudreaux back to reality, like a time traveler bobsledding at warp speeds down a dark, icy tunnel. His first stop was the hot, smoky desert floor where he had first seen Ballantine's face. Next was an apocalyptic battle in a steamy jungle valley, his last memory as Zachary Garrett.

"I must be living right." A distant voice invaded his reverie.

And now, a Canadian trout pond in Quebec Province.

"Hello. Captain Garrett."

Zachary Garrett pulled out from the day dream. He tried to shade his eyes from the lamplight, but realized he was handcuffed with what seemed to be a plastic flex cuff much like a trash bag tie, though much stronger, when his hands wouldn't respond. He wiggled them behind his back only to feel the sharp edges of the plastic cut into his wrists. His ankles were tied to the legs of the chair. He struggled to bring the face hovering above him into focus.

"We meet again. But this time we are on a different battlefield. Mine."

Zachary surveyed his confines. He noticed the large rafters in the ceiling of what looked like a cabin. There were the usual accompaniments of a lakeside cabin: a wooden table and chairs; some older, overstuffed furniture; and a wooden stairway to a loft above the kitchen.

He vaguely remembered a mission to snatch a target from his command post. The memories of his two worlds were overlapping, not without a fair amount of confusion. Then he grimaced, the face of his captor becoming clear, a dark woman standing next to him. "You . . ." he said.

"Yes, Mr. Garrett. Me."

"Ball . . . Ballan—"

"Ballantine. Jacques Ballantine. You should remember a man's name when you murder his brother."

Zach struggled to remember, vague images playing in the back of his mind like an old home video poorly shot on a 16mm camera. "What does this have to do with me?" he asked, confused.

"We have, as you like to say it, 'taken the fight to the enemy.'"

"I'm all ears," Garrett said.

"We have initiated a plan which, you may care to know, you have only been temporarily successful in averting—"

Again Zach struggled. As Boudreaux he had a mission to kill this man. He knew little about what Ballantine was planning to do, just that it was important to kill him . . . and that he had failed.

Ballantine smiled.

"Tell me, Garrett, we all heard you were dead. How is it that you have been brought back to life?"

"Frankly, I don't remember much about that."

"Let me refresh your memory about one particular aspect of your history."

"Please," Zachary said through clenched teeth as his restraints suddenly seemed much tighter.

Ballantine lowered himself so that he was eye-level with Garrett.

"You killed my brother, shot him in the face."

Garrett's eyes lowered to the floor much as they had twelve years earlier in his armored personnel carrier.

"That I could never forget," he said in a whisper.

"Nor will I ever let you forget it," Ballantine shot back. "Your brother should be here shortly, and I intend to let you watch him die at my hands, just as you did to me. Then, I suspect I will let you live so that you can experience the years of never-ending pain that only seems to grow as time passes."

Garrett lifted his head and met Ballantine's stare.

It had been a long time since he had consciously thought about his younger brother, Matt, and their days of growing up on the farm near Charlottesville, Virginia. Though he suspected warm thoughts of young Matt were always there, hidden away, to have the memory come rushing back so rapidly caused a visible reaction.

"I see that I have your attention now," Ballantine said.

"Why would Matt be coming here?"

"Because we have caused it to happen that way."

"Who has caused it to happen that way?"

"You would be very surprised."

"Surprise me." Zachary studied the scar on Ballantine's face as his rival began to speak.

"We've got inbound!"

Ballantine and the dark woman snapped their heads toward the door. A tall man wearing a camouflage hunting outfit and carrying an M-16 rifle came running up the steps. "Our radar showed a four-propeller airplane flying slow at twenty thousand feet," he said. "Drop speed and altitude for jumpers."

Ballantine looked at his watch and said, "They are early."

He turned toward Zachary Garrett and said, "When was the last time you saw your brother?"

"How do you know he's coming?" Zachary said.

"I just know," Ballantine said, his eyes turning dark as coal. "I just know." His voice trailed off as he turned toward the messenger.

"They'll be coming from the landing strip area either down the ridge or along the lake. Place one team on each approach ready to ambush. But I want Matt Garrett alive at all costs. Do you understand?" Ballantine said.

"Yes, sir."

"Virginia, you stay here with Garrett. I will return with his brother."

"Gladly," she said, fondling her pistol.

Ballantine secured his rifle and turned toward Garrett. "This is really better than I could have ever hoped. Finding you has given me new life, new purpose. Now I even care about the other things that are about to happen."

Then he was gone into the Canadian evening.

"What does he mean about the other things?" Zachary said, turning toward the woman. She was wearing a dark khaki outfit that blended neatly with her chocolate skin. *Attractive woman*, he thought. *What the hell is she doing with Ballantine?*

"Why should I tell you anything?" she said with a laugh.

"Because we're both Americans, and Ballantine is up to no good."

"What makes you think I'm American?" she laughed again. "And even if that's the case, why the hell would I support such a corrupt government?"

"You'll get no argument from me on our government, but it's the way of life, you know. Democracy and all that good stuff."

"Your government chooses to murder innocent people all over the world and does so in the name of freedom or democracy or vital interests. Well, we've turned that to our advantage."

Zachary raised his eyebrows. Anything to compel her to talk. He needed information.

"We could not stop what has been set in motion now even if we wanted to."

Zachary let the thought sink in for a moment, connecting this new information from this current identity with his programmed information from his previous identity. He smiled inwardly, thinking that it was a challenge to have to sort through two personalities. He had to achieve consensus with himself to figure out what he was thinking. He smiled.

"What's so funny?" she asked.

"Have you ever met my brother Matt?"

The black woman smiled. "No, why? Is he a big bad ass or something?"

"There's that, but he's also the smartest man I know."

"Can't be too smart if he's in Canada, right here in our base camp," she said.

"No, no. I think you're wrong there, Virginia. He's got to know something neither of us knows."

She paced along the wooden floor, her long legs reaching out slowly as she walked. Zachary couldn't help but notice her perfectly honed body, like that of a jungle cat, with absolutely no fat.

"Tell me about the war. I've heard it all from Ballantine. I'd like to hear what you have to say."

"I was doing a job for my country. I had no bone to pick with the Iraqis or anyone else over there. My company was attacking his division. We had been briefed to capture the commanders of any Republican Guards units. I saw a command post vehicle and went for it. Ballantine and I met in hand-to-hand combat. His brother came to his defense." Zachary paused a second, then continued. "So I shot his brother dead. It was war."

"Yes, I understand that, and it is very similar to the story that Ballantine tells."

"The war is over."

"Maybe you don't know that now, twelve years after the first Persian Gulf invasions, your country has again attacked Iraq; this time without provocation. We, Ballantine and the rest of us, are the counterpunch."

He didn't respond to her statement. His mind spun, searching for a tangible piece of information that could either confirm or deny her statement. *Had the U.S. attacked Iraq unprovoked?* If so, Zach was certain that there had to be good cause. But then what the hell was he doing here in Canada? Confused, he watched her circle the room.

"How do you think it will feel?" Virginia asked him. Her face was less than a foot from his. He could see in detail the softness of her lips, her smooth skin, and her striking facial features.

"How what will feel?"

"To watch your brother die," she whispered coldly, "and then live with that memory."

Zachary went cold at the thought, his curiosity about Iraq vanishing into the black void of his mind and replaced with the unfocused image of his brother's face.

Surely there was something he could do.

CHAPTER 30

MONCRIEF LAKE

Matt watched the ground rise toward him, his rusty parachutist skills kicking in. The irony was not lost on him. Twenty-four hours ago he was getting onto an Air Force jet to fly to a counter-terrorist summit. Now he had just jumped from an Air Force plane to help destroy a terrorist cell.

He looked over at Rampert's man, Hobart, who signaled him with a thumbs-up that it was time to deploy their parachutes. Pulling the rip cord, Matt felt the familiar yank of his canopy inflating and his leg straps crushing his testicles. Images of Mindanao and Ron Peterson flashed through his mind as he briefly recalled jumping into the C-130 crash in the uncharted rain forest a year ago.

Remembering his lucky landing amidst the wreckage, he reached over and pulled down on the two toggles. Suddenly his parachute flared, slowing his descent. Keeping his feet and knees pressed firmly together, he kept his eyes focused on the horizon. His body instinctively prepared for impact every two or three seconds, creating an anxious feeling that made him want to reach toward the ground with his feet. But he had learned long ago to avoid doing that at all costs.

Suddenly, the ground grabbed him before he had a chance to think about it again. He tumbled lightly and rolled away from his fluttering parachute. He felt a sharp pain in his left ribcage near where he had stowed his weapon. Once the pain dulled, his first thought was the same as it was for every jump: *That wasn't so bad.*

Matt pulled his parachute down quickly and stowed it in a kit bag. That chore completed, he carefully scanned above the high weeds and spotted Rampert. The colonel was a solitary dark figure silhouetted against the soft night hues. He grabbed his bag and weapon and raced to Rampert, who had already packed his gear and was speaking quietly to no one that Matt could see. Then Rampert turned toward Matt.

"We've got movement toward the lake and just to the east of the drop zone. Ballantine's goons are setting up two ambushes. Our man is being held in the cabin nearest the lake. We can loop east, north, and then west to avoid the ambushes. Our two other men are already moving in the opposite direction. Stick with me." Rampert whispered when he spoke and used subtle hand and arm signals.

Matt followed the quickly moving Rampert, leaving the two kit bags behind. Flipping down his night-vision goggles, Matt picked his way through the sparse wood line like a running back through a defense and listened as Rampert talked quietly to his two other men.

Two *other* men. As if he was one of Rampert's men. The thought brought back memories of all the missions with the Agency and the wounds that had ended that career path.

He saw Rampert stop and lift his M4 with a silencer. Matt scanned ahead of his own weapon for possible targets. He saw two darkened figures moving slowly toward them in the light-green haze of his night-vision goggles.

"Confirm you are not near checkpoint two," Rampert whispered, obviously talking to his other team over the radio net that special operations employed.

After a brief wait, Rampert said, "Roger. If you are, stop now."

Matt watched as the two men in his vision continued to saunter toward them with no particular sense of urgency. It was clear, though, that they were carrying long rifles.

The two whispers escaping from Rampert's M4 were welcome sounds. If Rampert had waited a few seconds longer, Matt had been poised to shoot.

He heard in the distance the unmistakable sound of two bodies falling to the ground unimpeded. Matt and Rampert moved quickly to the two dead men, Rampert shining a small flashlight in their faces. While Matt knew that Rampert was conducting a quick search of the enemy, he also suspected that he was confirming that he had not shot his own men.

He had not. Matt continued to scan the horizon while Rampert checked the equipment.

"Let's move," Rampert whispered. Matt noticed Rampert had secured two small radios, one from each man. "Hang onto this. It may be helpful," Rampert said, handing Matt one of the small devices that looked and felt like it might have been purchased at Radio Shack.

They moved quietly along a small ridge, angling down the slope to the north. He knew this was the direction they needed to be going. An instinctive flare ignited within him. Something from the Philippines, the memories, the smell of gunpowder, the dead bodies.

His brother.

Could it be true? Was Zachary actually alive?

They stopped at the edge of the tree line before it gave way to an opening occupied by five cabins.

"Cabin nearest the water is our target," Rampert whispered to Matt.

"What's the plan?" he asked, the quiet night air interrupted by a zipping noise.

Matt turned and looked at Rampert as the colonel slumped forward, obviously hit by the single, silenced gunshot. Matt moved quickly, dragging Rampert behind a hardwood with a large trunk.

"Find Hobart. Tell him he's in charge. Get Boudreaux. It's critical we get Boudreaux before his memory returns," Rampert gasped in short breaths.

Another shot tore at the tree directly above Matt's head. He turned to find the shooter's location. Scanning the wood line with his night-vision goggles, he noticed movement near the intersection of the lake and the tree line. He quickly checked Rampert's pulse, weak but noticeable, and wrapped a gauze bandage from the colonel's first aid pouch around the seeping wound just above the right pectoral.

"Find Hobart," the colonel whispered again, "and get Boudreaux."

"Roger," Matt said, moving silently back to the north and then looping toward the lake. The M4 was a comfort in his hand. The scar in his abdomen tightened as flashes of combat in the Philippines leapt through his mind and he spotted the large lake through the green haze of his night-vision goggles.

He knelt by a thick pine, scanning to the north. He noticed a slight reflection of a faint moon off the lake when he heard the distinct sound of AK-47 gunfire coming from across the clearing to the west. Fearing a trap, he avoided focusing in that direction and moved toward the east again, preventing anyone from trapping him against the lake and the cabins.

Taking a knee again, Matt clipped the radio he had secured from Rampert onto his belt, placing the earpiece in his right ear. He flipped the switch on the control box before speaking.

"Hobart this is Garrett. Rampert is hit."

"Say again, call sign," came the response.

"Rampert's hit. Don't have a call sign. This is Garrett. I jumped in with you."

"Roger, what's your status?"

"On the east side. I've moved Rampert from where he was hit, and I've circled back to try to find the shooter. What's your status?"

"We've killed two and are pinned down by a team of two to four."

"Roger. We killed two on our way to the objective. You should be fighting the remnants. How can I help?"

"See if you can move back toward the cabins and flank them from the rear."

"Roger. Where are they located?" Matt asked. He had a general idea, given the shots he had heard, but wanted their perspective.

"They're between the last cabin and the lake, almost a hundred meters into the wood line."

"Moving now." He found the water's edge and moved slowly into the frigid lake. Quietly, he lowered himself into the water until only his head was above the surface. He held his weapon and the small radio set above the water as he smoothly glided parallel to the shoreline. Soon Matt noticed the clearing with the cabins off to his left and the dock with small fishing boats just ahead. He could feel the soft clay slide beneath his feet. He paused, grasping a wooden railing as he guided himself around the outer edges of the dock.

Matt could hear more gunfire, this time much closer. Bright spots flared as hot white spots in his night-vision goggles. He focused on a small copse of trees thirty meters to the front as his destination. Sliding smoothly, silently, through the water, he felt his adrenaline surge. He dialed in on his mission, focusing on the gunfire, his index finger rubbing absently on the trigger guard of his weapon.

Matt stumbled just a bit as he closed in on the shoreline, his feet fumbling on the steep bank. He slowed his movement as he emerged from the water, allowing his clothes to drain slowly. He centered himself in the small grouping of pine trees and waist-high shrub, scanning the horizon and feeling strangely secure in his covered and concealed position. It didn't take him long to find two of the terrorists who were holding Hobart and his partner at bay.

Matt secured the headset and switched on the radio as he slid the monitor in his vest pocket.

"Are you there?" It was Hobart's voice.

"Yes, I'm in position. I need you to fire two shots so I can get your location. I think I see two of the enemy," Matt said.

"Roger. Where are you?"

"Don't shoot in the direction of the lake."

"Roger."

Matt waited patiently while Hobart positioned himself to get a decent shot that would not wind up toward his location. He heard two loud pops and saw the muzzle flashes nearly fifty meters up the ridge. Just as quickly, he saw three muzzle flashes return the fire, surprisingly only twenty meters to his direct left. In fact, the enemy was using an extension of the same group of trees.

"You got us?" It was Hobart's voice.

"Roger," he whispered, mindful of his proximity to his targets.

Matt reached slowly to the muzzle and switched on the AN/PAQ-4C Infrared Aiming Light. He shivered against his icy, water-soaked clothes. If he didn't move soon, it would not be long before hypothermia set in. Though cold, he refocused.

Matt trusted that Rampert had properly adjusted his aiming light as he drew a bead on the first target. His hand absently turned the silencer, testing to make sure it was properly seated and would muffle the sound of the subsonic bullet he was about to launch into the skull of this unknown person.

The man's body was a dark mass with mild distinctions. Matt watched the aiming light dance across his target's forehead for a brief second and then he squeezed the trigger. Before the man dropped dead on the ground, Matt had placed the aiming light on his partner, who was now just turning toward his fallen comrade. Matt had a perfect face shot from about twenty-five meters. The aiming light hung perfectly on the man's nose as Matt squeezed the trigger again.

The second man dropped dead about the time he began to receive heavy fire from what he presumed was the third member of the ambush element. He felt a spray of bark from the tree as he whispered into his headset, "Give me some help, guys."

"We're on it," Hobart said.

Matt crawled low to another position ten meters from his last location. Hearing a heavy volume of fire come from Hobart's location, he slowly raised his head to notice he actually had a better view of the enemy from his new vantage. He watched as the third member of the team slumped against a pine tree from the precision fire.

"Looks like you got him," Matt said into the radio.

"Roger. Keep your PAQ-4 lit and turn it skyward. We'll link up in thirty seconds."

"Roger."

Matt turned his muzzle skyward so that Hobart could zero in on the infrared beacon. Watching through his PVS-14s, he noticed the skill with which the veteran warrior led his wingman through the scrub toward his position. Hobart moved in quick, silent movements, like a bobcat.

He heard two whispers cut through the still Canadian night like a zipper closing. His stomach sank as he watched Hobart and his partner drop like shot quail. Unsure of their status, Matt quickly shut down his infrared aiming light, fearing Ballantine, or whoever, had night-vision goggles.

His caution was well-founded. Tree bark sprayed against his forehead.

He rolled and then low-crawled toward the lake. He didn't relish the thought of reentering the cold water but realized he might have no other option. Two more shots whipped through the trees from where he had just departed. He slowly inched into the dark water and moved quietly toward the dock. Finding the dock again, he rested.

Then it occurred to him that it was he, Matt Garrett, against Ballantine in the Canadian outback. He was, perhaps, the lone survivor of a commando raid to retrieve a compromised operative who also just might be his brother.

Freezing his ass off in a Canadian oxbow lake, Matt realized life was full of tremendous ironies. The surge of adrenaline served as a catalyst to remind him that it was a year ago that his brother rescued him from a revolution in the Philippines. Suffering near debilitating guilt since his return and Zachary's death, could he really be facing an opportunity to save his brother? Could God be giving him this chance at redemption?

Deciding that it would be best to save Boudreaux, whoever he might be, he tucked away the blossoming hope and the pressure that would surely accompany the notion. He quietly pressed the magazine release button and surmised that, after his brief firefight, he had at least five rounds remaining.

Standing on the wooden ladder that thousands of tourist fishermen probably had climbed with coolers full of lake trout, Matt scanned the open terrain around the cabins less than a hundred meters away. Noticing movement near the tree line he had just fled, he watched as a tall man crouched low and scanned the lake. The man appeared to be backing away from the wood line and moving ever so slowly toward the first cabin. It had to be Ballantine.

Matt slid his magazine back into the weapon with a barely audible click, then raised his carbine in the general direction of his target. He could see through his own night-vision goggles that his target was wearing some form of night-vision device as well. Noticing this, he realized that he would only be able to turn on his infrared aiming device briefly before the target would be able to see it and respond.

He waited patiently as Ballantine finally turned toward the wood line again. Matt swallowed some dry spit and leveled the weapon to a height where he thought the infrared light would shine behind Ballantine, if it was

Ballantine, so that he could walk it over to his target. His thumb felt absently at the safety selector switch, his mind registering that the weapon was in the FIRE mode. His other hand rested on the PAQ-4C selector, slowly rotating the switch to the ON position to avoid any metallic click.

The infrared light appeared as a bright white streak, a laser beam of light invisible to the naked eye. The aiming light shone about ten feet behind the target. Matt slowly walked the light across the surrounding terrain until it pointed directly at Ballantine's midsection. He knew a head shot would kill him instantly, but he wanted the certainty of a torso shot.

Matt steadied his aim, the light dancing in tight circles. He slowly exhaled and then held his breath as his finger began to squeeze against the hair trigger.

He saw Ballantine's head drop quickly and then snap back up, looking directly down the beam of Matt's aiming light. Matt's shot kicked the weapon back into his shoulder. The brief flash of flame emitting from the muzzle momentarily blanked out his field of view, causing him to lose sight of Ballantine.

Once his goggles came back into focus, he could see a figure slumped over on the ground, slowly inching into the wood line. Matt had hit him but had unfortunately not killed him. He trained the light on the crawling body again, which was moving more quickly toward the trees.

Matt's second shot struck Ballantine in the leg just before he disappeared into the trees. Determining that he had little time to waste, Matt pulled himself up onto the dock and began moving quickly to the first cabin. He kept his carbine trained on the scrub area where his prey had disappeared while he sprinted to the side of the first cabin, gun up, elbow out, sighting along the infrared laser through the green kaleidoscope of his goggles, legs pumping, lungs working at max capacity, adrenaline cycling through his body like raging rivers.

Matt Garrett. Back in the game. Alone.

In search of his brother.

CHAPTER 31

Leaning against the wood frame, he caught his breath. Acting purely on instinct, he moved toward the back of the house, realizing this could expose him briefly to Ballantine.

Not knowing if anyone was guarding the cabin, Matt felt it would be best to try to enter from the top floor. He surveyed the deck, which had stairs leading up to the second floor balcony. Moving swiftly and quietly, he ascended the stairs and crouched low.

Reaching up with his free hand, Matt slid open the heavy glass door. He felt the warmth of the cabin brush against his face. He stayed low to avoid reflexive fire from anyone who might not welcome his entrance.

He was in. A weak light shone below the loft so that he could see on his level an unmade bed, a chair, and a television. There were a few clothes strewn about the dusty hardwood floors.

Matt crouched low in the corner behind the door and rested. He could hear his heart racing and thought it might actually explode. Crashing thoughts, extreme physical activity, and danger all combined to release adrenaline and lactic acid into his body, pushing his heart to its limit. As he rested, he could hear muted voices from the first floor. They became clear as he caught his breath.

"So where is it?" Matt heard a female voice ask.

"Where is what?"

The second voice was a man's. And it was a familiar one. Matt leaned his head closer to the crack in the door so that he could hear more clearly.

"The backpack. Ballantine's backpack. You stole it from him, perhaps as a war trophy?" It was the female voice again.

Ballantine. War trophy. These were all clues and indicators to something, yet they were pinging off his wall of denial, his massive defenses, like tennis balls off a tank.

"Why is Ballantine concerned about a stupid backpack?" the man said.

Matt's mind was reeling. The voice, the inflection, the tone were all so familiar. Images of Zachary's face began swirling through his mind, breaking his concentration.

"You didn't find the tape?" the woman asked.

"What tape?"

"Never mind. You know he told me he saw you when you were watching them in the prisoner of war interrogation room. The colonel came out and talked to you," she said.

"Yeah, who was that guy, anyway?"

"The colonel?"

"Yeah, him."

"Someone I think you should know very well, actually," she said.

"Really? I can't quite recall him."

Matt stood slowly, moving toward the door, and accidentally kicked a heavy brass door stop.

"Is that you, Jacques?" the woman called.

Matt quickly repositioned to the entertainment center, which sat next to the stairway leading up to the loft. From that position, he could ambush someone moving upstairs unaware.

"Jacques?"

There was silence, then the man's voice again.

"Might be Special Forces coming to rescue me. Then again, it might be the wind. One in the same, really."

Now it was clear. Though the male voice was speaking in a different room on a different floor of a house in which Matt had never been, it was unmistakably his brother's voice. He stared open-eyed at the sliding glass door through which he had just entered, trying to hold back a wave of emotions. Was it really Zachary, or was he just hearing what he wanted to hear?

A movement reflected in the glass door caught his eye and brought his mind circling quickly back to reality. He gripped his M4, waiting as he watched a woman's reflection ascend the final stair. She took two steps into the center of the room, clearly focused for the moment on the fact that the sliding glass door was ajar by about three feet.

Matt studied the woman in the dim light. She had sharp, stunning features. Her eyes were wide, cat-like ovals. She was a dark-skinned woman, perhaps African or from the Indies. She moved with the grace of a mountain lion, taking another step toward the door, then pausing.

"Jacques?"

Matt sprang forward from his hideout, catching the woman as she brandished a pistol. He tackled her before she could aim the pistol at him, but that didn't prevent her from pulling the trigger. The shot flew wide, into the center of the television screen, shattering glass all over the room.

Matt raised his weapon and smashed it into the skull of the woman. She went immediately limp in his arms, a slight gasp escaping from her mouth. He grabbed the pistol from her hand, stuffing it in his trousers as he quickly moved toward the stairway.

He scrambled down the stairs, trying to keep his body moving ahead of the myriad thoughts that threatened to crash down upon him like boulders blocking a mountain pass. *Keep going, Matt. Keep going.*

At the bottom of the wooden steps, he spun to his left, keeping the front door to his right. The downstairs was as bare as the upstairs. In the distant corner, across the dingy throw rug and dusty, gray wooden floorboards, Matt saw a darkened figure, huddled and bound in a wooden chair. A shadow cut across the figure's body, making it difficult to truly determine who was in the chair. But his instincts began to clatter as loudly as a fire truck speeding down the highway to an apartment-building blaze. His slow, careful walk developed into a gait. The desire to see who the man he prayed was his brother collided with the realization that he had a very small window of opportunity to get back to the drop zone and safety.

Approaching the bound man from behind, Matt grabbed the back of the chair and spun it around until he was staring into the wide eyes of his brother.

No question. It was Zach.

Matt pulled a small knife from his belt and cut through the ropes and plastic zip-ties, trying to stay ahead of those thoughts. Those emotions he had been bottling up for months could burst free at any moment.

For a brief moment, Zachary Garrett was speechless, looking into the focused eyes of his brother. But it was unmistakable. He recognized his younger brother's smattering of fading freckles and sea-green eyes.

"Yes, Zachary. It's me, Matt," he said, quickly removing the rope from Zachary's hands and ankles.

His brother stuttered a moment, then said, "I think I remember you."

Matt paused, understanding what Zachary was saying. "Come on, we need to move out. Here, I'm sure you remember how to use this," he said, handing him the woman's pistol.

Zachary looked at him with a thin smile and said, "Naturally." That was the signature Zachary Garrett smile and comment, which almost caused Matt to lose it. But the bullet from Ballantine's gun that came crashing through the rear window and smacked directly into Zachary's back got his attention focused again. His brother slumped forward into Matt's arms, dropping the pistol on the floor. Matt quickly returned fire through the window.

A rocket-propelled grenade blasted through the window, knocking Matt fifteen feet toward the front door. Through the smoke and haze, he could see his older brother lying on the floor, blood oozing from his back. And he was sliding.

Away.

Sliding backward, as if pulled, Zachary looked at Matt like a wounded deer being hauled away from his den by a hunter, eyes wide and doubting. Matt was trying to move, pushing his arms to grab a weapon; but nothing was working; nothing was happening.

He could hear more firing from outside the cottage toward the wood line.

"Zachary!"

"Matt," came Zachary's weakening voice. Matt watched as his brother slid through the enveloping smoke from the fire that was beginning to build. In an instant, Zachary's face had vanished, and all Matt could see was smoke.

Through the background noise of machine-gun fire, he heard the words, "The colonel . . . get the colonel." Straining against the concussion that the rocket-propelled grenade had caused, Matt finally regained motor skills, thinking he had wasted a huge amount of time. It may only have been a minute or two, but it was too much. As he raced forward into the smoke and fire, he realized Zachary was gone.

Standing in the burning cottage, he stared out of the shattered window toward the lake and woods. He could see a limping figure carrying a body disappearing into the woods. Matt quickly found his weapon, the metal hot to his touch. He raced and leapt through the open window and tumbled to the ground as a hail of bullets chipped away the deck directly above him.

He performed a combat roll into the open and brought his carbine up, but there were no targets. The firing had ceased. He slowly elevated and began moving toward a shrub line to the west of Ballantine's cottage.

More machine-gun fire shredded the hedge row directly above him, scattering branches and leaves over him as if he were in a blender. Again he rolled away from the concealment and found the tree line. He flipped down his night-vision goggles and could see the faint outline of two moving figures in the distance, about four hundred meters away.

A stupid quarter mile was between him and his brother. Another burst of energy shot through Matt as he began racing through the woods, leaping stumps like a running back through a defensive line.

After sprinting a considerable distance, he found himself galloping down a hill sufficiently steep to make him decide to stop and gain control. He scanned with his goggles a full three hundred and sixty degrees, picking up no movement.

Walking slowly forward, M4 in hand, he briefly flashed back to the Philippines, moments before he had been severely wounded. He remembered:

Jack Sturgeon and Johnny Barefoot had been laying down a suppressive base of fire against nearly a hundred Japanese soldiers who were charging their positions. It was a math problem. They had three weapons with about thirty rounds of ammunition per weapon. The enemy had a hundred weapons with probably significantly more ammunition per weapon. Even if they hit them all, there would still be about ten enemy survivors.

And that's about what happened, Matt recalled.

The remaining few had broken through when he was down to only a few rounds of ammunition. An enemy soldier had approached him from the rear, causing him to spin as the man's bayonet moved toward him. It had thrust into his stomach, and the soldier pulled the trigger, blowing a hole out his back. It was only later that he learned Zachary and his infantry company had arrived in the nick of time to ward off the remaining terrorists and get Matt onto a medical evacuation helicopter.

His memory was interrupted by the sound of a small engine. For a moment, he had the curious notion that he was listening to a lawnmower or even a model airplane.

Ballantine's Sherpa.

Matt sprinted in the direction of the airplane, tripping and stumbling down the hill until he was standing knee-deep in a creek. To his rear, the creek opened to the lake. To his front it widened into the rocky shore, Ballantine's landing strip. The crescent moon hung in the southern sky like a misplaced ornament above the opening in the tall fir trees.

The sound of the airplane grew in intensity. With his back to the lake, he saw the Sherpa bouncing along the small river rocks, lifting ever so slightly into the air, and then finally gaining altitude as it buzzed directly over his head.

Matt turned and watched the airplane fly across Lake Moncrief into the night. The airplane looked different, though. It seemed darker, and the wingspan looked like bat wings.

With a certainty he had not felt in a long time, he knew that his brother was on that airplane. With that knowledge, he cemented his conviction to find a way get him back.

Alive.

CHAPTER 32

FORT SHERMAN, PANAMA

Frank Lantini was kicked back in an old metal chair that had two legs digging into the plywood floor and two legs angled up in the air. His AK-47 rested on his thighs. He sat in the corner of the cinderblock hut watching enemies of the United States plan and debate the next moves of what they were calling Phase Two.

He had grown a full beard that grayed toward the tips of the uneven strands of hair and stood in contrast to the dark brown hair on his head, now longer than when he had been CIA director last year. He wore old olive-colored pants, a black T-shirt, and a tan fishing vest in which he carried ammo. He passed as a simple, mute guard.

Lantini caught Tae il Sung's eyes ogling his beautiful assistant, Sue Kim. Sung was the North Korean leader of the Central Committee and knew Lantini as "Ronnie Wood." He had an understanding with Sung. He provided information and access where possible, which at times was substantial, in addition to strategic guidance.

As Lantini watched Sung stand to address the group that included representatives of Russia, Colombia, Serbia, Angola, Cuba, China, Iraq, and North Korea, he reflected on his path to this particular spot.

He recalled watching Matt Garrett lying in the snow with his team watching over a small village in Pakistan. Then Garrett linked them into his sniper scope via a USB-port uplink, and they were all staring down the length of the scope, looking through the interrupted cross hairs at al Qaeda senior leadership.

Lantini knew that his personal involvement in the Rolling Stones conspiracy last year was witting, yet forced. His guilt over guiding in the JDAM to Garrett's position and denying the kill chain had racked him. Lantini viewed himself as a patriot, yet his career aspirations had left him no options, he believed.

So last year, his life in disarray, he had fled when he heard that Matt Garrett had returned alive from the Philippines. If anyone knew how to beat the system, it was the director of the CIA. He had the passports and credit cards and identity-altering materials in a go-bag. Last May as the *Shimpu* was diverted from Los Angeles harbor with its rogue nuclear weapon, he used that focus as a magician uses misdirection. Lantini secreted himself in his 40-foot Chris Craft Roamer and used the two 200-gallon fuel tanks and twin Volvo IPS 500 engines to power along the Intracoastal Waterway down the East Coast. From Florida, he popped into the Caribbean Sea, all the while changing his appearance.

And thinking.

Like Fox and Diamond had done to Stone, the real Ronnie Wood had done to him. Wood maintained an E*TRADE account in Lantini's name with his social security number, and his home address that showed 10,000 shares of AIG short trades in the first week of September 2001. The trades were covered in January of 2002. He suspected that the money generated by the faux account had either been piped into the Philippine deal last year, or pocketed by the man who had held the weapon to his head as he called in the kill-chain denial to Garrett. After all, government employees, particularly military officers, didn't make much in the way of salary, and the frame job would have been entirely believable, not to mention impossible for him to refute.

And then he was given three options: Accept the role as Ronnie Wood, endure the embarrassment and prison sentence from the short trades, or die. He chose the path of least resistance and had remained a skeptic through their deliberations. Did the other Rolling Stones know he was a coerced participant? He didn't know. What he did know was that the real Ronnie Wood was a heartless megalomaniac.

But he could do something about it now. Last summer as he cruised south, he passed to the north of the main island of Puerto Rico, skirted the east side in the channel formed by the island of Culebra, and then cruised to the east of Vieques Island, which at one point had been a Navy bombing range.

And was sparsely inhabited.

He had circled the twenty-mile-long island once and then settled on anchoring in Sun Bay, just off shore from the coastal town of Esperanza. Vieques had been his target all along, it was just a matter of where he would anchor. The south side gave him a quick escape route into the open waters of the Caribbean, relative shelter from most hurricanes, and, most importantly, open portal access to the radar station managed by the Joint Interagency Task Force for Counter Drug Operations.

The satellite dishes on his boat weren't simply piping in HBO and XM Radio; rather, he had taken the effort to have a private contractor for the CIA build a state-of-the-art communications suite into his bridge. From this platform, he had been able to conduct sufficient eavesdropping operations to piece together the communications traffic of the Central Committee, determine their plan, and infiltrate the dilapidated Fort Sherman prior to their arrival.

The pressures inside the beltway were enormous for those who cared about career advancement, legacy, and such. A Navy admiral, Lantini remembered, had shot himself when a reporter was about to break a story that he had worn a medal that he had allegedly not earned. Lantini knew he was not a saint, nor was he a martyr. He was a survivor, at all costs.

He had sold his soul to the man with the pistol to his head, and now he was hoping for a bit of redemption. Then he would disappear again, because the E*TRADE records were still out there, and too much conjecture had occurred regarding his role as Ronnie Wood.

And the last thing he wanted was Matt Garrett salivating at the mouth with an opportunity to slit his throat after what had happened to his brother.

He knew what Garrett was capable of doing.

No, he would get his revenge and then disappear. But first, once this meeting was concluded, he had some people he needed to talk to.

CHAPTER 33

FORT SHERMAN, PANAMA

And Lantini watched the plan develop.

As it was not lost on him, he was certain the irony was not lost on Tae Il Sung. They were sitting in a concrete-slab and cinderblock building with no air conditioning in the middle of Fort Sherman, a former military base in a country owned and operated by the United States for the better part of the last century.

Now North Korea's greatest ally, the People's Republic of China, had achieved near sole proprietorship. Once the United States had turned over the canal, China began snapping up land and facilities in Panama as if the country was holding a going-out-of-business sale.

Lantini watched Sung survey the assembled crowd.

Sung smiled inwardly at his own brilliance in being able to gather such a diverse group of statesmen and criminals. He had never found Saddam Hussein a likeable person, but the former Iraqi dictator had been Sung's peer in the field of terror and Machiavellian statesmanship. And, Tae Il Sung did possess a certain affinity for Hussein's former regime emissary,

Hosni Aswan. How Aswan had avoided being included in the infamous deck of cards, he would never figure out. Perhaps it was the same way that Jacques Ballantine had avoided scrutiny. Regardless, Sung found Aswan to be direct and business-like. Sung preferred it that way. There were enough games to play just maintaining power within one's own country, so it was nice to be able to relax among fellow members of oppressive regimes.

An axis of evil? No, this was simply a coalition of nations and trans-national actors sensing a window of opportunity to give back to the United States what it had, in their view, been dishing out for the past two decades. A group of wolves that had been wandering through the geopolitical hinter-lands who had now found ample prey.

And like wolves or Serengeti dogs they stayed close, sniffing, appraising, thinking, and developed a plan of attack that was proceeding nicely.

Aswan looked up at him from across the table and shrugged, as if to say, *When do we begin?*

The last man had finally arrived, each accommodating another's tar-diness, given the circuitous they were required to take to arrive. But finally, Sung decided to speak. Those that required them had interpreters mumbling quietly in their ears.

"I think it best," Sung said, giving the interpreters time to echo his words, "that we all introduce ourselves, since many of us have never met. But first let me say that we are all here today to conduct the final coor-dination and come to ultimate agreement on a work that has been in progress for many years. Our objectives are mutually supporting, and indeed, our forces will be operating together. It is my understanding that each of you has the power to speak on behalf of your ruler, and that your word is binding."

He surveyed the room of nearly twenty men. He was impressed that they all had arrived and seemed dedicated to the alliance. Yet he had expected more of each man. Having left the country of North Korea only a few times himself, he had a grander image of these men than how they seemed in person. Nonetheless, they were present and ready to commit.

The room had a low ceiling and large, square, open-air windows. Plain-clothes guards were posted outside, leaving the diplomats to do their business. The men sat in folding metal chairs around a large, unfinished plywood table. Sung sat at the head of the table. He was a short man with black hair combed precisely. He had not changed his dark suit in the twenty-four-hour trip from Pyongyang to Panama City. His private jet had landed at Honolulu International Airport and then in Mexico City for refueling before making the final stop on the Atlantic side of the island at Fort Sherman.

"Let us begin with a quick update, which will be provided by my assistant, Sue Kim," Sung said.

Sue Kim stood from the table and addressed the assembled crowd. She wore a black silk business dress, which complemented her midnight-black hair. Her face was an oval-shaped, tanned mask punctuated by two onyx eyes and full, sensuous lips. While Sung had initially been simply attracted to her looks, he had become profoundly impressed with her balance and sharp mind.

"Our friends in Iraq have fully engaged almost seven U.S. Army divisions and, more importantly, a significant portion of their organic logistics. Likewise with Afghanistan, an entire army division is entrenched there. Bosnia and Kosovo are still consuming their forces, also. What's left in the United States is reorganizing. We believe we can get a foothold before these units can react."

She motioned at the map with a metal pointer as she listed each military unit. She rattled off which units were deployed in combat and which were refitting at their home stations in North Carolina, Kentucky, and Texas.

"We assess that it will be difficult, but not impossible, for these units to respond to an internal threat."

She paused, then said with emphasis, "We intend to apply an old North Vietnamese principle against the United States. For a time in the early portion of the war, the Americans were able to defeat the North Vietnamese armies by using superior technology such as jets, bombs, and artillery. The North Vietnamese overcame that advantage by applying tactics. The tactics were those of closing with the Americans in battle so that the bombs could not be called in without killing Americans as well. This technique proved to be very effective, and, thus, our entire campaign plan is based upon this principle. By introducing military force into the United States, the Americans will not only have to make decisions about the use of force within their own country, but also about the limits of destruction they are willing to accept."

The cinderblock hut was still. Sung could hear a pack of monkeys in the distance screaming and cackling, as if to amplify Kim's point. The Central Committee had been clever and resourceful up to this point. The news of the destruction of the Metroliner, the mall, and the sports arena was especially welcomed. It meant that the timeline was in effect and gave Sung confidence that many of the variables they had been questioning, such as internal American support, were indeed accounted for.

"Thanks to our Iraqi friends, in particular General Ballantine, we have begun Phase Two operations. The Texas state capitol building will be destroyed next, and we expect to have the same effect as the other attacks. There is one American that does seem suspicious of who might be behind the attacks. His name is Mr. Matt Garrett. He has been to the Canadian headquarters site with what we believe to be a small CIA paramilitary team. Ballantine had to evacuate last night, so operations from Canada were compromised."

Sung turned to Kim and asked, "What do we plan to do about this Garrett?"

"Not to worry. Ballantine has indicated that he will take care of that issue. He is in full communication and remains capable."

Sung nodded. "Continue."

"The American government has chosen to continue limited airline operations. This is better than we could have hoped and should provide us the necessary cover for the remainder of our operations.

"In closing, I should say that we will remain here at Fort Sherman. Lodging has been prepared for everyone. We have security. No one is authorized to have communications outside of our command center. Our guards have orders to kill anyone who is caught trying to depart." Kim sat down with a perfunctory cross of her legs.

Sung stood and began speaking. "Let me first say that it is a genuine pleasure to be teamed with so many admirable allies. I would like for us all to say our names, what our countries' objectives are, and where we are in stages of preparation. As for North Korea, we have the necessary personnel and supplies to conduct our part of the operation in this hemisphere. Inside of the United States, we have infiltrated our special operations personnel. Thanks to Mr. Cartagena's supply routes, we have all of the necessary equipment to conduct operations in the Northwest. Are there any questions?"

The men were silent, many still listening to their own interpreters and processing the information. Sung let what he considered sufficient time to pass and then opened his hand to Aswan, indicating for him to speak next.

"Good morning, gentlemen. My name is Hosni Aswan. I am here on behalf of all members of Saddam Hussein's former regime."

Hosni Aswan was a young Iraqi who had fought in the Persian Gulf War in Ballantine's Tawalkana Division. His loyalties ran deep not only to Ballantine, but also to Hussein. It was no mistake that Hussein had called upon the services of both Ballantine and Aswan. Aswan was a short man with olive skin, typical of his people, and a slashing scar across his left arm. The wound was the result of artillery shrapnel. He wore a short-sleeve, white madras shirt and black pants.

"Our grievance with the United States is well-publicized and much understood amongst this group, I am sure. Our objectives are to retaliate for the unlawful invasion and occupation of our country and exact revenge for the war crimes committed against our people. We have Ballantine, who is conducting Phase Two operations out of Canada. He has begun these operations with the attacks already described. As you just heard, he is in the process of moving to an alternate command post and will continue his operations, God willing. Our area of operations is the northeast region of the United States, including Boston and New York."

The light murmur of interpreters continued for a few seconds, and then the room fell silent. Sung noticed that most of the men were nodding their heads in agreement. A twinge of satisfaction and excitement flickered inside of him. He motioned to the next man.

"My name is Stephan Radovic. I represent the great leader of the Serbian people, Slobodon Milosevic." Sung watched Radovic speak. He had a large face, indicative of the man's impressive stature. His nose was that of a boxer's, contorted and bent in two places so that it was nearly parallel with the rest of his face. Sung concluded that Radovic would easily kill anyone, man, woman, or child, who obstructed his path. The Serb wore a white T-shirt beneath an ugly maroon sport coat that shrouded him like a prize-fighter's robe. He spoke in heavily accented but passable English.

"Our goal is to inflict great suffering upon the people of the United States, who sat by while their government was killing innocent civilians in Serbia," Radovic said. "We wish also to bring about an end to American arrogance and dominance in the affairs of other countries. We also have forces ready to execute Phase Two operations. Meanwhile, we intend to attack the current NATO Kosovo forces to engage them in battle.

"On behalf of President Milosevic, I wish to express two things. First is his desire to ensure that post-conflict matters and spoils, should there be any, are divided according to participation in this operation. And, second, he wishes for me to thank all of you in advance for your united effort in ending the tyranny of the oppressors."

"Thank you, Mr. Radovic," Sung responded. "First, before we leave this room today, we will all sign a document that addresses the very issue that you raise, the one of post-conflict matters. As we review this issue, some of us may not desire to possess some of the post-conflict spoils, as warfare is often a matter of chance. It may not bring what we wish."

A few of the men shrugged, understanding Sung's point that they may not win the fight, and therefore might suffer the consequences of an angry America.

"However, when the remainder of Phase Two operations begin, we will go forth with the Joint Document of Retribution, which we will all sign here today. This document accords to each country, in relation to the size of its participation in this operation, both the responsibility for the consequences of our forthcoming actions and the burden-sharing demands in the event of victory."

Sung paused and then continued. "As we all know, the G-8 is meeting next week in Helsinki, and by the end of the week, we should be able to force a UN Security Council vote on our Joint Document of Retribution."

"This is good," Radovic said.

Sung nodded at Radovic, an understanding passing between the two men, then opened his hand to a slight gentleman sitting across from Radovic.

"My name is Jorge Cartagena. Three nights ago, I crossed the border from Colombia into Panama paddling a canoe along the Rio Balsas through the Darien region into Yaviza. On my way, I visited my native friends in the mountains of Panama just to the east of here," he said pointing out the window. Cartagena spoke in rapid tones with just a whiff of Hispanic inflection.

"I then traveled by jeep through the impoverished hinterlands of this country along the Pan American Highway until I reached our location here this morning. While not an official of the Colombian government, I represent a great many Latinos who believe the Americans have prospered for too long by standing on the backs of our people. They say that I belong to a so-called drug cartel; however, we only traffic what the Americans desire. They are a society of consumers, and we provide a product.

"It is in our interest to be involved in this operation. We seek independence from the Colombian government and the recognition as an entity entitled to international money for infrastructure development. Our children need food and schools. The native Panamanian children need food and schools. We need help to lift ourselves up from this impoverishment that has been imposed upon us. We mostly are providing intelligence to the operation and the network to travel and communicate. In fact, Aswan's operative is using many of our lines of communication and operation to orchestrate his project."

Sung had deliberated carefully before allowing Cartagena and his Colombian band of drug pirates into the consortium. He knew the Americans had dedicated a significant amount of resources to spotting and tracking drugs and drug suppliers coming out of Colombia. But Cartagena's infrastructure in the United States was invaluable. All of the routes of ingress, as well as the internal supply routes, had proven vital. The Americans may have picked up on some of the movement, but their intelligence indicated that there was no reason to believe it was not simply drug trafficking.

"Thank you, Mr. Cartagena. We are delighted to hear from Mr. Lin, representing the great nation of China."

Bruce Lin was a tall, thin man who had been living in the United States for the past fifteen years. The one advantage that people like Lin, Sung, and Aswan had over their adversaries in the United States was their circular view of life, as compared to the extraordinarily linear and shallow view possessed by most Americans. Confucian and Islamic ideologies overlapped sufficiently both in theory and in practice to allow these strangers to find some common purpose.

Sung remembered meeting Lin some thirty years earlier. Sung had been a part of the North Korean military team that had brutally attacked and killed the American soldiers pruning a tree in the demilitarized zone in the summer of 1976. The Americans were clearing fields of fire as Sung had poured from the back of the military transport truck with twenty of his comrades, all wielding picks and axes. They had caught the Americans completely by surprise.

Sung had never forgotten the lesson of the attack. The Americans carelessly believed there was no threat and had accordingly placed no security to provide early warning.

After the massacre, Sung and his fellow attackers were rewarded in a ceremony in Pyongyang. Lin was an assistant to the Chinese ambassador to North Korea and had approached Sung after the ceremony. Lin had wanted to know about the attack, yearning for information and wanting to participate in the afterglow of victory against the Americans. Lin, wearing a gray silk Armani suit, spoke in smooth, well-practiced English.

"Thank you, Comrade Sung, for this opportunity. The Chinese government brings to the effort the most advanced technology, capable of doing great damage to our many targets. It has been our honor to extract from our adversaries the many secrets that have contributed to the development of these most dangerous weapons. All of our assets are in place, and we await only the message to execute. We have all of the necessary equipment and personnel in position to achieve the effects we desire in the southwestern and eastern portions of the United States. And, of course, I hope you find our accommodations here in Fort Sherman suitable."

Lin paused before continuing and then looked at Sung. "The *Fong Hou* is ready as well," Lin said.

"Yes, the *Fong Hou*," Sung whispered as he looked skyward. "The *Fong Hou* carries the most precious cargo and is crucial to our overall success. She is on schedule?"

"On schedule," Lin confirmed.

"Good. Now I turn the floor to our friend from Angola," Sung said.

"Hello, my name is Jay P. Kahtouma. I am a member of the National Union for Total Independence of Angola. While our oppressors have been primarily the Portuguese, the imperial policies of the United States have kept our people in a continual state of poverty. We have many points of contact in the southeastern United States that will execute the appropriate actions when the word is given."

"Thank you, Jay P. We appreciate your contributions to our effort," Sung said.

He then turned to Igor Krachev, a hard-line Russian who had spent many years in Afghanistan fighting that most horrible war. Many of the Russian commanders, such as Krachev, became worn down by the conflict. Toward the latter half of the war, they struck deals with the local Afghans to trade protection of their troops for the assurance that their occupying forces would not attack villages. He had spent most of his career in the Russian paratroops and had migrated away from the democratic reforms when he saw black market corruption take control of his country. Krachev held out a diminishing flicker of hope that this current course of action would help restore Russia to its rightful, preeminent place in world geopolitics.

"Commander Krachev," said Sung.

"Thank you, Comrade Sung. We have necessarily kept a low profile, but are ready to execute our portion of the plan. Everything is in place and we will perform with precision." Krachev sat back in his chair, his large shoulders slumping over.

Eduardo Sanchez stood as the final speaker. The Cuban nationalist was a tall, light-skinned man sporting a pencil mustache just above his thin upper lip.

"Everyone understands Cuba's role in this operation," Sanchez said. "We have been preparing for this for many years. Our country has been suffering the economic and political sanctions of the United States for nearly fifty years now. They have driven my countrymen into economic despair and we stand ready to unite with all of our brothers and sisters across the globe to destroy them. On order, we will begin operations to initiate the remainder of Phase Two operations and support Ballantine's actions as well."

Sung stood and spread his arms wide. "I thank you all for your commentary and for your support in this operation. I intend to speak with General Ballantine soon." He paused for effect and translation. "Our thoughts and best wishes go out to all of our men and women who are about to begin the remainder of Phase Two operations. We will await the code word from Ballantine, indicating that conditions are set, before launching our attacks."

Everyone nodded. They had been over this portion of the plan before. They all had agreed that Ballantine's final attack must be successful before they would sacrifice their soldiers. Destruction of the United States' command and control architecture would facilitate their attacks greatly.

"Together we conquer the enemy!" Sung shouted, holding his fists in the air.

"Together!" they responded, each in their own language, raising their arms and pumping their fists.

Sung lightly touched Sue Kim's arm as he guided her outside into the muggy Panamanian early morning darkness. The monkeys howled in the background, as if to signal the joy that was to come.

Sung, Aswan, Sanchez, Cartagena, Radovic, Kahtouma, and Lin had all waited a long time to strike utter fear into the heart of the United States. In retrospect, they viewed the events of September 11 as unfulfilling. Fear had not reached any level of resonance to which their citizens were accustomed. The American people had simply moved ahead with their lives while their volunteer military fought on their behalf. "Go shopping," their president had said.

With Sue Kim lightly grasping his arm, Sung proudly walked to his cabin.

As the group dispersed one man remained in the corner, sitting with his chair propped up against the wall, an AK-47 across his lap like a sleeping pet.

CHAPTER 34

MIDDLEBURG, VIRGINIA

"Meredith, get in here now!" Hellerman shouted down the hall of the operations center.

She rounded the corner, holding her cell phone and needing to hear the words over and over again.

"I saw Zachary, Meredith. He was alive when I saw him!" Matt's voice was hoarse from his lack of sleep, but his words were laced with adrenaline.

"What happened, Matt? Is he okay?" she asked, stopping before entering Hellerman's office.

"He's been shot, and Ballantine took him."

"What! Are you okay?"

"I don't know. Who cares? Are you guys trying to track down Ballantine? He's got Zachary, and I want in on anything going after him. He can't be too far. A Sherpa can only fly so far on a tank of gas. Do you guys have the airports and air-fueling sites covered?"

"Matt, slow down. We're working it. I know how important this is. Trust me."

"Okay. I'm at Walter Reed now. They flew me here early this morning. The Pave Low came in with a rescue team and got me, Hobart, Van Dreeves, and Rampert. All three are wounded. I got lucky. You seen

Peyton? She was hurt, too."

"She briefed Hellerman this morning, but she's resting now. She's a bit shook up. The Pave Low landed her back at Andrews. They took her to Walter Reed, too. Treated and released. She was grazed by a bullet somewhere along the way."

Matt's mind was racing ahead, his words following suit. "Okay, tell her I'm okay and that I need to talk to her as soon as possible."

Meredith hesitated, feeling a twinge of jealousy. "I'll do that." She figured it was no time to let petty issues get in the way. "I'm glad you're okay, Matt. And I'm glad you saw Zachary. We'll find him."

"Meredith?"

"Yes, Matt?"

Matt hesitated, considering his words, then chose a conservative statement.

"Thanks. I might have never gotten on that plane if it hadn't been for you."

Meredith's rushed response was the antithesis of Matt's. Her self-imposed emotional blockade since breaking off their engagement suddenly dissolved. "Matt, I love you."

He paused and whispered into the phone, "I love you too, Meredith. Very much."

"Meredith, get in here now!" Hellerman shouted.

Meredith dropped her head, shaking it, wondering why she couldn't grab thirty seconds of intimacy with this man Matt Garrett.

"Matt, I've got to go. Please be safe."

"Bye."

She pushed through the doors into Hellerman's office.

"We've got serious—" Hellerman said.

"Did you hear that Zachary Garrett—"

"—problems."

"—is alive?" Meredith finished. She instantly quieted when she noticed the dour look on Hellerman's face.

"Ballantine is on the loose, and we can't seem to stop these attacks. Thousands are dead, and the number is only going to grow. The press is all over our ass, and the president has a press conference in two hours. Our allies are concerned and are taking precautions within their own countries. Yet there have been no attacks anywhere but here, as far as I've heard. We have a video teleconference with the National Security Council in fifteen minutes. Now what ideas do you have?"

Meredith had rarely, if ever, seen the vice president so flustered. Even during the Philippines situation last year, he was the one who had kept his cool and steered the neophyte president through the crisis.

"Mr. Vice President, I think we need to find Ballantine's airplane. We're already mobilizing the National Guard across the country and calling up the Reserves. What few active-duty forces we've got stateside are preparing to move out and protect key sites, such as nuclear reactors and power plants. We probably need to review Posse Comitatus as well."

"Right. Have you and Palmer discussed that?"

"Yes, sir," Meredith said. "He's talking to the president about it right now. The president is not keen on allowing the military to be involved in police activity. You know that once you lift those restrictions, we really have a police state."

"Let's crank up this VTC."

The communications operator in the Middleburg alternate command post pressed some buttons, and a large plasma television screen lit up. Immediately, Meredith could pick out several of the National Security Council members seated at the cherry meeting table in the basement of the White House. She saw Air Force General Shepanski; the current chairman of the Joint Chiefs of Staff; Dave Palmer, the national security adviser; FBI Director Peter Dortsch, Secretary of State Catherine Arends; and Secretary of Defense Stone.

Meredith cringed at Stone's presence, but knew that she had parlayed her knowledge of his involvement with the Rolling Stones last year into a high-level position in the White House National Security Council. Besides, Stone's voice had been muted post-Philippines. She moved on, eying the assorted aides situated in a few chairs around the periphery of the small room, noticing all of them had a tense, almost wild-eyed, look about them.

"The president will be down in a couple of minutes," Palmer said.

"We're up over here. What's the agenda?" Hellerman asked.

"We've got you loud and clear, Mr. Vice President." Palmer continued,

"General Shepanski has developed a few positions . . ."

Meredith watched on the VTC as the president entered the Situation Room.

"Gentlemen," President Davis said.

"Mr. President," Palmer said after they had all stood and begun to sit down again. "Sir, we've got the vice president and his team up on VTC from the alternate command post."

The president looked strained. "What do we have?"

Hellerman immediately took control. "I would like for General Shepanski to give you a quick status report on what we know about the enemy activity, friendly losses, and then a couple of courses of action."

"Fine. Shark, go ahead," Davis said.

Shepanski had replaced Admiral Sewell as the chairman of the Joints Chiefs last summer. Sewell had stepped down in protest after the president had not fired the secretary of defense in the wake of the Philippine action last year. Meredith found it instructive that Davis had turned to Shepanski and not Stone.

Shark was Shepanski's call sign when he flew F-15s. The general was typical of modern-age Air Force generals. He had been an F-15 fighter pilot most of his career and had logged a hundred combat hours during the Gulf War and Kosovo.

"There have been more attacks. The Texas Capitol has been destroyed, and three more shopping malls have been attacked. Luckily, Atlanta police, with the help of the Georgia National Guard, uncovered a series of bombs set to destroy Lennox Square Mall and Phipps Plaza simultaneously. Two bombs exploded in Phipps Plaza, the less occupied of the two, and claimed at least five hundred lives and still counting. Burlington Mall near Boston and Seattle Mall were destroyed completely by a complex series of command-detonated bombs, killing thousands in each location. We've had three apartment buildings destroyed, the first in Seattle and two in Chicago.

"The operation to capture or kill Jacques Ballantine was not a complete failure, but neither was it a success. Our operative got close but was captured. We still do not have control of our operative, and Ballantine has escaped despite the best efforts of some very brave men."

Meredith felt a twinge of pride knowing that Matt was one of those men.

General Shepanski continued, "We are still getting spot reports on that operation, but we have secured the command post and accompanying equipment. Our intelligence analysts are going through everything as well as talking to two captured Ballantine operatives. Ballantine himself escaped, we know, in his plane. We've got radar teams scanning everywhere, but it is an impossibly small aircraft that is quite difficult to pick up on radar, so we're not optimistic in that regard. Also discovered, thanks to Matt Garrett and Peyton O'Hara, was a Predator UAV terminal. There is no indication of where the actual UAVs are. As you recall, at least two of these ground control stations went missing a few years ago, we believe to the Chinese."

"Shark, do we know how much contact Boudreaux had with Ballantine?" the president asked.

"No, we do not. But it was apparent that he was in captivity for several hours at a minimum. Boudreaux was last seen alive and is believed to still be in Ballantine's captivity."

Meredith watched the men talk, again thinking it odd that they would be discussing a single commando. She logged that part of the conversation away and continued to listen.

"As I was saying, we have found reference to eighteen missing Predator Unmanned Aerial Vehicles. There was a chart in the command center indicating employment in some capacity of multiple UAVs across the nation. The question remains, What would be their purpose? UAVs are primarily reconnaissance platforms. However, this particular technology allows for the transportation of a payload as well. Each UAV has a range of approximately 500 miles from the control station. What we know is that there is one terminal still out there that can control all the missing drones."

"What kinds of payload?" the president asked.

"Lots of things, sir, but most worrisome is the fact that chemical or biological weapons could be deployed from these vehicles. We know they were used in the Charlotte and Minneapolis attacks. I just received a report from the special operations team searching Moncrief that they have found a cave or old mine. It appears that chemical and biological weapons were being stored and manufactured there."

"It has to be the missing weapons of mass destruction. Hussein must have smuggled them out before we attacked," Meredith said.

"Strike fear into the heart of America by hitting the malls, apartment buildings, state capitols, and sports arenas, and then send UAVs with weapons of mass destruction in to high population centers to strike the knockout blow. Is that what we're dealing with?" Hellerman asked.

"That's certainly a scenario, sir, which we seem to be two-thirds of the way through."

"But who is behind it?" Hellerman asked.

"Well, obviously, Ballantine has an elaborate network of operatives across the country. We don't know if this is al Qaeda or not. We do know that Ballantine is Iraqi. He has to have been planning this for several years, maybe even initially in Iraq. His fishing guide service has been operational for two years, so he has had ample time to hop in and out of the country with his airplane, distributing supplies for the operation."

"Do you think that Ballantine is acting alone or with the support of the exiled Iraqi government? What is the goal of this operation, General? And how the hell did we miss this guy?" the president asked.

"In my view, this is an act of revenge. Ballantine's brother was killed in 1991 during the first Gulf War by an American officer. But also, I think this was originally planned by Hussein. So it seems the weapons of mass destruction were in Canada, not Iraq, which affirms our policy of going after Hussein. But now we find ourselves with over half our military committed in remote lands."

"What were the conditions of the killing of Ballantine's brother?" Catherine Arends asked.

Meredith watched the secretary of state on the plasma screen, wondering where she could be going with such a question. Whatever direction, it was not a good one. The secretary of state was infamous for continuous efforts to "put the military in its place," as she was once overheard saying.

"We're not sure, but it was at close range," Shepanski said.

"Was it an execution? Was it something illegal, where if we found the person and held him up for a war crime, it might help us convince Ballantine to back off?"

Meredith thought she might vomit. "Surely we must presume that the soldier acted properly and was executing his mission as assigned," Meredith said, a hint of disgust in her voice.

Arends, the only other woman in the meeting, did not enjoy being challenged. The fact that Meredith was a young, attractive woman did not help. The portly woman turned slowly in the direction of the camera, her hawkish nose leading the way, and leveled her stone-cold eyes at the screen.

"Secretary Arends, we must give the benefit of the doubt to our service men and women," Hellerman said.

"Tell that to the victims of My Lai, Vietnam; No Gun Ri, Korea; Vitina, Kosovo; and now in Iraq," she shot back. "If our defense was an adequate deterrence, we would not find ourselves in our current position, now would we?"

"Perhaps, Madame Secretary, if our diplomacy were adequate, we might find ourselves in a different position as well," Shepanski replied.

"General, don't ever speak to me that way again," she snapped, feeling somewhat outnumbered. Her Northeastern roots were always near the surface, and Meredith could see she wasn't about to lose the chip on her shoulder any time soon.

"As my favorite judge used to say," Hellerman interrupted, "order in the court, or I'll have all your asses thrown out."

"Charming," Arends replied.

"At least I can see you haven't lost that tremendous sense of humor, Catherine," Hellerman said dryly.

"Let's get back to the briefing, General," the president said impatiently.

"As I was saying, we are faced with the difficult but not impossible task of tracking down Ballantine."

"Excuse me," Meredith said, raising her hand and giving the VTC satellite delay a moment to register her words. "It appears to me, sir, that the operation is continuing even though Ballantine may be out of contact. Is it possible that the codes were delivered to the operatives, and they are now on autopilot?"

"It's possible, Meredith, but we still think it's very important to find the mastermind to the plot, primarily because we're not sure where it ends," Shepanski said.

"Well, a Sherpa has only so much range . . ."

"Right. We've covered every refuel stop within a five-hundred-mile radius of Moncrief Lake. But that doesn't address the thousands of open fields, lakes, rivers, highways, etcetera in which he could land and transition to ground transportation."

"We have to assume that Ballantine had several contingency plans for his escape. Why not shut down the airlines? It should make it easier to spot a small, slow-flying airplane," Meredith said.

"We asked for that to happen right away," Shepanski said.

"That's about a $10 billion hit to the economy, and half of those companies are already about to go bankrupt," the president said. "This war is as much about preserving our economy as it is anything else. That's our way of life we're talking about."

The room was silent. It was clear to Meredith that most believed the industry should be shut down for a few days, at least until they could get a better perspective on the depth and breadth of the attacks.

"Let's give it another day. So far there have been no attacks against the airlines," the president said.

"I really think we should do it now," Palmer said.

"Let's let this play out for another twenty-four hours, Dave." Hellerman was quick to support the president. "The airlines have already selectively shut down about 50 percent of their operations."

"That's my point. What will it hurt to shut down the other 50 percent?"

"Most are already bankrupt," Hellerman said. "We don't want to destroy the industry. It's mostly smaller airlines that are operating, anyway. We've beefed up security with the National Guard at airports."

"In my speech, I'll announce that we've gone to limited operations but continue to fly some commercial routes, particularly cargo," the president said.

"I think that's a good plan," Hellerman chimed in. "It will show we're not deterred." Then he turned to the row behind him. "What is the general reaction of the people? What are the polls saying?" Hellerman asked. "How do the American people feel about this?"

Meredith watched as a youngish male aide stood from the outer ring of seats and cleared his throat.

"Sir, right now polling data shows that 82 percent of Americans feel threatened and insecure. Seventy-eight percent have said that they seriously question the government's ability to protect them, and 64 percent admit they will avoid public places for the near term."

"We've got to keep the airline industry going, though. We've got to push through this," Arends said.

"Shit, more people than that voted in the last American Idol contest. The real issue is whether the country is pulling together versus being divisive and blameful," Hellerman interrupted.

"Our polls show that most Americans blame the government, and that is fairly evenly divided between blaming the administration, the military, and the intelligence community."

"Is there any sense of outrage?" Hellerman asked. "Is there any sense of coming together to defend our nation against this rogue threat?"

"Sir, quite the contrary. The divisions within the country seem accentuated. Blacks blame whites; whites blame liberals in the government; liberals blame the military." The young man briefly lifted his eyes toward Secretary Arends' image on the plasma screen. "One thing that is certain is that there is a fair amount of finger-pointing going on."

"So really, what we need," Hellerman started, "is a call for unity, a call for rising up as one nation against this rogue threat. What we need now is a clarion call to come together, to fight off this spiritual stagnation, to unify against this external threat to our security. Sir, I recommend strongly that you step forward during your speech, declare war on this threat, and begin to lead from the front."

"Against what threat, though? All we've got is Ballantine that we can put our finger on," Shepanski said.

Hellerman stood and leaned on the glossy table, hands pressing firmly into the wood, as he peered into the video camera. "There's more to it than that, for sure. The threat is the coordinated efforts against our freedom-loving people. Our national security strategy lists as its primary vital interest the defense of American lives and our way of life. What could be a more direct threat to our way of life than the brutal murder of thousands of Americans on our own soil by a terrorist network? What else do these people need!"

Meredith watched as Hellerman's faced turned red, veins popping in his neck.

"What else?" he said, his voice trailing off as he sat back down.

"Shark, I agree. I'll take the lead on this and try to bring the country together. We need to work Congress, get bipartisan support going forward here," the president said.

"Mr. President, all you really need to do is step forward, and they will follow. They will have no choice. But if we don't do it soon, I'm afraid these divisions will harden during this crisis and will prevent us from going forward. And, frankly, I think we might be looking at bringing back the draft," Hellerman said.

"You're kidding, right?" Arends fumed.

Hellerman gave Arends a disgusted look, then turned to Shepanski. "Shark, I need you to follow up on these unmanned aerial vehicles. They have me concerned. Eighteen, maybe more, Predators out there somewhere with at least one control station and chemical weapons could do significant damage."

"Right, we're working that now. We understand that as our number one priority right now."

"Meredith, anything you want to add?" Dave Palmer said.

"It's an interesting look at what kind of country we've become," Meredith said, backing up the vice president's reasoning. "It's pretty sad that we have such a short memory as a nation."

"I think we're better than that, Meredith. Maybe the message after Nine-eleven shouldn't have been 'It's okay, go shopping,' but by the same token, if we change the whole of our existence because of these attacks, we lose." Davis paused, and when no one else countered, he continued. "Our message, then, is three-fold. First, we've got crisis response teams at all of the attack sites treating wounded and accounting for casualties. Second, we've got an interagency task force led by the Department of Defense analyzing the threats and going after both the head of the operation and the distributed cells. To back that up, we've attacked and seized the terrorist headquarters in Canada and believe it's only a matter of time before we capture the elusive Mr. Ballantine. And third, I call on all Americans to come together in defense against this vile enemy."

Meredith watched Hellerman's eyes narrow. He was focused, perhaps thinking about his Rebuild America plan. She understood everything Hellerman had been talking to her about over the last few months. He had schooled her on his views of the downward spiral on which he believed the country to be sliding. Over 50 percent of the voting-age population did not care enough to vote, he had pointed out. Hellerman told her that, when he was serving in the first Persian Gulf War as an intelligence officer processing enemy prisoners of war, he had taken the time to reread Walt Rostow's book *The Economic Stages of Growth*. He explained Rostow's idea of the final stage beyond "High Mass Consumption" as being that of secular spiritual stagnation. In other words, nobody cares about anything but themselves. The apathy then leads to the divergence of rich and poor, and coupled with the professional, volunteer military, to a nation out of touch with its moorings. The Rebuild America Program was borne out of Hellerman's drive to unify the country.

"Of course we'll need to add some beef to it," Davis said, turning over his shoulder toward his speechwriter. "Until then, let's get after this thing. I want an update ten minutes prior to my press conference." The plasma screen went blank.

Meredith scooped up her notebook and darted back to her office. She could feel Hellerman hot on her heels. She spun around to see him closing the door behind her.

"See what I've been saying? Could I have been any more right?" Hellerman said.

"No, Trip, there's nothing right about all these people dying."

He leaned over and kissed her on the lips. The familiar feeling sent electrical shocks along her spine, but she recoiled.

"Get away! What are you doing?" She pushed him back.

"I know. I couldn't help myself," he said, straightening his tie. "We have to think about what's happening now and what's going to happen over the next few days."

"What are you talking about?" she said, crossing her arms. "I mean, people are dying. Our project was supposed to bring the country back together through programs and policy."

"That is what our program is going to do. I have no idea why all these attacks are happening, but the opportunity is unbelievable. This was made for what we're trying to do. We've got to be strong, Meredith. If we play this right, we've really got a chance to reunify this country. This is what Rostow was talking about."

"There's no opportunity in tragedy, Trip." An edge of anger tinged Meredith's voice.

"On the contrary. Never waste a crisis. People died in the Revolution, they died in the Civil War, and they died in the two world wars. People die every day. I would rather seize this *tragedy* as an opportunity than be a cold, timid soul that is too scared to act. James Madison said, 'The tree of liberty must be on occasion nourished with the blood of the free.' This was unavoidable." The vice president looked at her and then departed, his eyes wild with adrenaline.

Meredith walked to her window, suddenly fearful of what she believed the future would hold. The uncertainty was eating away at her. *Where is Matt when I need him?*

Probably the same place she was when he needed her.

CHAPTER 35

VERMONT-NEW HAMPSHIRE BORDER

"Hello," Ronnie Wood said into the small Kyocera phone powered by a Qualcomm CDMA chip and protected by U.S. encryption technology.

"This is Ballantine," the voice said, distant but clear.

Wood sat up in his bed. "Good. Do you have an update?"

Ballantine's voice was distorted over the secure phone. "I have been compromised, but I escaped. All other operations are set. I have one enemy captive. I am moving to my alternate command post and will wait for transmission of the signal."

"Tell me more about this compromise. We have seen the news," Wood said.

"They sent a special operations commando after me and my crew. I captured their agent and questioned him. A second team arrived and tried to rescue him. I am wounded but am healing and will be fine for tomorrow's operation."

Ballantine looked over his shoulder at the bound and gagged Zachary Garrett. He had hog-tied Garrett and stuffed him in the cargo compartment behind the pilot and copilot seats.

"What kind of condition is your captive in?" Wood asked.

"He will live. I shot him in the upper back. Flesh wound only. Bleeding has stopped." Ballantine spoke in deliberately concise sentences to minimize airtime on the phone, despite the secure connection. He knew the technology existed to intercept the traffic and decipher the coded signals. He had also just lied. The pool of blood gathering on the floor of the airplane provided an indication of Zachary Garrett's dire condition.

"What about your television appearance? Do you have the facilities for that, or do we need to execute the backup plan?" Wood asked.

"My facilities were captured. The backup plan is a go," Ballantine said.

"Are you certain you can execute?"

Ballantine seethed for just a second at his contact, letting the fuse burn, and then affirmed, "Absolutely."

"Your picture is on every television station in the world. The news media are providing the public with your aliases and your Muslim name. Without your secure facility, how do you intend to make an international statement without the risk of getting compromised?"

"I have a plan," he repeated, this time with less patience.

"Don't screw it up."

"I won't."

Ballantine pushed the END button on the satellite phone, removed the battery and stuffed both components in his pocket. He then banked the airplane toward a small set of lights to his south. He was glad that he had at least accomplished that task. He had considered not calling the contact, but he was concerned that the news programs might cause delay or even postponement, which he could not afford. While most of the Phase Two operations seem to have been completed with a success rate of about 80 percent, these next missions provided the most hope for achieving victory to his personal satisfaction.

Ballantine replayed the scene in his mind: the two commandos in his sights, moving along the woods toward the cabins. His first shot struck the lead man in the chest; the second shot narrowly missed the wingman. He fired successive shots, but the team to his rear was being overrun, diverting his attention long enough for him to lose sight of the other operative. Then, very quickly it seemed there was enemy fire coming from the small set of trees next to the pier. Hit once, he labored to hide in the woods until he could recover.

After a short while, he had moved toward the cabin. He saw a man untying Zachary Garrett and fired immediately, hitting Garrett in the back. He followed the small arms shots with a rocket-propelled grenade to stun whoever was in the house. There was only time to take the one captive, as he was receiving fire.

The trip back to the Sherpa had been a struggle. He had wrestled with the stealth gear, affixing his wing shapers into place. He had ensured the Chinese had used the same stealth technology on his Sherpa that they had used on the Predators. He had quickly fastened two triangles of fiberglass to his wings that angled toward the tail. The United States had achieved radar avoidance through aircraft composition, speed of flight, and shape. His Sherpa now looked like a poor man's stealth aircraft. Knowing that the United States would have an all-points bulletin on his plane, he intended to do everything he could to evade detection. It was critical to mission success.

Once in the aircraft with Garrett bound, he flipped the remote switch to ignite the previously rigged demolitions to destroy his operations center.

He was exhausted.

His adrenaline had carried him this far. He was flying to a small apple farm on the Vermont-New Hampshire border. He cut a low path through the cool spring morning, his mind trapped somewhere between controlling the airplane, seeking revenge, and adapting his plan to execute the remainder of the overall scheme. He was flying through the valleys no more than a hundred feet above ground level and under 70 mph to avoid radar detection.

This could be quite interesting, he thought. He was experiencing a moment of surging happiness offset by the loss of his command center, and perhaps Virginia as well. Nonetheless, the plan was coming together with an added bonus of the massive leverage of having Zachary Garrett in his possession. The American saying "what goes around comes around" popped into his mind. Garrett had killed Ballantine's brother while he watched, and now Ballantine could stage a replay for the brothers Garrett.

He slipped on his night-vision goggles as he carved through a valley, granite cliffs to his starboard side. While it took much longer than he desired, it was better to arrive later than not at all. He spotted the two infrared lights he had asked his wife, Regina, to leave on for him. They were sufficient to give him a good approach at a slow speed with the Sherpa.

Thinking about asking his wife to turn on the infrared lights made him absently wonder about Virginia. *Was she dead or alive? Had they captured her, and were they now extracting information from her? Would she crack?* He didn't believe so, but he wasn't sure.

He noticed through his goggles the rows of apple trees on either side of the strip. At the northern end was a house with a single light on in the upstairs bedroom.

The Sherpa's wheels found the grass, slipping a bit to the right, but the slide was easily controlled with a mild maneuver in that direction, like skidding on ice.

Ballantine pulled the aircraft into a small barn situated between the orchard and the house. As the engine sputtered to a stop, he dragged Garrett's body out of the airplane and carried him fireman's style.

Before he reached the steps, Regina came bounding out of the house, across the covered porch, down the wooden steps, and froze.

"What is this?" she said, shocked.

"Someone who tried to kill me. He's been shot, and we need to fix him."

"Why . . . what? You're hurt, too," she said, stepping back. "What's been going on?" she asked.

"I got into some bad stuff with some guys who weren't fishermen." Ballantine laid Garrett on the porch, and she hugged him on the neck.

"What do you mean? Not fishermen?" she said, pulling away and looking at Zachary Garrett.

"They were trying to run drugs on my airplane, smuggle them in from Canada. We saw them, and they suspected we knew too much."

"And who's this, the man who shot you? One of the drug runners?"

"Yes."

"Why would you bring him here?"

"Because he's our insurance policy. These drug guys know where we live, and if we keep him alive, I think they'll leave us alone."

"What do we do with him?" Regina asked.

"Regina, quit asking so many questions. You will operate on him and then me. Tomorrow I will fly him to his people. That's the deal, as long as they promise to leave me alone."

"I'm a veterinarian, Jacques, not a doctor," she said.

"You know what to do."

"Why not just call a doctor?"

His faced flinched once as the anger flashed inside him. *Don't release now*, he told himself. *It's not the time or the place.* "Just do as I say."

"Islam, right? Well Islam will grant us this one exception to call a doctor to work on at least you," she protested.

"Not this time, not ever," he said. "Now let's get him in the house, and you can fix him and then pull this bullet out of my shoulder."

"You must be horrified," she gasped.

"You have no idea," he replied under his breath.

Ballantine put on his best face. It had been a week since he had seen her. He routinely returned on the weekends to keep his cover alive and to keep her satisfied. While Regina was an attractive woman, she was also simply a means to an end. Fearing raising suspicions by purchasing land himself, he knew he needed a surrogate. It took him all of two months in Burlington to find a suitable mate who would marry him for the money he generously, but discreetly, spent on her. He had scanned the desperate legions of women on Internet dating sites. Regina had run an ad titled, "Submissive vet seeks dominant man."

After a few e-mails he had learned she was a veterinarian who had reenrolled at the University of Vermont. She was a second-year master's student earning a meaningless degree in Islamic studies. She told him she was trying to better understand the root causes of 9/11. She had a small veterinary business—mostly cats, dogs, and cattle—that helped pay for her studies. She lived by herself in a small two-story house on five acres thirty miles from the university.

Their Internet conversations quickly gave way to a cup of coffee and a fast, storybook romance.

"I missed you, honey. I wanted us to have some time together."

"I missed you too, Regina," Ballantine said, squeezing her back, wincing at the pain in his rib and thigh.

Regina was about five and a half feet tall and a bit heavier than she wanted to be, but not by much. She had a cute face framed by a bob cut of straight black hair that fell to her shoulders. She was wearing a UVM sweatshirt and blue denim pants.

Walking up the steps with a slight limp, he noticed a folded newspaper on the end table next to the rocking chair. He slowly opened the front fold, scanning the headlines and pictures quickly.

"I haven't had time to read it, yet. Since you cut the satellite off two weeks ago, I haven't had any news. Thought it'd be nice to know what was going on in the world when you got back."

"Did you go into town?" he asked.

"Yes," she said, sheepishly.

"And?"

"I was only there a few minutes. I took the old station wagon, bought some groceries, and picked up the newspaper on the way out."

He grimaced from the pain throbbing along his left clavicle. She naturally responded as if he was angry with her, as he had been a few other times. He had tamed her, in every sense of the word, to be an obedient wife. She had adopted Islam as her religion, or at least his version of the religion, believing she was to minimize her contact with the outer world and that no one else could be trusted. He had taken her to Canada to be married.

Chasteen had presided over the "ceremony," dressed in ceremonial Muslim garb. They had stayed two nights at the cabin and then flown back to Vermont, where she purchased, in her maiden name, the apple farm from an elderly gentleman who was moving to a nursing home. Of course, the marriage was not legitimate, but she believed it was, and that was all that mattered.

"Please, Jacques, understand," she whispered, fear shrouding her words. She took a step back and tripped on the door jamb leading from the porch to the front door.

Ballantine looked at her leaning back against the storm door. Another time he might have smashed her through the glass panel simply for violating his order to never go into town without him. But his primary concern was with whether to kill her or not. *Had she seen anything?* He had purposefully scrambled the satellite code and removed the fuse from the television so that she could not watch any cable or network television.

"Regina, what did I tell you about going into town?"

"To never do it alone. . . . I swear to Allah I will not let it happen again."

She was nearly hysterical.

"And what did you see? Any bad people, any television, any radio?" His eyes were black coals burning through her.

"Nothing. Nothing at all. I just needed some groceries and wanted to be able to catch up with you." Her hands were pressed firmly into the glass, which was fogging around her sweating fingertips.

He grimaced with pain as he raised his right hand and slapped her across the face with the back of his wrist. "Don't ever do that again. Get inside," he ordered.

Regina's head had snapped back, tears spraying against the glass. "Thank you, thank you. I'll never do it again, I promise," she cried, opening the door, trembling. She *was* thankful he had not gone mad.

They dragged the limp, bleeding body of Zachary Garrett into the house. She operated on him, removing a bullet from his left scapula. She stitched him up and gave him a shot of morphine to ease the pain.

"How are his vital signs?" Ballantine asked, still in pain himself.

"He's weak but hanging in there," she said. Her voice was calm and focused. She knew what she was doing. She was busy picking up used medical supplies and gauze.

Ballantine secured Garrett tightly to the bed and then handcuffed both his hands and feet.

"He will try to escape if we don't do this," he said, looking at Regina.

She didn't respond but poked an intravenous fluid needle in Zachary Garrett's arm to attempt to hydrate him.

"What are his chances?" Ballantine asked.

She grabbed a new scalpel and held it in front of him as she pushed Ballantine onto a single bed with a white sheet.

"Fifty-fifty. He's lost a lot of blood. I can tell this happened several hours ago. At some point, I would like to know what really happened, Jacques." The gleaming scalpel in her hand perhaps had given her some confidence to speak her mind to the man that she believed to be her husband.

She administered some anesthesia and began to carve away at Ballantine. The process took nearly an hour, but she finally pried the bullet from his left clavicle. He had nearly passed out from the pain, but the morphine sustained him. He lay back on the white sheets, now stained with blood, his arm laid atop his chest in a desert-sand-colored sling. His head hit the pillow, and his mind quickly spiraled toward sleep, trusting completely that Regina would clean up the mess and obediently go about her business.

As he drifted away, his last conscious thoughts were that the plan would be okay. He had survived and would live to fight another day. Images of Zachary Garrett blowing Henri's face to pieces briefly replayed in his mind, causing a weak adrenaline surge that was suppressed by the sheer exhaustion of the last forty-eight hours.

He was reassured by the simplicity of his new plan.

He was going to kill Matt Garrett and let Zachary Garrett watch.

CHAPTER 36

The distant ring of the phone clawed at the back of his mind like a dredge raking across the sand. It was too soon to wake up, his mind was telling him. He attempted to move in one direction, then another, causing pain to rocket unimpeded through his body as if through fiber optic lines.

He glanced at the alarm clock, not believing that he had slept for ten hours, his body making a very convincing case otherwise. His left arm and shoulder were completely immobilized, causing him to lose balance as he sat up.

He picked up the cell phone and clumsily pushed the encryption button.

"Yes?"

"We have a problem."

"We? Thought you went solo, Wood? Didn't we just talk?" Ballantine coughed, still not fully alert.

"I know you're drugged, but that wasn't me you talked to. Anyway, someone is alive who we both thought was dead. His presence complicates matters extensively. I want you to . . ."—the voice searched for a word—" . . . handle the problem rather quickly."

"I know about the problem. I will handle it while we execute the rest of the mission," Ballantine responded, more clearly this time.

He was confused though, certain that only hours ago he had communicated with Ronnie Wood, his contact. There was one phone number he called. The encryption technology masked the voice sufficiently to give him pause. Was he talking to the same person? He had received this call, though. He checked his cell phone display window: Private Number. Ballantine scratched his beard, his mind still swooning from the surgery and Regina's drugs.

"Operations may be in jeopardy if we don't act now. This individual may know, or worse yet, remember something from his past that very quickly could get in our way."

Ballantine decided to press ahead despite his curiosity. "Why didn't you know he was alive? You have access to everything."

"I have less access than you might imagine, especially from my new location. Even so, the special operations files are sometimes so secretive one section doesn't know what the other is doing. Never in my wildest dreams did I envision this possibility," said the man who called himself Ronnie Wood.

"It is your job to think of such things. It is my job to execute," Ballantine said. What he was really thinking was that Wood did not sound too believable.

Ballantine understood that his acquaintance on the phone already knew that he had been shot. He figured the phone call was as much to gauge his status as it was to give him the information about Zachary Garrett.

"We need to fix the problem in the next forty-eight hours," Wood said, trying to focus Ballantine.

"Right. Are we still on track for the full plan?"

"Full scale. Is there a problem with that?"

"I need to check the equipment," Ballantine said. "I haven't had time since I got back."

"Check the equipment, and get on with it. But you know your base camp is compromised, right?"

"I know," Ballantine said, expressing some frustration. "Let me ask, have operations so far had the effects you desired?"

"It's like Orson Welles all over again, only this time the spacemen are real. If anyone ever doubted U.S. intentions to attack your country, they surely will be convinced soon that preemptive war was the best option."

"This is a dangerous game you are playing, Mr. Wood. My intentions are to do as much damage to your country as possible," Ballantine said, wheezing at the pain.

"Have at it," Wood said. "The more aggressive, the more convincing."

"Let me ask. Were there any survivors from the camp?"

Wood hesitated and said, "Yes, one. Too bad. Quite the looker."

Ballantine thought about Virginia and all that she had meant to him. He knew what had to be done, and he surprised himself when he felt a flutter in his chest. A symptom of sorrow? He had left those senses for dead a long time ago. Poor Virginia. He was stuck here with moronic Regina, and he wished there was something he could do, some way he could save Virginia. He understood, though, that the voice on the other end of the secure wireless connection would help Virginia meet an untimely death. She knew too much. Way too much.

"Are you there?" Wood asked.

"Yes, I am here," Ballantine said.

"Good. For a moment I thought you were going soft on me."

Ballantine lay back on his bed and rode the wave of sadness. "Never. I will take care of your problem."

"Good. Now, do you have the operative? Rumor has it that you might."

Ballantine hesitated. "Not at this time."

"That's a problem."

"I know."

"A big problem if he goes public."

"I know. If he remembers." Ballantine had seen the confusion on Garrett's face. He seemed . . . different. "In which case *you* will have a problem."

"Then we're both screwed," Wood said.

"I understand. I'm leaving tonight," Ballantine said.

"You know you missed him," Wood said.

"Missed who?"

"Matt Garrett. I put him there in your base camp, and he's still alive. I delivered as you requested."

"I know . . . I know. But he will be dead soon."

Ballantine shut off his phone and closed his eyes. Yes, he would keep the fact of his possession of Zachary Garrett from his contact for now, primarily because he now had questions about the real identity of Ronnie Wood.

Or were there two, playing off each other?

He pressed his one free hand against the mattress and then paused. He heard voices.

Standing slowly, he remembered he had tucked his pistol between the mattress and box springs. Pain stymied him on his first attempt to remove the weapon from its ready position. Gritting his teeth, he used his opposite arm to secure the pistol. He moved quietly to his door, which was cracked slightly. Leaning forward, he listened intently. It was a woman's voice, but not Regina's.

He peered around the corner and saw an elderly woman holding a small poodle in one arm. What got Ballantine's attention, though, was the newspaper she held in her opposite hand. He watched as Regina looked to where the woman was pointing at the newspaper. Then he saw Regina hold her hand to her mouth and begin to shudder.

Without hesitation, he walked from his bedroom door into the foyer of the home. "Good afternoon, ladies."

Ballantine was practically catatonic as he pulled the trigger of his pistol exactly twice. Both women dropped to the floor with bullet wounds to the head, the poodle jumping nervously from its owner's arms.

Where cell phones and e-mail ruled the day, Ballantine had already risked too much by trusting Regina. Her limited contact with her customers had been her undoing, and he had known it would only be a matter of time before he killed her.

Just to stop the yapping, Ballantine shot the poodle as well.

He walked back into his bedroom and kicked Zachary Garrett in the ribs. "Get up. We're moving."

Ballantine led the shackled Garrett to the barn, where they would wait for darkness.

CHAPTER 37

FORT SHERMAN, PANAMA

Frank Lantini stared at his satellite phone as he leaned back against a palm tree on the perimeter of Fort Sherman, Panama. Hundreds of thoughts cycling through his mind, he stuffed the phone in his shirt pocket and looked over the minor waves that lapped almost noiselessly against the sand. He could hear just a slight curl of the 12-inch breaker that rolled with a zipping sound into the shore. The bay beyond Fort Sherman was glassy smooth, the small breakers a function of the tide shifting. His Chris Craft was not far.

Lantini was a slight man who had served as an intelligence officer in the U.S. Air Force for many years, transferred to the Defense Intelligence Agency as a brigadier general and, then upon retirement, was selected by President Davis as the director of the Central Intelligence Agency. He had "seen combat," as he referred to it, during the first Persian Gulf War in 1991 as a lieutenant colonel. With the plethora of prisoners of war—called detainees in politically correct circles—Lantini was deployed from his soft assignment as a State Department Fellow in Foggy Bottom to Saudi Arabia to assist with the massive interrogation efforts. Not only did the Department of Defense and CIA have a need to question as many prisoners as possible, but they also needed to develop a database of those who had been captured. The general feeling was that the Middle East was going to be the center of attention for quite some time and that cataloguing the enemy prisoners of war might bear fruit as the region continued to unfurl from the rigidity of the Cold War.

Last year he had discreetly allied himself with Taiku Taikishi, a Japanese businessman, Bart Rathburn, a former assistant secretary of defense, and Bob Stone, the current secretary of defense. They had used the moniker Rolling Stones to provide cover to their conversations as they diverted forces and intelligence assets from the Iraq buildup to the Philippines in an erstwhile attempt to derail the single-minded drive toward Iraq. To a man, the Rolling Stones believed the country had veered away too quickly from Afghanistan and, more importantly, Islamic Extremism. Instead of focusing on crushing bin Laden and his thugs, the military found itself straddling the Middle East, without clear focus in either locale or on either enemy.

Lantini watched the harmless waves lap near his boots as he pulled on a Sol.

"Shitty beer," he said to himself.

His mind spun back again to the video feed piped through the Predator drone that fateful December 2001 day. This time with more clarity. He could see Matt Garrett's team well camouflaged in their white parkas as they nestled in the snow overlooking a nondescript Pakistani village nearly 15 kilometers from the Afghanistan border. Through Matt's fiber optic snipercam he could pipe his sight picture up to the drone, which could relay back to whoever could access the downlink. The ultimate 8,000-mile screwdriver.

Lantini, as CIA Director, was the primary recipient of the feed.

And what he had seen was a short Egyptian man with a prayer callous on his forehead just above his spectacles directing a team of AK-47-toting Arabs carrying a wounded six-and-a-half-foot Arab with a gray beard.

He had invited Stone and Rathburn to join him by secure videoteleconference as they all watched the snipercam. Lantini knew that Colonel Jack Rampert from special operations and several in the White House Situation Room were also watching the feed. "Kill TV," they had called it. The ultimate in reality television.

Garrett's improper incursion into Pakistan had put the Rolling Stones on the horns of a dilemma. Do they let him kill al Qaeda senior leadership, whom Garrett clearly had in his sights? Or do they allow the transnational henchmen to go free, preserving their strategic flexibility?

"If he kills him," Stone had said, "we can't do jack shit about stopping the buildup for Iraq. It's going to be tough as it is."

"Takishi has an idea," Rathburn had said. Meanwhile, Matt Garrett's voice could be heard, a mere whisper through a small microphone 9,000 miles away, "Request kill chain."

And so they had, in harried fashion, as Garrett laid his finger on the trigger of his sniper rifle, discussed the pros and cons of letting the operative take the shot.

Ultimately, they had determined that it was best to let al Qaeda live to fight another day so that they, the Rolling Stones, would stand a chance, however slight, of keeping the nation focused on Islamic extremism as opposed to whatever the *causus belli* in Iraq was purported to be.

"Should've taken the shot," Lantini lamented, sitting in Fort Sherman, Panama, tantamount to a traitor. "Should've taken the damn shot!" he added and hurled the beer bottle into the yawning bay.

He grabbed his AK-47 and walked toward the cinderblock hut where Sung had recently held his meeting.

What to do? Lantini mused. *What to do?*

Interrupting his reverie was a vibration on his satellite phone.

"Wood," he said.

"Wood," came the response.

"Yes?"

"You tracking?"

"I am."

"Good. More to follow."

"Roger, out."

Lantini closed his phone and turned back toward the bay. The moon was a bit higher, casting a yellow carpet onto the tranquil water. Lantini thought about Secretary of Defense Bob Stone, Dave Palmer, the national security advisor, Trip Hellerman, the vice president, and Colonel Jack Rampert, who had performed many sensitive missions for him as the commander of Joint Special Operations Command. All good men, he thought, trying to do the right thing.

Now, in hiding, he had to carry out his mission vicariously through cut outs and third parties. *Patriot or traitor?* That was the most bothersome question. Put it up to a vote, he thought, and it would be 51%-49% one way or the other. Regardless, he had to proceed.

He played along with the idea of a second Ronnie Wood who was in contact with Ballantine. For the time being, he was letting the situation develop. It was Frank Lantini who was walking the edge of the razor at the moment. While he conceptually agreed with his alter-ego counterpart, were they like two serial killers, twinning in their drive to satiate utopian desires?

The Philippine action had been all about keeping focused on trans-national Islamic extremism. The present course of action offered a gambit of a different flavor. He was inside the Central Committee, perhaps not a fully trusted member, but close. Could he pull off his plan?

Hero or goat?

He sensed a presence hiding in the dark shadow of the cinderblock command center. He tightened his finger around the trigger of the unfamiliar weapon. Hell, if it wasn't an F-15, it was unfamiliar to him. Still, he had, like a kid, gone to an open field on the Pacific side of the isthmus and "popped caps," as he called it. While not the most accurate rifleman to ever use an AK-47, Lantini had learned the functionality of the weapon and was confident in his ability to use it as necessary.

"Mister Wood?" Her voice was a whisper, no louder than the lapping waves he had just left behind.

Lantini saw Sue Kim step from the shadows of the cinderblock building, her black hair framing her alluring face. He saw the crinkle of her eyes and her thick lips form a smile.

"Sue Kim," Lantini said responding to her use of the Stones' moniker.

"This way," she said and then vanished.

Lantini followed her along a minor trail that led south through a tight section of jungle. At its end the trail gave way to a small opening framed by two large banyan trees. Lantini could see a large hammock strung between the nearly touching branches of the two trees. Her destination.

"The guards will not see us here if we are quick," she said, fumbling with his belt buckle.

Looking beyond her bowing head, Lantini scanned the horizon and said, "But I am one of the guards."

His pants around his ankles now, she was pushing him onto the hammock, ready to slake her desires. She lowered herself onto him, steadying them in the shifting netting by grasping with her hands either side of the hammock above Lantini's head.

"You are much more than guard, and you know it," Sue Kim gasped as her rhythm increased.

"And you are much more than mild-mannered assistant to Sung," Lantini said, joining her motion.

The two lovers remained silent as they intently focused on their personal pleasures, a rare, delicious moment amongst this double-layered job he was doing.

First, he was a most wanted man in the United States.

Second, he was still a patriot. He knew how to get his country back on the right path.

Sue Kim gasped, as quietly as possible, as a frisson of ecstasy shuddered through her. Lantini was not too far behind and they collapsed together into the netting, breathing hard as they had first begun doing in Seoul, Republic of Korea.

"Never forget," Sue Kim said. "I am the reason you are here." She paused enough to lift her head from his slick neck. "And that you are safe."

Lantini lay back in the hammock, their sweat binding them together, and looked at the stars through the thin canopy of trees.

"And never forget, Sue Kim, without my contacts, none of these people would be here."

CHAPTER 38

GARRETT FARM, STANARDSVILLE, VIRGINIA

Matt stood silently by the upstairs foyer window that provided him a panoramic view of what he and Zachary, as kids, had named the Razorback, a north-south running spine of the Blue Ridge Mountains. The morning drive from Washington, D.C., had been less hassle than he had anticipated. He was thrilled to have spent less than twenty-four hours at Walter Reed Army Medical Center.

"Hey stranger." His sister Karen gave him a firm hug. "It's all kind of hard to believe. With Zachary's death and your injuries last year, this is just kind of mind blowing. Something inside me is having a hard time believing it, as much as I desperately want to be happy about this."

"It's still settling over me, too, Karen. Meredith contacted me two days ago and told me she thought Zachary might still be alive. Luckily, things were moving so fast I didn't have much time to think about it."

"The things you told me last night on the phone. I'm so proud of you, Matt. I know you'll get him back," she said, hugging him tightly.

"I have a lot to make up for," Matt whispered into Karen's hair.

"Maybe in your mind, but I always knew you did your best. And you'll do it again. You'll get him. We'll get him. It will be good to have both of you back," she said, crying into his shirt.

He knew that his sister truly did mean *both* of them. He had been gone and might as well have been buried in the ground next to Zachary's grave. In the last eight months, he had been home exactly once and had spoken on the phone with his family less than five times. He had slipped deeper into his darkness when Meredith started her new position at the White House and began drifting away from him.

"I hope you will give yourself a break now," she said.

"Well, I can't rest until we've got Zachary back. Plus, I think there is something bigger going on here. No way Ballantine could do all of this on his own."

The nation was under attack in the most unconventional way, but out here in the foothills of the Blue Ridge Mountains, it all seemed so far away to Matt. And so unrealistic, as if the television transmitted a series of fictional episodes.

"Why don't we go get some coffee," Karen recommended.

He was hit with a blast of nostalgia as they sat down at the same pine table at which the entire family had eaten for the past thirty years. He saw the notches he had made with his knife to mark the boundaries for the late-night paper football games he and Zachary had played.

Karen put on a pot of coffee, then turned toward Matt. "What makes you think there's something bigger going on? The president came on TV and said he thought things were going to be under control soon. On the news they said there were no attacks in the last twenty-four hours. Maybe that's a good sign."

"I haven't had a whole lot of time to piece it together, Karen, but look at the range of this campaign. It's too big, too well-planned, too well-executed, to be just one guy pulling all of this together."

"What else could there be?"

"I've got a few things rattling around in the back of my head. I mean, listen to this: Meredith called me when I was in Vermont."

"You mean when you were with this new girl, Peyton?"

"How did you know about that?" Matt asked.

"I have my ways," she said.

"Meredith called you, didn't she? She's the only one who knew about Peyton."

"So tell me about her," Karen said.

"There's nothing to tell. We were on assignment together. That's it."

"Where is she now?"

"She's in D.C."

"Really?" Karen fought back the smirk growing on her lips as she looked through the kitchen window at a blue SUV moving slowly along the gravel drive that cut between the house and the barn.

Matt followed her gaze. "What's that all about?"

"At least she's prompt," Karen said looking at her watch.

"Who's prompt? What are you talking about?" Matt asked.

The footsteps on the front porch provided the final clue that Peyton was actually here and not in Washington, D.C. He walked to the door, opening it as Peyton's hand was about to knock. He smiled at the awkward pose in which he had captured her, small fist stretched outward, as if shaking it in rage.

"What are you doing here?" he asked.

"That's a hell of a welcome for an Irish lass who's traveled so far."

"Right. Sorry. Please come in."

"Thank you."

He watched Peyton slide through the doorway, cat-like, and step into the foyer. She was wearing a tight pink angora sweater and light blue denim jeans. Her hair fell loosely on her shoulders, providing a backdrop to simple diamond earrings that seemed, oddly, to fit the ensemble. *Country elegant*, he thought.

"You look nice," he said without thinking.

"Well that's more like it." Peyton smiled, leaning up to give him a quick peck on the cheek.

Where did that come from? he wondered.

"Glad you're okay," she whispered.

"Back at you. Ducati in the shop?"

"Weatherman predicted rain." She smiled.

"Hi, Peyton. I'm Karen."

"Hey, Karen," Peyton said, giving Matt's sister a quick hug. "Great directions, by the way. Drove here like I've lived here all my life."

They walked into the den and sat on the sofa.

"You did great the other night. We all have hope that we're going to find Zachary soon and that he's going to be okay," Peyton said, looking at Matt.

"I hope so," Karen said, standing. "Listen, can I get you anything? Water, coffee, Coke?"

"Whiskey?" Matt said.

"Actually, it's been a tough week, and a Bailey's and coffee would be nice. Help me unwind from the drive."

"Coming right up," Karen said.

Matt's dutiful sister went about the business of playing hostess, a task she had honed over the past year since their mother's death. Karen delivered the coffee, then excused herself.

"I'll let you two talk. Matt, I'm going into town. Do either of you need anything?"

"No, thanks, sis. See you when you get back."

Karen pulled a set of keys from a hook on the hall stand and the screen door slapped the wood frame of the house as she crunched across the gravel.

"Nice sister you have there," Peyton said.

"Thanks. How's your arm healing?"

Peyton looked down at her left shoulder. "No biggie."

"Your sister okay?"

"She's fine. Thanks. Had decided to take the Saturday train, thank God. She's still at my place."

"So, to what do I owe the pleasure?" Matt asked. "Or is this truly a social visit?"

"Mostly social."

"Figures. Who sent you?" he asked.

"I sent myself but told Hellerman. When he found out I was coming, he wanted an 'official' report on you and for me to tell you that we are going to find Zachary very quickly," she said.

She used her hands to form quotation marks when she said "official"—a move he normally disliked, but one that somehow made her appear sexy. It might have been the sweater.

"I see. He doesn't expect me to be back for a while, does he?"

"No one knows what he's looking for right now. I think we're all waiting to see if Ballantine has anything else up his sleeve. The media's obviously all over this thing, but it has been quiet for the past twenty-four hours. So it's either the calm before the storm or Ballantine's done."

"I don't think he's done," Matt said.

"Why don't we take a walk? You can show me around this farm of yours."

"Sure thing."

They walked onto the porch and down the wooden steps. To their left, two hundred yards away, was a red barn, and to their right was an open field where cattle were grazing. The sky was pale blue, etching a beautiful line along the soft ridges of the mountains to the west. Matt grabbed Peyton's hand and led her around a rough spot in the gravel drive as they walked toward the barn.

"You okay, really?" she asked, slipping her arm through his.

"Not really. I had him in my hands, Peyton," he said, lifting his free hand to emphasize the point. "In my arms. I had him."

"What was it like in there? Did you see or hear anything that would give you a clue as to what happened or where Zachary is now?"

"Nothing that I can think of. It's all running together. Just lots of gunfire, lots of adrenaline, and a black woman."

"A black woman," she said, surprised. "Where was this?"

"In the cottage. She must have been guarding Zachary while Ballantine went out to fight."

"In the cottage?"

"Roger. Why do you find that so interesting?" Matt asked.

"No reason. Did she say anything?"

"Nothing important."

They continued walking past the horse stable on the left, angling toward a small creek on the right. The land dropped precipitously behind the stable toward the South River. The trees that hugged the river were still leafless, a few just beginning to bud. An infrequent evergreen spotted the forest as it gave way to the open hills. Matt was putting on a good face, but inside his mind he was wrestling with the possibility that he had lost his brother again. Unlike the Philippines, this time he was right there and had been unable to protect him. Naturally, his happiness at seeing Zachary alive was offset by the fact that he had seen him shot and then taken away.

"Wait a minute," Matt said, stopping.

"What?"

"I did overhear something about a backpack and a tape."

"Go on."

"I'm not sure what she said exactly, but the woman asked Zachary if he had the backpack and had found the tape." Matt was talking in measured cadence, staring at the barn. "Then she said something about a colonel."

"A colonel? You mean a military colonel?"

"Yes, like a colonel in the Army. You know, the rank directly before general."

"I know what a colonel is," Peyton said.

"What about the backpack and the tape? What's that all about?" Matt spoke more to himself than to her. Then he looked at her with an obvious flash in his mind. He remembered something.

"What?" she said.

"Zachary, back in the Persian Gulf War, the first one, had captured Ballantine. Remember, I told you this. General Ballantine, the same Ballantine who was in Canada," he said rapidly, the words rushing into one another. "He mentioned something about a war trophy. In all the madness of Desert Storm, he never turned it in and rushed back to the front lines. As they were redeploying he just stuffed it in his duffel bag. So he just kept it. He just kept the backpack."

Peyton had a terrified look on her face as she processed the information.

"So where is this bag?" she asked.

"The Army packed all of Zachary's household goods and shipped them back from Hawaii when he was killed . . . when they *thought* he was killed. We put it all in the barn."

They looked at the barn and began moving quickly in that direction.

Inside the barn, Matt climbed a wooden ladder. He remembered watching Karen and Blake stack all of Zachary's personal effects in the loft.

Peyton was directly behind him as he started sifting through the boxes.

"Start over there. Look through that stack," he said, directing her to the back corner.

After fifteen minutes of ripping open boxes, he found a dusty old green backpack in the bottom of a box containing other military equipment.

"Got it!" he said.

Peyton moved toward Matt where he was holding up a grimy, oil-stained backpack with barely noticeable Arabic writing on the side.

"Well, open it," she said impatiently.

Matt slowly unzipped the bag, opening the mouth of the zipper, and whiffed the musty aroma of old, unkempt things. He pawed lightly through its contents, extracting a small copy of the Koran and held it up to the light.

"This is a Koran. It has got to be Ballantine's backpack."

He continued to dig and found a small, single-bladed knife in a leather sheath. It had an Arabic inscription on the blade. Further on, he found a pair of socks and a brown undershirt.

"Do you find anything scary about going through Ballantine's bags, like he might actually be looking for this thing and be pissed knowing that we're going through his stuff?" Peyton asked.

"I think that's a possibility . . . that he might be pissed and that he might be looking for this, if indeed it does hold something relevant."

"Why would he take something so important into battle?" she wondered aloud. The warming spring sun caused some expansion in the wooden slats of the barn's roof, which emitted an audible squeak. Matt looked up, remembering the incident in Sheldon Springs and then returned to the grimy backpack.

"Maybe he thought there was no one else he could trust to watch it."

"Or maybe it had value, like currency, and he thought it could help him after the war," she said.

Matt looked at her. "If he was captured."

"It's a possibility."

His hand found a small, tin lock box secured by a tiny padlock.

"Okay, this has got to be it." Matt held the lock box up to her.

"Be careful," she said, taking a step back.

"What do you mean?"

"I've seen this kind of thing before with the IRA. It could be booby-trapped."

He held the small box in both hands, studying the padlock.

"Hand me that hammer," he said, pointing across the loft at a sawhorse where they had been doing some minor repairs.

"No, don't do it. The more I think about it, the more I'm convinced we should turn this over to docex," she protested. Docex was the acronym for the document and media exploitation teams that interpreted capture tomes, most meaningless, and computers, which held infinitely more value.

This was a small tape that could point to a conspiracy 12 years ago and possibly to one today. Further, Matt thought, he did not know who he could trust, including the alluring woman standing directly before him in her form-fitting sweater, flattering jeans, and wafting Givenchy. *Just like Meredith*, he thought.

"Don't be ridiculous," Matt argued, as he moved toward the sawhorse. He laid the box down and, grabbing the hammer, lifted it high above his head. Then he brought it down hard on the lock, sending it spinning across the floor next to Peyton's feet.

"If this blows up, I'll kill you," she said.

"Now there's a point worth debating." He gave her a thin smile and flipped the lid off the lock box. Matt stared inside the container, getting a view not only of its contents, but of the world of Jacques Ballantine.

There was a small framed picture of a man and woman—Ballantine's parents, Matt guessed—and two boys standing near the Eiffel Tower in Paris. They were all smiles and, Matt thought, very atypical of the average American's perception of a Muslim family. The gold frame was tarnished and spotted, the glass cover cracked. Beneath the picture were a few pages torn from a book, most likely the small Koran he had just tossed to Peyton. Some coins littered the bottom of the box, surrounding a small cassette tape, the type found in an answering machine or handheld recorder.

"Bingo," he said.

"You got it? You found the tape?" Peyton asked.

"Yes, the tape. Let's go listen to it."

They stuffed everything into the backpack, and Matt jammed the tape into his pants pocket. Once back at the house, he found an old tape player he had once used to record lectures in college. Sitting at the kitchen table, he popped the tape into the small, battery-powered machine and pressed play.

The voices sounded like geese squawking but were understandable.

Male voice: Hello, May. How are you?

Female voice: Fine, fine. Things are heating up here a bit, though. Do we have any guidance?

Male voice: Just got done talking to the secretary.

Female voice: Really? This is good. Finally getting some guidance on the build up of Iraqi forces on the Kuwaiti border?

Male voice: He wanted me to relay to you that we are staying out of this.

Female voice: You mean, staying out, like it's okay if they attack Kuwait? You know that's what he's talking about doing—taking the Rumallah oil fields and maybe even the entire country?

Male voice: Yeah, we know. If you look back at history, those oil fields all the way down into Saudi Arabia really belong to Iraq.

Female voice: What about the cost of oil and gas. Won't it skyrocket if Iraq takes these fields? Aren't we concerned about the economy?

Male voice: Yeah, yeah, we are. We don't think he's going past Rumallah, so it doesn't matter. Keeping Hussein on our team against Iran is more important than protecting some minor kingdom.

Female voice: Do you need me to talk to the secretary about this?

Male voice: No. He specifically asked me to relay this to you.

Female voice: Did the president clear this? Does he know?

Male voice: Indirectly.

Female voice: Indirectly? What the hell does that mean?

Male voice: You know exactly what it means.

Female voice: Sounds like I might be left holding this bag . . .

The sound became a static buzz, then resumed.

Matt looked at Peyton, whose eyes were the size of saucers and the color of the Caribbean Sea.

Male voice: Just make sure you communicate as clearly as possible to Hussein that we will not oppose him or take issue with any action he takes in the region.

Female voice: Okay, I understand.

The tape went blank, and Matt hit the stop button.

He stared at Peyton for a long time before either of them said anything.

"So, who are they?" he asked.

"Well, my guess is that the woman is the ambassador who took all the heat for telling Hussein it was okay to ransack Kuwait."

"Right. Who's the guy?"

"The tape quality is too poor to determine anything either way, even if you knew the guy," she said.

"Do you remember what she said, that tape they kept playing out of Baghdad?" Matt asked.

"Something like, 'We won't take issue with Arab disputes.' That's not exactly it, but it wasn't too far from what we just heard," she said.

"She said, exactly, 'We have no opinion on your Arab-Arab conflicts, such as your dispute with Kuwait. The secretary of state has directed me to emphasize the instruction, first given to Iraq in the 1960s, that the Kuwait issue is not associated with America.'"

Peyton looked at Matt and nodded, impressed.

Matt picked up the tape recorder, looked at her, and said, "Memorized it. If you really take a look at it, we gave them the green light, almost baited them into attacking Kuwait."

"Well, we've got the conversation that started it on tape. Clearly it's not the secretary of state because he references 'the secretary.' But it's most likely someone high up because she's not questioning him too much. She's an ambassador, and she's dealing with him instead of going to the main man," Peyton pointed out.

"Right. So what does this tell us? Why would they be discussing this particular tape? Zachary specifically said, 'Get the colonel' as he was being pulled away. And I overheard the talk of the backpack and the tape. Could the colonel and the tape be connected?"

"Did the tape sound at all like Rampert?"

"Rampert was a lieutenant colonel during the Gulf War, but the ambassador wouldn't have been talking to him." Matt didn't sound convinced of his own comment.

"Well, maybe," she said, "but these special ops guys do some wild stuff. How do we know it wasn't the political adviser for Schwarzkopf on the phone or someone like that?"

"Good point," he said.

"And Zachary did say, 'Find the colonel."

"Right. But the tape really only tells us what we already knew," Matt said, thinking out loud.

"Unless what we know isn't the truth. You never heard the secretary of state take any grief for any of this. May Sandford, the ambassador to Iraq, was hung out to dry, perhaps even set up. Maybe he never gave those instructions."

Peyton had this way, he was learning, of cutting to the chase, getting right to the point. He liked that about her. Not only was she exceptionally attractive, she was bright, had a quick mind, and might even have a sense of humor hidden in there somewhere.

"But why would someone tell the ambassador to tell Hussein it was okay to take Kuwait?" he asked.

"Why did Admiral Kimmel not act when he heard the Japanese were going to attack Pearl Harbor?"

"I get your point, but Kimmel was incompetent. This seems more deliberate. Like someone wanted Hussein to attack," Matt said.

"Why would someone want Hussein to take Kuwait?"

"Someone looking for a war."

Matt's words hung in the air for a moment, circling like a hawk. Their analysis seemed right to him. Could Zachary have tumbled upon a conspiracy?

"So let's assume that someone told the ambassador to say these things to Hussein for the purpose of starting the war," Matt said.

"That sounds about right," she said.

"The next level of detail is, why would someone want to start a war?"

"Well, we've been focusing on Rampert. There are theories about the military trying to start wars to prove their viability, test new weapons, show their stuff—you know, that kind of thing," Peyton said.

"My experience has been that the military, the actual men and women in uniform and on the ground, are the least likely to be looking for a war. They've seen it up close and personal. That wouldn't make sense."

"Maybe Rampert, if it is Rampert, was told by someone to say these things."

Matt stood and paced toward the kitchen stove and then turned around. "But again, why would someone want to start the Persian Gulf War? Who benefits from that?"

"Oil companies, for one," Peyton said.

"The president and secretary of state at the time both had big oil connections. That's a possibility, but would seem too obvious. The president then was a better man than that. I don't think he'd send young Americans to their deaths so that his buds in the oil business could make a buck or two. Doesn't flush."

"Maybe it wasn't that high up. Maybe someone knew that the president would react if Iraq attacked Kuwait. So they kept the intel about Iraqi maneuvering below the noise level of the National Security Agency."

"That's certainly a possibility," Matt said. "But again, why? Who?" Matt stared at the spine of mountains then moved his line of sight toward the South River that framed the north side of the property. Its banks were full from the spring thaw, which always brought new growth. In the last year he had believed he lost a brother and a mother, both supposedly buried in the soil upon which he stood. He had also lost Meredith's love as she found herself more suited for the ultra-powerful circles in which she now operated. *Just like Kari Jackson,* Matt thought to himself, thinking of his college girlfriend who had moved to the Manhattan financial district. But really, who could ever love a man whose goal in life was to kill every son of a bitch that wanted to do harm to his country. There was that edge . . . and also the mere logistical fact that he was usually away conducting missions.

"Who?" Matt said again. His mind drifted to Rampert, an unlikely possibility, in his view. And then he latched onto something, like a gear catching.

Lantini. Frank Lantini had been involved in detainee interrogations in the first Gulf War when he was an Air Force officer prior to working his way into the CIA.

"Ronnie Wood," Matt said more to himself than to Peyton. "It has got to be Ronnie Wood. Lantini."

Peyton ignored the comment, stood and walked over to him. "Can I do something?"

"It's Frank Lantini, aka Ronnie Wood, the former CIA director. I can see it now. He met Ballantine and began conspiring with him. For what, I don't know. He started that war in the Philippines, and he's got something to do with this one. The bastard is one of these academics with a vision. Smart by half."

"Let's forget about these Rolling Stones," Peyton said. She lightly clasped his jacket lapel with thin, well-manicured fingers. "Can we? That's wrapped up."

She wrapped her arms around his neck and hugged him. Matt hesitated a moment, then slid his arms around her waist. She felt good, and he liked the way she smelled, clean and light. He noticed just a whiff of perfume as he nuzzled his head into her hair.

"What brought this on?" Matt took a step back.

"I think we bonded in Vermont." She smiled. "C'mon."

Matt followed her into the house and up the stairs. After a quick trip to the restroom, he peeked in Zachary's old room. The bookcases were lined with football and baseball trophies, not unlike Matt's room. Zachary had hung some of his military memorabilia on the wall when he had left the service and moved back home during the peacekeeping years of the nineties. After 9/11, of course, Zach had eagerly accepted returning to active duty at a lower rank than the rest of his West Point classmates. And now, Matt had been led to believe that he had paid the ultimate sacrifice.

Fond memories started to snake their way back into Matt's mind. Strangely, when he had no opportunity to save his brother he felt fully responsible, yet when he had his brother in his arms and was knocked back by a firefight, he felt as though he had done well. Not good enough, but he was confident that he would retake Zachary. Something inside him told him that Ballantine wanted the duel with him, not Zachary. Matt figured that Ballantine might now see Zachary as the bait and would therefore try to keep him alive, so long as he didn't become a liability.

He walked across the hall into his room and saw Peyton sitting on the bed kicking off her leather shoes. He did the same, and they stretched out on the quilt.

As Matt lay his head back against the pillow, he had an unwelcome thought: *I'm close to something, am I being moved?*

As Peyton laid her head on his chest, a tear slid down her cheek as she thought of what might happen next. Was there anything she could do to stop it? she wondered. *Anything?*

The ringing phone startled her as she wiped the tear away. *It couldn't be him calling, could it?*

Listening to Matt's heart beat she clutched him tightly, fighting her confusion and frustration more than out of any desire to pull him closer.

CHAPTER 39

Matt groaned with displeasure as the phone interrupted a promising moment with Peyton's head resting peacefully on his chest.

"Hello," he said without much enthusiasm.

"Matt Garrett?" the familiar voice said.

"Yes?" Matt replied, trying to place the voice. He felt Peyton stir and pressed his right arm into her to keep her from moving too much. This could be about Zachary.

"This is Colonel Rampert," the voice on the phone said, "from special operations."

Matt motioned to Peyton with his hand, and she moved tight against him. She leaned next to his ear, straining to eavesdrop on the conversation.

"Yes, Colonel. What can I do for you? Are you okay?" He could hear a distinct thumping noise in the background, though he couldn't quite place it. Images of Rampert conspiring to start the war in Iraq sprang into his mind quite easily, much to his surprise.

"I'm fine, thanks for asking. Well, two things actually," Rampert said. Matt noticed his voice was not the same, crisp commander's voice he had heard in the airplane.

"Okay, go ahead," Matt said.

"First, you performed very bravely during that mission, and I've recommended you for a Presidential Medal of Freedom."

Matt, newly suspicious, paused, thinking, *Okay there's the bait.* "And the second?" he asked.

"Well, I thought you'd be happy about the nomination for the medal. It's the closest thing a civilian can get to the Medal of Honor. You put your life on the line for us."

"I could really give a rat's ass about a medal," Matt said, impatient.

Rampert paused and then said, "The second item is that we need to get our operative back. I need to talk to you about what you saw in the cabin."

"Your operative is my brother," he said. "So let's be honest. And I was hopeful that this call was actually a notice as to his whereabouts."

After another brief pause, Rampert said, "I understand. I can tell you more about your brother. I've got a helicopter heading up that way right now."

"How soon will you get here?"

"About five minutes."

"Need directions?"

"No, but thanks." Rampert sounded amused.

"How many of your friends are you bringing with you?" Matt said.

"Don't worry about it."

He could hear the ice in the colonel's voice. He pictured the man in his battle gear, stone-cold eyes set on the horizon through the windscreen of the helicopter. Something was different. Amiss. Matt's instincts were wailing louder than the obnoxious chop of the helicopter rotors he heard in the background.

Why was Rampert so interested in getting his hands on Zachary? Could it be the "no man left behind" credo to which he and others in the special operations communities adhered? Or, as his instincts were telling him, was Zachary a liability? He imagined the colonel smiling wickedly like the haunting sliver of a diminishing moon on a cold February night.

"Now, I'm going to discuss with you how to get him back," Rampert said. "And it's imperative that no one else know about any of this. We are way beyond Top Secret here."

"Well, Colonel, how do I know to trust you?"

Matt listened to the chopping noise of the helicopter rotor blades, muted through the telephone transmission.

"I can help you. I know some things that perhaps you don't. It is important that we talk. And, of course, you can help me as well."

Matt hung up the phone and looked at Peyton.

"We need to move fast. Rampert's almost here."

Peyton looked at him. "You're serious, aren't you."

They quickly gathered themselves.

Inside the living room, Matt walked toward the gun case and opened the glass door. He grabbed two weapons, a Remington shotgun and an AR-15 semi-automatic rifle. He handed the shotgun to Peyton.

"Give me the one with no range, huh?" she asked.

"Just have it somewhere you can get to it. If Rampert's the voice on the tape, this could get ugly."

Matt and Peyton stood in the living room and watched through the bay window as the helicopter hovered briefly before shooting straight down to the ground.

"Look at that," Matt said. "Makes me think Rampert's our man. But there's Lantini, too. Are they working together?" His questions were more rhetorical than anything, tumbling from his mind like an overstuffed closet door suddenly opened. Lantini the planner, Rampert the operator. Made sense.

They watched Rampert disembark from the helicopter and walk around to the front porch. They heard a knock on the door.

Matt looked at Peyton. "You can't say the man doesn't have style."

"Figured all your friends did this." Peyton smiled. There was something electric about her smile, as if she was about to enjoy something. Beyond the emerald-sea beauty, there was hardness in her eyes.

"I'm going to check and see who this is." He walked down the hall, attempting to be as calm as possible. He had initially been worried about Peyton's loyalties, but he could see now that he could concern himself with other matters.

Matt opened the door with his right hand, his AR-15 in his left. Colonel Rampert stared back at him wearing an Army combat uniform, or ACU, as Zachary called it, and a maroon beret that somehow made him seem even more menacing.

"Good evening, Colonel. May I help you?"

"Yes, may I come in?"

Matt considered his request. Standing next to the colonel, Matt saw that he was the man's equal in stature. Matt's shoulders were probably broader, though the colonel may have been half an inch taller.

"Listen, if you invite me in, I can answer some of your questions about Zachary," Rampert said.

"The first thing I want to know is, Why is Winslow Boudreaux buried next to my mother out back?"

"I'm sorry about that, Matt, truly I am. And I can tell you more."

Matt slowly opened the door.

"Are you always this hospitable to your guests?" Rampert's words were accusatory.

"You're not a guest." Matt's adrenaline was pumping. His muscles were taught. He was ready. Memories of the Philippines and the surges of emotions were flashing back in his mind.

"This house reminds me of my parents' home," Rampert said, following Matt down the hallway.

Peyton stood across the living room, shotgun clearly visible by her side.

Rampert nodded at her. "Peyton."

"Colonel," she responded.

"Please, have a seat," Matt offered, pointing at the wooden chair across from the overstuffed sofa. "Drink?"

"No, thanks, I'm in uniform." He smiled wryly.

"Okay, so talk," Matt said, sitting on the sofa, the AR-15 propped against the end table. Matt watched Peyton pick up the shotgun as Rampert reached for his pistol. Matt snatched the rifle, feeling the breeze from Peyton swinging the shotgun up to her eye level.

"I'm putting my weapon on the table!" Rampert's voice was authoritative.

Peyton's shotgun was leveled at Rampert, but he knew it was not a stretch to move it an inch or two. He played out a course of action in his mind where Peyton and Rampert were teaming against him for the tape. It was not implausible.

"Is she really necessary?" Rampert asked, hooking his thumb over his shoulder at Peyton.

Matt paused a second. "Peyton, it's okay."

"You people are sure jumpy. What the hell is going on?" Rampert said.

"After a bunch of Rolling Stones last year yanking everyone's chain, are you kidding me?"

"Well, that's over with," Rampert said.

"So you found Lantini?"

"Of course not. He went deep. Completely disappeared. His trail is colder than bin Laden's."

"Don't play mind games with me about bin Laden and The Shot," Matt said.

Rampert shrugged and looked at him. "Since when did you start following instructions Matt? You had the shot."

Matt turned away, sensing this was Rampert's negotiating routine: get him off balance and then make some outrageous demand. "Tell me about Zachary; what you think you know." Matt wanted to get to the point quickly.

"Well, I assume that there is some quid pro quo going here, and that you'll reciprocate in kind with information that will help us."

"This is the quo, my friend. The quid was me letting your ass in the house," Matt said. His face was stern, jaw set, eyes locked with Rampert's.

"Right, well, perhaps we can make some progress, then. This is top secret stuff, but I'm trusting you. So here goes. Your brother commanded the rifle company in the Philippine action, and he was executing exceptionally well. I had a small team in the wood line near the last battle. We were calling in the attack aircraft. If it hadn't been for Zachary and his company, the Marines would have been crushed. His company destroyed just about every enemy attack helicopter and artillery piece. Classic light infantry stuff. Our strength against their weakness and all that. But they finally wised to Zachary's tactics and chased him with the likes of an infantry battalion. It was about 300 bad guys massing against them.

"I had Winslow Boudreaux with me, along with Hobart and Van Dreeves, the two men with us in Canada. Winslow was about fifty meters away and caught a mortar shell not five feet from where he was standing. The explosion nearly vaporized him. Your brother's action was about a hundred meters away, and we saw him get hit about the time the weather cleared enough for us to get the A-10s in there to provide air support."

Matt watched Rampert speak with authority and authenticity. Matt could picture the scene Rampert described as if he had been watching a movie. A thin film of sweat broke across his brow. Matt was traveling back in time.

"Anyway, Winslow was dead. Hobart and Van Dreeves covered me while I pulled your brother out of the fray. His radio operator was also dead. Good man as well. We recovered Zachary. Van Dreeves, who is primarily a medic, literally saved his life. We kept him on oxygen and plugged his holes until the medevac aircraft got there a few minutes later. Last thing I did was switch dog tags and uniforms between Zachary and Winslow. Don't ask me why, I just did it."

Matt was having a hard time remaining calm. The emotions were so overwhelming that they seemed to be tripping over themselves. It did occur to him that Rampert was luring him in with the seduction of the story. *Hold on. Don't feel like you've got to give anything back.*

"We learned that Zachary was going to make it, but he was in a coma. He had taken a gunshot wound to the head, mostly a glancing blow, but enough to knock him out for a couple of months. He had other wounds that, coupled with the two to his head, caused enough nervous system damage for his brain to shut down for a while, until he could recover from the trauma. At first, we were simply trying to keep him alive, but then he started making a miraculous recovery quite unlike anything any of our doctors had seen before."

"So instead of contacting us," Matt interrupted, "you let us believe Zachary was dead. What right did you have?" His fire was back, his trance broken.

"First of all, young man," Rampert said, leaning forward and sensing his first small victory, "your brother would certainly be dead if it were not for Hobart, Van Dreeves, and me. I was the one who placed my team in that spot to support Zachary's company."

"That's your job. Your duty."

Matt's eyes broke away, if only for an instant. Rampert had the momentum now. He knew that Matt felt guilty that while Zachary had been able to save him, Matt was not there for Zachary in the Philippines.

"Maybe so, but *I* was there. Where were you, boy, when your brother needed you?" Rampert said, knowing exactly Matt's remorse and grinding the thought in a bit. "I pulled him back to safety and got him the medical help he needed. I've got proprietary rights, you might say." Rampert smiled a thin, evil grin.

Matt fumed in silence at Rampert's smugness. "That's bullshit."

"Maybe so, but, there's more," Rampert said.

Matt stared at Rampert, waiting.

"I was doing some deep black stuff during the Persian Gulf War. I've been face to face with Ballantine. I know what he wants."

"I know what he wants also," Matt said, regaining his composure. "My question is, why do you need Zachary so badly now?"

"Ahh. The $64,000 question, as they say." Rampert was acting the petulant bully now. "Your brother knows things that, left unguarded, could be very troublesome."

"Such as?"

"We're not going there, but the things he knows, if they come back to him, will be difficult for some to deal with. And he will become a liability."

"A liability? Proprietary rights? You talk about Zachary like he's a piece of real estate." Matt's voice was low, nearly a growl.

"It is what it is." Rampert gestured with his hands. "I'm truly on your side. I'm out to protect Zachary. I've invested the last year doing just that and I have no desire to stop now."

"Why don't I believe you?"

"I can't answer that. So tell me what you know about what happened at Moncrief."

Matt began, "I had Zachary in my arms. He was shot in the back, by Ballantine, I presume. Then a grenade came through the window and stunned us for a couple of minutes. I saw Ballantine drag him away before I was able to do anything about it. I chased them down to the river about the time Ballantine took off in the Sherpa."

"How do you know it was Ballantine who did all this?" Rampert asked.

"I don't. I'm assuming. Anyway, we need to be checking the area around Vermont and New Hampshire. Even Maine. Possibly New York," Matt said.

"We're watching the area with unmanned aerial vehicles, U2s, and other assets. Nothing so far. It's a pretty big area, you know," Rampert said.

"So where do we go from here?"

"I need to ask you, Matt, for your own safety, of course, if during the time that you believed Zachary to be dead, you went through any of his things and perhaps found anything you believed to be unusual?"

"Well, yes," Matt replied.

Peyton's eyes darted to his, squinting as if to say, *What are you doing?*

"Yes?" Rampert said, curious.

"I found out that my brother had two girlfriends, one in Hawaii and one in North Carolina. That dog. I found love letters from Kaoru, a Japanese chick who works as a consultant in Honolulu, and Stephanie, who I believe is a stripper in Fayetteville. Maybe you know her?" Of course, Matt knew that Zach had loved Riley Dwyer and his daughter, Amanda. But he was not giving Rampert any useful personal information.

"You don't realize who you're messing with, son." Rampert's eyes were hot coals.

"Maybe you don't realize you've got a shotgun trained on your head right now. I believe it's called tactical advantage, Colonel."

"Do you want Zachary back or not?"

"Absolutely," Matt said. "I'm ready now."

"It's not that simple."

"But you're supposed to be good, Rampert. I've heard about you. Seen you in action. And if you help me find my brother, we might just find what you're looking for." If Rampert wanted the tape badly enough, Matt thought, then he could bring to bear the full weight of Fort Bragg's intelligence-gathering assets behind the effort to find Zachary. It would be a major victory.

His instincts were telling him that Zachary was supposed to be dead and that the military would not be knocking itself out to find him. The government would be even less eager to find him and perhaps determined that he not return. The ploy of plausible deniability would be blown.

Zachary was hugely expendable, and if the tape might increase his survivability, then Matt would pursue that option.

It was all he had.

CHAPTER 40

ATLANTIC OCEAN

Ballantine's body was numb with painkillers. Because he needed both hands to fly the Sherpa, he had taken Percocet, one step down from morphine, and he was fighting the drowsiness.

He reached down and cut the trim, attempting to smooth out the bumpy, low-level flight as much as possible. He snatched a bottle of water from the console. Swallowing against a swollen tongue, he let the water trickle down his throat.

He had been airborne for several hours. He knew that the Air National Guard was patrolling and that AWACS airplanes were searching for him. Ballantine had also launched two of the Predators, one to fly up the St. Lawrence River. The other was flying toward Detroit, Michigan. Both were diversions.

Because his ground control stations had been destroyed in Swanton, all he could do is set the computer to launch them from his barn in Vermont. Two hours after he departed in the float plane, the first should have taken off. Another hour later, the second. It was a classic scatter strategy. Limited U.S. resources would get multiple spot reports of low flying aircraft and have to set priorities. With one focused on shipping lanes and another on Detroit, Ballantine figured it would place his aircraft, if detected, as the third priority.

Also, convincing the Central Committee to not attack airplanes or airports was proving as key to his ability to fly as the stealth technology and tactics he employed with his Sherpa. He believed the Americans focus on avoiding economic ruin, as almost happened after 9/11, and would want to continue to fly their airplanes. His calculation had led him to persuade Tae Il Sung to hold off on threatening the airline industry. So far, their plan had been devoid of attacking anything dealing with air travel.

Ballantine flew across the glimmering water of the Atlantic Ocean, low enough and slowly enough that if he was detected by radar, it would probably read him as a boat. He was surprised to make it this far, but not overconfident of his chances at making it all the way. To avoid the intense air defense coverage and scrutiny of the capital region, he had slipped off the Atlantic coast through the less populated areas of southern Massachusetts and then paralleled the coast over twelve miles offshore, just outside the United States' territorial limits.

His global positioning system told him he was due east of Chincoteague, Virginia. He had heard about the wild ponies that swam the channel at low tide, and he actually registered that it was something he might like to see one day. The possibilities for a painting were limitless. Soft pastel colors of a setting sun against the earth tones of the sand and swaying reeds as spotted horses galloped through a knee-deep strait to reach the island. Fascinating.

Banking to the west, Ballantine would soon be entering an area heavily monitored and patrolled by military aircraft. He would arrive at his destination in about twenty-five minutes, if everything went according to plan.

He spotted a small light in the distance, his sight of it enhanced by his night-vision goggles. His adrenaline began to surge for no apparent reason. So far the Percocet had done an excellent job of both numbing his pain and suppressing any emotion. He had lost many friends and the only woman that he might have ever loved in Canada. He knew that, as an international terrorist, emotions were needless burdens; but in his mind, at this moment, he was just an artist.

And he was a man whose brother had been murdered in cold blood by the American in the back of his airplane. He glanced over his shoulder at the bound and gagged Zachary Garrett. Frankly, he was surprised the man was still alive.

Ballantine determined the flashing light to be a buoy. He was about to enter the mouth of the Chesapeake Bay, which was surprisingly quiet and vacant this evening. The quiet din of the modified turbine engine droned along, causing him to experience a form of highway hypnosis. He was tired, but he knew it would be tragic for the mastermind of the greatest terror attack in history to fall asleep at the controls and bore an insignificant hole into the ocean with his little Sherpa.

He noticed through his goggles that the peninsula to his right was beginning to narrow, an indication that he was nearing the south shore, where the twenty-five-mile-long Chesapeake Bay Bridge-Tunnel would begin. His instructions were to key off the third and fourth islands that connected the second tunnel with the bridges. He looked at his fuel gauge, the red needle resting slightly above the E. Flying low, where the air was thickest, his having to fight the swirling winds had eaten into his fuel supplies. He figured he had about fifteen minutes of fuel before he would need to land.

He picked up the string of lights that dotted the bridge for several miles. The lights stopped for about two miles, began again, and then, in the distance, stopped for a brief span. His contact had told him to look specifically for the lights. Just east of the north tunnel would be his landing strip.

He was flying so low that he could see the white caps on the bay surface, and he received an occasional spindrift against his windscreen.

"Lily Pad one, this is Dragonfly one, over."

Ballantine waited for the expected response, and, when it did not come, he repeated his message.

"Lily Pad one, this is Dragonfly one. Over."

"Dragonfly one, this is Lily Pad. Over."

"This is Dragonfly. Inbound. Over."

"This is Lily Pad. Acknowledge visual. Stay low and hit the runway early. Over."

"Wilco. Stand by."

Ballantine searched the horizon, his weary eyes straining against the metal night-vision goggle rims. They saw nothing. Hearing a noise that was both unfamiliar and unsettling, he looked at the fuel gauge, the red needle falling below the empty line. He had used all 770 miles worth of his gas.

The propeller sputtering and straining, Ballantine ripped off his goggles and searched for the reserve tank switch. Frantically, his scrambling fingers found the toggle and flipped it downward. He pressed hard again, ensuring the switch was set. After a moment, the turbine picked up the steady hum, indicating it was receiving adequate fuel. He quickly set his goggles back to his face.

He still could not see his landing strip.

He determined he might be too low, so he gained altitude to increase his visibility.

"Dragonfly, this is Lily Pad. Acknowledge visual. Over."

"Lily Pad, this is Dragonfly. No visual. Low fuel. Over."

"Stand by."

Ballantine suddenly noticed a string of dim lights to his right front. He could see the bridge-tunnel about five miles ahead.

"Lily Pad, this is Dragonfly. I acknowledge visual. Over."

"Roger. Winds twelve knots from the southeast. Heading two-seven-zero degrees. Standing by. You must make touchdown within first fifty meters."

Ballantine flew past the landing area and then banked hard to the north, making a hairpin turn in the air, his starboard wingtip almost touching the water. He gained altitude, leveled his approach, and picked up the two rows of runway lights. These lights were different. They seemed to be moving some, swaying back and forth, and they seemed to end abruptly, well before he knew he would be able to stop his airplane.

As he neared the landing strip he knew he would have to perform one last tricky maneuver, much like landing in the creek bed near Moncrief.

He came in just above the first lights and then pushed down on his controls, nosing over just a bit before pulling up to a level position. The Sherpa's wheels grabbed the landing strip, lurching him forward but maintaining a steady roll toward the end of the short runway. He throttled back and pressed on the brakes, skidding hard and diving into darkness. He could not see beyond the windscreen. It was completely black.

Ballantine's heart was beating powerfully against his chest. Then he realized, Lilypad had built a concealed runway with containers stacked three high on either side and wide enough for his airplane. *Ingenious.*

He had made it. Miraculously, he had made it.

The deck of a merchant ship had been converted nicely into an aircraft carrier.

CHAPTER 41

CHESAPEAKE BAY, VIRGINIA

Native Virginia Beach resident Gary Austin knew that cobia was best caught near the rocks that supported the Chesapeake Bay Bridge-Tunnel. But there was a current this cool evening as the tide was flowing out to sea, and he didn't want to run the risk of drifting into a concrete pylon while he focused on pulling in a twenty-pound cobia. Cobia tended to hang around structure, so Gary chose a floating buoy just outside the mouth of the bay to target.

Gary's father had been the chief pilot, running the pilot boats out of Lynnhaven Inlet, where small crews of navigational experts would come about the merchant ships dotting the mouth of the bay like an armada awaiting the signal to attack. The pilots would board the ships and steer them through the obstacle course that included the bridge-tunnels and the tight channels. The navigational challenges were too many to risk a marginally trained ship captain from, say, Thailand, to negotiate. One wrong turn and a bridge or tunnel would be destroyed, stopping road and sea traffic for weeks.

"Red right returning," Gary muttered aloud to himself, repeating the seafarer's reminder of where to keep his boat in relation to the red light when returning to port. He stalled the engine and dropped anchor as a small sliver of the moon looked down at him with a haunting smile. In theory, he wasn't supposed to be out tonight, as the recent attacks had caused the Hampton Roads Port Authority to issue a warning against all small craft from entering the bay. At 25 years old, Gary had two things in his favor. First, he was a certified merchant-ship pilot, and it was his night off. So if he ran into anyone, it would most likely be someone with whom he worked. Second, he thought the order to keep small craft out of the bay was stupid. With many friends in the military he knew that the more eyes and ears you had out and about, the more likely you were to deter bad things from happening.

"Screw 'em if they can't take a joke," he said.

He opened the Igloo cooler and pulled a frozen mullet from the chest. Taking his filet knife, he cut the fish in half, leaving two six-inch pieces of fish. He took the one with the head and ran a large hook through the lips of the fish. He then shut off all of his lights, to keep from spooking the cobia, and pulled on a pair of night-vision goggles he had purchased at the Army-Navy surplus store. The goggles were first generation and relied on starlight, but they were a vast improvement over the naked eye.

With the night-vision harness on his head, he picked up his rod and lobbed the baited hook over the side, watching the current pull the bait toward the buoy. He let the bait drift for about a minute, then reeled it in and repeated the process. It had good action fluttering in the current. He let the bait drift again, then locked the spool on his reel once it was directly aside the buoy. Putting the rod in a trolling rig, he set the line so that if a fish took the bait, it would set the hook.

In the same cooler, he found a Budweiser, popped the top, and kicked back in his captain's chair, looking toward the sky.

Where had the years gone? he wondered. He recalled standing at his father's knee as he would steer their boat through the wicked currents and how his dad was always able to find the best fishing spots. He had learned well, though, and today he was the younger, salty spitting image of his father. Blonde hair, tanned face, bitten fingernails, and the same Cape Hatteras drawl. He had already begun his career as a ship pilot, following in his father's footsteps, though a penchant for good-looking women had landed his career in jeopardy a few weeks ago in Baltimore. While docked there, he had allowed the crew to enjoy a few "ladies," which, after an accident a few years back, was strictly verboten.

Snapped back to the present with the sound of another boat sputtering around the bay, he could hear the distinct hum of a gasoline engine somewhere in the offing.

He heard the equally distinctive snap of the fishing line against the trolling rig. Gary snatched the rod out of its holder and heaved it skyward. He had a cobia.

"Yeah, baby, give it to me," he said, talking the fish toward the boat. He could see through his goggles that it was not just a cobia. It was a *large* cobia. Maybe forty or fifty pounds. Cobia were actually members of the shark family, making them terrific fighters. Moreover, their ability to produce thick fish steaks good for grilling made it worth the effort.

As he worked the fish toward the edge of the boat, the engine he had heard became louder—so loud that he had to stop what he was doing, holding the rod high in the air to keep the hook set while he looked skyward.

Gary found it hard to believe, but there was a small, single-engine airplane flying about twenty meters off the water, and it had just turned less than a quarter mile from his anchor position.

Through his night-vision goggles, he suddenly saw bright lights shoot upward from a ship about a mile away.

The cobia kept pulling at his rod but was wearing down. Gary kept his eyes on the airplane as it flew directly at the ship. *He's going to hit the ship,* he thought. Grabbing his cell phone, he prepared to call 911.

Then the strangest thing happened. The airplane lifted a bit in the air and dove straight for the deck of the ship, almost like—well, exactly like Navy pilots do on aircraft carriers. He had watched about a million Tomcats take off and land on carriers and at Oceana Naval Air Station. What he was watching seemed, in theory, no different. He watched as the plane blended with the ship, thought he heard a slight noise of rubber screeching on metal, and then quickly reeled in his fish.

He unhooked the cobia, stumbling with it a moment, and stuffed it in the live well, still flapping, and then drew in his anchor.

Gary cranked the engine and sped toward the ship, slowing and slipping into idle as he neared. He kept his night-vision goggles on and the running lights off.

He drifted close to the ship, close enough to see the name under the moonlight: *Fong Hou.*

He recognized the name from the long list of merchant ships on their "to do" list. China, he recalled. About fifteen down the list of ships that were going to enter the Bay, up to Baltimore, he thought.

He pulled away from the ship to get a better angle, but saw nothing out of the ordinary. As he throttled the engine he looked over his shoulder and began to wonder if he hadn't just lost sight of the plane as it continued to fly up the Bay. Or had he really seen a small aircraft land on the deck of the *Fong Hou*?

During the hour-long trip back to the Chesapeake Bay Pilots Quarters just inside Lynnhaven Inlet, his confidence faded in what he had seen. It was dark and his goggles weren't the best. There were maybe twenty-five ships anchored in between the mouth of the Bay and the Ocean. And he had a giant cobia in his live well. Maybe the screech of the wheels had been the pull of his drag on his reel.

He tied his own boat up to the pier and bounded up the steps to the Pilot Quarters. Opening the door he saw Rich Burns and Blake Sessoms. Burns was the second in command and on duty tonight. Sessoms was a volunteer who liked to hang around the 45-foot twin-diesel boats. Gary thought Burns was a decent boss, but a bit strict. Sessoms, on the other hand, had surfed Hatteras with him a few times, was rich, had his own rig, and was trying out as an apprentice pilot, Gary thought, just to have something cool to do.

"What are you doing here, junior?" Burns asked, putting down a deck of cards. They sat at an old picnic table that had been in the Quarters since Gary's dad was the chief pilot.

"Gary," Sessoms said, acknowledging his friend.

Austin grabbed a seat and looked at Burns then Sessoms.

"You guys may think I'm crazy—"

"No doubt," Burns said, holding the deck in his hand.

"That's been established," Sessoms added, looking at the two cards Burns had dealt.

"Listen you dickweeds. I was just out doing some Cobia fishing—"

"Catch anything?" Burns asked.

"He ain't got nothing," Sessoms said. "Every time he catches a minnow, he brings it up here like it's a citation."

"Guys, quit giving me shit, here, okay?"

"Then what did you come in here for on your day off?" Sessoms quipped. Then, to Burns, "Hit me."

Burns flicked a card at Sessoms and then looked at his own.

"I think an airplane just landed on the *Fong Hou*."

"*Fong Hou*?" Sessoms asked. "Is that like, 'One Hung Low'?"

"Bite me, Sessoms," Austin said.

"*Fong Hou*'s number seventeen on the list," Burns said, looking at his cards. "We've got four operational boats. Takes a day per ship. We'll get to it in five days, junior, *if* we get the word to move 'em."

"What'd the plane look like?" Sessoms asked.

"It was small," Austin said. "Wings above the fuselage and some kind of crazy v-shaped things between the wings and the rest of the airplane. Like bat wings."

"Like a flying saucer?" Burns joked.

"You can bite me, too, Burns."

"Listen, Austin. After the hookers in Baltimore and the alcohol on your breath, I think you ought to be a bit more," Burns paused, obviously looking for a big word, "circumspect."

"I'm telling you, man." Austin shook his head in dismay.

"Alright, dudes. I'm out of here," Sessoms said, throwing his cards on the table. He stood, his long sandy hair flowing down to his shoulders. "Going up to the mountains early in the morning to catch up with, Matt."

"Garrett?" Burns asked.

"Yeah. His sister sent me the S.O.S."

"It's been a while. Say, 'hey,' for me, will you, Hope he's okay," Burns said. By now, they were both ignoring Austin, who had walked to the digital docket that displayed the long list of ships awaiting pilot assistance.

"Sure. Hey Austin," Sessoms said. "Wanna show me that cobia?"

"Might as well," Austin sighed.

"Later, Burns." Burns and Sessoms did a knuckle punch and then

Sessoms walked out with Austin.

"You don't believe me, do you?" Austin asked.

As they approached Austin's twenty-five-foot Dixie, Sessoms said, "Why wouldn't I? How big?"

"I'm talking about the airplane," Austin said.

Sessoms stopped and put his hand on Austin's shoulder. He was over six feet tall and towered above the younger man.

"Look, Gary—"

"This ain't got anything to do with bringing a couple of chicks on the pilot boat, man." Gary looked down at the ground.

"Probation is probation, man. I wouldn't push it with Burns."

"But what if it's something?" Austin asked.

Sessoms looked at the glassy water of the Inlet then back at Austin.

"Okay, let me think about it tonight and then we'll chat tomorrow. I'll call you. Deal?"

"Thanks."

"Least I can do is give you some top cover with Burns."

"He's just pissed 'cause he ain't getting any."

"He's still your boss. And no matter who your old man was, you've still got to be careful."

By now Austin had opened the top of the live well. Blake stayed on the pier as Austin lifted the enormous cobia.

"Steaks tomorrow night?" Sessoms asked.

"Deal. Thanks, bud."

"Good land there, Austin. I'll catch you tomorrow," Sessoms called over his shoulder as he walked one pier over to his Boston Whaler.

He cranked the engine, backed away from the pier, and throttled his way quickly to his home on nearby Broad Bay.

As he navigated the channel, he remembered three things: *Fong Hou*, small airplane, and bat wings above the fuselage.

CHAPTER 42

THE VICE PRESIDENT'S MIDDLEBURG MANSION

Meredith pulled her car into the familiar driveway. She parked next to the other cars in front of the guest cabins that the vice president had converted into the alternate command and control center.

She could see the lights on in the center cabin, which was the primary communications center. Behind the "command post," as Hellerman called it, were the other two cabins. All three were constructed in a stone cottage style that made them look like they had jumped off a Thomas Kinkade painting. The other two cottages primarily housed staff and Secret Service personnel, who stayed on site twenty-four hours a day.

The size of nice suburban homes, the cottages each had bedrooms, bathrooms, kitchens, and all the usual amenities of a house. The big upgrade had been in communications equipment. A communications team had spent months installing satellites, laying fiber optic cables, and essentially digitizing every phone, radio, television, computer, and camera. The entire compound was wired with Top Secret phone lines and Internet connections.

Meredith looked across the field about a quarter mile to the mansion, which was strictly off limits to everyone except herself and some select Secret Service. The mansion was a medieval-looking stone building, like the cottages, but five times the size. Meredith thought that it seemed like a dark and brooding father watching over his three children. Tonight the mansion was dark but for a room on the second floor.

She entered the command post and could hear the steady rhythm of an operations center. Fax machines were chugging away, CNN and Fox News were playing on two separate televisions, phones were ringing, and there was a computer running at every desk. She saw Jock Evans, Zeke Jeremiah, and Stan Rockfish from the Rebuild America discussion group and waved.

"Hey guys," she said, walking over to the flat panel display monitor that summarized significant activities. "What do we have tonight?"

"A shit storm, like usual. All trading was suspended on the stock market today, and the world markets are diving everywhere. No doubt we're going to be heading for a major worldwide recession, if not depression," Evans said, shaking his head.

Jeremiah continued. "The president is shutting down all of the shopping malls, and everywhere in the country people are to avoid places of public assemblage. And he finally decided to shut down the airlines. It's about time. This Ballantine guy is going after everything."

"So much for our twenty-four-hour respite," she said.

"We've mobilized the Reserves and the National Guard, but there's really no plan for dealing with something like this. We'll be making it up as we go."

"That's reassuring," Meredith said.

"Right, but we've got Special Forces Command as well as all of Fort Bragg going over contingency plans right now. There are some leads, but they're rather thin. Problem is that we've committed the bulk of our forces abroad. Not much left to deal with stuff at home."

"Not much of the elite ones anyway," she said, remembering Zachary.

"We've also picked up a low-flying airplane moving up the St. Lawrence River. Could be Ballantine. Actually the Canadians found it first. We're sending some jets up there now to check it out."

"Good. Good," Meredith said.

"Here's your briefing packet. The vice president wants his update in the mansion tonight for some reason."

"That's unusual, but he's the boss," she said, shrugging. She knew exactly what he wanted.

She grabbed the packet and rifled through its contents. On one PowerPoint slide was a map of the country with little red starbursts indicating the locations of attacks. Having it graphically displayed made an impact on her, allowing her to see the genius of the attacker. North Carolina, Minnesota, Georgia, Arkansas, Colorado, Washington State. It was diverse and unpredictable. It was terrifying.

"Okay, let me go do the deed," she said, shaking her head. While they understood her to mean one thing, her comment actually meant more than what they gathered.

She walked across the parking lot, carrying the manila folder, following a stone sidewalk that led from the cabins to the mansion. Black, wrought-iron gas lamps lit her way as she ascended the steps to the mansion. The spring evening was mild with just a hint of chill in the air.

She rang the doorbell and waited, then rang again. She looked through the window to the side of the door and could see no lights on in the front of the house.

She had been here before and knew he wouldn't want her waiting on the porch. So she let herself into the home and quickly punched the security code on the pad in the coat closet. She paused, took off her coat, and then hung it in the closet next to some others, including a few of his wife's coats. A bolt of guilt shot through her but quickly ran its course.

Meredith had rationalized this a long time ago and had convinced herself that it was the right thing to do. She was wearing a turquoise business suit with a diamond butterfly broach and matching earrings. Her hair was up in a bun, because he liked it that way. The small Rolex watch that he had given her slid gently on her wrist as she walked into the large foyer and then into the den. She flipped a light switch and then threw the manila folder onto the coffee table.

She noticed that she was more nervous this time than she had been the others. Her mind quickly flashed back to a year ago when the secretary of defense had invited her to his house. She had refused. With Hellerman, though, it was different. She was a willing participant in the affair. As they got to know each other, she became completely infatuated with his vision and plans for reuniting America. Meredith was a patriot, and she was devoted to both the vice president and his special cause to bring the country back together.

But now, after today, she wanted to call it all off. She was going to tell Hellerman she still loved Matt.

She moved around the room like a cat, regaining familiarity with her surroundings. She stopped in front of the large fireplace, the slate rock chimney climbing all the way to the vaulted ceiling. A Civil War-era musket hung above the hearth with a powder horn on one side and a bugle on the other. The entire room was tastefully done, reflective of Hellerman's personality and past professions. There were the appropriate law books in the study, international relations books in the bookcase in the living room, and assorted paintings depicting faraway lands scattered throughout the home.

Meredith waited another fifteen minutes and thought about departing but decided against it. Walking into the kitchen, she noticed the door to the basement was slightly ajar with a hint of light seeping from below. She tucked the loose strands of her hair behind her ears as she did when she became focused and peered down the dimly lit stairway.

Having just watched the movie *Scream* for the first time a few weeks before, she laughed at herself for feeling nervous. Here she was in the home of the second most powerful man in the world. Security systems were everywhere, and the Secret Service stood watch out front. What could happen to her?

She stepped slowly down the steps, pulling at the beaded chain hanging to the right and causing the single light bulb to flash on next to her head. She found the concrete basement floor and turned toward a small room in the far corner. Having never been down there before, she felt as though she was violating the vice president's privacy a bit, but she pressed on anyway.

She pushed on the wooden door to a small room, and the weak light became somewhat brighter, giving her a full view of what looked like a military operations control center. Radios were banked atop one another, and two television screens showed news channels.

On the wall was a white dry-erase board on which someone had marked the days of the current week and the next week. Red slashes were through the days that had already passed and a list of events was itemized in each box representing a day. Last Friday's box, she noticed, had *Mall of America,*

Lennox Square/Phipps Plaza, Charlotte Coliseum, Capitol Building Tallahassee, Florida, Puget Sound Apartment Tower/Seattle. The next day had similar events. Hellerman was clearly using the board to track what had happened and keep tabs on the events.

But she had never seen this set-up before. She figured he probably came down here to study the patterns, being a former military intelligence officer. She knew it helped her sometimes to get away from the maelstrom and insulate herself so that she could follow her own instincts instead of the leanings of so many others. She remembered listening intently to his stories of interrogating high-ranking prisoners during the first Persian Gulf War. She assumed he felt comfortable in this kind of closed-in environment with the radios and maps.

She smiled when she realized she really did admire the man. As she scanned the room, her eyes drifted to the desk and chair. There was a laptop computer with its monitor shut atop the keyboard next to the bank of phones. Next to the computer was a pad of paper and it appeared the vice president had been doodling some circles and the letters RW. The letters were bored into the paper exactly twice. RW RW, overlapping almost.

Huh, Meredith thought, with a twinge of jealousy. *Who could that be?*

Their relationship truly started when Hellerman had asked her to work on his Rebuild America plan. He had pulled together the likes of Rockfish, Smithers, Evans, Jeremiah, and O'Hara. The group was focused on the best way to bring the country together again and shed the many divisions. It was all about defeating the secular spiritual stagnation that his favorite author, Walt Rostow, had predicted.

"Pretty interesting, don't you think?"

Meredith jumped at the voice floating through the darkness behind her. She found herself ten feet further into the room.

"You scared the hell out of me!" she said sharply to Hellerman.

"Well, now, Meredith, God might thank me for that." He smiled, emerging from the darkness, his face a theater mask that was half smiling, half frowning.

"My heart's racing a mile a minute," she said, leaning against a table and placing her hand on her chest.

"I usually have that effect on you, don't I?" he whispered in a low voice, sliding toward her and firmly grasping her hand.

"Of course, but I have to pull my stomach out of my throat first," she said, surprised at the firmness of his grip. She followed him out of the room into the darkness of the basement. He stopped and locked the hasp on the door.

"How long have you been here?" he asked.

"About thirty minutes," she replied.

"Down here, thirty minutes?" he asked tersely.

"No. No. I was only down here a couple of minutes," she said. "I waited for you upstairs for about a half an hour. Remember, I'm supposed to brief you in the mansion tonight?" She leaned forward and kissed him on the lips gently, trying to take the edge off him.

He responded to the kiss as he always did. She felt him relax considerably in her arms.

"Yes, right. So what do you think of my tracking center?" he asked, pulling her away and heading up the stairs.

"I think it's great. What do you do, just sit down there, think about what's going on, and anticipate the terrorist's next move?" She glanced over her shoulder at the small enclave. Something was not quite right. Something had registered in her mind as not fitting, not being precisely in place, but he had startled her to the point that the thought escaped her, perhaps forever.

"Exactly," he said, smiling. "That's exactly what I do."

They climbed the steps, and she held his hand the entire way, trying to calm him back down the way she had learned to do. They sat comfortably on the sofa in the great room, facing the fireplace. He poured them each a glass of Chianti.

"Meredith, as you know, these bombings have taken a terrible toll on the nation and, in particular, on the administration. But the Rebuild America Program has oddly benefited from these tragedies."

Meredith studied Hellerman. He was holding his glass of wine with his arm cocked on the back of the pillow of the leather sofa.

"I've been thinking about that. When you were in my office the other day, you said, 'It's all coming together like we planned.' You seemed so excited by what was happening. It kind of scared me."

"I know. It was more the adrenaline. We've been so close to Ballantine, and I thought we had him. I really thought we had him," he said, his voice trailing off as he looked away.

"Our plan, Trip, is still achievable," she said. "Reuniting this country is a worthy and noble cause. It will be even more important on the heels of this crisis."

Meredith had a brief flashback to the day that the vice president entered her office and shut the door nearly eight months ago. Last summer, he had sat on one of her blue sofas in her White House office and told her to sit down. He didn't ask her, she recalled, he directed her. She had been struck by his command presence, especially because she almost instinctively obeyed.

"I've been tossing around a concept," he had said. His summer tan back then contrasted with his flashy white teeth. "I think the country is clearly split into two halves, and we need to find a way to bring them together. Rostow's spiritual stagnation has set in. Hell, no one even knows we're fighting two wars in Afghanistan and Iraq. Everyone just drives on with their business, riding around in their Lexuses and Beamers."

Most of her friends certainly felt that way, she knew. But how would he do it? How do you reunite a country of 280 million people?

"People don't see the real threat to our nation," he had said, jokingly, she thought. "We have to make them understand, so I'm pulling together a team to work on some ideas for how to bridge the gap. You look at these national elections we're having, and everything is split right down the middle. You've got those trying to hold on to some core American values, and you've got those that are convinced that changing into a new image is the right way to go. Only no one knows what that image should look like, only that it should be different. The Republicans are on one side of the issues and the Democrats on the other. It doesn't matter who is right; it's all party politics. If we cut through the chaff, we can get at what everyone wants: a better, more unified country."

"What is the unifying mechanism?" she asked.

"That's why I'm pulling all you braniacs together," he said.

Hellerman's light stroking on her arm pulled Meredith back to reality. Over those eight months, she had left Matt and begun an affair of the heart and mind with this man. Generally a very conservative woman, she had surprised herself when she decided to follow Hellerman's path. It had started rather slowly with the weekly brainstorming session in the basement of the Old Executive Office Building, but then gradually it had progressed to private office visits with him and finally secret rendezvous at his Middleburg estate.

The sex had begun one night after a bottle of champagne. No doubt, she was attracted to him. Then, about four months ago, sliding off her dress, she noticed her slip catch on her engagement ring. The pangs of guilt had rippled through her, and the very next weekend she told Matt they needed to take a break.

They really had not accomplished much in the eight months. More ideas than substance. Everyone seemed to have a good handle on the problem but no real solutions. She was initially most impressed by Hellerman's driven conviction to solving the problem. His unbridled passion was, in her mind, his most attractive feature. He was seductive, and she was drawn to him like an eager student to a wise professor.

"Trip, I hate to admit it, but it almost seems like these things that are happening are tailor-made for what we have been talking about. I mean, the country is horrified, searching for leadership. Now is your time."

"You're right, Meredith. Now is the time to capitalize on what is happening. In my view, we have an opportunity here to bring the nation together, to achieve a common purpose and establish a new national identity that can serve as a foundation for the next two hundred years," Hellerman said.

She could see the intensity in his eyes.

"I agree, Trip. In a sense, if we could seize this opportunity, these deaths might somehow mean something. I'd hate to see so many people die in vain," she said.

"Me too, Meredith. So while the president goes about his plan, I've been asking the group to begin pulling together a few ideas. We will develop an internal protection team to take volunteers around the country to do basic security work. Naturally, we'll have to train them for a few weeks to give them the basic skills, so we intend to use the National Guard to put literally hundreds of thousands of civilians through a 'boot camp' of some sort. Right there we start the foundations of a shared experience.

"Next, we'll activate every stateside Army division and mobilize them to secure key and essential targets around the country. They guard churches in Kosovo. Why can't they protect important facilities here? As we do this, we make sure that we've cut across all the socioeconomic lines so that we build the bonds between people necessary to propel us into the future on common ground."

"These are all things we've talked about in the past, Trip, and it seems to make sense that we go forward now. The real question is how much the president should know and how much we should just keep to ourselves."

"Well, the key, Meredith, is that the president has to sign the laws and enact the legislation—call up the Reserves and all that—but we are the drivers of those actions. We have to work Congress to get the votes, but I know the votes are out there. And, the president can decree a lot of this stuff the same way FDR did with all of his alphabet soups."

"We can do that, but can we talk about something else first?" Meredith asked.

Hellerman wasn't even listening to her. "We've already started. I've got Jock Evans working tonight on finalizing the details of the legislation for the Internal Protection Corps. I figure each state will need about ten thousand folks, give or take, depending on the size. We'll mobilize the National Guard within twenty-four hours, and they'll develop cadres in each state with a standard three-week program of instruction. We'll target mostly eighteen-to-thirty-year-old men and women. They're the future of the country. We can adapt a military pay scale and give the organization a military rank structure."

"Trip, I need to talk to you about us." She realized their conversation had become surreal. So far, she had simply agreed with everything he was saying to make this part of the conversation go a bit easier.

"Congress will have to appropriate the money, of course. They'll want to do a special tax increase. I think we can convince them to divert away from some unnecessary funding and refocus the money on this national priority. Everyone knows there's a ton of fat in the budget, and everyone knows where it is. I'm thinking that in a time of national emergency, there will be some players who want to trim some of their own fat to avoid scrutiny later on. Plus, they'll see this as a temporary deal, which, of course, is the intention. At least initially."

Meredith watched the vice president's eyes jump with excitement as he spoke about the plan. To this point, most of the discussions had been pie-in-the-sky, with no real substance. But this was substance of the best kind. Hellerman was pushing his agenda forward in the face of a national calamity. She felt like a child trying to get her parent's attention.

Hellerman stepped from his soapbox and reached for the wine bottle, as if he were shifting gears. The *Eagles*' "Hotel California" played softly in the background, adding a touch of irony to the discussion: *"Good night," said the night man, "we are programmed to receive. You can check out anytime you like, but you can never leave."*

How true, she thought. She might be able to check out from this affair with Hellerman, but she knew she would never be able to escape his spell.

"Have you heard from Matt lately?"

"Yes, this morning we spoke about Zachary and the fact that he's alive. It's pretty exciting," she said, trying to hide some of her emotions. "That's what I wanted to talk about."

"Yes, that's great news about Zachary," he said. "I was quite surprised to find out he was alive, much less in special operations. Do we have any ideas where he might be?"

"Only that he was last seen being dragged from the cottage at Moncrief. Ballantine's certainly got him somewhere," she said.

Hellerman stood, brushing off his pants and raised his arms in the air, stretching.

"Let's take a walk," he said.

"I need to talk to you," she said as the vice president grabbed her hand.

Meredith wasn't sure how they had found their way upstairs into the bedroom, but they had. She had every intention of telling him that she could not see him anymore and that she was going back to Matt, but when the moment came, she was unable to resist his magnetism. The evening had been captivating. He had taken her with a reckless abandon, and she had responded likewise.

His ideas, his thoughts, his clarity of mind during these most violent times were absolutely breathtaking. She was in the arms of a historical man—someone who was making history as they lay in bed together. Someone she could not ignore.

As she drifted off to sleep and felt him ease out of bed for his trip back to the Naval Observatory, and his wife, she got mad at herself for capitulating. She was a stronger woman than this. But then again, she might be out of her league.

As her mind tired and she began to swoon, she found herself replaying scenes from that mysterious room in the basement. Something was not right.

If only she could remember.

CHAPTER 43

GARRETT FARM

Matt left Peyton sleeping and walked along the riverbank that framed his family property to the north and east. To his left the river pushed smoothly over the rocky bottom and ran full with fresh snow thaw from the spring melt. Young poplar trees spotted the high, rocky bank, along with a few oaks and ash. A level area stretched out to his right, creating a flood plain during unusually heavy rainy seasons. They had actually grown corn and sorghum on the fertile plain in recent years. The sun was cresting the hill to the southeast. He heard the distant crow of a rooster from a neighboring farm.

A cool spring breeze swept off the mountains, causing Matt to huddle against himself. He could feel his cheek redden from the wind, and he absently longed for those times that he and Zachary could just kick around the farm.

"Where are you, Zachary?" he wondered aloud. His words floated meaninglessly into the morning ether, to be chased away by the wind.

He stepped onto a large rock and looked twenty feet below into the rumbling stream. The water bubbled and churned to the east toward the Rappahannock River and eventually Chesapeake Bay, over 200 miles away. He had caught many trout in the stream as a child, though he had never developed the patience or the technique for fly fishing. Stuffing his hands into his pockets, he recalled the time he and Zachary had been sitting on the very same rock nearly twenty years ago. Located at the outer limits of the property, they talked about a world they knew existed out there and what they might want to do one day.

"Go to West Point," Zachary said.

"You'd be good at that, Zach. I think I just want to play baseball."

"You're good at baseball, and you'll do well, Matt, but you're too smart for that."

"What the hell does that mean?"

"It's most important to make a difference, do something important."

"Baseball's important to me, Zachary."

And it had been. Even today, Zachary's maturity at that point in his young life seemed impressive. At the time, though, Matt was one of the best shortstops in the state and was already receiving hints from the head coach at the University of Virginia, where he had always known he wanted to go.

"Then you should play baseball. And when you're done with that, you will be chosen to do something else. We all have our talents and our destinies, Matt."

Matt remembered those words: *You will be chosen to do something else.* As if it wasn't his decision. There was a larger force at work, directing him, determining his calling. Was it his admiration for Zach that had led him into the CIA after college, or was it Providence. Was this his lot in life? If so, he found satisfaction in the difference he had made, so far.

He started back up the hill, picking his way through the high grass and finding the minor trail they had worn into the rise over the years.

What was it that he needed to do now? The country was under attack, the Reserves were mobilizing beyond what they had done in the wake of the September 11 attacks, the nation was at war abroad, and his brother was alive. The conflicting emotions collided inside him, causing him to question his own instincts.

His only true instinct was to find Zachary. In the end, he presumed, Zachary was all that mattered. The World Trade Center and Pentagon attacks had been so chillingly brilliant in their execution that the nation was stunned to the point of disbelief. And for many Americans, while tragic, it was a distant event.

Now it was coming home to everyone. It was not New York and Washington, D.C. It was the American heartland that was being terrorized, fear undermining a sense of security in every citizen. The economy was in a nosedive that was comparable to the enemy freezing American assets, Matt thought. The Coalition has seemingly sped to victory in the Iraq War yet was actually caught flatfooted with so many troops deployed around the world in combat. There was not much left to defend the home front. With that notion, the spark of an idea lit in his mind.

But it was chased away quickly by the idea of what might be next. Surely the end game was something even more spectacular than what they had seen so far.

What would Ballantine do? What would Hussein have planned, even as he may have expected his demise?

Matt crested the hill and stared at the house, stopping as he pondered the two questions he had just asked himself. How could an enemy of the U.S. make the most headway against her? Sure, psychological terror is one thing, but what is the physical manifestation, the ultimate goal?

Through the morning fog, he saw a motorcycle turn much too quickly onto the dirt and gravel road that served as a driveway up to their home. He smiled. He knew he wasn't alone anymore.

Matt walked quickly to the house, greeting Blake Sessoms as he dismounted the motorcycle.

"Am I glad to see you," Matt said.

"Well, my brother, it has been too long."

Matt looked away, at the mountains. "I know. I'm sorry."

The two men hugged and then walked into the kitchen, where Karen was making coffee. Blake looked every bit the surfer. He was taller than Matt by about two inches. His countenance was clear, his face handsomely tanned. He was smooth and polished, intelligent, and a gentleman.

"Hey, Blake. Long time no see," Karen said.

"Karen, how are you pretty lady?"

"Not pretty enough for you. Never was, you know?"

"Not true. You were always too good for me. That's for sure."

Karen smiled and then handed them each a cup of coffee, excusing herself. "Time to do some chores."

"Thanks for the heads up," Blake said to her as she departed.

"Doing *my* job," she called over her shoulder. Karen had called Blake and told him Matt needed a friend.

Matt turned a chair around and sat down, leaning against the back. Blake followed suit.

"Need to get inside your head, bro. I know when you're not okay. So tell me what you know, starting with Zach "the Z-man" Garrett. Karen told me he's alive."

Matt smiled at Blake's nickname for his brother. He had not heard anyone call him that in a long time, and just hearing the name gave him a sense that his brother was nearby. He grabbed his coffee and kicked back.

"Okay, I'll start, as they say, from the beginning." He began talking, slowly and deliberately at first, leading off with the Rolling Stones fiasco and then Zach's funeral a year ago, the conversations with Hellerman, his depression, meeting Peyton, the breakup with Meredith, the plane crash, escaping the terrorists, Dr. Insect, the firefight, and then the jump into Moncrief, Canada.

Blake nodded and gestured. On occasion he stared out to the deck, still listening, thinking, piecing together the mosaic that Matt was describing. Of course, he mentioned Lantini, almost obsessively so . . . *that bastard.* At a significant pause, Blake motioned for him to stop.

"You mentioned the vice president sent you on the no-notice mission to link up with some special ops guys at Fort Bragg, and then you have this Colonel Rampert guy coming to your house asking about Z-man, right? And you're still worried about these rocker dudes, the Stones, right?"

"Right," Matt said.

"Okay, first question is, Why have you talked more about Lantini, Hellerman and Rampert than you have the enemy?"

Matt stared at him a moment.

"Think about it. You've got Zachary in the hands of an international terrorist and the nation under attack. Your instincts are the best I've ever seen, and you're talking about these three bubbas. What gives?"

"They're central to everything," Matt said slowly.

"How central?" Blake asked suspiciously.

"That, bro, is the question."

"Sounds like we need to go to wide field of view."

Matt smiled. It was just like when they would hang out every day as teenagers. Blake was always good at helping Matt see the forest through the trees.

"Let me read it back to you," Blake said. "You've got Zachary in captivity somewhere, probably being held as a hostage in exchange for something. You've got a special ops commando colonel with intense interest in the Z-man. Then you've got a tape that sounds like it might be a conspiracy to start the first Gulf War." Blake was ticking off the points as if he were responding to an oral comprehensive exam for a master's degree. "You've got some missing Predator drones, and then you've got this Dr. Insect guy that you think has done something to make the Predators able to communicate."

"Don't forget about Lantini," Matt said.

"We'll get to him in a minute. So what you're dealing with is the fact that your brother is both in captivity and expendable to the government. You may have uncovered a conspiracy, and you may have the information to prevent a major, perhaps cataclysmic, attack on the country."

"About right."

Blake added another layer of analysis. Matt listened and was reminded that Blake had a rare acumen for discerning the precise heart of the matter.

"You're trapped. You've got two or three people that you think might be involved in a conspiracy not only twelve years ago, but maybe even today. I agree. There's some connectivity between the tape and today; otherwise, they wouldn't be looking for it. Bottom line is, you want Zachary back alive, but you also have a conscience with respect to your service to the nation. And you can help. You know some things that can help. It's just a piece of information or two that you need."

"Again, right on."

"So tell me what you think the gouge is," Blake said.

"Well, I'm trying to be objective about this, but I can't help but think Lantini is driving this bitch from somewhere afar. Then I think about Colonel Rampert from special ops. Zachary said, 'Get the colonel.' And Rampert was in the first Gulf War. He mentioned to me that he had met Ballantine. 'Face to face' is how I think he put it. He also operates in circles that would have access to ambassadors and intelligence operatives. He would be able to reach across the spectrum of political and military heavyweights with a fair amount of gravitas and authority."

"Face to face? Huh." Blake scratched his chin, then offered a counterpoint. "Maybe Zachary was saying, 'Get the colonel so he can help us'? Or maybe there's an entirely different colonel? It would make sense to me that the colonel he is talking about is someone who he knew from Desert Storm or before. Weren't all these bubbas 'colonels' in Desert Storm? But what I'm hearing is that we have to figure out whose voice is on that tape, and that should crack the code as to who might be allied with Ballantine, correct?"

Matt thought a moment. "Roger, they were. And, correct, it seems plausible that it could be Rampert to me," Matt said. "Maybe I'm just too focused on Lantini."

"You don't say that with a whole lot of conviction, bro. Who else could it be? Think about all of the new points of contact you've had in the last few months. Anybody?"

"Well, there's Peyton."

"You still need to introduce me. My question is, Where'd you first meet her?"

"When the vice president called me and told me to go to Fort Bragg, she was already at my house," Matt said, his voice trailing off toward the end.

"The vice president?"

"Yes, you know, Hellerman."

Blake took a sip of his coffee, smacked his lips, and looked at Matt. "Isn't that a little unusual?"

"What's that, meeting with the vice president?"

Blake nodded.

"Maybe," Matt said. "He wanted to use me on a special task force for terrorism."

"How did he contact you?"

"Well, that's actually how I met Peyton. Like I said, the vice president sent her out to my house to get me to come to the meeting. I had disconnected my phone."

"She works for the vice president?" Blake asked suspiciously.

Matt looked at Blake without speaking, then nodded. "I see your point."

Blake gave him a quizzical stare and stood. He walked over to the door, opened it, and stepped outside, looking up at the sun. "Man, we've got a problem," Blake said.

Matt stood and walked onto the deck, taking in the chill and the sun hanging low to the southeast. "I don't think there's any way that she is involved in this, or that the vice president is, for that matter."

"Theoretically speaking, the vice president could be our man, and O'Hara could be his spy," Blake said.

Matt considered the comment. "Okay, I'll play along. If your theory is correct, that would mean he has contact with Ballantine and is involved with the terrorist attacks on America—theoretically speaking—and that would make him our man on the tape as well."

"It would. Hence, we've got a problem." Blake ran his hand across his face and then through his long hair. Matt sat in one of the deck chairs, observing the fog lifting ever so slowly from the crags in the mountains.

"And that brings us to Zachary," Matt said, "who is my main concern."

"Naturally. I think we needed to work through all of that to get to what is important. Whether it's Lantini, Rampert, or Hellerman, Zachary is alive and that's huge."

"That's right, and I think Zachary was a surprise to whoever the contact is."

"But he was with Rampert for the last ten months, you told me," Blake said. "How could that be a surprise?"

"Right. What probably happened there, if it is Rampert, is he knew, but wanted to keep the secret from Ballantine, though that doesn't really make sense."

"Unless he's a cruel son of a bitch who likes to play games and wanted to feed Zachary to the lion's den up there and give his buddy Ballantine a crack at him before he came to kill you. I mean, what is this nonsense about a one-man mission? I'm not in the military, but I've read enough to know you don't ever send one guy to do anything," Blake said.

"Good point. Rampert told me that Zachary had been in a coma until recently, when he became fully functional again. Apparently, physically he was okay a long time ago, but psychologically he was slow to recover."

"So the actions with Zachary indicate that it might be Rampert," Blake said, trying to nail down a point.

"Right, I'll buy that. Rampert could have been grooming him to go into Moncrief as part of some type of deal he cut with Ballantine. Your 'no one-man missions' theory. He hides my brother from us, retrains him, gives him a new identity, and then sends him on a suicide mission." Matt paused, shaking his head.

"Doesn't make sense unless he wanted Zach dead, really," Blake offered.

"But, then again, the actions with me might indicate it was Hellerman," Matt said.

"How so?"

"Just look at what happened. As you pointed out, all of a sudden I get a visit from a good-looking babe. Then I get a phone call to meet Hellerman at the airport, and I'm off to Fort Bragg, but my plane gets hijacked to Vermont. It's almost as if he knew what was going down."

"As if he was feeding *you* to the lion's den."

"Right. An eye for an eye. Zachary killed Ballantine's brother. Maybe his goal is to kill me. But he didn't kill Zachary, he *took* him. Why?" Matt said.

"To exchange for the tape?"

"I've thought about that, but the tape seems to benefit the contact more than Ballantine, though it could be a sort of insurance policy for Ballantine, to hold the contact in check," Matt said.

"I agree."

"And it's not likely that Hellerman would have known about Zachary being alive. If Rampert's a good guy, he wouldn't tell a soul."

"That's reassuring," Blake said, scoffing at the notion.

"Then there's Lantini. Maybe he's orchestrating the entire thing," Matt said.

"But can you really believe that any of these guys would actually participate in the killing of thousands of Americans?"

"Lantini helped start a war in the Philippines, and he denied me the shot on AQ senior leadership," Matt replied.

Blake nodded and took a moment to think, then said, "Could be a financial motive, could be something else. Ideological maybe."

"Not sure I buy the financial motive thing." Matt stopped talking and stood. He walked over to the railing of the deck, staring straight ahead at the mountains. The thought came tunneling back to him like the Metro train barreling into Union Station.

"What is it, bro? You've got that look," Blake said.

"The meeting that I went to with the vice president at Dulles airport. He asked me to think about this thing called 'secular spiritual stagnation,' a condition envisioned by Walt Rostow . . ."

"Yeah, I know, his sixth stage of economic growth," Blake said. "Rostow's fifth stage was high mass consumption, where we just buy stuff. Very materialistic. Because he wrote the book in the late fifties, he didn't know what would follow, but predicted it would be a kind of 'every man for himself,' lack-of-spirit, lack-of-unity environment."

"Right, forgot you were a genius. Anyway, the vice president went on about how the nation is adrift—no national spirit, and so on. Not sure I agree, by the way, but come to think of it, he seemed to know an awful lot about Ballantine. Of course, that could have been intelligence."

"So we've got three suspects," Blake said, "that could lead us to Zachary. You've already said, though, that Rampert didn't seem to know where Z-man is. But that could either be a ploy, or the possibility exists that Ballantine may be jacking with Rampert. Then Lantini, who you seem fixated on. Is there something there?"

"All three are plausible."

"That's right," Blake said. "And don't forget that you may be the target."

Matt nodded.

"Maybe I can talk to Meredith about him, see what she thinks." Matt looked away. The thought of Meredith caused him to pause.

"Think that's a good idea? What's that *X-Files* saying? 'Trust no one'?"

Matt smiled. "I think it's 'The truth is out there.'"

"Depends on which show you watch, I guess. So where do we go from here?"

"We?"

"Yeah, we," Blake said. "You don't think I'm going to let you do this alone, do you?"

Matt paused. He had been away too long. He had pushed away his family and his friends so that he could wallow in his self-pity. That had to stop.

"Yeah, man. I'm glad you're here," Matt admitted, looking at Blake.

"I've always been here, bro," Blake said, hugging Matt. "It's going to be okay. We'll find him."

Matt broke the embrace and walked down the steps of the deck to the field in the back. Blake followed. "First, we need to confirm who the voice on the tape is. That will give us some leverage against both Ballantine and the contact. For the time being, we need to assume that all three—Lantini, wherever he is, Rampert, and Hellerman—are all bad guys. Assume the worst."

"I agree."

"Okay, then we need to find the contact, once we confirm his identity, and use the tape to get Zachary back. I've already planted that seed with Rampert."

"The tape for Zachary? I like it. Okay, let me head back down to Virginia Beach. I've got a couple of rat-holes I want to check. I'll get back with you tomorrow. My sense is that we don't have much time."

"That's right. And Blake, there's something much larger hanging in the balance here. I can feel it."

"Well, if you can feel it, then it's happening. I know that much, dude."

They walked around the front of the house, where Matt noticed Blake's new Honda Super Hawk. "Sweet."

"You can touch her, but I'm afraid we're going to have to wait for you to take her for a spin. I've got a mission." Blake grabbed his helmet and said, "I'll call you tonight. In the meantime, be careful about your bed partners."

"No problem."

Blake revved the engine, pulled down his face shield, kicked the bike into gear . . . then stopped. The engine sputtered. Lifting his face shield, he said, "Almost forgot. The dudes at the Pilots Quarters said, 'hello.'"

"Burns and that crowd?"

"Yeah, he and Austin."

"Burns getting any yet?"

"No, but Austin's got hooker problems from Baltimore," Blake said.

"That crew's always got something going on."

"You're telling me," Blake said, laughing. "Get this, Austin was out fishing for cobia last night—caught a killer about thirty pounds—said he saw a plane with *bat wings* land on a merchant ship . . ."

"He smoking weed or what?"

"No, he gets kicked around being a legacy there and all—what?" He stopped in mid motion of popping his visor back down when he saw Matt's eyes widen.

"Wait a second," Matt shouted, holding up his hands. "Wait just a second. What did that plane look like again?"

Blake took off his helmet. "He said it was small."

"Were the wings below or above the fuselage?"

"Above. Why?"

"Bat shaped, like a stealth plane?"

"He didn't mention stealth, but he did say bat wings."

"What was the name of the ship? Country of origin?"

"Chinese I think."

"That could be Ballantine's Sherpa."

"Wait a second, Matt—"

"That bastard landed on a Chinese merchant ship? Are you kidding me? China is involved in this thing?"

"No way. Could have just been an executive getting there from the shore."

"No, it was Ballantine," Matt said. "I saw him fly away from Lake Moncrief."

The two friends stared at each other for a moment.

"And if Ballantine's there, Zachary is there," Matt continued.

"Sounds like we need to contact some authorities," Blake said.

"No. *Trust no one*, remember?"

"Right."

"No. Ballantine wants me," Matt said. "This is personal. I'm not letting Zachary down again."

"I hear you, bro, but you never let Zachary down to begin with. If you want to do this, then count me in. I'm sure we can develop a plan in the next few hours. Why don't you follow me to the beach?"

"I like it. We'll take your boat out tonight, scope it out, and come up with a plan. You go ahead, and I'll meet you at your house."

"You bringing this Peyton O'Hara?"

"She's been with me from the start," Matt said.

"Could be part of the issue, but your call."

"Sure you can't remember the name of the ship?"

"The 'One Hung Low,'" Blake laughed.

"I'm serious, Blake."

"I know," he said, shifting his helmet in his hands. He looked at Matt with a shrug. "*Fong How*, something like that."

Matt paused, remembering the Japanese ship *Shimpu: Divine Wind*. And he knew what *Fong Hou* meant as well. He nodded, recalling what the insect scientist had told him.

"What?"

"Queen Bee. *Fong hou* means 'queen bee' in Mandarin," Matt said.

"If that's right—" Blake started.

"It's right, and making more sense by the minute. Listen, I'm going to tighten up some things here, get some supplies, and then meet you at your house this afternoon."

With that, Blake slipped his helmet back over his head and popped down his visor. The Super Hawk's engine roared to life and sped along the gravel.

Matt watched him turn to the south and disappear. He walked to the back of the house again and came up the deck steps, crossed the deck, and stepped into the den. He stopped, cocked his head, and stepped back outside, looking directly above him.

The curtains from his open bedroom window were swaying with the breeze.

CHAPTER 44

FONG HOU CONTAINER SHIP, CHESAPEAKE BAY

"How did you do it?" Ballantine asked Admiral Chi Chen.

They were sitting in the captain's quarters of the *Fong Hou* as it moored in the deep water of Chesapeake Bay. Chen was dressed in a white uniform with an unbuttoned coat. He held a glass of sake, a Japanese rice wine that he had come to enjoy.

English was the only common language between the two men.

"Do what?" Chen asked, looking out the large circular porthole.

"Turn this thing into an aircraft carrier."

"Would you like drink first?" Chen asked.

"No, I want to get acquainted with the ship," Ballantine said. He really did want a drink to dull some of the pain. He had slept most of the day after the precarious landing in the darkness and awakened a few hours ago, stiff and unable to move his left arm. He had downed another Percocet and was still waiting impatiently for it to bestow its numbing effects.

"Very well, follow me," Chen said, standing.

They walked out of the small cabin and down a narrow set of stairs. Ballantine had not spent any time on a ship and was surprised at how little room there actually was to maneuver. It was single file everywhere he went. They continued down a circular staircase and then popped out onto a deck that overlooked the shipping containers.

As they walked, Chen turned to look at Ballantine. "Your injuries, serious?"

"No. I'll be okay."

"You're brave warrior, Ballantine. I am happy to be allied with you," Chen said.

"And I with you," Ballantine responded.

"And your friend in brig, what is his purpose?"

"He is simply a means to an end."

They reached the railing of the deck that overlooked the entire ship. Ballantine could see containers stacked nearly seventy feet into the air, almost eye-level with the bridge.

"*Fong Hou* built to exceed size of largest merchant ship in world, *Sovereign Maersk.* Danish ship," Chen said. "This ship three hundred eighty meters long and fifty meters wide," he said, pointing in both directions across the ship's bow.

The superstructure of the ship was positioned all the way at the aft end, and they looked out over 300 meters of ship to their front.

"Three hundred thirty meters only one thousand feet of runway. No problem for Sherpa, but Predator require two thousand feet for takeoff. So we make like aircraft carrier, with catapult."

"I see. Good job on building these containers to conceal the runway," Ballantine said. "I was unprepared for that when I landed. Good thing that I didn't come in too high."

Chen smiled. "My instructions to stay low, right?"

"Yes."

"These containers," Chen said pointing at the top row, "they have openings. Forty-millimeter Bofors inside—anti-aircraft guns can quickly rotate out and elevate. We can use them in anti-air or anti-ship mode."

"Impressive."

"Yes, best of Chinese engineering to develop this ship past ten years. Most impressive is runway to solve problem of length. Come, I show you."

"When can I see our precious cargo?"

"Soon," Chen assured him as he motioned Ballantine forward.

They returned to the stairwell and spiraled all the way down to an exit door that opened to a giant garage-like structure. Ballantine looked up and could see the ship had been built with a shell that stepped from the rails on either side upward to the center. Huge I-beams created an inverted stairway of sorts that allowed Chen to stack containers on top of the shell that made it appear to the outside observer that the ship was full of containers. In reality, though, there existed a 100-foot-wide and 1,000-foot-long runway inside the shell.

"Amazing," Ballantine said. He saw his plane parked to the side. A ground crew had pushed it into a corner.

"Look here," Chen said, walking him onto the runway, complete with centerline striping.

"Unbelievable," Ballantine said.

"Centerline groove holds catapult, just like aircraft carrier. Our flight engineers modify Predator landing gear so we can control during takeoff. We tested in Pacific Ocean on way over."

Ballantine looked at him.

"It worked perfectly. Because Predator only needs one thousand feet to land, we bring it aboard safely using tail hook and cable system as added precaution."

"So you still have all of your Predators?" Ballantine asked.

"Yes, of course. Mission calls for this. And yours? You still have them?"

"The Predators are hidden in a cave, but the ground control station was captured by the Americans," Ballantine admitted. "So my two are useless for now."

"How do we strike those targets?"

"Well, I may have to take one down with my Sherpa," Ballantine said.

They walked along the centerline catapult. Ballantine could see that the lane went the length of three football fields. "Why does it look like we are enclosed?"

"Ah, we make other addition." Chen walked to the wall and pointed at a series of buttons not unlike a garage door opener. "These control bow of ship. They make flat. Add forty meters more to runway. Allow Predator to stabilize after leaving catapult. And of course, runway completely concealed from satellites."

"You have outdone yourself, Admiral," Ballantine admired. "Let's look at our cargo."

"Of course."

They reentered the stairwell and walked down another level into a much smaller compartment about the size of an underground parking garage. Ballantine immediately saw the Predator UAVs.

"Here they are." Chen swept his hand across the UAVs sitting on the flight deck like angry hornets. Their inverted wings and large heads made them appear decidedly insect-like—hibernating wasps inside an evil lair. "Fifty-foot wingspan, thirty-foot length. UAV can fly five hundred miles from ship and, if target area is bad, we can recall home. We use stealth technology from downed American aircraft in Kosovo air war in 1999. Combination of structural makeup and low-speed flight capability help in radar avoidance. Through ground control station, we can program each for specific grid coordinate. Once in air, they can fly to target alone . . . and have ability to converge in pairs on separate targets or mass on single target."

"What about what the scientist gave us. Is it reliable?" Ballantine asked.

Chen stared at Ballantine a moment. "Predators programmed appropriately to swarm if target is identified. If not, they destroy priority targets in sequence. However, I must admit, I am concerned that your 'Dr. Insect' has been captured."

Ballantine looked at Chen. "I think it will be okay."

"Now, this switch"—Chen was pointing at a similar device used for lowering the bow of the vessel one level up—"opens deck above, and this switch raises platform."

"Just like an aircraft carrier," Ballantine confirmed.

"Only better. Everyone thinks I have plastic Barbie dolls on board, not Predators and weapons-grade uranium."

"How have you containerized the material?"

"Our scientists only have enough material to create four bombs. Others will carry nerve gas," Chen said.

"So the ruse worked. Develop these chemical and nuclear weapons, secretly ship them to China and Canada, and then entice the Americans into Iraq. Brilliant. Have you reviewed the target list?" Ballantine asked, running his hand atop one of the Predator drones.

"Yes, we have prepared UAVs with preprogrammed grid coordinates. One dirty nuke, as you say, will go into Fort Bragg 212 miles from here. Another will hit naval base only twenty miles from here, and another will hit Pentagon 190 miles to north. Last is for target of your choosing."

"Thank you. And the chemical bombs?" Ballantine asked.

"Chemical bombs go into Philadelphia to north and Raleigh, North Carolina, to south. That should sufficiently set conditions for follow-on attacks," Chen said.

"I should say so. How are our communications with our sleeper cells?"

"They are good. We will go to communications center next. I believe you will be satisfied and that you will find it suitable for your international television appearance tonight."

"I will be satisfied when our mission is complete, Admiral." Ballantine's voice was dark and tense.

They reentered the spiral staircase and climbed to the top of the bridge into a Plexiglas enclosed communications hub. It contained computerized digital display screens, radio banks, satellite hookups, television screens and two digital cameras.

"Before this camera is where I will make my presentation tonight?" Ballantine asked.

"Yes. Has satellite uplink, and we can tap into major cable stations such as CNN and Fox News. We tested ten-second broadcast last week. We blasted digitally into their bandwidth and dominated spectrum. We watch on our satellite televisions and see our encoded message."

"What was the message?" Ballantine asked.

"Phase Two."

"Phase Two? Don't you think that's a bit risky?"

"Perhaps, but Americans have no sense of this threat. Their soldiers fight and die overseas. Right now, they huddle in their gated communities."

Ballantine shook his head. "Okay, I will broadcast at 2100 hours tonight. Nine p.m. As the Americans say, prime time."

"Okay, we relax for while, then. Satisfactory, General Ballantine?"

"Yes, Admiral Chen, quite satisfactory. I believe we can have that drink you mentioned."

CHAPTER 45

ABOARD THE FONG HOU, CHESAPEAKE BAY

Zachary Garrett felt a surging pain rocket through his upper back as he rolled over. He wasn't sure where he was, though he seemed to be realizing *who* he was. A step in the right direction, he figured.

The room faded in and out of view as if his mind were a camera, recklessly zooming in and out. The image of Matt hovered in his mind like a rising sun crawling out of the ocean's horizon.

His short-term memory allowed him to think back to two nights before, when he had been bound to the chair. The black woman had left the room, and then suddenly Matt had appeared from nowhere. Then they were separated just as quickly.

His mind began to steady a bit. He could feel the tightness in his back and he remembered being shot. Having been shot before, he knew the feeling of a bullet slapping him in the back. He remembered falling into his brother's arms and how good it felt to be held by him, if only for a moment. He could see in Matt's face the anguish, the hope, and the love of a brother who had probably not accepted his disappearance. For all he knew, Matt and the rest of his family had considered him dead and would have had a funeral service for him.

Zachary sat up, the drugs wearing off enough that he was able to steady himself. He studied his new environs, trying to make sense of the white walls and bars, like an animal cage. He found himself laughing inside, wondering whether he could possibly be in a zoo, but somehow he knew that was not right. He had so many conflicting thoughts and emotions that he was having a hard time making sense of anything.

He couldn't hear anyone and saw nothing but a sterile hallway beyond his cell. He continued to feel a bit groggy, lightheaded. He slid onto his knees and slowly crawled over to the edge of the cage. Now he really did feel like an exhibit at the zoo, crawling around, dragging his heavy legs, limping on his left arm as he tried to maneuver himself.

Reaching the edge of the cage, Zachary stuck his face between two bars, pressing against them until he could go no further without getting his head stuck. He shifted his eyes to the right and then the left without noticing anything of significance.

He began to pull back, then wedged his face in again, this time until it hurt. He turned his head just a bit to the right to try to understand what he thought he had seen.

A fire hose and axe were encased in glass on the opposite wall about twenty feet away. While that was unusual, the most interesting part of his discovery was that Chinese or Japanese characters were inscribed beneath the casing.

Zachary pulled his head from between the bars and slid back to the far wall. He looked around again. There was nothing.

A cage. A fire hose and axe. Chinese writing. Where the hell am I?

CHAPTER 46

MIDDLEBURG

Vice President Hellerman paced the grand living room of his estate, the plush carpet sinking beneath his feet with every step. It was Tuesday afternoon. He had taken a break from the alternate command post across the lawn, the incessant activity of attacks, reports, analysis, and meetings all proving to be a stimulant. He needed to step away from the operations center before he became too excited.

As he stood in his living room, he could feel the eyes of James Madison and Thomas Jefferson upon him as they peered down from their portraits. He thought about the paintings that hung in his official mansion in the Naval Observatory in Bethesda. So many vice presidents, forgotten men who did so little. He could hardly name five of them, and he was a history buff. The thought put a fine accent on the moment, this moment in time.

Yes, the people would remember him as the one who had reunited the country for generations to come. But, frankly, it was not so much the recognition that would rightfully fall his way, but the resurgence of an ideal borne out of repression and tyranny over 230 years ago. They would begin to mix his name with the likes of Revere, Madison, Monroe, Jefferson, and Hamilton—all great statesmen willing to risk everything for a greater good.

Who could argue with the need? The country was polarized, he mused as he stared at a fifteenth-century Chinese Ming vase. He didn't think it was anything special, nothing a third-year art student couldn't do with some practice.

He stared at James Madison's portrait. Looking like so many of the others from that era, he had the white wig and the pale, angular face that the artist touched with a hue of pink. A white ruffled shirt protruded from beneath his top coat. Madison had a hand placed lightly on a chair.

"Mr. Madison," Hellerman said, smiling as he spoke to the portrait, "the violence of factions, as you accurately predicted, have begun to undo us. You founded our government very wisely upon the very principle that factions at both ends of the spectrum would undermine the majority mainstream. These factions, you predicted, would try to morph the government into something that best looked after their respective interests."

He stepped away to take the picture in, almost waiting for Madison to nod, as if to say, *Go on.*

Hellerman continued. "As you so eloquently commented, it was the creation of government institutions that provided for the channeling of the very violence that those factions propagated. That's what made the American form of government work, the diffusing of anger, the outrage, and discontent through representatives at the local, state, and federal level. Any American has multiple people with whom he can express his disgust on any given topic."

He was enjoying himself now. He visualized Madison there, taking him in, pondering his genius and his ability to connect it all.

"But all of that was predicated on a firm center. That firm center, in my view, has eroded and given way to a polarized nation, like the heavy weights at either end of a barbell. And what has done that, Mr. Madison, is the media. In your time, it would take days for the word to get around. Legends were built upon myths that, as they circulated, became even more adrift from reality. Today, the television is reporting news as it happens and manipulates the public opinion instantly. People are bombarded with spinners that constantly lie in order to push across their agendas. They are the very factions you envisioned. It is a tangent that wants to become the primary."

He swirled his drink in his hand, then placed it atop a felt coaster on the antique sofa table that ran behind the leather davenport. Maker's Mark bourbon and Coke. He'd been drinking it since he had sneaked flasks into college football games to watch his jock buddies play.

"Your institutions have done their job well. This is the greatest nation on earth. We are the beacon of democracy and hope for so many, yet few understand our genius. Your genius, my genius. They don't understand the essence of what makes this country great, and now we are under assault by a decaying moral spirit. We are retreating from our foundation. And what is filling the void in the wake of our retreat is cynicism and opportunism."

He shook his fist at the portrait, his emotions overtaking him.

"What is it that we must do as a nation to return to our foundation?" Hellerman asked Madison, his voice filled with rage. "What is it that people cannot see? There is no shared sacrifice! There is no attachment to the idea of democracy, only an assault on its principles in its own name! There are those in this country who have put under siege the very courts that you, sir, created. They are using those courts to manipulate and pervert the very Constitution that you framed. All in the name of contemporary expediency!"

His arms were outstretched, fingers spread in tense anger.

"How do we reunite the country and create that common center? What would you do?"

And he knew precisely what Madison and the others had done. They had revolted and, in the process, changed the world. They had seen the wrong, and they righted it. He was doing nothing less.

Hellerman heard a noise behind him, snapping him from his soliloquy.

He saw her standing in the foyer, and it was clear she had been there for some time. Something seemed odd about her appearance. It was spring time and not overly cool, yet she was wearing a long, black overcoat that hung just above her bare ankles. Studying her, he saw she had on black heels, two inches high. Her hair was combed back and out, framing her face the way a cobra's neck flares when it is ready to strike. In one hand, she was holding a bottle of Dom Perignon. In the other she was holding a small bag.

"Hi, Trip, how are you?"

"Fine, fine," he said, a slight sheen of sweat covering his face, a product of his passionate discussion with Mr. Madison.

He walked to the sofa table, snatched his drink, and walked over to give Meredith a quick peck on the lips. Then, after stepping back, he waded into her, giving her a long kiss. She responded by dropping her long overcoat, revealing her completely naked body.

She walked past him carrying the Dom and stretched out on the sofa. She peeled away the foil covering the cork and slowly, but seductively, worked the cork out of the bottle. It popped about the same time Hellerman thought he might. The foam was running down the bottle and oozing over her warm skin.

"Want some?" she asked. She poured a steady stream onto her flat belly, a pool of the tan liquid gathering in her navel.

He was upon her, drinking the champagne from her body. They worked hard at it, sliding all over the sofa. He was normally much more careful than this, but what an entrance. And he wasn't even expecting her this afternoon, which made it seem that much more reckless, dangerous, and . . . appropriate.

At some point, Meredith had retrieved two champagne glasses from the china hutch and poured the remaining champagne into them. Hellerman excused himself for a few minutes. She presumed he was either in the restroom or popping another Viagra. She had achieved the effect she was seeking. As he dragged himself up the stairs, she watched him disappear. She quickly reached into her overnight bag, and pulled out a small vial of powdered diphenhydramine hydrochloride, the active ingredient in sleeping pills. It was enough to knock out a small pony, but she had been assured that it wouldn't kill him.

She hesitated, weighing the significance of drugging the vice president of the United States and then dumped a little over half the powder into the drink. The man had told her she could use the entire bottle and not worry about it, but better safe than sorry, she figured. Half should do the trick, erring on the side of caution. She sloshed it around as she quickly returned the vial back to her overnight bag.

She held up the glasses, checked the clarity on each, and assured herself that he wouldn't be able to tell the difference. Placing the glasses back on the coffee table, she felt a wave of sadness wash over her. She had promised herself she wouldn't get weak. Part of the reasoning behind the entrance attire and sex up front was so that she would feel detached from herself, the actions being so completely out of character.

She ran her hands along her naked body, feeling the stickiness of the champagne. She felt cheap and whorish and was glad. She deserved it. She needed one last dirty episode before she cleansed herself of this demon.

"You look great there on the sofa, like a mountain cat, sleek, stalking," he said, obviously energized. Maybe he *was* taking Viagra, or probably some amphetamine.

"Thanks, you look like a stud bull just earning a day's pay," she said with a chuckle.

He laughed as he sat next to her and rubbed her leg with one hand while reaching for the champagne with the other.

Her heart raced when she saw him snatch her glass off the table. He looked at her with a knowing grin and said, "Here you go, my dear." He handed her the glass and then retrieved his from the table.

"Cheers."

They clinked the glasses, chasing away the bad spirits, she hoped. Meredith watched him finish his champagne. He was an impatient drinker and typically downed glasses of $200-a-bottle champagne like it was a beer mug full of Stroh's Light.

It took about five minutes and was more natural than she thought it would be. Hellerman yawned and said, "Well, wildcat, I think you wore me down to a nub. I'm suddenly very tired. I think I'll take a short afternoon nap."

He settled next to her on the sofa, but she quickly stood and retrieved the quilt from the rack in the hallway. It was a typical country patchwork quilt with a sunrise design, the dawning of a new era.

He snuggled into the leather pillow and was breathing heavily by the time she placed the quilt over his naked body. She stood back and watched him for a second. His face was drooping and sagging. He made a few spasmodic twitches here and there as his body reacted both to the drugs and the stress. She surveyed the room and shook her head. The scattered clothes, empty champagne bottle, empty glasses, naked bodies, and the smell of sex reminded her of college. Except champagne bottles had replaced box wine.

She quietly retrieved her bag and slipped into the blue jeans, tennis shoes and sweat shirt she had brought along. Carrying her bag over her shoulder, she eased toward the basement door and slid down the steps. She found the door, which was unfortunately locked. Expecting this, though, she pulled out an electronic lock-picker she had purchased online.

It was a simple device that looked like a key. Once she inserted it into the keyhole, a small laser scanned the ribbing inside the lock to determine the shape. A micro blast of air then replicated the key shape, the force depressing the tumblers. The entire process took about thirty seconds. She pulled down on the lock, slid it off the hasp, and was inside Hellerman's lair.

She had not figured out what had been bothering her about last night's visit until she saw a report on the latest tallies of deaths and injuries across the country.

A Florida Bureau of Investigation team had picked up a cell-phone transmission that indicated a possible terrorist attack on the State Capitol building during a full session of the legislature. The details were sketchy, but a combination of extra security, pushing the perimeter out, and having blocking forces to prevent escape had worked. Once the terrorist vehicle entered the perimeter, SWAT teams captured two U-Haul trucks filled with explosives. They were being operated by four Latinos that, authorities later learned, had connections to Cartegena's Colombia drug cartel. This was the first real clue that the attacks were bigger than Ballantine.

Meredith had gone jogging that day during lunch and, as she rounded the Lincoln Memorial, it suddenly occurred to her. On Hellerman's list were the bombings of the Mall of America, the other malls, the Charlotte Coliseum, the apartment buildings, and even the averted one they all knew about in Atlanta.

Meredith remembered seeing Tallahassee, Florida, on the calendar as well. Nothing had happened there, and the intelligence report had just come in this morning. She checked the date and time on the message and called the Florida Bureau, who told her the arrests had gone down the previous afternoon at about five p.m. The Florida authorities had kept it top secret at the state level, fearing who might be intercepting the information at the federal level. Once the operation was complete, they were more than happy to share the information.

So unless Hellerman had some unknown connection in Florida's Bureau of Investigation, he had known about the attack before it had happened. She had been beating herself up all day trying to figure out how he could have known about it, trying to find a loophole. She kept coming back to the same place . . . that he somehow knew ahead of time.

She pulled out a small disposable camera and took two pictures of the same poster. This time she noticed a small question mark next to *Tallahassee*. While not completely incriminating, the question mark indicated that at some point today he had wondered what had gone wrong. Of course, there was still the remote possibility that it was a note to himself to follow up on an intel feed he had received.

Her gut told her she was right. He was involved. She had no clue how, but she came here to find out.

She took a quick snapshot of the radios, all displaying a different frequency. There were two Qualcomm Globalstar satellite phones in a recharge pack and two other, more normal-looking, cell phones plugged in as well. She snapped a picture of those. She opened the drawers of his desk and began opening files and snapping pictures no matter what they said. She wasn't reading any of the files. She was a one-woman assembly line. Open file, snap picture. Open file, snap picture. She was beginning to get nervous now. She had been in the basement over twenty-five minutes, and something felt wrong. Aside, of course, from the fact that she had drugged the vice president and was secretly in his basement gathering evidence that could possibly indicate a conspiracy.

When she felt that she had thoroughly canvassed the room, she turned to leave and then stopped. There was a laptop computer plugged into a modem. What the hell, she figured, so she steeled herself up and reached down, popping out the hard drive of the laptop and tossing it in her bag.

She turned off the light and closed and locked the door. Then she stopped and waited, standing perfectly still and listened.

Nothing.

She waited some more.

Still nothing.

She slowly climbed the stairs and then waited at the top of the last step before opening the door that led to the kitchen.

Still nothing.

She pushed slowly, the door making a slight creak that stopped when she had pushed it past a forty-five-degree angle. She stepped into the kitchen and slowly closed the door behind her, the squeak playing its octaves in reverse. *That's interesting*, she thought.

She stopped. Still nothing.

She stepped into the connecting hallway between the kitchen and the living room, where she could see the high back of the sofa, which was a comforting feeling. While she could not see him, she felt in her planning that if she got to this point, she could just sweet talk her way out the door. She watched the sofa as she walked toward the foyer. Despite her progress, something did not seem quite right.

She hit an angle where she could see lengthwise along the sofa.

Hellerman was not there.

She froze. The room started spinning around her like a top, large sections of the house panning toward her quickly and then away like in the horror flicks. She could hear the screeching strike of Norman Bates' knife with each image racing at her. She was hyperventilating and began to sweat.

Then a thought occurred to her.

Maybe he left. Maybe he woke up and left. After all, it was still daylight outside.

While completely irrational, it was enough to get herself under control. She still had not moved since noticing the sofa was empty. She tried moving onc leg, then another toward the foyer. It was working. She was moving. She was going to make it.

"I thought you'd left," Hellerman said from the dark recesses of the foyer, his face half-lit by a splash of sunlight cutting through the dining room window.

"I just changed," she whispered.

"Why are you whispering?" he asked, stone-faced.

"Sorry," she said louder. "When I left you were asleep and I guess I was in my 'be quiet' mode."

"Where were you?"

"I went into the kitchen and changed, honey. Didn't want to wake you. You were such an animal today, thought you'd need to rest up for tomorrow," she said, sounding better and proud of herself.

He seemed to consider that and then said, "I went into the kitchen and got some water, then took a leak in the hall bath. I didn't see you."

She swallowed hard.

"Well, I was there getting dressed and have to head back now, honey, so why don't we just drop the inquisition here and be grateful we both had some of the greatest sex in our young lives," Meredith said, moving toward the door.

"What's in the bag?" he said, moving forward.

"My coat. These clothes I'm wearing used to be in there. Remember, I showed up naked and we screwed our brains out?"

"Don't talk to me like that," he spat.

"Then quit treating me like this. You screw me until you drop, and then I'm quiet and respectful of your need for sleep, and you are giving me the third degree."

"I just didn't see you."

"Well, I saw you, thought you might be sleepwalking," she chuckled and immediately knew she had said the wrong thing.

"Why are you lying to me, Meredith? What's in the bag?" He moved closer. He was only five feet away now.

She held her key ring in her hand.

"Go to hell. You treat me like garbage and now accuse me of coming in here and stealing something?" she asked incredulously.

Hellerman lunged toward her, hands outstretched in anger. She lifted her keys and gave a long squirt of mace directly into his face, causing him to double over and scream.

She grabbed the door, darted through the entrance, forearming the storm door. As she raced down the steps, she heard the door smack back onto him.

Safely inside the car, she glanced at the front door and saw Hellerman glaring at her. She shook it off and drove slowly along the quarter-mile driveway, not wanting to alarm the Secret Service agents present.

She passed a black Lincoln Continental parked at the end of the driveway. She smiled and waved at Alvin Jessup. Jessup was no fool. He had known long ago what was going on between his boss and her. She turned east, as she always did, and could not stop the emotions escaping her as she accelerated.

She needed to talk to Matt right away. Pulling out her cell phone, she punched in his number and let the phone ring.

Then she started to cry.

CHAPTER 47

NORTHERN VIRGINIA

Jacob Olney would do just about anything for Meredith Morris. He had developed a crush on her the first day she stepped into the Pentagon two years earlier and found her way to his cubicle to sign up for a pass and a photo. He remembered how she had smiled at him, engaging him like he really mattered.

Even though it only took a minute to complete the form and then take the mug shot, she shook his hand and talked to him for what seemed like an hour, but was probably closer to ten minutes. She had asked about him, what he liked to do. He immediately launched into a nervous dissertation on his photography business and gave her his card. She had called a couple of times just to check up on him and had even stopped by once since she had been at the White House.

Jacob was a wiry, pimple-faced, thirty-year-old man with shaggy black hair. He knew she was out of his league, but he loved the way she made him feel. And even though they hadn't chatted for several months, he was delighted to receive her phone call this late afternoon. He was even more than happy to oblige her unique request to meet her at his place for him to develop a roll of film.

Tonight, she was walking into his basement with him.

"This must be why they call it a dark room." Meredith smiled nervously. They were standing in the room with only the eerie black light to see by.

"Right, it is a room, and it is dark, ergo a dark room." Jacob's voice was squeaky, as if puberty were just around the corner. She was ready to laugh, thinking it might be a joke, but she could tell he was serious. He was focused as he pressed the film into the solution in the pan.

"How has your business been lately, Jacob?" She was wearing the same clothes she had on when she left Hellerman's house and felt dirty.

"Great, Meredith. I'm making about eight hundred bucks a week on the side, lots of it tax free." He looked at her seriously. "But don't tell anybody."

"You have my word," she said, holding up her hands to emphasize the point.

"So why the big rush to get these developed?"

"They are for a project I've been working on, and I have a terrible deadline."

"Got anything to do with all these terrorist bombings?"

Meredith paused.

"Sorry, sorry, I know I shouldn't ask," Jacob said. "But I was just kinda wondering, you know. They've hit everywhere but here. North Carolina, Washington, Georgia, Boston, even Minnesota, for crying out loud. Don't you think they'd hit here, too?"

Meredith thought he sounded almost disappointed but knew it was just the way he framed his question.

"I doubt very seriously that they're done," she said.

"Really? You think they'll strike again?"

She watched as he continued to push the film around and asked, "Why don't you have one of those processors like they have at the one-hour places? Wouldn't it help your business?"

"No way," he said. "I would never let anything I take pass through one of those destruction machines. I've seen works of art destroyed because of a misfeed, and there's no way to get it back. The picture, the moment, is lost forever."

He looked at her solemnly and said, "And you know, that's a long time."

"Yes it is." She nodded. Jacob was a bit odd, but right now she needed his help.

"It'll be about thirty minutes if you want to go upstairs and have a soda or something," he said.

"Sure, but do you have a computer I could borrow also? I've got my hard drive here and was curious if I could get at some information." Meredith held up the hard drive, showing it to him.

Jacob looked at her, took the hard drive, and said, "Sure, I've got that capability, I think."

"But let's have that drink first." Meredith playfully punched him on the shoulder.

She found Jacob cute in a nerdy sort of way. He was clearly smitten with her and proud to be showing off his work. She adored how nervous he seemed when he asked her upstairs for a Coke. Seeing how she had just slept with the vice president of the United States and then sprayed him with mace, she was having a hard time feeling anything but disgusted.

"Would you prefer some wine?" he said, his voice quivering again.

Meredith was also overcoming a champagne hangover but didn't want to disappoint Jacob, so she agreed to a small glass of wine.

"Great," Jacob said. "I'll let you pick it out."

She followed him out of the dark room, which led into the main portion of the basement. They walked directly across the basement into another small room, this one cooler and darker until Jacob turned on the lights.

Meredith gasped. There were at least two hundred bottles of wine sitting labels-up in a handmade oak wine rack that covered both walls from floor to ceiling. She saw that he had organized the wines, with whites such as Sauvignon blancs, Pinot grigios, Chardonnays, Chablis, and more on the right side. On the left were the reds—the Merlots, Pinot noirs, Cabernet Sauvignons, and so on.

"Jacob, I had no idea."

"Yeah, most people just think I'm this little, geeky guy but . . ."

He didn't finish the sentence, but she almost thought he was going to say, "But I'm really hung like a horse." She chuckled. "This is fabulous."

"Thank you. Take your pick."

"Well, are you collecting, or do you drink it also?" She immediately knew this was a stupid question, one that brought him back to his point of everyone thinking he was a geek.

"I'm a connoisseur, Meredith. In addition to my photography, I like to travel to wine tastings all over the country and buy special wines. I've even cruised the Rhine during wine season and tasted all the different varieties from Frankfurt to Strasbourg."

"That's really something, Jacob," she said, then pulled out a 1972 Pinot grigio from Vicenza, Italy. She looked at him and shrugged, "Is this okay?"

"Absolutely, an excellent choice. If you recall, in 1972 Italy experienced a winter with one of its heaviest snowfalls ever, and the vineyards were able to feed off the cool mountain waters trickling into the valley from the Alps for an extra month. The grapes are a perfect mixture of tart and dry, with a slight almond background that makes for the absolute best Pinot grigio I've ever tasted."

They went upstairs and drank the wine. She had to admit that it was delicious. Before she knew it, they were back downstairs in the dark room, and the pictures were perfect, just like the wine.

"How can I ever repay you?" Meredith was pulling out her wallet as Jacob was holding up his hands, warding off her gesture.

"Please, this has been my pleasure, both to help you and to entertain you," he said. "You owe me nothing other than, perhaps, another unexpected call in the future. That way it will give me something to look forward to every day until the next time."

Meredith almost cried. Jacob was simple and sweet, but she had business to take care of, and she was ready to get to her house and review the pictures. Then it occurred to her that Hellerman would be sending the Secret Service after her, or something much worse, and the first place they would look would be her home.

On the other hand, they would never think to look here at Jacob's place. She paused and then said, "You are so sweet, Jacob, and I do have one more favor."

"Anything."

"I'm working on a sensitive project." She held up the manila envelope. "And there are some bad guys that are trying to find me."

"Really?"

"Yeah, well, I'm afraid if I go back to my place . . ." Saying the words made Meredith realize how much danger she was facing.

"Meredith, I insist. Stay here. And I have a garage, so you can park your car in there."

That was a good point, she thought. She had not considered that Hellerman would be putting the full-court press on to find her, which would include the police looking for her car.

"Jacob, I don't know what to say, but thank you."

"I have a very nice guest room with clean sheets on the bed. You can have all the privacy you need to work on your project."

She went out and drove the car into the garage, Jacob standing at the garage door watching with his hands stuffed in his pockets. She followed him in, through the kitchen this time, and down a long hallway.

"This is your room," he said. "You have your own bath, and there are some clean towels."

"I don't know what to say," Meredith said, truly at a loss for words.

"Don't say anything. I know you've got work to do, so I'll get out of your way. If you need anything, I'll be in my room," he said, pointing across the hall at his bedroom. "And in the meantime, I'll see if I can't get that hard drive squared away for you."

"Thank you," she said, giving Jacob a quick peck on the cheek. She turned and entered her room, closing and locking the door behind her. She quickly dumped the pictures out on the bed, turning on the lamp sitting atop the nightstand. She did a quick once-over of the room. It was décor-ated with a country theme, including rustic oak bookshelves and a sleigh bed. There was a tan oak bureau along the wall opposite the bed. The comforter on the bed had a pattern that included men with beards wearing top hats riding in buggies pulled by high-stepping horses.

She turned to the contents of the envelope, holding each picture up one at a time, squinting to read the writing, which was surprisingly legible. The first few were routine notes and indiscernible scribbling, almost like scraps of paper from doodling on the phone. Like the RW RW she had seen earlier. Who or what was RW? She could see Hellerman there plotting with his co-conspirators, them boring the hell out of him while he scribbled nonsense on the paper.

The next picture was of a message over secret cable from China. Her heart froze. Was there a connection between China, Ballantine, and the missing Predator drones? And then there was the Colombia connection with the aborted Tallahassee bombing.

The message read: *Must end all contact. Operation is ready. Glad to help an old friend. Must depart for passageway that connects our worlds.*

The message was dated just before the bombings began. Had Hellerman enlisted the aid of international terrorists to attack inside the United States?

She tucked her hair behind her ears and flipped through the pictures. She stopped at a picture of the wall with the calendar. She confirmed again that Tallahassee was marked and had a large question mark next to it. Her memory had been good. She next saw the pictures she had taken of the communications gear. Hellerman had a tactical satellite phone and radios with cables that ran out the back of the office. He had a satellite television installed and guessed he was using that satellite to also feed his telephone.

What did he need those communications platforms for? The long-distance equipment was state-of-the-art and would allow him to talk to anyone in the world who had a similar piece of equipment and the correct encryption technology.

The last two pictures were even stranger than the others. They were photos of a document written in Chinese and a sketch of a ship. She studied each photo, the Chinese characters unfamiliar to her.

She saw a single line of English letters which read TOP SECRET, SPECIAL CATEGORY on the very bottom of each page in fine print.

Flipping back to the sketch, she could see it was a cargo ship. But it had a long, narrow aisle drawn down the middle of its deck, almost like a road. *Curious*, she thought.

China, Iraq, Colombia! Huh, she moaned to herself. *What could it mean? Why would Hellerman be at the center of this coalition? They had been seriously concentrating on the Rebuild America project. Could this be his way? Let an attack on American soil wipe out the apathy and reunite the country in popular defiance?*

She lay on the bed, the men with top hats staring at her from the comforter. She was exhausted from all of the physical and mental activity of the last twenty-four hours and began to fade, her instincts trying to keep her awake. She had a firm grasp on some decisive information.

But perhaps it could wait.

It would have to.

CHAPTER 48

NORTHERN VIRGINIA

Vice President Hellerman struggled out of the bathroom. He had spent the last hour washing his face and cleaning the mace out of his eyes. He was slowly recovering from a drugged, drowsy feeling and could see, though his vision was a bit cloudy.

He had dressed in khakis and a sweatshirt with tennis shoes. He moved slowly but purposefully down the steps into the kitchen and through the door leading to the basement. Negotiating those steps, he was encouraged when he saw the lock on the hasp.

He pulled out his key and unlocked the door. *Has she been down here?* Everything appeared to be in order. He opened the file cabinet, and all of the files were where they belonged. In fact, there was nothing that seemed to be out of place.

Not a single item appeared to be amiss. Had she been telling the truth about changing in the kitchen? Perhaps he had been a bit scary the last few days, he figured. Maybe she did feel threatened by something he had done.

He looked at the televisions, the maps, the chart boards, and the computer. He leaned over and pressed the button to turn on his computer. He waited for it to boot up, which it usually did fairly quickly. He saw that the monitor screen was still blank, so he pressed the button again. Still nothing.

He lifted the laptop and immediately saw that the hard drive was missing. His heart sank. She had his hard drive. That was a big problem.

Everything he had done in the last fifteen years was recorded on that hard drive. He had scanned old notes and copied them in PDF format. Also, he had copied old floppy disks and CDs onto thumb drives and then had consolidated everything onto this one hard drive. After copying them, he had destroyed all of the notes, papers, disks, and drives. But having backup was not the issue.

He immediately grabbed his secure satellite phone and hit a memory button.

"Bandit, this is Rawlings," he said, using his call sign that referred to the baseball maker.

"Rawlings, this is Bandit. How nice to hear from you."

"I need you to track down Meredith Morris. You've got a file on her with her address, home phone, and cell-phone numbers, as well as some of her closer friends. She has something of mine, a hard drive, which I need back."

"Sounds simple enough. Do we need Miss Morris back?"

The voice was eerie and unnerving to Hellerman. He pictured the delight with which this particular individual enjoyed killing. He paused and thought of Meredith, then spoke. "No, Miss Morris' presence is not required."

"Fine and dandy. I'll call you soon. I presume you need your computer up and running shortly?"

"Tonight. No later than tomorrow. Got a big project I'm working on."

"Anything else?"

"Yes, if you have to find her using CallScan, then do it. It's that important," Hellerman said.

"My, that is important. Will do."

Hellerman hung up the phone. Having just ordered Meredith's death was enough to make his weakened body tremble. He felt like he might vomit, but then regained his composure.

What is one more death in this quest for national unification? he thought.

Meredith had served her purpose as both a sexual diversion and someone to keep him company as he developed his plan. He picked up his cell phone and called Alvin Jessup, who he knew was probably sitting in a car at the end of the driveway.

"Alvin, I need you to find Miss Morris. She may be in a bit of trouble, and we need to get her back here on the compound."

"Yes, sir. She left about an hour and a half ago. We'll find her," Alvin said.

"Thanks, appreciate it. It's pretty urgent," Hellerman said.

"Yes, sir. I'll let you know when we've got her."

Hellerman shut his phone and then double-checked to make sure that the hard drive really was missing. This time his stomach couldn't hold back as he ran into the basement bathroom and unleashed the poison in his stomach into the toilet. He wiped his mouth, brushed his teeth, walked back into the command cell and opened the file-cabinet drawer.

Even though he believed that he honestly had nothing to hide, he pulled the files out and began running them through his crosscut shredder one at a time.

Next he called Zeke Jeremiah, the tall Naval Academy graduate, over to his residence.

Jeremiah stood before him in a blue suit, white cotton shirt, and light blue tie, all hanging loosely off his lanky frame.

"Zeke, I need to let you in on something," Hellerman said. It had taken him only a few minutes to clean up the living room prior to Jeremiah's arrival. He motioned Zeke onto the facing davenport.

"I'm listening, sir," Zeke said, pulling out a small green notebook.

Hellerman coughed, leaned forward, and said, "I've intercepted the enemy's plan. I have evidence of a conspiracy involving former CIA director Frank Lantini to aid terrorists in attacking the United States."

Jeremiah put his pen in the crease of his notebook and looked at the vice president.

"You don't want me writing any of this down, do you, sir?"

"That's right. I've been holding onto this information until I was certain what it meant. After the Rolling Stones incident last year, I don't trust too many of our agencies these days. Being a former intelligence officer, well,

I've been doing the analysis down in my basement."

Jeremiah nodded.

"You do look a bit . . . overtaxed, sir."

"That's why I'm calling you into this thing. I need a first-rate mind helping me here. I'm concerned that once this wave of attacks is done, something bigger is heading our way."

"What could be bigger?"

"That's what I need you to figure out. I need you to work in isolation to read through this file here and tell me what you think it means." Hellerman pushed a manila folder across the table to Jeremiah, who reached out with his long, black fingers and pulled the file toward him. "Don't take it to the ops center. Just need you over here, maybe down in the basement, studying all of this."

"The basement?"

"Follow me," Hellerman said. They stood and the vice president led him downstairs. He opened the door to his lair and showed Jeremiah the basic components. "Here's the tracking chart. They were supposed to hit Florida, but never did. I think local law enforcement got in front of that one. But as you can see, the others have panned out."

Jeremiah stood, awestruck, at the vice president's research and his elaborate maps and matrix.

"How did you crack this code, sir?" Jeremiah asked, never removing his eyes from the data displayed on the wall. He took his right hand and touched each of the large squares with predicted attacks and then touched the map where the attacks had occurred, or not.

"Combination of signals intercepts and some tracking I've had some folks do to find Lantini. Pretty embarrassing, you know."

Jeremiah finally broke away from the charts and looked at the folder in his hand.

"How can I help?"

"I need you to find the link. It's in there somewhere, but I'm certain Lantini is behind this thing. He's working Ballantine, you'll see."

Hellerman paused.

"But I also think Colonel Jack Rampert is connected to this thing.

That's what I need you to find out. Spend some time down here reading through those reports.

"And find me a link to Rampert."

CHAPTER 49

VIRGINIA BEACH, VIRGINIA

Matt Garrett pushed the Porsche to 100 mph down the long, straight stretch of Interstate 64 between Richmond and Williamsburg.

"Dial this number," he said handing the cell phone and a slip of paper to Peyton, who was sitting in the passenger seat. He was wearing black dungarees and a dark navy button-down shirt with a black turtleneck underneath. She was wearing a similar outfit at his request, though she had a dark-blue denim jacket atop her black turtleneck.

"Yes, sir," she said, saluting him with her right hand.

She punched in the number and then handed him the cell phone.

"Meredith?" he said.

Peyton snapped her head toward him and mouthed the word, "What?"

He held up his hand, warding off her suspicions.

"Meredith, this is Matt. Can you hear me?"

He waited.

"Bad connection," he said, turning toward Peyton.

"I'm crushed," Peyton said.

"Meredith, I can barely hear you."

Peyton looked at him and rolled her eyes. She saw a road sign that said NORGE and figured it was no wonder he had a poor cell phone connection.

They were in the middle of nowhere.

"What? . . . Who? . . . I would hope Hellerman knows what's going on," Matt said.

Peyton looked at Matt with a quizzical expression.

"Tell her you'll call her back when we get to civilization," Peyton said.

"We're heading to Blake's. I'll call you when I get there," Matt shouted into the phone, as if that would help her understand him better.

He looked at Peyton and flipped his cell phone shut.

"Can't believe we're in the twenty-first century, I'm on an interstate, and I can't talk on the cell phone," he said.

Peyton put her hand on his leg and said, "We'll be there soon."

"Do you think we should call Rampert?" he asked her. He had been debating the issue since Blake had given him the information about the Sherpa landing on the Chinese ship. He could feel the tape in his pocket. He had some definite ideas as to whose voice was on the tape, but had not revealed those thoughts to Peyton.

"The tape for your brother. That's your plan, right?"

"Right."

"If that's the plan and you think Rampert can help you find your brother, then I think it's a possibility. You know you can't trust any of those guys, though, right?"

"I know," Matt said. He was thinking about the value of the tape. If the voice on the tape was who he thought it might be, then it would be very good evidence in a treason trial. And while it was clear that Ballantine was not acting alone, what was not so clear was whether he had inside help. The connection between the tape and the current events, he figured, could be very real.

"I'll think about it." What was hanging in the balance, it was clear, was not only the retrieval of his lost brother, but finding the possible inside man on the attack plans.

Matt continued driving, lost in his thoughts, watching familiar landmarks tick by. They passed the Hampton Coliseum and then found themselves negotiating the Hampton Roads Tunnel, cutting through Norfolk, and getting onto the Virginia Beach Expressway. They hit Atlantic Avenue and then found Blake's house in the Bay Colony subdivision.

Blake's home backed up to Broad Bay and the Lynnhaven Inlet, a deep-water tributary that fed into Chesapeake Bay near the Bay Bridge-Tunnel complex. They drove along a paved road that led them past several large mansions and ended at Blake's driveway.

"Wow, your friend Blake has it going on," Peyton said as she eyed the two-story brick home. "Nice pad."

"Blake did pretty well a couple of years ago during the stock market bubble. Got in and out at the right time."

"I'd say so," Peyton replied, stepping from the Porsche and looking beyond the house to the broadening inlet. She could see the elevated bridge of Shore Drive that spanned the mouth of the inlet where it fed into Chesapeake Bay. Silhouetted by the setting sun was the barely noticeable bridgework of the Chesapeake Bay Bridge-Tunnel.

They walked along the sidewalk, framed by a well-manicured lawn on one side and high Boxwood shrubs sitting beneath the home's tall windows on the other.

"Hey, guys, you made pretty good time," Blake said as he stepped from the front door and walked down the slate porch. He had changed from his motorcycle garb into the type of black wetsuit worn by surfers.

"Blake, this is Peyton."

"Peyton, how are you?" Matt noticed Blake was not his usually charming self.

"Doing well, thank you," she replied.

They walked inside the well-decorated home. Sandi's touches were visible everywhere. There was a mixture of surfing and beach artwork coupled with more traditional colonial themes. Somehow the couple had made the mixed decor work.

"Matt, you remember Sandi, right?" Blake asked.

The blond woman was standing next to a surfboard in the foyer. It was artwork but would probably hold up well in the waves, also. She, too, wore a dark wetsuit.

"Sandi," Matt said, kissing her on the cheek.

"Good to see you again, Matthew. We'll take care of this business." She placed her hand lightly on Matt's arm.

"Sandi, this is Peyton, a friend from Washington, D.C."

Peyton stepped forward, shook Sandi's hand, and said, "Nice to meet you."

"Okay, let's go over some initial thoughts: weapons, cameras, and so forth," Matt said, ready to get down to business.

"I spent some time on that already," Blake said. "Got a bag full of guns here and a good digital camera for nighttime pictures. Boat's out back, ready when you are. But I need to talk to you upstairs first."

They went upstairs while Sandi intercepted Peyton.

They walked into Blake's study, which had a large teak desk in the center of the room. A flat-panel computer monitor the size of a television sat in the middle of the desk facing the leather chair. Blake had furnished the room with large globes, maps, and military artwork. He was a man of many interests, boating and sea navigation ranking on the top of his list.

"I got a fax from a secret admirer of yours." Blake handed him a sheet of paper. "From none other than your former girlfriend, Meredith Morris."

"And?" Matt raised his eyebrows.

"Well, she called down here trying to reach you and said she needed to talk to you. Said you told her you were heading to my house. Telling her you were heading to my house was a questionable move in my judgment, but sometimes you get lucky."

Matt was getting impatient with his friend. "Okay, let me have it."

"She sent you this," he said, sliding three pieces of paper toward him across the desk. Matt picked up the pages and saw the photographs of the *Fong Hou* sketches that Meredith had taken in Hellerman's basement. She had scribbled a note on the first page.

Not sure what this is all about, but a large container ship with a runway down the middle could only mean bad news. Remember what Zachary saw at Ballantine's cabin.

"What did Z-man see at Ballantine's cabin, Matt?" Blake asked.

"He saw lots of things, but his first report was about some missing unmanned aerial vehicles," Matt said. Then it dawned on him. "Ballantine's got a Trojan horse with those UAVs on it. He's going to launch them with a payload right at D.C. Eighteen missing—which is enough to destroy the entire government."

"Um . . . we need to call someone," Blake said, backing away from his desk.

"Normally I'd say call Rampert and Fort Bragg, but we don't know if Rampert's involved with this tape or not," Matt said.

"Let's think about this."

Matt walked to the bay window and looked out at the lights marking the Bay Bridge-Tunnel's route across the mouth of the Chesapeake Bay. In the reflection of the window, he could see Blake's profile, his face drawn with worry.

"The ship is right there." Blake pointed through the window. "And if Hellerman or Rampert, or both, are involved in this thing, they know every move you are making, which means they know that you are at my house. They probably haven't had time to bug my stuff, so we're probably okay there, but everything up to this point has to be considered compromised."

"Right. Except our face-to-face conversations," Matt said.

"Right."

"Well . . ." Matt said slowly. "We might even have a problem there."

"Say what?"

"Roger. Remember when we were talking on the back deck of the house?"

"Yeah," Blake said, looking worried.

"Well, after you left, I went around to the back of the house and came up the deck. The window to my bedroom was open."

"As in 'Peyton opened the window to listen to us' open?"

"Possibly," Matt said.

"I opened the damn window to get some fresh air," Peyton said, walking into the room.

Blake and Matt snapped their heads in her direction. They had been so focused on the boat in the distance that they had not heard Peyton come up the steps.

"This is a private conversation," Blake said.

"I've been involved in this from the start, and I'm not going anywhere but onto that boat with you guys," she said, hands on her hips.

"How do you know about the boat?" Matt asked.

"I was sitting on the porch today when you guys were out front. Nice bike, by the way," she said to Blake.

"Thanks. So you heard everything?"

"I heard you say you saw an airplane fly onto the ship. I agree with Matt; that has got to be Ballantine. It makes sense," she said.

"What value do you add to this operation?" Blake asked. "Why do you need to come along?"

Matt stepped in. "Peyton's been by my side the entire way."

"That could be part of the problem," Blake said, still looking at her.

"Could be, but it's not," Peyton said, locking eyes with Blake.

"Where did you come from, O'Hara?"

"I'm from Boston, Sessoms," she said. "What are you worried about, the fact that the vice president sent me to Matt's house, or the fact that I'm part Irish and actually knew a few IRA freedom fighters?"

"What bothers me is that you're next to my best friend and I have to trust you completely, because if anything happens to him, then I'm going to be really pissed off," Blake said.

"Okay, team, let's just cool it here," Matt said. "While we're at it, though, Peyton, tell me why you *really* need to be here."

"You guys are both such jerks," she said. "I want to be involved in this thing because I have a stake in this, too!" She had raised her voice now. She poked her finger at the ground to emphasize her point.

"What stake is that?" Matt asked.

"It's my country, too, Matt. Damn it, why can't you trust me?" she shouted. "Tell me that. Why am I a suspect when all I've done is try to help you?"

She was crying now, the tears streaming down her face. Matt walked over to her and pulled her close. She crossed her arms, and he pressed her into his chest, feeling her heave against him. She was strong, but she still had emotions. There had been an enormous amount of stress, and even Matt wondered how he was able to hold up.

Then it occurred to him that Peyton *had* been by his side, and that was one reason why he had crawled from his shell and was able to operate now. Peyton had been there for him.

Why couldn't he have seen that? How could he have been so unfair?

"I'm sorry," he said.

"You're damned right, you're sorry. I've done nothing but support you and asked for nothing in return," she whimpered into his chest.

Blake quietly slid out of the study and waited in the hall just outside the open doors.

"It's okay. I appreciate what you've done, Peyton. I really do. I know I've been focused on so many other things—"

"Stop. Don't. You don't need to explain anything," she said, pulling away and wiping her eyes. "I know what you're facing, and I know what the country is facing. The odds are terrible, and I am just quietly trying to support you."

"I understand."

Blake returned. "Is it safe to come in? Are we good?" he asked, looking from one to the other. "Okay, then. With that out of the way, we should probably get going here."

As they broke the embrace, Matt noticed Peyton's eyes dance with alarm as she looked at the sketch of the *Fong Hou* that Meredith had faxed. Matt motioned to Blake, who was loitering in the hallway just outside the study door.

"Okay," Matt said, pulling out a piece of paper from Blake's printer and leaning on the desk. "We'll head out of the inlet to the ship." He drew a rough sketch of the inlet, the bay, the bridge-tunnel, and the location of the ship in relation to those geographical features.

"Moon is coming out at eleven p.m., so we need to be away from the ship before that. Gives us about two hours to scout it out," Blake said.

"Okay, we're looking for hull ladders. Every ship has ladders that go up the hull," Matt said, pointing upward with one hand. "We want to identify our point of entry and exit."

"What precisely are we looking to do tomorrow night?" Blake asked.

"Well, we have two objectives. The first is to get Zachary back, alive," he said, looking at Blake. "The second is to destroy the ship's ability to launch those UAVs."

"Right, but how?" Peyton wondered aloud.

"This ship plan here . . ." Matt said, pulling Meredith's fax onto the desk. "This thing shows the runway down the center aisle of the ship."

"It's weird, bro. Gary said he saw containers stacked to the sky on that bad boy," Blake said.

Matt looked at him.

"Maybe it's just a shell. Maybe the runway is beneath the shell of those containers," Peyton said. "They would have to know about our satellite capabilities."

They both looked at her and then at each other. Matt thought it was possible, but it was a huge engineering feat that would have required years of thought, planning, and construction.

"I think there's a good possibility you're right, Peyton. China's no friend." Blake patted Peyton on the back lightly.

"That would mean this conspiracy dates back at least ten years," Matt said. "Kind of makes you wonder what else has occurred in those ten years—what other Trojan horses are out there."

"So we find the runway and these UAVs," Blake said.

"No. The ground control station is what we're after. The UAVs are useless without the terminal. So instead of having to take out eighteen UAVs, we need to disable one ground control station. If we get the station, I think we'll destroy whatever capability Dr. Insect built into these Predators. The station looks like this," Matt said, pulling out a sheet of paper with a picture on it. "This isn't exact, but it was the best I could do on the Internet yesterday."

"Looks like a computer terminal inside a refrigerator," Blake said.

"Right. But the distinguishing feature of this puppy is that it has a unique antenna on it that looks like the Space Needle. We find that antenna on the ship, we know the general location of the ground control station," Matt said.

"You're a genius," Blake acknowledged.

"I know."

"Now for Zachary," Matt continued, moving to the next sheet of paper. "This shot of the ship's interior rooms is almost like a blueprint."

"Okay," Blake said, staring at the diagram.

"Anyway, there's a section of rooms right here that are labeled," Matt said, pointing at the diagram. "It shows these rooms here as service rooms. And everything else, if you think about it, kind of fits what we believe that thing really is, which is an aircraft carrier. These rooms are the only place they could confine someone."

Matt's finger smacked the map emphatically.

"He has to be there," he said.

"So, we look for the ladders that will get us closest to where Zachary and the space needle are," Blake said.

"Roger. Let's rock," Matt said, pushing the papers away and walking toward the door.

Blake, Matt, and Peyton walked out the back door along a dimly lit path to the dock and stepped into Blake's Boston Whaler.

"Why not the Zodiac?"

"Save that for tomorrow night. I'd rather only run that puppy one time past the big boat."

They shoved off with Blake cranking the low humming engine and the Mercury 200 shaking in the water on low throttle.

Matt looked at Peyton, who was staring into space, arms folded and a decidedly worried look on her face. She was an enigma. She had come out of nowhere, crashed into his life, and suddenly his fate and the fate of the free world hung in the balance. Was it just coincidence, he wondered, or was there something more to it? Was she by his side because of Providence? Or had she been delivered to him by someone with more nefarious intentions? Was she good or evil?

As the Boston Whaler carved a quiet path into the broadening waters of Lynnhaven inlet, Matt could see the boat docks and yachts dotted along either side of the waterway. The still water of the inlet met mostly bulkheads, which gave way to well-manicured lawns and estates ranging from contemporary to traditional. Was this evidence of Hellerman's notion of high mass consumption, or were these mansions symbols of freedom matured and refined over the years? The country was so insulated, so disconnected from the military and the global war. It was almost as if the country's spirit *was* adrift.

Matt froze at the thought. There was no question in his mind that Hellerman was connected to Ballantine somehow. He could feel his adrenaline pumping, not unlike standing in the batter's box at the bottom of the ninth inning with two outs, needing a hit to keep the rally going.

Blake made the turn past Chick's Bar and Restaurant and aimed for the Lynnhaven Bridge. Matt felt the boat toss and pitch as Blake maneuvered the small craft through the rapid current where the Chesapeake Bay funneled through a narrow gap into Lynnhaven Inlet. He recognized the DANGER, NO SWIMMING and DANGER, FAST CURRENT signs flanking the passage. There was even one featuring the count of how many people had drowned in this very small area.

"Up to forty-eight, huh?"

"Yeah, pretty sad, man. Had a kid, maybe fifteen, a few weeks ago think he was invincible. Tried to swim the channel on a dare," Blake said, pointing a football field away to the north where the shore reappeared and the Lesner Bridge reconnected with land. "Kid was maybe thirty yards into the water when he shot out to the bay like he was being dragged by a shark. They were doing it at night. All his friends on the shore were screaming. By the time they found him, he had drowned."

"No place to screw around, that's for sure."

Blake navigated the bridge pylons, each one a different angle, appearing like some nouveau form of artwork. As they cleared the bridge and officially entered Chesapeake Bay, Matt saw the Duck Inn off to his right and the lights from the Bay Bridge-Tunnel ahead and to the left.

The quiet hum of the Boston Whaler's Mercruiser engine was the only noise against the peaceful backdrop of a black night and the still waters of Chesapeake Bay. Matt looked at Peyton again, who seemed fixated on the distant horizon, many things no doubt running through her mind. Could he trust her? What was it that made him think he could not? Ballantine was ruthless, yet she had received medical treatment in captivity. And then there was the Irish Republican Army connection. Was that a true story? If so, had she gone native, as they say? What was her purpose in this operation? And there was something else, he couldn't put his finger on it just yet, but it was close. Was her presence near him Hellerman's way of keeping him close?

Or was she Lantini's intermediary? His cutout? These thoughts darted through his mind like tossed boomerangs, always circling back.

One thing he did know, however, was that when a batter stepped into the batter's box, he had to believe he was going to rap a line drive into the gap. He had to know he could beat the pitcher, no matter how good his stuff. So, there was no time for a lack of confidence or doubts about partners.

"Over there. See that giant black spot against the horizon?" Blake said, pointing.

"Roger, I've got it," Matt said.

"I see it," Peyton echoed.

"That's the *Fong Hou.* We'll swing wide like we're going through the channel and then come back on its bow."

"Okay. That should give us a view of the UAV antenna, and then we need to start looking for ladders," Matt said.

They closed in on the black mass that quickly took the shape of an enormous commercial cargo ship with containers stacked high on top.

"Geez, they've got enough containers on there, all right. How the hell do they land an airplane on that thing?" Matt mused aloud.

"Like I said," Peyton replied. "This ship could have just a shell with the containers stacked all around, leaving enough room for the UAVs."

"Thought a UAV needed more room than that," Matt said. "Blake, take it a bit closer. Angle over toward the third island there," he said pointing at the giant boulders that constituted the entrance to the tunnel nearest the Eastern Shore, called the Baltimore Channel.

"This is when we need that damn Zodiac," Blake muttered to himself, turning the wheel of the boat. He downshifted the gear box and slid the throttle into neutral, letting the boat drift. Then he shut off the engine, the absence of the motor making them feel utterly vulnerable, as if their voices could be heard for miles.

"This is as close as we want to get," Blake said, whispering. The Boston Whaler was about a football field's distance from the *Fong Hou.* Matt picked up Blake's night-vision goggles and held them to his eyes like binoculars.

"Okay, there it is. The satellite antenna. Damn, right there," Matt said quietly, then stopped. "Man. Chinese merchant ship? Iraqi general? Predators? Is this a strategic counterattack?"

They stood motionless in the boat, swaying with the subtle rocking, thinking about the nexus of the three vectors Matt had mentioned. Matt looked at Blake, whose face was drawn and worried. Clearly he understood the implications. Peyton's face was stern, as if she were facing a firing squad with defiance.

"China and Iraq?"

"That's the big picture," Matt said. "Has to be. The French helped us during the Revolutionary War; why would it be a stretch for China to help Iraq? It's all geopolitics. We've gone guns blazing into Iraq. Why not absorb the blow that we telegraphed for a full year and have a counterattack planned?"

They continued rocking in the boat until Peyton broke the silence.

"I see the antenna. And there's a ladder over there." Peyton pointed to the aft end.

"Let me see." Matt grabbed the goggles. He surveyed the ship, top to bottom.

"Okay. We need to get closer, though, to see if we can reach the bottom of that ladder," he said, shaking off the concept of an alliance between two powerful countries that hated the United States.

Blake looked at him. "Dangerous stuff, bro."

"Yeah."

Blake reached into a duffel bag and extracted two new Les Baer AR-15 rifles with close-combat optic red-dot scopes and infrared aiming devices.

"I would say this is a good start," Matt said, handling the AR-15 before giving one to Peyton and picking up a Ruger Model 77 bolt-action rifle. "And this is even better. Seventeen caliber, right?"

"That's right. Sniper rifle. I've mounted the infrared laser. There's some pistols in there, too."

"Where'd you get all this stuff?"

"I called some friends. The Ruger is mine, but the AR-15s . . . I had to cash in some chips."

"Big chips."

"Big mission."

The boat was about twenty yards now from the ship and drifting closer, much closer than any of them believed they should be to the *Fong Hou*/*Queen Bee*, but there they were.

"What's that noise?" Peyton asked.

They listened and could hear the screeching of metal moving.

"Sounds like an anchor lowering, but not exactly," Matt said. He pressed the illuminating dial on his wrist watch and saw it was nearly nine p.m.

Prime time.

Then it hit him. The terrorist radio from the barn in Vermont, the voice on the other end had asked, "Is *he* dead?"

Not "Are *they* dead?" or "Is *she* dead?" but is *he*, singular, dead?

He looked at Peyton and stepped onto the gunwale of the boat.

PART 4:
GRAVE NEW WORLD

CHAPTER 50

PANAMA CITY, PANAMA

Ambassador Sung's sleep had been fitful. Nightmares preceded the biggest decision of his life. He awoke, got dressed, and walked through the stale, muggy Panama night air to the cinderblock hut where they all waited.

Sung eyed Ronnie Wood in his familiar position in the corner. He turned to his comrades and said, "Gentlemen, we are about to make history."

He walked to the window of the Fort Sherman headquarters. In the moonlight, he could see the palm trees sway and the waves lap gently against the rocky beach. He knew that the next morning the sun would rise on a better day for these enemies of the United States.

"The Americans have most of their military deployed overseas and in the Middle East. They have very little capability to respond. Some of our riskier missions, such as the military transports, may be intercepted, but even with those, we have been able to hack into the military flight schedule system, and all of our attacks are legitimately scheduled flights."

His consortium of evil stared at him from around the table. A soft Caribbean breeze blew through the open windows.

"It is time for the next phase," Sung said. "Give the orders to your subordinate commanders to prepare for attacks."

Lt. Col. Yeung Park sat proudly in the back of the C-141 troop transport aircraft. He surveyed his 120 paratroopers, who wore grim looks on their faces. They were ready to fight. They knew this mission was most likely their last. Park thought about the ten other aircraft loaded in the same fashion. Eleven hundred paratroopers were invading the peaceful city of Seattle. How delightful.

The North Korean soldiers had departed from several different locations in the Caribbean Sea, where they had staged over the past year, training and rehearsing their attack plan. When given the word, they would take off and link up with the other transport aircraft in flight. The planes would meet twenty miles outside of Seattle just before the airborne invasion.

Park thought of his family, waiting for him in Pyongyang. He was certain he would never return, but he kept a small picture of his wife and two little children in his pocket. He removed the picture as they taxied along the runway of a Costa Rican airfield. One of his soldiers watched as he stared at the photo. His wife was beautiful but had aged rapidly over the years as a result of limited food and harsh living conditions. Their life was a difficult one.

And even he had to admit this plan was a bit extreme.

Their purpose was to seize Seattle-Tacoma International Airport, killing as many people at the airfield as possible, before transitioning to an attack on wealthy neighborhoods east of Seattle.

The planes would converge on the same flight route before the air traffic controller realized what was happening. In their rehearsals, they had practiced the call signs and maneuvers of American cargo-plane pilots. They would be aiming for McChord Air Force Base and veer away at the last minute to seize the Seattle airfield.

The Chinese soldiers had infiltrated Houston over the last five years, sometimes one at a time, other times in small boats. Most had made it, though some had not. The Chinese slave trade had been the perfect cover to inject determined soldiers and operatives into the inner city. They had gathered slowly, increasing in size to two battalion's worth, or nearly 900 soldiers. The weapons had been the easy part. There were plenty of those to be had. The liberal immigration laws and the incompetence of the Immigration and Naturalization Service had combined to make for an almost effortless infiltration.

This evening, the two battalion commanders talked on cell phones as they coordinated their attacks on a variety of targets. They had elected to concentrate their efforts on two areas. One battalion would focus on the government buildings and leadership, while the other battalion would attack the wealthy Woodlands area and kill as many civilians as possible. This would achieve the dual effect of crippling the command and control architecture and causing significant pain.

Their instructions were to hold the areas they secured, repel counterattacks, and, after forty-eight hours, go to Houston's Bush Intercontinental Airport, where military transport would pick them up. Phu Chai, the 1st Battalion commander, realized that the last portion of the plan, the extraction, was not likely to happen. And he was okay with that.

His men had waited years for this moment. They had practiced and rehearsed, much like the Japanese had for the Pearl Harbor invasion.

Phu Chai looked across the dingy crack house he and his men inhabited. Other members of his team lived in many dilapidated buildings throughout the slums of Houston. If the U.S. government had cared about its people, Chai figured, they would have discovered him and his plan a long time ago. But Chinese intelligence had told them it was best to melt into the inner cities because no one cared about those places. The police rarely stopped, taxis would not venture there, and there was no commerce other than drugs—all indicators of institutional neglect. To Chai, the fact that 900 soldiers had been able to enter the United States through Mexico and across the Caribbean Sea relatively intact and prepared for a military mission spoke volumes about the American system.

He held his satellite phone in his hand, awaiting the call to attack.

The Serb soldiers had waited a long time for their revenge. Able to muster nearly two thousand men and women, they had stowed away on a ship that departed from the port of Split in Croatia two months earlier. Tired of defecating in the cargo hold and sleeping right next to it, they were sufficiently fed up to attack the first thing they saw.

However, their mission was Jacksonville, Florida, and the Mayport Naval Station.

Stefan Ilic, a former colonel in the Yugoslav army, who had lost his entire family in the Kosovo air war, walked along the deck of the large container ship. She was a Liberian flagged vessel that had made frequent legitimate ports of call to the Balkan area and had always checked out.

After Sung had contacted Ilic four years earlier, it had taken him almost a year to find a ship that was not constantly monitored by American or British intelligence. With the insurgency in Macedonia, NATO intelligence had shifted its focus to the former rump country of Yugoslavia, and Ilic had ironically found a ship through Albanian contacts he had developed in Kosovo before the war.

Ilic had stockpiled thousands of AK-47s, RPK machine guns, light anti-tank weapons, and 82mm mortars along with the appropriate ammunition for each weapon system. Like the others, Ilic's force was designed to be light and mobile.

Their objective was to seize the Mayport Naval Air Station and destroy all of the F-14 fighters to deny the U.S. military a rapid reaction to the internal threat they would soon discover they faced.

Standing atop the deck of the ship, Ilic could see the port of Jacksonville on the near horizon. Once notified to attack, it would take about two hours for the ship to move into the port and unload the personnel and cargo. He was certain they would have to fight their way off the ship.

Ilic looked at the stars and thought he could see the satellite that would deliver his message . . . and his freedom.

Rafael Hernandez leaned his head forward and studied the faces of his Cuban comrades as they sat in the mesh webbing of the Russian-built Anatoly aircraft. He saw determined, nervous young men who were prepared to make the ultimate sacrifice to help unlock their country from the grip of the United States. His men bounced silently in the cabin of the aircraft, parachutes on their backs, weapons tied carefully to their sides, as they taxied into position on the runway.

The Cuban soldiers would take off in fifteen cargo airplanes headed directly for New Orleans International Airport. It was a one-hour flight, and the pilots thought they would be able to avoid detection because of the short duration. Their mission was to seize the airport and use the airfield to bring in aircraft and supplies to sustain the attack. Primarily, though, their mission was to inflict as much damage and pain as they could.

Of all the participants in the mission, Rafael figured they were the ones who had the most legitimate reason for participating in the operation. For over fifty years, the United States had been ostracizing, quarantining, blockading, and embargoing their country.

Rafael looked at the load master wearing his helmet and visor. The man gave Rafael a flat palm signal, indicating the word had not come yet. He was looking for the thumbs-up sign.

Awaiting the word to attack, Rafael ran his hand down the stock of his AK-47, reassured by its presence.

His revenge would be sweet.

The African coalition soldiers had traveled by ship, much the same way their ancestors had been transported as slaves. The difference was that this was a liberating mission. While it might not liberate a single African, it would liberate the soul. They were at one with their kindred spirits, who were calling these warriors forward with ghostly, outstretched, bony fingers, seeking their revenge.

Johnny Igansola from Nigeria paced slowly among his men, all as black as the mahogany of the African forests. Their oily, sweaty faces shone up at him; their wide eyes following, questioning.

"When do we attack, Commander?" one man asked from a squatting position beneath a porthole. The brilliant starlight punched through the window above the man's shaved head.

"This evening we should land in Port of Baltimore. We are only a few miles out and have slowed our speed considerably so that we are not too soon. We await the call."

The Colombian insurgents were at first reluctant to risk using their intelligence networks and infiltration routes for the coalition's purposes, yet they immediately saw the longer-range benefits of cooperating closely with the leaders of the coalition.

By allowing the alliance to use their secretive drug distribution routes, Cartagena's cartel would benefit richly. They had readily agreed to supplying guides and route information throughout the Caribbean Basin and within the United States.

With Sue Kim seated next to him, Sung felt grand and powerful. As soon as he got word from Ballantine, or the backup caller, should Ballantine be compromised, Sung would issue the order. They all had agreed that Ballantine's Predator attacks needed to be successful to wipe out the command and control architecture and radar warning systems to allow the airplanes and ships to arrive at their final destinations without interruption. Sung would follow the plan and await the call, as hard as that would be.

All they needed to do was get a foothold, and they could bring the economy of the most powerful nation to a dead halt. Once that objective was achieved, the Americans would have no option but to sign the international framework the Central Committee had drafted. The end result would be a redistribution of American wealth to the member nations.

Sung looked at Sue Kim. She looked across the room at Ronnie Wood, who nodded ever so slightly at her. Sue Kim turned to Sung, her almond eyes returning his gaze.

"We are ready, sir," she said. "We await only the call from Ballantine."

CHAPTER 51

2100 HOURS, CHESAPEAKE BAY, ABOARD THE FONG HOU

The drink had done him some good. The Percocet was kicking in full strength, and he was feeling just fine. Ballantine looked around the communications room and noticed the many flashing lights, radios, televisions, and Internet switching devices. He was sitting in the middle of a state-of-the-art communications platform.

He had memorized his speech, but thought he might speak with emotion and stray from his prepared remarks. This would be historic, the most widely recorded event in history, he was certain. Mentally rehearsing his opening line, he watched as Admiral Chen gave him a hand signal that he could begin.

He stared directly into the camera with the most hateful look he could muster. It was not difficult. He wanted to achieve a hard edge mixed with aloof humor. A sort of catch-me-if-you-can attitude. Daring, yet calculated. Though he believed his actions to be justified, he wanted the Americans to see him as the evil man in the dark corner of a dark house. *Their house.*

"Good evening, citizens of America. I apologize for interrupting this broadcast, but you all are about to die, and I wanted to be the first to tell you," Ballantine said in a thick Middle Eastern accent. He watched himself on the television screen upon which the digital camera sat. His face was dark and sinister. His black eyes burned with the hatred that he wanted the American people to see and understand. *They will finally comprehend*, he thought. Their lives had been so easy and protected. These people would finally understand some of what his people and other Arabs had endured for many years.

"Right now your country's intelligence apparatus has no idea where I am, and so far they have been unable to stop any of our attacks, except the one in Tallahassee, which is of little consequence. Make no mistake, we are very happy with our progress. And you should know that our success would not have been possible without the cooperation and assistance of a very high-level United States government official."

Ballantine looked at Admiral Chen, who was nodding in agreement.

"Tonight we will begin to unleash attacks on your forces around the world in Iraq, Bosnia, Kosovo, Afghanistan, Somalia, Yemen, the Philippines, Germany, and many other places, as well as here in your homeland. Yes, I said *here* in your homeland. I am amongst you. Why, you ask, have I stolen your satellite time and forced my message into your homes?"

He paused for effect.

"Because I want you to feel the fear that every Arab feels every day. I want you to know that we are in your country and that your government is not only incapable of stopping us but has betrayed you through the cooperation of Mr. Ronnie Wood."

Ballantine stared hard at the camera, pausing again, selecting his words carefully.

"Tonight begins the final destruction of America. This country all of you love so much will collapse upon itself because you are weak. We attacked your country on September 11, the Day of Independence, as we call it. All you could do is send a small force to Afghanistan, of all places, to martyr some of our freedom fighters. And then we lured you into Iraq to set the conditions for this phase of our operation. Your military campaign was as unimpressive as your lack of popular support for your war. Very few wanted to leave their comfortable lifestyles and make a sacrifice. Well, I tell you tonight that you all will sacrifice."

He looked away and then back at the camera.

"Prepare to die."

Those words were the cue to the cameraman to cut off the digital camera.

"Very well done, General," Admiral Chen said.

"Thank you, Admiral. Do you think I have their attention?"

"Certainly, but these people, as you say, they are weak."

"If others could be so lucky to have half the blessings and freedoms of the Americans . . ." Ballantine muttered.

"We should begin."

"Yes."

Ballantine stood and walked, feeling liberated. Perhaps this was how the American soldiers felt as they were unleashed from the border of Saudi Arabia and Kuwait during the two Gulf Wars. Like the Americans had done, he was now advancing toward the objective after months, even years, of waiting.

As Ballantine followed Admiral Chen to the launch deck of the *Fong Hou*, though, his most savory thought was that surely his live broadcast would bring Matt Garrett back into his lair. There was only one person who could deliver Mr. Garrett to the *Fong Hou*, and surely he would succeed. Zachary Garrett would serve his purpose as bait.

Ballantine watched Chinese sailors rig the crude nuclear bombs inside the payload housing in the domes of the Predators. He approvingly walked from Predator to Predator, briefly inspecting the handiwork of the Chinese engineers. The bombs looked like small black boxes with a few protruding wires. The sailors locked each bomb into place, using metal clasps and bungee cords. The only difference Ballantine could make out between the nuclear bombs and the chemical bombs was the size of their housings. The nuclear bombs were about two inches larger in diameter.

"Please have your sailors bring Mr. Garrett to my Sherpa, and activate the nuclear bomb on board," Ballantine said to Admiral Chen.

The admiral looked at Ballantine and smiled. "You are brave warrior, Ballantine."

Minutes later, Zachary Garrett walked through the small metal door, hands bound behind his back, ducking his head as he was pulled by one captor and pushed by the other. His footsteps rang like shots in the dim flight-operations dungeon of the ship.

"Mr. Garrett, so nice of you to join us," Ballantine said as the sailors walked Zachary to the Sherpa. Ballantine walked over to the small airplane, resting his hand on the fuselage and looking a bit like Charles Lindbergh might have after his successful flight.

"Can't say it's my pleasure," Zachary said through gritted teeth. In addition to securing his hands behind his back, his captors had shackled his feet with chains. He still wore the tactical clothing from the jump, including his lightweight, tan combat boots.

"Yes, well, you will observe these eighteen Predators, all loaded with nuclear or chemical bombs, fly off of our aircraft carrier and attack your country. Then, if our timing is good, and I think it is, you will watch me kill your brother," he said. "And then you and I will take a little flight." Ballantine enjoyed describing the events to Zachary Garrett.

"Let me ask you a question, Ballantine. Kind of a last request kind of thing," Zachary said, his words echoing in the chamber.

"Anything, but we don't have much time," Ballantine said.

"Why couldn't you just accept defeat? We beat you in the Gulf War. You were wrong, we were right. The whole world rose up against you," Zachary said, stalling for time, taking in his surroundings, observing what was going on around him. Though, he also was truly uninterested in Ballantine's response.

"Not the whole world," Ballantine said. "There are many countries who despise you, and we are allied against you. The war never ended. You have seen only the beginning."

"Yeah, but who else is there? You guys hate the Iranians more than you hate us. There's maybe the Chinese. These guys look sort of Chinese, don't you think?"

"Of course, there is China, North Korea, Angola, Colombia, Serbia, and others. I believe the American term for this is *blowback*, no? Then, of course, there's this," Ballantine said, sweeping his hand across the ship's interior deck, "which is only part of China's contribution."

"Really," Zachary said. "Since we're all going to die here, why don't you enlighten me as to the genius of your plan?"

"We've wasted enough time. I'm not sure what you're trying to do, but events will happen much too quickly for any of your friends to respond, if that's what you're thinking," Ballantine said sharply. "Next time you see me, your brother will have a knife to his throat. My brother died coming to rescue me, and yours will die coming to rescue you."

"Sweet justice, it seems. But then what?"

Ballantine stopped and turned. "Nothing else matters, Garrett. Nothing else matters."

He stepped away as two guards held Zachary. The ship surgeon produced a syringe and clicked it twice with his index finger. "This will keep you docile."

Zachary watched through bloodshot eyes as the doctor rolled up his black shirt sleeve and slipped the needle beneath his skin without the slightest pinch.

Only seconds passed before his vision narrowed and his head grew too heavy to hold up. He felt his mind swoon a bit and began hearing dislocated voices saying the words, "Predator One," "Predator Two," "Hellerman," "Signal to go," "Radio," and so on.

"In the Sherpa," Ballantine ordered.

The voices floated around as two people maneuvered him into the cargo compartment of the Sherpa and placed a large, black box next to him. He watched as best he could as the sailors drilled and filed for several minutes, using power drills to screw long bolts into the floor, countersinking the device. Then he watched as they connected wires from the box to what appeared to be a timer.

Though drugged, he instinctively knew he was staring at a nuclear bomb.

CHAPTER 52

CHESAPEAKE BAY

With one hand grasping the rusty iron bar of the hull ladder and one foot still on the rail of the Boston Whaler, Matt Garrett was looking over his shoulder at Blake when his cell phone began to vibrate.

"Garrett," he whispered into the phone.

After a pause, he heard Meredith's voice. "Matt, turn on your television. Something's going down. It's big time. Ballantine cut into all the news channels and broadcast a message."

"No TV. Hang on. . . . Blake, find a news channel on the radio." Matt's voice was a low whisper that blended with the tide lapping against the hull of the small boat.

Blake bent over and turned on the boat radio, selected AM, and turned the dial until he could hear a man's voice talking clearly.

"What's going on?" Peyton cocked her head forward.

"Okay, got it, Meredith. Something about a public statement."

"Right. Ballantine essentially said he was attacking us tonight. I think he truly enjoyed just scaring the hell out of two hundred million Americans."

"Look, I have to go." Matt didn't want to spend a lot of time on the phone. Plus, he didn't need the distraction of Meredith and all that came with visualizing her.

"Matt, look, Hellerman is in on this thing. I know it. I saw his command center, and he's somehow calling some of the shots," Meredith said.

"We'll deal with that later," Matt said. "I want to get Zachary back first."

"Ballantine also mentioned he was working with Ronnie Wood. You may be onto Lantini."

Memories rushed through Matt's mind like bats from a black cave. Meredith had cracked the code on the Rolling Stones last year and Lantini, the one they speculated to be Ronnie Wood, had fled. That was also a time of great sadness as the loss of Zachary offset the budding love they each had begun to feel for one another. Now, all of the variables were in play again, only they were skewed. Zachary was alive, but in peril. Meredith had drifted away, perhaps pulled by some impossibly strong force. Ronnie Wood was reappearing.

And Matt was at the center of it all. *Lantini, that bastard.*

"Thanks, Meredith," was all he could manage.

"Call me when you have a chance. I'm staying at a friend's house, but I'm on my cell," she said.

"Okay."

Matt flipped the phone shut, stepped back into the Boston Whaler, and stared at the mammoth ship. After a moment, he opened the phone again, pulled a card from his wallet, and punched in a number.

"Hey, it's Matt Garrett. You should probably call Meredith Morris, get a copy of what she sent me, and head this way. I'm going in now."

He flipped the phone shut again.

"Who was that?" Peyton and Blake asked with raised eyebrows.

"Don't worry about it. We are ad-libbing from this point forward. Blake, according to what we just heard on the radio, Ballantine and his Chinese fire drill are going to launch those UAVs tonight as a precursor to some follow-on action. Ronnie Wood is in play—Lantini. His ass is mine. Their method of operation has been to sustain the terror over a prolonged period of time, making us believe he can operate with impunity."

"He pretty much has, hasn't he?" Blake said.

"Not really. What he did was execute a plan, developed over the last ten years, on autopilot. Now he seems to be in a phase where he has to give cues and signals, hence going on television. I think his next move is to launch those UAVs with some kind of payload, either biological or chemical. Maybe a nuke. Though, that would be tough. But with China in play, anything is possible."

"So what's your plan?"

"I'm going up there to kill Ballantine and Lantini and get Zachary back."

"That is not a plan."

"I'll make it up as I go," Matt said, "just like Lake Moncrief. Only this time I come back with my brother."

"You mean *we'll* come back with your brother . . ." Blake could see he was serious.

"Blake, you need to stay in the boat here with Peyton."

"Wait a minute," Peyton interrupted. "I missed out on Moncrief and flew back in that stupid helicopter. I'm going with you."

"I don't think that's any place for a chick," Blake said. "Why don't you stay with the boat while I head up with my bro?"

"You know that's not going to happen," she said.

"What is it with you guys? You argue like an old married couple. Now look, I'm doing this alone. It's my responsibility," Matt said.

"Since when was the fate of the free world your responsibility?" Blake said.

"Just doing my part, man," Matt said, grabbing one of the AR-15s and a Luger pistol. He stuffed the pistol into his belt and then slung the rifle over his shoulder and across his chest. Grabbing four magazines of ammunition, he slapped one into each weapon and stuffed the remaining two into his pocket. He took the night-vision goggles and slipped them on his head. He pulled on some gloves, reaching out with his hand as the boat drifted closer to the ship's metal hull.

"I'm going up. I'll let you two sort out who stays, but someone needs to stay with the boat and watch for me when I come hauling ass back down this ladder with Zachary. We may have to jump off the side, and people will probably be shooting at us, so I need someone with this puppy ready to go. Understand?"

Blake and Peyton nodded at him.

Matt gave Blake a quick hug. "See you in you in a bit, bro."

Then he stared at Peyton, her arms crossed, her face a dark mask against the ocean behind her. Now that Meredith seemed to have definitive proof that Hellerman was involved in this conspiracy, he was convinced that Peyton was a plant. Her mission might be to keep him close.

Operating under that notion, he gave her a long, sustained hug, sliding his hand into her back pants pocket. "You might want to hang onto this," he said.

She didn't reply for a moment and then said, "I understand."

He gave her a quick kiss and said, "Be back shortly." He turned, walked to the gunwale of the Boston Whaler, and said, "Later."

Matt reached up and grabbed the metal rung, the first of many that were spaced about three feet apart all the way to the top of the hull. Matt felt his weight pull against his arms as he stepped off the boat and was fully suspended by the ladder rung. Because of the curvature of the hull, Matt found himself being pulled directly off the ladder by the gravity. He was climbing, suspended from the rungs.

He could hear the muffled sounds of Blake and Peyton talking softly as he progressed higher on the ladder. He realized that the hull of the ship was much higher than he could have imagined when he was looking at it from a distance. He was in good shape, though, even if he could feel the scar tissue tearing away at his abdomen and forearm with every pull. The more recent flesh wounds barked at him as well. He felt scabs ripping open where the bullets had grazed him.

Still, he focused, thinking about his weapons and the small amount of ammunition that he had on hand. He had two twenty-round magazines for the AR-15 and two eight-round magazines for the pistol. He had the distinct impression that his ammunition load might not be enough to complete the job.

As Matt approached the top of the ship, he saw he would have to negotiate a small ledge that stuck out about three feet from the surface of the hull. He could see the outline of a hatch that, under normal circumstances, would be open for anyone traversing the ladder. He pressed against it and determined that it was locked. He looked down and could not see Blake's Boston Whaler, meaning they had repositioned or that he was simply too high. Clearly he would have to be very nimble to reach out, secure the ledge, and then essentially do a pull up while swinging a leg atop the outcropping.

Holding onto the ladder with one hand, Matt reached out with the other and grasped the gunwale. He could barely reach it and had to swing one foot out over the water to give him the leverage to fully grip the leading edge of the gunwale. He realized another problem in that the metal was about four inches thick, preventing him from getting a good handhold. He would have to simply use the strength of his fingers to support his weight, like a rock climber. He inched his hand forward to the point where he felt like he had a good grip and then mustered the courage to smoothly let go of the ladder with the other hand.

He now had one hand on the protruding gunwale and one foot on the ladder, forming a triangle with the hull of the ship and the outermost portion of the ship's gunwale. The tension against his fingers was enormous, only lessened a bit when he slowly moved his other hand to the ledge and grasped tightly next to his supporting hand. As he was moving his hand, Matt reached a point where his foot on the ladder had to come free. He was hanging by two hands, a rifle slung across his back, feet pointed straight down at the water, and certain danger awaiting him as he crested the rail.

He lifted himself as if he were doing a pull-up, scar tissue really becoming a factor. He hadn't realized until this point how severely wounded he had been. A bullet had pierced his stomach and all associated muscles and organs less than a year ago. The bayonet cut across his forearm had healed, but the tendon and ligaments were stiff and unwieldy. He was thankful at this very moment, however, that he had been doing batting practice, working his wrists and forearms hard, rebuilding them.

Matt lifted his leg slowly. It was harder this way because he couldn't get any momentum going. He had to rely on pure strength and adrenaline, of which he had plenty. Hooking his left foot onto the ledge, he continued pulling with his arms until he could reach out with his left arm and slide it along the riveted metal. All of this was going well until he felt something loosen in his belt and had the sickening realization that his pistol was sliding loose.

There was absolutely nothing he could do about it except accelerate his climb onto the ledge. He did, but it was too late. He felt the pistol pop out of his waist and visualized it falling. About the time he would have expected to hear a small splash, he heard a dull thud. Either splashes registered as thuds this high up or the pistol landed in the boat. He hoped he hadn't just killed Blake or Peyton.

He was on the gunwale and quickly slipped over onto the deck of the ship. He found himself staring at a large container, but could see a pathway toward the superstructure of the ship. Stopping to catch his breath and ensure he at least had some ammunition left, Matt heard a high buzzing sound, like the sound of a weed eater.

The sound also reminded him of remotely piloted airplanes, the kind you see on the weekends in the open fields, with a father and son laughing and playing with the joystick as the small aircraft does barrel rolls in the sky. Funny he should be having that image pop into his mind as it occurred to him that Ballantine was launching the first unmanned aerial vehicle.

Destination unknown.

CHAPTER 53

ABOARD THE FONG HOU

Ballantine looked at the television screen and saw the darkened cave of the *Fong Hou* runway. Though he sat in a comfortable chair in the ship's command center, his visual perspective was that of a pilot looking out of the cockpit window of the Predator.

He and Admiral Chen had completed inspection of the crude nuclear bombs the technicians had affixed to four of the Predators. The remaining aircraft were carrying VX nerve gas as their payload. Chen and Ballantine kept their distance.

The technicians had then entered the grid coordinates into the global positioning system aboard each aircraft, allowing them to fly on autopilot once launched, much like cruise missiles shot from U.S. Navy ships. Because they could only launch one Predator at a time with the single monitor, Ballantine had elected to fly each aircraft for thirty minutes, get it on cruise path, and then release it to the Queen Bee's satellite control for digital guidance.

Flight time at 70 mph to Fort Bragg, North Carolina, would be three hours. The flight to the Pentagon would be about two hours, and then Ballantine would launch the chemical attacks on population centers, saving the nearby naval station in Norfolk for last. This would give him the opportunity to get in his Sherpa and fly it directly into the White House with a nuclear bomb aboard.

Sitting in the command center at the controls of the Predator terminal, he waited for the green light to flash, which would give him the signal to release the brakes on the Predator. The red light flickered to yellow.

Ballantine marveled at the genius of their campaign so far. It had been innovative and lethal. While in his view the Americans had come into Afghanistan with a muted and limp response to the September 11 attacks, this campaign could serve as a primer on how to attack a country in the twenty-first century. Start with terrifying attacks on the civilian population, follow with debilitating attacks on military infrastructure, and conclude with destruction of command and control capability.

Through the television screen, Ballantine saw Admiral Chen walk to the front of the Predator and stand at attention, saluting in strict military fashion. The admiral disappeared from sight as the small light at the bottom of his control terminal turned green.

Although Ballantine could not hear it, he could sense that the whining engine of the Predator had become deafening. He released the brake and the catapult shot the aircraft forward along the centerline of the runway. He gingerly handled the joystick as he watched the Predator bore through the cavern. Quickly, though, the Predator was free of the runway, dipping a bit off the bow's elevated ramp. He gained rudder control and pulled the joystick to the rear, gathering altitude as he left the throttle full. *Like playing a video game*, he thought, *though much more deadly*.

The nuclear bomb weighed about thirty pounds and pulled down on the nose of the aircraft, forcing him to fight against gravity. He had flown the Sherpa overloaded with fishing gear enough to know not to fight to gain altitude, instead nosing over and letting the engine catch up with the workload. Ballantine tipped the nose forward just a bit and immediately was rewarded with a smoother ride.

Through the camera, he could see that the unpiloted Predator was probably one hundred feet above the glimmering water of Chesapeake Bay. Headed east, he would soon bank the aircraft to the south and then to the west over Virginia Beach, setting it on course for the command center at Pope Air Force Base and Fort Bragg.

Ballantine tilted the joystick slightly to the right, bringing the Predator to a southbound course. He began picking up the lights of Fort Story and the strip along the beachfront, and then he turned the Predator some more. The aircraft was actually quite responsive and easy to maneuver. The sterile environment of the Predator monitor did not provide the hum of the engine and the bumps of the wind—those extrasensory items that give a good pilot the feel he needs.

After about twenty minutes, he leveled the Predator at 800 feet above ground level, the normal height C-130 and C-141 aircraft flying near Fort Bragg used when they conducted parachute-drop operations. He set the speed at 70 mph and locked in an azimuth of 207 degrees, a south by southwesterly heading. Through the camera, Ballantine could see the occasional house or cluster of lights indicating a suburb. He checked the global-positioning-system grid coordinate against the map on the wall in the command center and realized the Predator had just passed into North Carolina. He released the joystick, watching as the autopilot took over.

Ballantine pressed a small green button on the computer terminal and watched as a second computer screen started flashing computer-generated dots from a central position on the screen to a single moving icon. Ballantine was pleased to see that Dr. Insect's nanotechnology was working. The Queen Bee was communicating with the first Predator.

After about five minutes, he was confident that the aircraft would hold the desired course and, in about two hours, would achieve the desired effect.

Ballantine pressed a button labeled MONITOR ONLY, which turned off the camera display from Predator One but continued to display the grid coordinate progress of the aircraft. Placing Predator One in monitor-only mode allowed him to free up enough bandwidth to launch Predator Two using the video feed.

Ballantine thought back two years to the original e-mail from a contact in France with encoded messages pertaining to the *Fong Hou*, the Predators, and the final mission of attacking the listed targets with unmanned aircraft. He remembered reviewing the information on his Dell laptop using Microsoft Word after he had downloaded the e-mail and its instructions of terror from his Yahoo! e-mail account. He had been curious, but delighted, about the China connection. China brought to the table what all the other nations had been lacking—unlimited resources and ample technology under a veil of extreme secrecy.

The nuclear-grade material, the chemicals, and the germs were all refined in China. They were put on a simple merchant ship and were being transferred to the most surprising means of attack—American Predators—that anyone could imagine. Ballantine smiled at the thought, then spoke into his headset. "Admiral, prepare Predator Two."

CHAPTER 54

ABOARD THE FONG HOU

Matt watched through his night-vision goggles as the Predator whined and lifted slowly into the sky, eventually drifting out of sight.

One down, he thought to himself. *Ballantine is holding Zachary hostage on this ship while he launches nukes and God knows what else at the United States.* At least Matt had made a phone call to the one person who he thought might be able to do something about it. Maybe he was wrong, but it was worth the chance.

He walked slowly, hunched over, staying low to avoid what looked like firing parapets in some of the containers. He could barely make out the space-needle satellite antenna near the bridge of the ship. He focused on that while keeping an eye on the containers. Something didn't feel right about them.

Fifty feet from an opening that led to the bridge, he saw a muzzle slide slowly out of a small rectangular hole in the container on his left. The muzzle was no more than two feet in front of his face.

He froze and watched the bore drift toward him, stopping before the barrel of the weapon reached his head. It then slid slowly away from him. He gently moved toward the container so that he was flush with the wall. The muzzle swept its sector again and then retreated into the container.

Matt waited for a few seconds and then proceeded. He could hear talking as he passed below the firing parapet and paused long enough to recognize it as Chinese. He stopped near the ladder to the bridge.

Through his goggles, he looked up to the bridge and saw a bright spot inside the hexagon of a steering room. He could see four or five panes of square glass and a dim light, with other lights flashing, the way a television does as it changes images during a program. The lights were different hues of green through his goggles, so he lifted his headset and paused a second before opening his eyes again.

Matt remained focused on the six-sided command center, approaching the ladder with stealth. He was a bit concerned that it had so far been too easy. His general work ethic told him that if something was easy, it was probably not worth the effort. The harder the task, the more worthwhile the endeavor. Not that what he had been through over the past year had been easy, but this specific phase, this subset, was too simple.

As if it was a trap.

"Matt Garrett, I presume?"

The voice was a deep, penetrating baritone that rang an alarm bell inside Matt's most primal hiding places. And the words were followed by an audible click of a weapon hammer locking to the rear.

"Ballantine, how pleasant," Matt said without turning. "I thought I killed you back at Moncrief."

"You Americans think you have martyred so many freedom fighters that are still alive."

"Glad to have another shot at it," Matt replied.

"Cocky son of a bitch," Ballantine said with a chuckle.

"I have an idea, Ballantine."

Matt was still facing away from Ballantine and now he could feel the cool circular rim of some form of firearm pressed against his head.

"I like ideas, Garrett."

"You had Hellerman send me up to Moncrief so you could kill me up there, but I was always curious about why you didn't just come down to Stanardsville and kill me there. What gives?"

"You have such an inquiring mind, Mr. Garrett. And such an imagination, implicating your own vice president in our scheme."

"The way I see it, my brother Zachary captured you, fought you man-to-man," Matt said. "He killed your brother in the process, but, hey, it was war. Hellerman helped you out when you were a prisoner after Zachary captured you in Iraq. He was a Reserve officer in military intelligence when he interrogated you."

"Young men have such imaginations," Ballantine said.

Matt continued. "You told him that you had a tape recording of his voice telling the ambassador to go ahead and let Iraq attack Kuwait. See, Hellerman wanted the war for some insane personal reasons and, of course, Hussein wanted Kuwait for his own, shall we say, personal reasons."

"You are a bright young man, Matt Garrett. But while I appreciate this history lesson, we have business to attend to. I will kill you while your brother watches, and then he and I will both fly away in my airplane to attack your White House. Sound like fun?"

"Loads. But hear me out, Ballantine. Anyway, you promised Hellerman that you would give him the only copy of the tape on which his very distinctive voice authorizes the ambassador to tell Hussein it is okay to attack Kuwait. It was your insurance policy."

"Don't be so sure of yourself. I've received help from any number of accomplices."

"Well, Rampert's a soldier. Hellerman's a weasel politician. That's a no-brainer. Where's Lantini, by the way?"

"All politicians are weasels, no argument there. You'll see Ronnie Wood soon enough." Ballantine laughed.

Matt felt the barrel of the weapon push him toward the ladder.

"Good," Matt said, and with one swift movement he spun, lifting his left arm and cracking it against the pistol Ballantine was holding. The pistol fired one shot as Ballantine lost control of it, the shot going wide, striking metal with a high-resolution ping behind Matt's ear. The pistol made a loud clanking noise as it dropped on the deck of the ship.

Matt reached back for his AR-15, which was slung across his back. But he was met with Ballantine's boot to the ribs. Matt doubled over but found the strength to grab Ballantine's head and lift his knee into Ballantine's face as he watched his rifle skid across the deck.

Matt heard an audible crack, but quickly found himself being swept to the ground by a hand pulling at his heel. His head struck the hard, metal floor of the ship deck, causing him to black out for a moment, but leaving him the good sense to kick Ballantine in the balls and scurry to his feet.

"Ballantine, you want the tape. I know," Matt said, squaring off with his adversary as though they were wrestlers.

"Why would I want that stupid tape anymore?"

"You don't sound too sure of yourself," Matt said between rapid breaths. He saw Ballantine pull a knife from his waistband.

"Let's see if this is more convincing," Ballantine said, waving the knife in front of Matt's face.

Matt quickly recalled his own personal axiom of *always bring a gun to a knife fight*. He eyed his rifle about fifteen feet away.

"How about I trade you the tape for my brother?" Matt said.

"You think you have this all figured out, don't you?" Ballantine said. "Years of planning this invasion and a bit of personal revenge and you think you can climb up on my ship and change my mind?"

"Look, Jacques, your brother is dead, and I'm truly sorry about that," Matt said. He saw Ballantine's eyes flicker, just for a moment, with sadness, only to be replaced by boiling hatred. "But your deal with Hellerman, I presume, is to get this tape back to him. You get a new identity and probably a government-sponsored witness-protection-program vacation somewhere. Am I right?"

They were still circling like two collegiate wrestlers. Ballantine was quiet, his mind processing what Matt was telling him. Matt guessed that he was close and that his assessments were accurate. He had ruled out Rampert as a suspect when he remembered Hellerman was a Reserve military intelligence officer with the State Department during the Gulf War. Hellerman had access to everything.

When Matt thought about Hellerman's obsession with the Rebuild America project, it provided the perfect cover for his conspiracy. So he figured the tape, the last remaining bit of evidence that anyone had against Hellerman, was both Ballantine's ticket into America to conduct the terrorist attacks and Hellerman's chance to have his war with complete deniability, provided Ballantine retrieved the tape. The real question, to be sorted later, was, What was Lantini's connection?

"Now that you have me all figured out, it is a shame that you will have to take your secrets to your grave."

As they circled, Ballantine was always sure to keep Matt away from the rifle and pistol. In Matt's view, the Iraqi seemed to be enjoying the one-on-one. This was the reason Ballantine had not simply come to Stanardsville and killed him. It was the game. Ballantine's brother had been killed in war, the ultimate chess match, and now Ballantine wanted the same challenge, to prove himself every bit as capable and worthy as Zachary Garrett.

"You're not as good as my brother, Ballantine," Matt said, feeding off the thought.

"We shall see, Garrett. Right now your brother is on his death bed and will soon be vaporized as he plunges into the White House in my Sherpa."

Matt could hear a slight buzzing noise, like an active beehive. He swallowed hard. "How many Predators have you launched?"

"I think I hear the good admiral readying the second one right now."

"So are you going to kill me, or are we just getting to know each other?" Matt asked. "You're an artist, Ballantine. Are you trying to live up to some macho image or something? Why can't you leave it alone?"

"Did you leave it alone, as you say, when you thought your brother was dead, and you believed that you had not done enough to save him?"

Touché, Matt thought. Ballantine had done his homework. He would know from Matt's silence that he could chalk one up in his column.

"I didn't go to the Philippines to try and find the guy who fired the shot. I dealt with it in my own ways, privately," Matt said. It occurred to him that they were two people who had experienced similar emotions. They had both shared a battlefield with their brothers and each had lost—or in his case, believed he had lost—a brother there.

"Then you are the weak one. If we do not avenge our family, what do we have left?" Ballantine said.

In a way, Matt understood exactly what his rival was saying. Matt, too, had wanted to reach out and strangle anyone that had anything to do with Zachary's death.

"But you have to admit that death on the battlefield is different than this," Matt said.

"That is where you are wrong. The battlefield is everywhere. Warfare has changed, and I am most disappointed in you that you do not acknowledge that. This is the battlefield," Ballantine said, sweeping his hand across the ship.

"Maybe your battlefield, but to what end?"

"To rob from the rich and give to the poor. Isn't that a great Anglo-Saxon fairy tale?"

"Robin Hood was a common thief and beggar," Matt said. "And I'm getting tired of this conversation." He heard a whining noise and watched as the second Predator wobbled off the bow of the ship.

Having relinquished his Predator-piloting duties to the admiral, Ballantine turned his head ever so slightly, wanting to watch.

Matt seized that moment to dive toward his rifle, sliding across the deck, feeling the rivets tear through his shirt. He felt the butt stock of his rifle and then lost his grip as Ballantine kicked it away, arching the knife downward into the steel next to his throat.

Ballantine held the knife against Matt's neck, breathing hard.

"Garrett, you are a dead man. Just accept it. There is nothing you can do to save yourself, your brother, or your country. If I wanted, I could slice your jugular in half a second, and you would bleed out in two minutes right here. But I want your brother to watch. I want him to experience the horror and pain, if only for a short while."

Ballantine lifted Matt to a standing position, the knife pressed against his neck, drawing a trickle of blood.

With his back to Ballantine's side, Matt could sense that though Ballantine was a big man, he was about two inches shorter and a not as well built as Matt.

As they began walking toward a metal door, Matt saw a slight figure in the darkness, standing on the deck, holding a rifle, her hair blowing in the stiff bay wind.

It was Peyton O'Hara, watching the action unfold.

"Where have you been? I thought you'd never get here," Ballantine said.

Matt's heart clanked on the ship's deck.

And for the first time he began to lose hope.

CHAPTER 55

MH-60 BLACKHAWK COMMAND AND CONTROL HELICOPTER, ABOVE CHESAPEAKE BAY

Colonel Jack Rampert looked over Chesapeake Bay from beneath his communications headset.

"Tomcat one six, this is Delta six," Rampert said into the small mouthpiece. He could see the lights of the Bay Bridge-Tunnel and the dark mass that was the *Fong Hou* just to the east of the third island. Matt Garrett's phone call had come at a time when the nation was at its highest state of alert. Rampert had contacted Meredith Morris, and she had described for him the most harrowing scenario he could ever imagine. He had thought he had seen it all.

But as he watched through his night-vision goggles, a Predator unmanned aerial vehicle glided effortlessly off the deck of the *Fong Hou*, and he became a believer. The curious events of the past week were culminating, not necessarily here, but perhaps primarily from this location. He was still thinking about how it would all play out when the voice came back to him through his headset.

"Delta six, this is Tomcat one six."

Rampert shook his head. The pilot of the Navy F-14 Tomcat didn't sound a day over twenty, and here he was flying an aircraft launched out of

Oceana Naval Air Station. There were no flight wings present at the station as they were all on carriers around the world fighting the War on Terror. But two F-14s had been returned to Oceana for significant repairs in the last two months. When Rampert got the call from Matt, he ordered the commander at Oceana to launch what he had.

And this was it. One F-14 with four Maverick missiles and five hundred 20mm rounds. Pitiful.

"Tomcat, this is Delta. I've got visual on one Predator flying east over the bay toward Fort Story. We believe it is armed with a crude nuclear device and is preprogrammed for detonation at a high payoff target somewhere on the East Coast. I need you to shoot it down, avoiding the nose of the airplane and making sure it lands in the water."

Rampert knew that he sounded like an over-controlling bureaucrat, but they had to get this one right. "And I think you've probably got about one minute before you lose the capability to destroy it over the water."

"I don't even see it yet, Colonel," the pilot shot back.

"Well, find it, son, or lots of people are going to die."

That was more like it. Mission orders were always best. Just give people a mission and let them do their job.

"Roger."

Rampert continued to circle in his Blackhawk, wondering how many Predators had been launched. He called back to Oceana on his headset.

"Radar control, this is Delta six, over."

"This is radar control, over."

"Do you have any indications of aircraft flying anywhere in the area?"

"We have your aircraft and Tomcat one six. Nothing else. We do not, say again, do not observe on radar the Predator you see."

"Okay, I need you to start searching a three-hundred-mile radius around this point and tweak your radar so that you can find slow-moving aircraft."

"We can lower the resolution, but we'll start to pick up birds and other ground clutter."

"There will be a lot more ground clutter to pick up if you don't find these Predators. Do what you have to do."

"Roger."

"Sir, Tomcat one six is calling you," Hobart said. His most trusted operator was listening to the other radio net, tracking the F-14.

"This is Delta six," Rampert said into the mouthpiece.

"This is Tomcat one six. I think I've got visual on a Predator. It's actually banking to the north over the mouth of the bay. It's heading up to the peninsula there. I've got a clean shot and just want you to confirm your authorization to shoot."

"Guidance stands. Shoot it down. Avoid the nose. Observe its impact into the water and laser a grid coordinate. We have boat teams heading into the bay right now."

"Roger. Be back in a second."

"Roger. Just shoot it down. Now. Out."

Rampart switched his intercom to internal. "Mike, can we get this thing turned so my window is facing the east by northeast?" he asked to his helicopter pilot, Mike Jamison.

The pilot turned the aircraft so that Rampert could observe the action. He slipped on his night-vision goggles again and peered through the large square window. He could see the afterburners of the F-14 glowing brightly in his goggles. He watched the jet aircraft maneuver as it pitched forward and leveled its nose at the target.

Rampert felt a surge of adrenaline as he watched bright green streaks of light cut across the black sky. He saw burst of 20mm chain-gun fire. Suddenly he could see the Predator, highlighted by a small fire on what he hoped was the tail section.

He watched as the Predator first angled toward the ocean and then began a slow spiral out of control. He saw the F-14 pilot pull up and bank so that he and his navigator could observe the impact. It fell into the ocean with an unceremonious splash. Rampert watched the laser from the F-14 immediately find what remained of the aircraft.

"Delta six, this is Tomcat one six," the F-14 pilot said.

"Delta six, go ahead. Over."

"Roger. Target destroyed. Impact observed. No detonation observed. Grid coordinate follows."

Rampert wrote down the grid the pilot reported and then said, "Continue to loiter and watch the bow of the ship for other Predators."

He then radioed the patrol boat captain, who had alerted his fleet of six harbor boats to move from Little Creek Amphibious Base into Chesapeake Bay toward the *Fong Hou*.

"Anchor six, this is Delta six. Precious cargo at the following grid coordinate. Move to that location immediately and recover Predator aircraft with possible rigged nuclear explosive device. Device could have timer."

"This is Anchor six, wilco."

Rampert switched his radio set back to the F-14 frequency.

"Tomcat six, this is Delta six. Prepare to destroy the ship, using Maverick missiles on my command."

"This is Tomcat six, standing by for your command," came the pilot's more confident voice.

One battlefield kill against a drone with no pilot or weapons, and he thinks he's the Red Baron, Rampert mused. But the weight of the task before him quickly took hold.

Rampert knew that Matt Garrett and Zachary Garrett were probably on that ship. It was quite a dilemma he was facing. He could solve a slew of problems with a couple of well-placed Maverick missiles. And he didn't have much time to make his decision.

CHAPTER 56

NORTHERN VIRGINIA

Francis "Trip" Hellerman III sat in the command bunker at the guest quarters with Jock Evans, Zeke Jeremiah, Stan Rockfish, and Ralph Smithers, all watching Fox News and monitoring reports coming in from Colonel Rampert. Hellerman was privately concerned about Rampert's sudden appearance near the *Fong Hou*, but he watched and waited. This was a game of chess, and his sole drive now was to retain freedom of maneuver to avoid getting pinned.

"They turned a damned commercial ship into an aircraft carrier and used our UAV technology against us," Jeremiah said, shaking his head at the enemy's ingenuity. Though having sifted through Hellerman's ingenious interception of the enemy's plan, he had special insight into what was happening.

"If you thought someone's legacy was in trouble before, how about now? With all his China links and the fact that we know China got these Predators at about the same time that administration got millions in campaign contributions, wow," Evans said.

"Well, children, we can blame whoever we want, but we have a war to fight," Hellerman said, his voice commanding and reassuring.

"Yes, sir," Jeremiah said. Hellerman exchanged a knowing glance with him.

"Zeke, we've destroyed one Predator. We know he had at least eighteen. That leaves seventeen, and we don't know if he launched any before this. We think he had one or two at Moncrief. These damn things are impossible to pick up on radar. Make sure we're tracking what our air traffic controllers are reporting. We've got all air traffic shut down, correct?"

Jeremiah nodded. "Roger, sir. That and we've alerted the F-15 squadron at Langley, but the Air Force general there said they aren't prepared to do anything for two hours."

"This thing will be over in two hours. Who gave him the authorization to do a standdown with our quick-response force?"

"I asked him that, and he said he thought another wing was covering the quick-response mission."

"Keep working it," Hellerman said, frustrated.

"Sir," Jock Evans said, holding his hand over the phone, "it's Agent Jessup."

"Thank you," he said, taking the phone.

"Mr. Vice President, if you could meet me in the big house, I'd appreciate it," Jessup said.

"Be there in a minute," Hellerman said.

He handed the phone to Evans and walked out the door. He called over his shoulder, "Be back in a minute. Keep tracking the situation, team. Zeke, join me in a few minutes."

Walking across the driveway, Hellerman felt a renewed sense of purpose with the plan actually underway. The attacks on the civilian population had a large impact. Now that the Predators were on the way, the country was fighting back. Even if it was just one F-14, at least it was a start. He had never imagined that any of the Predators would reach their targets, anyway.

He walked up the steps and into the foyer of his mansion to find Jessup waiting for him in the living room.

"Sir, I don't know what's going on, but we tracked a cell phone call from Colonel Jack Rampert to Meredith Morris. We've got her location, and I sent one of my men out to get her and bring her here, just like you ordered."

"Great," Hellerman said. "When do you think she'll be here?"

Jessup raised his eyebrows as only he could do. "Hopefully within the hour, but I have to ask you, sir, do you have anyone else looking for her?" He was a big man and very respectful of the friend he protected every day, but he would not let himself drift beyond a certain line, no matter how strong the tide.

"Alvin, why would I do that?" Hellerman said, acting curious.

"Sir, the nature of the phone conversation indicates to me that you might be concerned about something she might say. And you're talking to me, not some green Secret Service agent. Sir."

"Meredith may be involved in some bad stuff. She's had some money problems and boyfriend problems that are pretty well known. We just need to get her and bring her here, that's all."

Jessup stared at his boss for a long moment. "Sir, I will do what you say, but I will not cross the line. I want to know if my agent is going into harm's way when he gets to Meredith."

"I would never expect you to cross any line," Hellerman said. "And I would never have you send an agent into harm's way unnecessarily."

On that note, he turned and left Jessup standing in the foyer as he descended into the basement.

JEREMIAH APPEARED A few minutes later.

"What have you found out? We've got Rampert up in a helicopter over this ship. Is he friend or foe?"

"Sir, then-Lieutenant Colonel Rampert was a Delta Force operator in the first Gulf War. Ballantine was interrogated by several different soldiers, but it appears that Lantini and Rampert were involved somehow." Jeremiah looked away for a moment and then back at the vice president. "And you talked to Ballantine also."

"Of course I did. I was in charge of that whole mess. Tens of thousands of enemy prisoners of war, and this hotshot lieutenant brings in a no-shit Republican Guard enemy commander. What else was I going to do?"

"The interrogation reports you gave me show that Ballantine proved of no significant intelligence value and with his French connections, he was released rather quickly. The reports show that Lantini interviewed him twice and that Rampert was responsible for releasing him into the wild, as they say."

"So, you think Rampert and Lantini are triangulating with Ballantine now?"

"Seems plausible."

"Pick up that phone over there and dial me in to Dave Palmer," Hellerman directed. When Jeremiah picked up one phone, Hellerman said, "No, not that one, the other phone." Jeremiah replaced the one in his hand in its cradle and picked up an identical looking cordless phone. Jeremiah punched in the numbers. "On second thought," Hellerman said, "never mind."

"Sir?"

"Let's get back to the command center," Hellerman said as he walked briskly out of the office and up the steps. He called over his shoulder, "Lock up when you come up. And shut down that laptop, will you."

He watched as Jeremiah punched a few buttons on the laptop, closed the lid with his long fingers, then grabbed the keys, moved the plastic chair into place, pulled the door closed, fumbled with it, and pulled it shut again, moved the hasp into place, touching the metal, grasped the lock, inserted the key, snapped it shut, tugged on it, leaving fingerprints over every conceivable surface.

Exactly as Hellerman wished.

Hellerman looked over his shoulder as he ascended the stairway and watched as Jeremiah pocketed the keys to the makeshift bunker.

Hellerman. Moving the pawn when he has to. Freeing up the queen to slide across the board for checkmate.

CHAPTER 57

NORTHERN VIRGINIA

Meredith Morris sat cross-legged on Jacob Olney's guest bed with her cell phone clutched in one hand. The phone call from Colonel Rampert was welcome, and now she was wondering how this scenario would develop.

She looked down at the pictures she had taken of Hellerman's lair and knew instinctively that some very bad people were probably going to be coming after her. Having grown up in southwestern Virginia, she was no stranger to hard times or even dangerous times. But the thought of a nameless, faceless human being with a specific mission to find her, and possibly kill her, was extraordinarily unsettling.

Rampert had been all business and not the least bit concerned about finding out where she was located, which was a good sign. He wanted the information that Matt had told him about, and that was all. He had kept the conversation short and to the point, avoiding unnecessary air time. She knew that the longer the call, the easier she would be to track using the government's CallScan cell-phone monitoring system.

She unfolded her legs and stood from the bed, walking into the guest bathroom off of her room. She closed the door to the bedroom and the door that led to the hallway, placed the manila envelope with the pictures on the back of the toilet lid, and leaned against the counter top, staring at the mirror. She could see lines of worry etched across her once-smooth and beautiful face, a face that Matt Garrett used to softly stroke as they lay in bed, solving the world's problems and building their dreams for the future. She had abandoned all of that because of her lack of discipline and inability to resist the power and seduction of the vice president of the United States.

Hellerman was attractive, successful, powerful, and magnetic . . . but so was Matt. Why, she wondered, had she been unable to resist the pull, despite so many evident reasons to avoid the man she now considered to be the devil?

She splashed some water on her face and decided a hot shower would do her some good. She stripped naked and cranked the shower to full blast, edging the selector knob toward the fat portion of the red line. She let the hot water build and stepped gingerly into the shower, recoiling at first at the searing heat but gradually accepting its cleansing effects.

As the hot rain bore down on her, she began to weep. It was impossible to feel any worse about herself than she already did. She had destroyed her relationship with a great guy, possibly the best guy she would ever meet, and had unknowingly helped to put him and the country in harm's way. She was a good woman, and perhaps only she would ever fully understand what had happened.

These last few hours, her bravery in pulling away from the magnetic reach of Hellerman's black hole, taking the pictures that helped break the case, and then vectoring Rampert to the right location, were personal salvation for her. But she knew that there were not many people who would see the big picture of what she had been trying to do versus what had actually happened.

She washed her hair and rinsed the soap from her now-bright red skin. She then sat for several minutes on the shower floor, tears mixing with the water and swirling down the drain.

How appropriate, she thought, as she watched the soapy water disappear beyond the metal sieve. *My life has long since washed away, stolen by Hellerman.* But she didn't blame him, only herself. If she had been strong enough, she could have resisted and possibly even cracked the Predator case earlier, or figured out what was going on before thousands of Americans died. Now was as good a time as any to blame herself for everything that had happened in the past week.

Strangely, she was at peace. Somehow she had gained some momentum in at least absolving herself of her sins. She figured that nailing Hellerman to the wall with those pictures would at least pull her out of hell and put her somewhere in between there and heaven.

Yes, taking those pictures to her boss, Palmer, or even the president, would be some form of sweet justice, bringing Hellerman to his knees. She had already hoped that Rampert had the good sense to preserve as much of the *Fong Hou* as possible so that things such as radio frequencies could be retrieved and matched with those in Hellerman's basement.

She stood and twisted off the faucet, letting the steam boil around her. Her skin felt rejuvenated. She reached a long, slender arm from the shower into the foggy steam and felt around for the towels that Jacob had pointed out earlier. Grabbing one, she patted down her skin and dried off.

She stepped from the shower into the steam, unable to see the mirror. She used the towel to wipe off a few streaks. She could barely make out her face in the haze, the worry lines soothed a bit, a fatalistic form of recognition coloring her countenance.

She pulled her jeans and sweatshirt back on and stepped into her shoes, the steam still swirling around the bathroom. And then something didn't seem right.

She heard a noise from the hallway or the bedroom, she wasn't sure which. It was a thud of sorts, perhaps Jacob closing his door, but more like the sound of something large dropping on something hard.

She opened the bedroom door, moving quickly, but then she stopped suddenly and moved back to the bathroom, remembering the pictures.

She reached into the dissipating steam, eyeing the toilet lid, and saw that there was nothing there. The manila envelope was gone.

A shiver crawled up her spine like a rattlesnake slithering toward its prey.

This is it, she thought. *I'm going to die right here, right now, and get blamed for being involved in Hellerman's conspiracy.* She steeled her resolve so she could step from her frozen state of fear.

She walked slowly into the bedroom and could see the door was slightly ajar. She looked around the room for some sort of weapon and remembered her mace, but even her purse was missing.

She opened a few drawers until she found a pair of scissors, which she clutched in her hand as if it was a Ginsu sword. More boldly, she moved toward the door, hearing another small thud coming from Jacob's room. Her quick mind raced with possibilities, the most logical being that Hellerman's hit man had found her using CallScan, searched a few houses, and found her car in Jacob's garage. Because the scan system would only give a grid coordinate and could not provide a precise address, it had taken some time.

Poor Jacob.

She peered from the bedroom door down the long, dark hallway and saw that Jacob's door was open and his room was dark. She tip-toed towards his room when she heard a noise behind her.

Blasting from the steam-filled bathroom was a man dressed in black with a ski mask covering his face and a glint of steel in his hand.

She bolted down the hallway and into Jacob's room, slamming the door behind her. The attacker's knife came piercing through the six-paneled, fiberglass door, inches from her face as she held the knob in place.

She locked the door and walked backward, holding the scissors with one hand, feeling her way in the darkness with the other. She found a wall and followed it away from the door until she found the back wall and a window. She frantically clawed at the window latch as a shot blew off the door handle. She hadn't seen the gun.

She was raising the window as the light came on in the room. Stepping through the window and looking over her shoulder, she saw Jacob lying on the floor next to her, a bullet hole in his forehead.

What else can I do wrong?

A bullet smacked into her shoulder, knocking her through the open window, her head smashing into the window frame. She fell into the bushes below, barely conscious. She mustered the resolve to move away from the window and stand alongside the brick exterior of the house. She had lost her scissors in the fall but saw a jagged piece of glass about ten inches long. She retrieved it, careful not to cut herself.

She watched as a dark head protruded from the window no more than two feet from her position. She gripped the glass and brought it up hard toward the neck but found instead the shoulder of her assailant. The glass cut deep into the bone of her hands, causing her to scream a long, anguished wail, more from the pain of so many bad decisions over the past year than from the present moment.

Her attacker instinctively recoiled and fled back into the bedroom.

Meredith slid down the brick wall, bleeding heavily from the glass shards embedded in her hands.

"Come get me, you bastard. I don't care," she muttered.

Then she passed out in Jacob's back yard.

CHAPTER 58

ABOARD THE FONG HOU

"Why were you expecting me, Ballantine?" Peyton O'Hara said, leveling her rifle at the men in the darkness. She could see the two of them, but they were too close together for her to have a clear shot.

"My sources tell me that you and Mr. Garrett here have become quite an item, and my research on you tells me that you're quite the aggressive one. So it only makes sense."

Ballantine continued backing toward the door until he found the latch for the galley stair that would lead them down to the Sherpa, where Zachary Garrett was waiting for them. As he turned the handle, the light from the stairwell silhouetted him and Matt Garrett.

The light gave her an instant where she thought she could pierce Ballantine's eyes with one shot, but they were moving too fast for her to be safe, so she deliberately shot wide, but close, squeezing off multiple shots, suppressing Ballantine as he dragged Matt down the steps. The door closed, but not before she could get a knife wedged in between the door and the frame. She pried the knife back, opening a small slit in the door. She heard a door below her open, shut, and then lock. She waited and then backed away from the stairwell, moving to the top of the containers and stopping to think.

What is he doing? She needed to move fast. She scampered over the top of the containers, feeling the wind and salt water spray across her face before she entered the stairwell on the opposite side from where Ballantine had taken Matt. She went up the stairs and found the door to the communications center. As she rounded the corner, she was confronted by two Chinese sailors with AK-47s.

Clean, well placed shots from Blake's silenced AR-15 cleared them out of her way. She stopped for a brief moment before she turned the knob to the control center and saw an elderly Chinese man wearing a white naval uniform standing in the center of a communications node with televisions and radios all around him.

He lifted a pistol and fired a round, but she dove out of the way and slid along the floor, raising her rifle in time to squeeze off two shots and then feel the disheartening lock of the bolt.

She quickly ejected the magazine and replaced it with her last twenty rounds, pressing the detent button and slamming the bolt forward. As she was changing magazines, the admiral escaped from the room. She stood and ran after him, hoping he would lead her to Matt.

The old man leapt through a small metal door and into a stairwell, turning to fire at her, two rounds pinging off the wall next to her head.

She fired back, aiming intentionally high so that he would continue. He went down another flight of steps, Peyton close on his heels. He burst through the door to the flight deck, Peyton popping another couple of rounds at the gap in the closing door. This time it worked. She found the door open and leapt through it, doing a combat roll on hard metal as she sought cover quickly.

She saw two Chinese sailors running for their weapons. She fired two rounds, dropping them in succession. She saw another sailor to her right as she moved to hide behind a Predator.

She fired another two shots at the sailor to her right, wounding him at worst, killing him at best. The admiral was running away down the long axis of the runway. He was harmless, she figured, but leveled the weapon at him and blew off one of his calf muscles from nearly seventy yards away. *Not bad,* she thought to herself. *He might be able to provide some useful information after this is all over if he doesn't bleed to death.*

"Peyton O'Hara!" a voice called out. "Peyton O'Hara!"

It was Ballantine. She knew it had to be. Then she saw Ballantine walking to the center of the runway, near the Sherpa. He was holding Matt close to him, knife to his throat. Behind them, she could see the Sherpa's open cabin door. There was a body in the back, facing the opening. That had to be Zachary Garrett, she determined. Her mind was racing. What to do?

"I see you, Miss O'Hara. So step forward, or I will slit your boyfriend's throat."

Peyton paused, then stepped forward holding the rifle to her cheek, sighting the best she could in the dim light. Ballantine had his right arm over Matt's chest with the knife to the left portion of Matt's neck. His head was almost directly behind Matt's head, and the only exposed portion of his body available for a shot was his right arm.

"See, if you kill me, you don't get your tape back," Matt said. He was looking at Peyton, who was walking slowly in their direction, rifle leveled at them both.

"Yeah, I've got the tape," Peyton said, picking up on Matt's lead.

"That's where you're wrong, O'Hara. I have the tape. Your brilliant boyfriend had it in his pocket."

"That's where you're wrong, Ballantine. He gave it to me before coming up the ship, and I've got it right here in my pocket. What you've got is a fake," she said, moving slowly.

"And we both know that you're not the martyr type. Never were, never will be. You want to live in peace in some country with beautiful pastels to inspire your paintings," Matt said.

Ballantine's silence was telling, Peyton thought. She added, "You want to make sure about that tape, don't you? Think about it. Why the hell would he come up here with that tape?"

"I'll just have to take my chances," Ballantine said. "Drop your rifle or I will kill him. Now."

Peyton figured their time had expired. She had moved slightly to an oblique angle where she could take more of a shoulder shot.

"Okay, you win Ballantine, but what do I get in exchange?" she said.

"I'll kill you first," he said, "so you don't have to watch."

She squeezed her trigger finger, feeling the hammer of the weapon fall and her mind willing the bullet to a specific spot. She saw the round impact a bit lower than she had intended but squarely into Ballantine's upper bicep. She immediately knew she had probably shot Matt as well, but if he got medical attention, he could survive. Maybe.

Matt spun away and she saw blood on his shirt, confirming her fear. Ballantine reeled back, the knife never leaving his hand, slicing into Matt's clavicle. Matt quickly grabbed at Ballantine's arm and, despite tremendous pain, thrust it downward while bringing his knee up, snapping Ballantine's forearm.

The knife fell to the ground. Matt quickly retrieved the knife, only to see Ballantine bolt for the airplane. Peyton had a shot, but Matt's movement blocked her line of fire, causing her to lift and shoot high her last bullet.

"Damn it, Matt. I had him," she shouted, tossing the weapon to the ground and running toward them.

Matt sprinted to the airplane and pulled at Ballantine, who was climbing into the pilot's seat and cranking the engine. Ballantine swatted at Matt, who was coming at him over the passenger seat. Peyton suddenly appeared on the other side of the airplane as the engine sputtered to life.

Matt lifted the knife and drove it into Ballantine's chest as the airplane began to roll forward. But Ballantine refused to give up, the blood pouring over his shirt and spraying from his right lung into Matt's face.

The plane was now moving along the centerline of the runway, gaining speed. Somehow Ballantine was still maneuvering the Sherpa.

Peyton was outside the pilot's door, hanging onto the lower wing stanchion with her feet barely inside the cockpit. She pushed Ballantine with her left leg. Matt retrieved the knife and drove it deep into Ballantine's heart, ending any doubt about his future status.

Matt pushed the dying Iraqi in between the pilot and copilot's seats toward the back, where Zachary was. Reaching across Ballantine's legs, he grabbed Peyton's hand and helped her into the airplane, now doing donuts on the deck.

Peyton slid into the pilot's seat and grabbed the controls, turning the Sherpa back toward the catapult.

"There are more sailors over there," Matt said, pointing. "And we're out of ammo."

"They still think Ballantine might be piloting this thing. We've probably got about two minutes until they figure it out."

They looked at each other and then down at Ballantine, who was rapidly dying, and Zachary, whose status was unknown.

"We've got one choice. When was the last time you flew one of these things?" Matt asked.

"Let me think," she said. "Never? Yeah, never."

"Never."

"I did helicopters, remember?"

"Okay, same thing, right? Rev it up real high and go into the air?"

"Let's hope so," she said, studying the instruments and controls.

Peyton reached full throttle and then released the brakes and shot along the centerline. Two Chinese sailors watched, raised their AK-47s, and began firing.

CHAPTER 59

CHESAPEAKE BAY

"Delta six, this is radar control, over."

Rampert's steady voice crackled over the radio net. "This is Delta six, over."

"This is radar control. We've been sorting through a lot of clutter down here over the last hour, but think we might have something. There's a small, steady mark on the radar heading southwest from your location at about seventy miles an hour. Those Predators can do that speed, which would be slow enough to take it off our normal radar procedures. The interesting thing is that it's flying at eight hundred feet above ground level."

"Have you mapped out where it's heading?"

"All we can do is follow the UAV's azimuth. If you look at the range of these things and the 207-degree azimuth it is on, well, it's going toward your command center at Fort Bragg and Pope Air Force Base."

Rampert thought for a second. That would make sense. Destroy the temporary headquarters of the homeland defense command system and then take on other targets. That would be the perfect first target. It had to be a Predator.

"Thanks."

Turning to Hobart, Rampert said, "What has Pope got that they can scramble?"

"Nothing. Everything's over in Afghanistan or Iraq. Langley's still on its butt. Be another thirty minutes before they can scramble a jet. Tomcat two six is still broke at Oceana. Tomcat one six is all we've got left."

"Are we broke or what?" Rampert said in disgust.

"We do have one option, boss," Hobart said, looking at him.

Rampert paused, knowing exactly what Hobart was talking about.

"Kill the Queen Bee . . . destroy Dr. Insect's software . . . keep the Predators from communicating," Rampert said, more to himself than Hobart. He had replayed the scenario in his mind once he had been able to believe it.

The two warriors stared at each other for what seemed an eternity, then Rampert pressed the talk button on his radio.

Jack Rampert said a brief prayer for the Garrett family and any other innocent souls on board the *Fong Hou*, then spoke into his headset.

"Tomcat one six, this is Delta six," Rampert said.

"This is Tomcat one six. Go ahead."

"This is Delta six. We have permission to destroy the *Fong Hou* container ship. I want you to first destroy the command and control cell in the bridge of the ship. Then I want you to put a Maverick through the bow of the ship where they have been launching those Predators. We don't necessarily want to sink it, but if that happens, we'll deal with it."

"Roger. Understand. Anything further?"

"Negative. Execute."

Rampert had Mike position them again for front row seats. This time it was to watch the destruction of the *Fong Hou*. He watched the F-14 circle once and rise into the air. He could see the missile release from its rack and leave a streaming vapor trail as it made its way to the bridge of the ship. Rampert was a soldier and he knew that he had just ordered the sacrifice of good men in the name of the greater cause. But the idea of which cause and for whom left him with the slightest flutter of doubt, an emotion utterly unfamiliar to him.

Despite Rampert's misgivings, the missile exploded with a brilliant impact, destroying the entire superstructure of the ship. The F-14 screamed overhead as it arched skyward from its first bombing run.

"Roger that," Hobart said into the headset, applauding the direct hit.

"Roger that," Rampert repeated in a hushed voice, knowing he had probably just killed some people that didn't need to die. "Zachary and Matt Garrett are heroes." He looked at Hobart.

"Heroes often die, sir."

"We wouldn't be here if it wasn't for them, but we've got to destroy this ship and get Tomcat one six on afterburners down to Fort Bragg."

"Tomcat one six, this is Delta six. Prepare for run number two," Rampert said.

"Roger. Out."

Rampert said another small prayer.

CHAPTER 60

ABOARD THE FONG HOU

Peyton sped the Sherpa along the centerline of the runway, tracers screaming past the fuselage and disappearing into the darkness beyond.

"It's tough to hit a moving target," she said under a forced breath, voicing more of a hope than a fact.

"You did pretty well back there with the admiral," Matt said.

"Yeah, but I'm an expert marksman. Shot expert in basic," she said.

Bullets were pinging off the Sherpa as they began to gain altitude. Suddenly they felt a shudder and heard an explosion to their rear that ricocheted through the cockpit.

"What the hell was that?" Matt said, hoping they had not elevated too early and hit the roof of the shell.

He looked back and saw the Chinese sailors running from a fireball that had blown off the doors of the stairwell and was seeking the oxygen of the bow opening.

"Fireball moving this way. Step on it, Peyton. Step on it!"

"I'm full throttle," she said, focused ahead. The plane began to lift again.

"Not yet!" Matt shouted. "We've got a roof over our head."

"Damn it, I'm doing the best I can," she said, wrestling with the controls.

"Okay, here it comes," Matt said.

"I've got it!"

Matt watched as she pushed forward on the controls to fight the aircraft's natural tendency to lift at these speeds. As they approached the bow opening, Matt saw the fireball on their tail and then, looking skyward, something that made his heart stop.

"What the hell . . . ?" Matt yelled.

"Don't say that. We're almost there," she said. The Sherpa popped into the clear. Matt watched the incoming missile as Peyton pulled back on the steering column, providing maximum lift to the light airplane at the same time it shot from the elevated bow. The billowing flames reached out for them, licking at the tail of the Sherpa as the Maverick screamed past them at supersonic speed, slamming into the bow of the ship.

Peyton struggled against the turbulence created by the second explosion.

"What was that?" Peyton shouted.

Matt looked to the rear as Peyton fought to keep the Sherpa above the waters of the Chesapeake.

"You don't want to know. Keep flying this mother," Matt said.

Peyton stayed low, fighting the airplane, pulling back on the controls and trying to cut the trim at the same time. "Are we okay?"

"I think so. How are your flaps? Flaps okay?" Matt said.

"This piece of junk doesn't have flaps!" Peyton shouted.

Suddenly she leveled it about thirty feet above the water. Peyton found the right combination of speed, altitude, lift, and pitch, and there it was.

They flew for another few seconds.

"Okay, okay, we're good to go," Matt said. "I'm going to put on the headset and try to make comms with somebody, because I'm sure anything that flies will get shot down quickly. Then I'll check on Zachary." He cast a glance at his brother, who he could see was breathing, eyes heavy with sedation, barely conscious. Then he looked down at Ballantine, who was a sharp contrast to Zachary.

He was dead.

"Fine, but where do you want me to go?" Peyton asked.

"Head up the Chesapeake Bay to the north. I think we've got one more bad guy to get before this thing is over."

"Hellerman?"

"Right. Hellerman," he said.

"If you say so, but this could get interesting," she said.

Matt looked at her. "Get?"

Peyton paused. "Well, I guess, it's already pretty interesting."

He put the headset on and began to conduct radio checks.

CHAPTER 61

MH-60 OVER CHESAPEAKE BAY

"Great shot, Tomcat one six," Rampert said.

"Hey, sir, you see that?" Hobart said, pointing.

Rampert looked where Hobart's finger was directing his attention. He saw a small airplane just beat Tomcat one six's Maverick missile into the bow of the ship. They watched the airplane wobble in the wash of the explosion and dive toward the water, then recover and dive again until it finally leveled out.

"That's Ballantine," Rampert said.

"Roger that. We can't let him escape."

"Radar control, this is Delta six. I need you to track a small white airplane flying low over Chesapeake Bay near the *Fong Hou*."

"Wait one."

"Standing by."

"Roger, Delta six, we've got a small single-engine aircraft doing about 150 miles an hour banking north up the Chesapeake Bay. We will continue to track, but the signal is very weak. If it slows down, we might lose it."

"Roger. Continue to track. Let me know if you lose it." Rampert switched to intercom and looked at Hobart. "How long until the F-15s are available?"

"They'll have two F-15s airborne in twenty-five minutes, loaded with Mavericks and chain guns," Hobart said.

"Good. We'll send Tomcat one six after the Predator and launch the F-15s after Ballantine's Sherpa with instructions to destroy on contact. Radar control should be able to vector them in quickly."

"Sir, you sure you want to do that?"

"No option. If Tomcat one six doesn't go now, he'll be too late. There's about thirty minutes of flight time left before the Predator hits the command center. It's an hour flight for the Sherpa up to D.C. We have to take the chance. It's been on-again and off-again on the radar. We have to get it now."

"Roger. I agree," Hobart said.

Rampert looked at the burning hulk of the *Fong Hou*. Two missiles had destroyed it, but there was still one rogue nuke heading toward Fort Bragg and one Sherpa loaded with bad intentions heading to the nation's Capitol.

Still, he wasn't convinced that this was everything the bad guys had to offer.

CHAPTER 62

CHESAPEAKE BAY

"Good job back there, Peyton," Matt said.

"Thanks," she said.

"Keep trying to make contact. I'm going to check on Zachary. Stay low. Don't get over 500 feet above ground level."

"You know they probably think we're Ballantine, going to attack the Capitol," Peyton said.

"I know, but if we don't stop Hellerman, he'll get away with this. And that is totally unacceptable."

"I agree, but if we get shot down in the process, then he'll definitely get away with it," Peyton said.

"You have the tape, right?" Matt asked.

"I thought you had it," she said, forcing a smile. She reached into her bra and pulled out the small cassette tape.

"Double Top Secret hiding place?"

She managed a weak smile.

"Yeah, he would have never thought to look there." Matt grinned, stepping over Ballantine.

He bent down on one knee and placed his hand against Zachary's neck. He felt a steady, strong pulse. "He's okay," Matt said.

"I'm glad," Peyton said, softly.

"Zachary, can you hear me?" Matt asked.

"What . . . ?" He struggled to open his eyes. "Matt . . . ? Where you been?"

"Are you okay?"

"Yeah, I'm okay," Zachary said. "I'm okay, Matt."

Matt held back a wave of emotions. It had been nearly a year since he thought he had lost his brother. In between kicking himself and mourning his brother's death, he had rendered himself dysfunctional. Now Zachary was safe. They were safe.

Well, almost, Matt figured. Even if something were to happen to them in the next few hours, he would cherish those words, *I'm okay, Matt.*

Matt ran his hand along his brother's face.

"Thanks, man. You did great." Zachary's voice was weak but clear.

Matt pulled the knife from Ballantine's chest and cut the ropes on Zachary's wrists, then unscrewed the shackles on his legs, rubbing each area to get the circulation back.

"But it's not over." Zachary turned his head to the rear of the airplane.

Matt stopped what he was doing and followed Zachary's gaze.

"It's a nuke." Zachary's voice was clear.

Matt's heart froze. He could see a small timer with flashing red letters counting down from thirty-five minutes. Now thirty-four minutes and fifty-nine seconds.

"Peyton?" Matt said.

"Yes?"

"Where are we, and how long until we get to Hellerman's Middleburg mansion?"

"We're over Tappahannock right now and about thirty minutes out," she said. "Why?"

"How long would it take us to get out to the Atlantic Ocean?"

"About the same amount of time," she said. "What's up?"

He looked at Zachary, who met his gaze. "We need to de-rig that thing, man, or drop it over the ocean."

Matt inspected the black box. Whoever had installed the bomb did so by drilling screws into the floorboard of the airplane and countersinking them through the housing of the bomb. Three-and-a-half-inch screws locked down each side of the box.

"If we dump it, we dump with it. This thing ain't going anywhere this plane doesn't go," Matt said.

Zachary looked at him with a clear countenance. "If that's what we have to do, that's what we do, Matt."

"It's not what we have to do. I'll de-rig it. We can have somebody talk us through this."

"If you don't make comms in a couple of minutes, I want you to take us out to sea, Matt. And I mean it," Zachary said.

Matt momentarily wished his brother were a bit more drugged.

"I've got him, I've got him!" Peyton waved her hand.

"Who, who do you have?"

"It's some radar control guy at Oceana."

Matt scrambled to the front seat and grabbed the headset from Peyton.

"What's going on back there?" she asked.

"Oh, that. There's a live nuke on board, that's all."

She stared at him for a moment in disbelief and then said, "Well, it finally got interesting."

"Radar control, this is Matt Garrett."

"Matt Garrett, this is radar control. State type of aircraft and intentions."

"This is Matt Garrett flying in Ballantine's Sherpa aircraft. We just launched from the deck of the *Fong Hou* about forty minutes ago. We are headed to a small dirt airfield in northwestern Virginia for a landing."

"I am tracking your aircraft. Stand by."

"Two other things you need to know about this aircraft are that we have Ballantine on board. He is dead. And there is a live nuke on board."

"A live nuke?"

"Yes. I need you to contact Colonel Jack Rampert and get a bomb specialist to talk me through neutralizing this thing. We have thirty minutes."

"I have communications with Colonel Rampert. Stand by."

Matt felt a surge of hope.

"Matt," Zachary said, sitting up. "If we can't shut it down, I'm telling you we need to turn east and get over the water."

Peyton looked over her shoulder at the man that had been Matt's obsession for the past year. She understood what Matt had been going through, having lost her parents when she was younger. And now, hearing Zachary tell his younger brother that they both might need to die to serve the greater good was about all she could handle. She was a tough woman, but she was a sap for nobility. She didn't know Zachary well, but she did know Matt, and she would set the plane on a course for a remote portion of the Blue Ridge.

Matt felt the plane bank just a bit. "What are you doing?" he said to Peyton.

She looked at him. "You know exactly what I'm doing."

They locked eyes for a long moment, each reflecting on the dynamics occurring on many different levels. Matt and Zachary. Peyton and Matt. The nuke. The right thing to do. Hellerman.

How would it all end, Matt wondered, waiting for radar control to contact him again.

As they waited, the hum of the plane's engine droned along, Peyton steering the Sherpa on a new azimuth that would give her the option of getting them over the Chesapeake.

Just in case.

CHAPTER 63

MIDDLEBURG, VIRGINIA

"Sir, we've got Ballantine's Sherpa flying north right here," Zeke Jeremiah said, pointing at a large map of Virginia, his finger touching an area just northwest of Fredericksburg, Virginia. "And there's a Predator armed with a nuclear device, we believe, about fifteen minutes out from Fort Bragg, just south of Raleigh, North Carolina, down here." Zeke's long, black finger circled an area on a North Carolina map about fifty miles north of Fort Bragg. "They both have primitive stealth technology, but we are getting intermittent signals. This is why we never tracked Ballantine coming out of Canada."

Vice President Hellerman stood staring at the maps. Jock Evans tapped him on the shoulder and handed him a phone.

The operations center was a humming machine of activity. At least thirty staffers were manning phones, fax machines, and computers. They updated slides and moved markers on maps. There was a high level of noise that accompanied the activity, allowing Hellerman to take this phone call directly in the middle of the command center.

Bandit's voice was firm. "Rawlings, I've got the pictures and hard drive. Miss Morris will not be joining us. It appears she had a falling out with a lover. Out."

The vice president flipped the phone shut and pursed his lips. A huge weight had been lifted from his shoulders. The pictures and his hard drive were on their way back to him, Meredith was no longer an issue, and now he might have Ballantine flying to his airfield to deliver the tape. *Pretty ballsy move,* Hellerman thought, *but things are way out of control.* The question was, should he just order the Air Force to shoot down the Sherpa and destroy everything that could implicate him? That was probably a good idea, he surmised.

"Zeke, get me the secretary of defense up on VTC," he said, turning toward the video teleconferencing camera next to the operations map.

"Roger, sir. He's up," Jeremiah said, pointing at the screen.

"Secretary Stone, can you hear me?" Hellerman said into the camera, looking at the screen that was projecting the secretary of defense and the chairman of the Joint Chiefs of Staff.

"Yes, Mr. Vice President, go ahead."

"The president is monitoring from his quarters right now, and I have control. I am going to take control of the F-15s coming out of Langley. Are they ready to go?"

Hellerman watched as Stone traded curious looks with Shepanski, then turned back to the camera.

"Mr. Vice President, right now Langley has launched a flight of two F-15 Eagles with a mission of finding the Sherpa airplane in which we believe Ballantine is traveling. Their communications are with Colonel Jack Rampert, the special operations commander. He is controlling the operation."

"Yes, Mr. Stone, let me say this a different way. That Sherpa is bearing down on my location. I will best be able to direct the F-15s, not Jack Rampert hovering over Chesapeake Bay. So switch command of the aircraft to me immediately. Do you understand that this is an order and not a request?"

After another exchange of looks with Shepanski, Stone turned to the vice president and said, "Yes, sir. The F-15s are on UHF frequency two-zero-five-two. Call signs are Eagle six and Eagle five. They are armed with four AIM-120 missiles and 20mm machine guns. They are under your operational control."

Hellerman clicked the remote, muting their conversation, and turned to

Jeremiah. "Get me Eagle six and five up on the UHF net."

Within a minute, Jeremiah gave the radio handset to Hellerman, saying, "Here you go, sir."

"Eagle six, this is the vice president. Over."

"Vice President, this is Eagle six. We are a flight of two F-15s currently on afterburners moving to locate a Sherpa with new instructions to observe and monitor."

Hellerman looked at Jeremiah, who shrugged his shoulders.

"Your instructions are to destroy the Sherpa," the vice president said into the radio handset.

"Negative. Prior to being moved to your control, we were told friendlies are on board the Sherpa. We are in monitor mode."

Hellerman looked at Jeremiah again and said, "Call Rampert and find out what the hell is going on, what kind of games he's playing."

"This is Eagle six. Also, was told that a nuclear bomb is on board the aircraft, and we are to avoid firing at all costs."

"Eagle six, you are under my operational control, and you will take all orders from me. Do you understand?"

"This is Eagle six. Roger. I understand that I will follow all lawful orders you give me."

Smart ass, Hellerman thought to himself.

"What have you got from Rampert?" Hellerman asked Zeke.

"Sir, can't reach Rampert, but Oceana radar control said he talked to one of the people on board, and the rumor is, get this, Matt Garrett is on board."

The noise level in the operations center quickly wound down, and muted television monitors flashed off the dumbfounded faces of the operations crew.

"I say again, Matt Garrett might be on board the Sherpa."

Hellerman looked stunned. He had assumed Matt and Zachary Garrett had both perished. The news that the pictures had been retrieved and that Meredith had been killed was welcome. His only concern now was the tape, the last remaining shred of evidence that could be used against him.

Ballantine had played the tape for him one day over the phone and then had sent him a copy during the early months of Desert Shield. He remembered listening to it and recoiling at the sound of his voice, so very clear and convincing, talking with May Sandford, the U.S. ambassador to Iraq at the time. It was clear evidence of conspiracy thirteen years ago. It would only circumstantially contribute to a case made regarding today's activities. He doubted, until now, that there was anyone who could implycate him in any foul play.

But now he had Matt Garrett out there, the man that Ballantine should have killed several days ago. That was the deal, to get Matt Garrett up to Lake Moncrief so that Ballantine could kill him. In trade, Ballantine would provide Hellerman the original tape. It seemed like good sport, and Hellerman benefited from Ballantine's organization of attacks on the country.

"Sir, did you hear that?" Jeremiah's voice slowly brought Hellerman back to reality.

"Yes, Zeke, I heard. Matt Garrett is on board. That's . . . that's great news."

"If it's true," Jeremiah said with raised eyebrows.

Hellerman paused, then said, "Yes, if it's true. What authentication did Oceana get?"

"None that I'm aware of, sir."

"Alternate command, this is Eagle six. Over."

"Eagle six, this is alternate command," Jeremiah replied.

"Roger. We've got this Sherpa on our radar, and it has banked hard to the west, following along just south of Interstate 66."

"Roger. This is the vice president. Your orders are to destroy the Sherpa once it gets west of Warrenton."

"Sir, this is Eagle six. Pardon me for asking, but why do you want me to destroy this aircraft with possible friendlies on it?"

Hellerman recoiled at the insubordination. "Eagle six, you are now relieved of command. Your orders are to return to base. Eagle five, you are now in command, do you understand?"

The pilot for Eagle five replied weakly, "Roger . . . roger, sir."

"Eagle five, this is the vice president. If Eagle six is not out of your airspace in one minute, your instructions are to engage and destroy him."

"Roger."

"This is Eagle six. Roger. I monitored, have copied this conversation on cockpit recorder, and am breaking station. Eagle six out."

"Eagle five, this is the vice president. Did you copy my last order to Eagle six regarding destroying the Sherpa once it has crossed west of Warrenton?"

"This is Eagle five. Roger."

Hellerman dropped his hand to his side, still holding the handset, and realized for the first time that the entire command center was listening to his conversation and had heard his orders.

"Okay, team, listen up," he said, authoritatively. "We don't know if Ballantine has a gun to Garrett's head and made him make the call or what is going on in the cockpit of that airplane. We do know that it has a nuclear device on board and that we need to destroy it in the next fifteen minutes or it could wind up anywhere. It's a loose cannon right now, and we can't have that. I have tough decisions to make, and if anyone here doesn't agree, well, this is not the time to question orders but to follow them."

He looked around the room, many eyes locked onto his.

"Matt Garrett has done a great job, and he will die a hero the same way we would have shot down any of those civilian airliners on September 11 if the Air Force had been able to get in the air soon enough."

He heard a few grunts of agreement and saw the general mood of the crowd shift. They needed leadership. They were confused and scared sheep.

"Zeke, track this thing. I need a moment."

Hellerman took a step back and looked at the map, ever the wolf.

If it was Matt Garrett in the airplane, who was flying? He knew that Garrett couldn't fly and didn't believe that Zachary Garrett could fly. Maybe it was Ballantine who had the gun to his head.

Why would Matt be taking the plane to the northeast? To go to their farm? No, they were too far away. The plane was flying a parallel path to the Chesapeake. He pondered the situation, and then it occurred to him. Matt Garrett was a good man, who would not want that nuke anywhere near large population centers. Their change in course meant a couple of things to Hellerman. First, they had only recently discovered the bomb. Second, they were having problems disarming it.

Francis Hellerman suddenly felt better about everything.

CHAPTER 64

NEAR WARRENTON, VIRGINIA

"Pay attention, Matt," Zachary said with a heavy tongue. "I watched them install this thing. I know you think you know your bombs, but let me walk you through this."

Matt was sitting next to the nuclear device, studying the timer and its four wires. He looked at his brother, whose heavy eyelids belied the fact that he was about to instruct him on how to disarm a nuclear bomb.

"Hey, guys, we've got a low fuel gauge coming on here," Peyton warned, looking at Matt. "It's been draining pretty fast. We must have taken a hit to the fuel tank."

"It's got a reserve somewhere. I think it's a fifteen-minute job. Just play with some knobs up there," Matt replied over his shoulder.

"Try this, Matt," Zachary said. "Take the knife and unscrew the timer from the face plate of the bomb casing."

Matt dug at each screw, the knife slipping and cutting his fingers twice, until the last screw fell to the floor.

"Now pull that bad boy forward." Zachary's eyes slipped shut for a second.

"Okay, I've got it Zach." Matt lightly shook his brother, trying to wake him.

"Right, right, now you should see the same four wires. Two should be leading to the timer. What color are they?"

"They're all the same damn color, Zachary."

"Oh. Okay. Then you'll see copper leads. Those indicate the end of the cables. Separate the ones that have the copper leads next to the bomb from the two that have leads next to the timer."

Matt looked at Zachary. His brother's voice was getting weak, the drugs obviously ebbing and flowing in his system.

"Okay. There are two that lead directly from inside the bomb into the timer and two that lead directly from the top of the timer to each end of the bomb."

"Right, that's the circuit. Each wire coming into the timer closes the circuit. When the timer hits zero . . . uh, where is it now, the timer?"

"It's . . . it's saying seven minutes, man. Come on, quit screwing around, Zachary. You used to pull this crap when we were kids."

"Hey, man, I'm drugged. Get off my case."

The engine began to sputter, and Matt could see Peyton frantically searching around the cockpit for knobs. Any knobs.

"Will you two quit fighting and deal with the problem, please!" she shouted.

"Oh, yeah, the reserve tank is between the seats. That little knob, just push it back," Zachary said. "Saw Ballantine do that on our way down here. Same thing happened."

Peyton found the knob and pushed it back, the engine sputtering and coughing, then regaining its steady hum.

"Am I good or what?" Zachary smiled weakly.

Matt looked at his brother. The man had not changed, even in death.

"Matt, you fixed that bomb yet?" Zachary asked.

"Yeah, okay. I've got the wires that run into the bomb."

"Right, they're the ones that close the loop. The timer, when it hits zero in about five minutes, will send an electronic pulse through the top wires into the bomb. The bomb will recognize that it is time to blow up and will check just to make sure with the wires coming into the timer. Those wires will complete the loop and confirm that it's time to blow up."

Matt looked at his brother. "And?"

"And, isn't it obvious which wires you're supposed to cut?" Zachary said.

Peyton looked back and said, "We've got a big town off to our south. We're passing it now."

"Must be Warrenton," Matt said.

"No, actually it's Fredricksburg. I cut up the Potomac since you seemed to be making progress. We're still over water and I'm going low. So get ready."

Her solemn tone served to cut through the brotherly jousting.

They flew in silence for about one minute, and Matt said, "Peyton? Ready?"

"Cut the loop-closing wires, Matt. Now!" Zachary's voice was clear.

Matt looked at his brother, who said it again. "Now, Matt."

Having taken orders from his older brother all his life, Matt lifted the knife and cut the two wires that led from the bomb to the timer. His hand shook as the knife sliced through the rubber-coated wires. He held the timer in his hand. It continued its countdown.

"Now what?" he asked, looking at Zachary.

Zachary's eyes were closed, and he was breathing heavily.

Peyton steered the small airplane so close to the docile Potomac that the exposed wheels created minor rooster tails.

CHAPTER 65

MIDDLEBURG, VIRGINIA

"Eagle five, this is the vice president. Give me the status of the Sherpa," Hellerman ordered into the UHF handset.

"Sir, the Sherpa has just banked north of Fredricksburg. I'm giving it some space before I take it down. My plan is to use guns, hoping that might limit the damage and prevent that nuke from going off."

"Okay, give it another two minutes, max. It ought to go down somewhere in the old Wilderness battlefield area. While not perfect, it would be acceptable."

"Roger. Understood," Eagle five said.

Hellerman stared at the map and paced, pinching his lips together, obviously in deep thought. Chess moves, these were all chess moves. This airplane was nothing more than an exposed queen ripe for the taking, a last gambit by a desperate opponent. The plane would be shot down, the nuke recovered, and the entire Chinese operation dismantled. The Garrett brothers would be dead, snuffing out any possible recrimination against him.

He could keep Rampert in a box, and Ballantine no longer appeared to be a threat.

Still, nagging at the back of his mind was the thought that no clever player ever offered up his prize without a counterstroke in mind.

The Ronnie Wood issue was still something he needed to contend with. Could that be it?

"I've got video lock on the Sherpa." The pilot's voice broke him from his strategic reverie.

He suddenly realized that he needed to get to his command bunker in order to survive the blast as well as continue to control the action. If the nuke detonates, everything is incinerated.

"Your command center there ought to be able to download this from the satellite, sir."

"Zeke, hook that up." Hellerman looked up at the blank screen. Then, after a moment, said, "Roger. Thanks. We're with you, son."

"Sir, we just got word that Tomcat one six shot down that Predator near Dunn, North Carolina. The report is that the bomb exploded and there's a radiation cloud about two miles in diameter. Small nuke, but what a mess," Zeke said.

"Listen up, everybody. Understand what I'm talking about here?" Hellerman shouted. He heard several grunts and "Yes, sirs." "This ain't child's play. This terrorist came to do business, people, and we've got to stop him."

Hellerman turned and looked at the large screen again. He could see the Sherpa flying level above some dotted lights on the ground. The picture was grainy but good enough to see one head in the pilot's seat. Just for an instant, he saw long hair hanging off the shoulders of the pilot. The video feed wasn't clear at all, but his instincts told him that Peyton O'Hara was flying that airplane.

"Eagle five, this is the vice president. Over."

"This is Eagle five. Go ahead."

"It's time. Get in position and knock this thing down. Go for the forward portion of the airplane," Hellerman commanded.

"Will comply. This is Eagle five assuming attack position."

On the screen, the operations group in the command center saw a quick rushing of land, losing sight of the Sherpa, as Eagle five turned the jet to close in on its tail. But then the Sherpa came back into view. It was closer now. The pilot had pulled up parallel with the airplane and was only a few feet away from the Sherpa's wingtip. The mesmerized faces of the operations group could plainly see the face of Peyton O'Hara huddled over the cockpit, straining to see beyond the windscreen in the night.

"I salute you," the pilot's voice came over the radio speakers. Then the Sherpa was gone from sight for the moment.

The pilot's voice again broke the deathly silence. "Going to guns."

Hellerman watched, waiting for the image of the Sherpa to reappear on the screen.

CHAPTER 66

NORTHERN VIRGINIA

"Now what, Zach?" Matt shook his drugged and exhausted brother, then muttered, "Unbelievable."

"Hey, Matt, we've got an F-15 out here on our flank," Peyton said.

"What's he doing?"

"Saluting me, I think."

"That's either good news or bad news."

Matt looked at the bomb timer. It had thirteen seconds to go . . .

00:32 . . .

00:31 . . .

00:30 . . .

"Okay, Peyton, I just want to tell you in case this thing doesn't work out that I'm really very proud of you, and I want to thank you for helping me get my brother back. If we die here in a few seconds, well, we saved him, and now we're saving others. That's not a bad way to go."

Peyton turned and watched the countdown.

00:03 . . .

00:02 . . .

00:01 . . .

The digital readout flashed zeroes for a few seconds and then began an upward count:

00:01 . . .

00:02 . . .

00:03 . . .

Matt and Peyton stared at the nuclear bomb.

"Now cut the other wires. You have fifteen seconds while the bomb tries to close the loop through the wires you cut, then it will reverse course and confirm the loop through the sending wires. If it can't confirm the loop, it won't blow up. I think."

Zachary's head rolled on the back of the Sherpa floor as he spoke.

"Damn it, why didn't you tell me that?" Matt flashed with anger.

"You were too busy sucking face with your girlfriend. Now cut the wires, man."

Matt scrambled for the knife, unable to find it, wasting precious time.

"Come on, Matt, hurry," Peyton said.

"Found it." He fumbled with the knife and grabbed both sets of wires, slicing them and then looking at the black box. The number fourteen frozen on its face.

The bomb sat idle in the back of the Sherpa. A few seconds went by, and they started to laugh. It was nervous adrenaline. For all Matt knew, Peyton was about to fly the plane into the Blue Ridge Mountains, but at least they had beaten Ballantine.

Then they heard the loud report of machine-gun fire.

"He's shooting at us!" Peyton said, banking the plane hard to the north.

"Where are we?" Matt asked her.

"We're about twenty miles from Hellerman's dirt strip. We'll never outlast this guy. He's in a fighter jet, for crying out loud."

"Take it low. Take it as low as you can go. He won't want to use Mavericks on us because he thinks the nuke is still live. He has a problem flying slow enough, so he'll have to keep circling and trying to get behind us."

Peyton pushed the airplane into a near-vertical dive, tracers ripping past the fuselage. The lower she flew, the less accurate the fire. She tilted the wings and followed the grid coordinate she had punched into the navigation system. It was as simple as lining up two small arrows, unless there was an F-15 fighter jet trying to shoot you down, she mused.

"Okay, what are you, about fifty feet off the ground?" Matt asked.

"Forty," she said.

"Okay, push it to about twenty," he said.

"I'll hit telephone wires at twenty. No way."

Another burst of machine-gun fire shot past the windscreen. Two rounds caught the right wing.

"Good thing we're low on gas," Matt said. "That's where the main tank is." He pointed at the two holes in the wing next to his seat.

"Speaking of gas, I'm getting the low-fuel warning again," she said. The engine began to sputter, as if cued.

"How far?" he asked.

"Five miles, five damn miles! And we would be home free, but this jackass is going to shoot us down—that is, if we don't fall out of the sky first!" she shouted.

Matt looked at her for a moment, then said, "Feel better?"

"Yes, actually," she said, shaking her hair behind her head and shaking off the fear.

They saw the F-15 race overhead and then pull upward, spiraling in the sky, and then loop behind them.

"Okay, here it is. He's not missing this time," Matt said. "You're going to need to zigzag a bit, like a running back, you know?"

"*This* airplane! *You* grab the handles and zigzag this bitch," Peyton hissed.

"Okay," Matt said, grabbing the steering column and yanking hard to the right about the time the F-15 spat a 20mm burst at them.

"See, it's not so hard," he spat through gritted teeth.

"Damn you!" Peyton shouted, regaining control of the airplane and leveling the wings. She put on the night-vision goggles that Ballantine had stashed on the dashboard.

"One mile. One mile. Okay, line up the arrows. One mile. There it is. There it is. We're going to make it," she said.

Peyton banked hard once, in the same style Matt had previously, avoiding another wide spray of machine-gun fire. Then the engine began to sputter and cough. They were out of fuel.

"Six hundred yards. Six damn football fields!" she shouted. "Keep going.

Get going, baby. Please keep going!" Peyton pleaded with the faltering machine.

"He's lined up on our tail, flat on our tail, Peyton. Do something!" Matt yelled, leaning out of the door and looking back. He could see the F-15 slowing almost to a stall, appearing to hover like an angry hornet. Then he saw a violent burst of machine-gun fire again.

The Sherpa rocked and swayed hard to the left and then came back to the right, its wings groaning beneath the stress of evasive maneuvers. Then the plane bucked and pitched hard to the right, pieces of sheet metal and hardware ripping off the light frame.

"We're hit, we're hit!" Matt shouted.

"I think I'm hit," Peyton said, looking down at her hip. Blood was seeping onto her pants. "Damn it, I'm hit."

"It's okay. You're going to be okay, just land this thing," Matt said. "He's going back around for another turn. We've got a window."

"I'm hit, Matt. I'm hit bad, I think," Peyton gasped, holding onto the controls, pushing the nose of the airplane lower. Her eyes were getting heavy.

"Hang in there, Peyton. We're going to be okay."

The plane banged hard into the ground, lurched upward, and then banged hard again, thrusting Matt's head into the ceiling. The wheels found purchase, though, and leveled the ride out.

She had found the runway and was guiding the plane as far north as she could toward the mansion. About one hundred yards away, the engine quit, and the plane coasted a few more feet before whipping into a tight ground loop and coming to a stop.

"Come on. Hurry, Peyton. Let's get Zachary and get out of here," Matt said.

He opened the sliding door to the Sherpa and pulled Zachary forward.

"I'm okay, Matt. Let's grab Peyton. Nerves of steel she's got, man."

Zachary wobbled, leaning on Matt, but able to control himself as he walked. They moved as quickly as possible to the other side of the fuselage and opened Peyton's door.

Peyton slumped into Matt's arms, unconscious. He pulled her from the cockpit, feeling her blood on his hands as he reached around her waist. He needed to get her to a doctor quickly and remembered that Meredith had mentioned that Hellerman always kept a medical team at the alternate command post. It only made sense.

Matt and Zachary carried Peyton away from the Sherpa about the same time they heard the F-15 thunder overhead with a deafening roar, a proud hawk circling its wounded prey. As they rounded the corner behind the mansion toward the three cottages that housed the alternate command post, Alvin Jessup stood in the dim light, holding a pistol.

"Halt or I will shoot you dead. And you know that to be true."

Matt and Zachary held Peyton, her gasps for air becoming weaker and fainter by the second.

"Alvin, it's me, Matt Garrett. This is Peyton O'Hara, and she needs a doctor, now."

"Step a little closer. Carefully," Jessup said.

They walked about ten steps, carrying Peyton.

"Who's that other guy?"

"That's my brother, Zachary," Matt said. "He was supposed to be dead, but he's not, clearly."

"What happened?" Jessup said, lowering his pistol.

"It's a long story. We need a doctor."

They were about fifty feet from the front door of the alternate command post. Jessup waved them forward toward the front door.

"Come on, let me help you," Jessup said, holstering his pistol and taking Zachary's place in helping to carry Peyton.

As they stepped onto the threshold of the alternate command post, Hellerman turned from his position near the large screen. He watched them as if it was the first time he realized the Sherpa had landed in his back yard. The camera images had been so fleeting, and with the pilot having to loop around so frequently, he had lost track of the Sherpa's actual location.

It was an awkward pause, but one that was very telling to Matt.

"I need a doctor for Peyton. Zeke, can you help me out?" he said. Jeremiah looked at Hellerman and then back at Matt.

"Absolutely." Zeke motioned to Jock Evans. "Jock, take Peyton to Doc Bell in the clinic right away. He's on call, resting in cottage two. Make it quick." Matt stared at Hellerman as he felt Jock gently remove Peyton from his grasp.

"Good to see you, man," Jock whispered. "Good job up there."

Matt kept his eyes on Hellerman and said, "Thanks, man. Take care of Peyton. She's hurt bad. Don't let me down."

"We got her, man. She's with us."

The alternate command center had gone strangely quiet, like a standoff in Dodge City, Kansas. Matt and Zachary Garrett squared off against the vice president.

Who would draw first?

Matt heard more commotion over his shoulder. Then he heard Dave Palmer, the national security adviser.

Matt stared at Hellerman and felt Palmer's hand rest on his shoulder.

"Matt, Meredith told me to get right down here, but she wasn't able to tell me why," Palmer said.

"Why couldn't she tell you everything? You in on this, too? Who are you, Brian Jones?" Matt accused, stepping back from Palmer. Brian Jones was a founding member of the actual rock group, the Rolling Stones.

"No, Matt. She didn't have time to tell me everything she wanted to. But she did manage to say, 'Tell Matt I really do love him.'"

No one in the room said a word, Palmer's message serving to silence the entire staff. The muted sounds of radio squawk boxes and fluttering images of rapidly changing television screens created a surreal atmosphere. There were volumes of activity but no movement. Sound everywhere, but silence. The blinking eyes of the televisions fluttered and faltered as if to faint at the information.

Meredith was dead.

CHAPTER 67

FORT SHERMAN, PANAMA

Frank Lantini surveyed his stockpile of weapons. The AK-47 was merely a stage prop. What he had been able to smuggle into the Central Committee's hideout was impressive.

He had a .300 Whisper sniper rifle, an M4 carbine with noise suppressor, two Beretta pistols, and enough ammunition to go down fighting. By his math there were nine primaries, each with a security detail of one guard and one interpreter. That was 27 people he needed to kill, but he thought that the interpreters might run, so 18, best case.

If he had any connections left, he would have simply called in a JDAM strike onto his location, annihilating this terrorist base camp as well as ending his own misery.

Lantini had served honorably in the Air Force in military intelligence and then had worked his way through the labyrinth of the CIA until he was nominated and confirmed as the director. Not an overly political man, he did maintain a deep and unwavering belief that Islamic extremism was the equivalent threat to democracy that Nazism had posed in the middle of the 20th century.

His witting participation in the Rolling Stones endeavor last year had been a huge mistake, but one he had been compelled to make. Literally, he'd had a gun held to his head when Matt Garrett's calls to receive kill chain approval on al Qaeda senior leadership came into his office. Despite the threat, he almost gave the approval.

Except that gun was there, held by the hand of the real Ronnie Wood.

But now he could do something about it. Redemption. This was all about redemption. He could square himself with his demons and then move on. Sure, he would continue to be on the run, but he would have evened the score.

Lantini had sent the communications team to Hellerman's alternate command post in Middleburg when the vice president had originally asked for the command suite in his basement. Hellerman was such a moron, Lantini thought, that he had no idea that Lantini would emplace the technology so that he could eavesdrop or intercept Hellerman's clandestine communications.

So he had nurtured this plan, never exposing it, so that he could ensnare as many of the nation's enemies as possible. Using a North Korean double agent, Sue Kim, whom he had known for many years, he had watched as the Central Committee began planning, monitoring Hellerman's conspiratorial tomes and messages all the way.

Lantini looked down at his Whisper and pulled it from the duffle bag that he had hidden in a spider hole covered with palm fronds.

No. He couldn't give a rat's ass about Zachary Garrett or even Matt Garrett. But he did believe in God and that redemption was possible. It was his soul he was most concerned about. Frankly, he didn't care so much about what the country was enduring. In a way, he agreed with the man with the pistol to his head who was orchestrating most of this with Ballantine.

Lantini handled the rifle and laughed. "First it was Ollie North, then the Rolling Stones, and now . . ."

He heard a noise about 50 meters away.

Lantini was kneeling in a tight stand of sugarcane growing inside the fort. His field of vision was a 270-degree arc that included the sleeping quarters, five of the six guard posts, and the cinderblock hut in which the Central Committee had been planning.

The first of the attendees for the meeting were beginning to appear.

Something was happening, and it was decision time, both for Sung and for Lantini.

Lantini's only question was, how much did he allow to happen? Put differently, how much *more* should he allow to happen?

As he slowly sighted the weapon, he determined that what happened in the United States was no longer his concern.

This was about survival.

The Russian walked into view and Lantini pulled the trigger. A silent subsonic bullet hit his skull, flattened and tumbled through his brain. Next was the Russian's interpreter.

Like a traffic accident, the others slowed and gawked in the open field, unsure of what was happening, providing superb targets for Lantini's self-taught marksmanship.

DOING THE MATH, Lantini determined that he had killed the bulk, if not all, of the foreigners, save Sue Kim and Tae Il Sung, who were in the planning hut. He kept his weapon trained on the pile of bodies as he used his peripheral vision to slowly stalk the command center.

Lowering his weapon, he opened the door and saw Sung and Kim sitting at the table.

Lantini nodded as Sung stared at the different weapon hanging by a sling across Lantini's chest.

As Sung began to push back from the table, Lantini shot the North Korean in the heart.

He spared Sue Kim, looked at her, and said, "We're done."

As they began to exit, Sung's cell phone rang, and they stopped in the doorway of the cinderblock bunker.

"I'll get that," Lantini said.

CHAPTER 68

MIDDLEBURG, VIRGINIA

"Dead?" Matt said the words as if he couldn't believe them, and saying them made them seem all the more unbelievable. *No, there must be some mistake.*

"Yes, Matt. I'm sorry."

"If Meredith is dead, I know only one person who would have motive to kill her," Matt said.

"It looks like a murder-suicide kind of thing. Maybe a spurned lover." Palmer didn't sound convinced.

"That might be what it looks like," Matt said, staring again at Hellerman, "but the vice president here can tell us exactly what happened, can't you, sir?"

"Matt, I'm glad you're okay, and Zachary, too. How wonderful it is to have Zachary back," Hellerman said.

"Don't patronize me, you murdering son of a bitch." Matt took a bold step toward Hellerman.

Alvin Jessup kept his eyes squarely on Matt and moved a bit closer to Hellerman. "Don't do it, man. I don't know what your beef is, but I will have to kill you if you threaten the vice president."

"Alvin, what would you do if I told you I had proof that he had full knowledge and helped plan all the events of the last few days?"

"I'd say you were smoking some serious shit, brother," Jessup said. The staff began to whisper the low rumble of disbelief.

"What about you, Hellerman? Isn't this part of your Rebuild America Program? Blow up a few buildings, destroy a mall or two, and then launch a few nukes to get us really concerned?"

"You're crazy, Garrett. You've gone completely mad. Alvin, arrest this man," Hellerman ordered.

"I'm afraid I have to agree, Matt. You're a bit stressed right now," Palmer said. Matt watched as Alvin Jessup pulled handcuffs from his belt and unshackled them.

"Wait!" Zachary broke his silence.

The entire room focused on Matt's brother, standing by his side.

"Wait. Matt's right. And I remember you," Zachary said, pointing at Hellerman. "You were a Reserve military intelligence officer during the Gulf War, weren't you?"

Hellerman looked amused. "Of course I was. I believe we even met there, but enough of this foolishness. We've got a war to fight."

"That's right," Matt interrupted, "this is your war."

"Arrest him," Hellerman said, flipping his hand at Matt.

"No, wait," Zachary said. "Matt's right. This is Hellerman's war. I captured Ballantine during the war and brought him back to the military intelligence center in Saudi. I was being debriefed in the next room and saw them together. I overheard Ballantine and Hellerman discussing this. Something about a tape that Ballantine had of Hellerman talking to Ambassador Sandford."

"This is crazy. Arrest them both, Alvin!" Hellerman spat.

Jessup took a step back, looked at his boss, and then back at Zachary, as if to say, *You've got thirty seconds to convince me.*

"Keep going," Palmer said, surprising everyone.

"Then, after Ballantine captured me at Lake Moncrief, I heard him say that Hellerman was to give the backup launch code if things went badly tonight."

“Launch code? What else could there be to launch?” Palmer asked. “We got all the UAVs and destroyed the Queen Bee. We confirmed that an hour ago.”

“Something about a ground invasion,” Zachary said. “I remember hearing at Moncrief that there is a ground invasion to follow the Predator attacks.”

“Give me a break,” Hellerman said. “Are you going to listen to these nut cases? For all we know, they’re the ones who are in on this thing.”

Hellerman dramatically paused a second, holding his hand up as if he were remembering something.

“Wait a minute. I caught Jeremiah nosing around in my basement earlier today.”

Jeremiah’s eyes popped wide, “Say what?”

“Alvin, check Jeremiah’s pockets.”

Jessup stepped toward Jeremiah and said, “Empty your pockets carefully.”

Jeremiah glared at him, pulling a set of keys from his right hip pocket.

“Haven’t seen those in days,” Hellerman said. “Just what the hell have you been up to, commander?”

Jeremiah, an African American in a white man’s mansion being framed for something he didn’t do. At least he could have been original, Jeremiah thought.

“Easy target, huh, veep?” Jeremiah said. “Black dude and all.”

Jeremiah paused, and pulled a small cell phone from his pocket.

“Watch it,” Jessup said.

“I’m not as stupid as I look,” Jeremiah replied.

“Hands out,” Jessup said as he began placing the handcuffs on Jeremiah. Jessup escorted Jeremiah to the side.

Jeremiah? Matt’s mind spun. Jeremiah was a mid-level action officer and a good guy at that. There was no way he could be the plant. Didn’t make sense. A diversion.

“Sir, I’ve got a tape right here,” Matt said to Palmer. “This proves what Zachary just said. This tape is a conversation between Hellerman and Sandford where he tells her to inform Hussein that it’s okay to invade Kuwait.”

“I got a tape, too,” Jeremiah shouted, his head a foot taller than all the others in the room. “Right here.” He shook his Blackberry.

Jessup’s head was cycling between Jeremiah and Matt now. Hellerman looked at Matt’s hand and thought there was a fifty-fifty chance that the tape was actually the conversation he had with Sandford. Then he looked at Jeremiah and figured the Navy man wasn’t such a dumb ass after all. To counter Jeremiah, he decided to call Garrett’s bluff.

Chess moves.

“I happen to have a tape player right over there,” Hellerman said to Matt. Hellerman walked over to a desk and pulled the small Sony from the drawer. “Alvin, lock up Jeremiah in the third cabin. Dave, you can be the honest broker here.”

Palmer looked at Hellerman and then back at Matt and Zachary. He walked over, grabbed the tape from Matt, then took the tape player from the vice president. He placed the tape in the cassette window and pressed play.

“Sir, we’ve got something coming in on the airwaves from Panama,” Ralph Smithers said. “This sounds pretty important.”

Palmer pressed stop and then turned to Smithers.

“We’ve got a call going out to about fifteen different places around the country to stand by for commencement of immediate offensive operations.”

Smithers removed his headset and stood from his chair in the middle of the circled gathering, feeling important for having contributed that significant piece of information. “The speaker said they were waiting on the authorization to go.”

Palmer looked at Zachary and then back at Matt.

Matt said, “Why don’t you go check the basement of the mansion? I think you might be able to speak directly to his friend in Panama. And Zeke has nothing to do with that.”

Palmer started the tape, and Hellerman’s voice was clear.

As everyone was focused on the tape and Jessup was guarding Jeremiah, Hellerman shot through the side door toward the mansion.

Matt dashed away from the operations group, chasing Hellerman. He was fueled by his anger at Hellerman’s manipulation. Only Lantini’s artful charade last year compared to Hellerman’s nefarious orchestrations. As that thought cycled through his mind, something caught, like a gear, then slipped away. Lantini. Hellerman. Lantini. Hellerman.

What was it?

"It's over, Hellerman. You've got to give the order to stand down!" Matt shouted. He sprinted across the flagstone path, followed Hellerman up the steps of the mansion, and they crashed through the front door nearly simultaneously. Hellerman escaped Matt's grasp and shot down the stairs into the basement, closing the door behind him.

Matt used his momentum, size, and strength to break through the weak hasp and enter Hellerman's small command and control cell.

"So this is it?" Matt said, breathing heavily. He stared at Hellerman, who was holding a cell phone. The gear released. Matt had figured it out.

"This country has gone to hell, Garrett, and no one cares anymore! But I care! I'm bringing us back from the brink of decline!"

"You're a sick bastard."

Hellerman produced a crazed, wicked smile, like a jack-o-lantern, as if to acknowledge Matt's discovery. He held a small satellite phone in his hand as Matt walked closer and closer.

"Give them the order to stand down, Hellerman, or I'll kill you myself."

"You don't scare me, Garrett. What's another twenty or thirty thousand? That's what it will take to make us serious about this, don't you see? Our soldiers are dying, and until civilians start dying, no one will care. You and I both agree that this country is going down the drain. Rap music, drugs, money, credit cards, SUVs, and instant gratification. It's all about people getting more and more stuff without ever having to work for it. You have to sacrifice every so often or you lose sight of what's important."

"You see the negative. I see the positive," Matt argued, now standing a few inches from Hellerman. "You worry about this generation? News flash: worry about something else. We're going to be okay."

"You're blind, Garrett. You don't understand my genius. Madison's genius. The roots of liberty must be nourished with the blood of the free!" Hellerman spat.

"Madison, I agree, was a genius, but don't place yourself in his category. Madison fought tyranny and oppression. You're fighting a phantom theory. It's over, Hellerman. Now tell me the code word to call it off."

Matt watched Hellerman, who began to shake, his eyes lifting to the white board on the wall. Matt looked at the white board and saw two words.

Cape Canaveral had a small check mark next to it and *Octagon* had a small *X* next to it. Matt turned back to look at Hellerman, but instead found the unwelcome sight of a Ruger pistol staring him in the face.

"It's your turn to die, Garrett, and my turn to save this country."

A shot bellowed loudly in the small cavern of the basement. Matt flinched, but as the smoke cleared, he saw Hellerman stumbling back against the wall. He looked over his shoulder at the angry face of Alvin Jessup, his right hand holding a Smith and Wesson Magnum, smoke wafting from its bore.

The Ruger dropped from Hellerman's hand, and he lifted the phone to his ear. His thumb pressed the send button and Matt could hear Hellerman's voice trying to make a *K* sound, trying to say a word.

"Damn it, he's giving the go-ahead order!" Matt snatched the phone from Hellerman's weakened hand.

"'Octagon, octagon. I say again, octagon," Matt said clearly into the phone. He heard mechanical voice come back at him, chuckling.

"Garrett, you just killed Ronnie Wood," the voice said.

Matt listened to the confirmation of his instinct. The vice president was Ronnie Wood, the co-conspirator who led the Rolling Stones and perhaps was complicit in the 9/11 conspiracy. And who was this?

"Now leave me alone. You'll never find me anyway."

"Lantini?"

"By the way, all these yahoos are toast. But you've got some fighting left to do in the States. Not my problem. My conscience is clear. Goodbye."

"Wait, Lantini. If you're not Ronnie Wood, then why the hell did you run?"

"Figure it out, genius. We were a viper's nest, each with enough to destroy the other. The best option for me to stay alive, which I intend to do, was to hide."

This time Matt heard the audible click of the disconnecting phone line.

He looked over at Alvin Jessup, who was slumped against the wall, his head hanging low.

"I just killed the man I was supposed to protect," Jessup said, his voice hoarse.

"You did the right thing. He's killed a lot of people, and I suspect you're more bothered by that right now than the fact that your friend is dead. Besides, if what Lantini says is true, Hellerman's the real Ronnie Wood."

"Pretty easy to blame it on a dead man," Jessup said, shaking.

Palmer came running down the steps and surveyed the scene. "What happened?"

"Sir, the bottom line is that we need to send special ops down to the grid coordinate in Panama that Ralph Smithers mentioned," Matt said. "Have some one raid the place where these guys planned this operation. Lantini was there. Says he killed them all. Might be good to go get him, too."

"Lantini?"

"Yeah. He was involved in this somehow. Just talked to him. Says Hellerman was Ronnie Wood. Makes sense."

Palmer stared at Jessup and then Matt.

Matt waited a moment, and when the bureaucrat had nothing to say, he patted Alvin Jessup on the shoulder and walked up the steps to find his brother and check on Peyton.

As he exited the vice president's mansion, he walked down the marble flagstaff to the servant's quarters that doubled as a medical clinic. He walked in and saw Zachary being treated for his wounds.

"Thanks, man," he said, looking up.

"You okay?"

"I'll live. Got some memory back too."

"How'd you get that scar?" Matt smirked.

Zach rubbed his chin where the pellet from Matt's shotgun had nicked him. He looked up with his trademark grin and said, "War injury, brother."

"Thought so."

The two brothers hugged and Matt turned to the doctor as they broke the embrace.

"Where's Peyton?"

"Peyton?"

"Peyton, the redhead Jock brought over here."

Doc Bell shrugged. "I know Peyton, but never saw her or Jock."

Matt stared at Zach, who shook his head.

"Ah, man."

"Gotta find this Jock dude," Zach said.

"If he's alive."

"There's that."

"Or he could be part of it."

Matt walked over to the window and stared into the darkness. How bad had she really been hurt? What was her motive?

Then he had a thought.

Lantini.

EPILOGUE

The white rubber tires created a low hum as they spun in opposite directions, ready to fire a fastball at Zachary. Matt watched his older brother from the deck as he held a cold beer bottle in his right hand. His left arm had been properly set in a sling by a stern doctor.

Matt continued to watch Zachary take solid cuts at the pitching machine, though he had tuned down the pitch speed to eighty miles an hour.

The tires slowed with a whine as Matt watched Zach punch the red button and flip the bat into the net. The machine spit a final ball out of the decelerating tires. The ball only made it about halfway to the plate and then rolled into the back net, causing Zach to look casually over his shoulder as he stepped from the netting.

"Beer?" Matt asked.

"That's a stupid question."

"Two left in the cooler," Matt said, but Zach was already twisting off the top of a Budweiser.

"Thanks." Then, "Blake okay?"

"He's fine, other than his pride. He told me that he had bent down to secure the weapons in the duffel, and when he stood up, Peyton was over the edge and climbing the ship ladder like Spiderman."

"Could have shot her," Zachary said.

Matt smirked. "Then who would have flown the plane?"

"Good point. Any clues on her whereabouts?"

"I'm thinking she's gone south. With Lantini. Either that or she was Hellerman's spy and bolted to save her ass."

Zach took a sip of his beer and pondered the notion.

"Or she was boning Jock Evans," Zach said with his characteristic frankness.

"There's that."

They remained silent a moment.

"Gotta watch that machine. Tires catch a thread sometimes," Zach said, staring into the backyard at the batting cage.

"Roger."

"We both got thrown curve balls if you think about it." Zach said.

"I've thought about it," Matt said. "Somehow we got out of the inning."

The two continued to talk in baseball analogies.

"We're okay, you know. A few hit by pitches, but we're solid again, Matt."

"Getting there, anyway."

"Sometimes I think of all these weasels throwing fastballs, junk, sliders, whatever at us, and they're our own guys, you know?"

"That's what makes it so hard."

"Ever think Hellerman was onto something?"

Tricky subject, Matt thought to himself. The man had highlighted the nation's complacency as a threat equal to Islamic extremism. But to attack ourselves to prove the point was over the top, to say the least.

"This whole stagnant spirit thing, he was probably right about that. But entirely dicked up in his approach to dealing with the problem," Matt finally concluded.

"How would you have approached the issue?" Zach asked, a bit of challenge in his voice.

"Not sure, man. I mean, there are only a few, less than one percent, of us who are fighting these wars. So that's ninety nine percent who don't feel the sacrifice, the cost of liberty. How can you know the value of something if you don't fully understand its cost?"

"Right about that. Maybe a draft or something like that to get everyone's attention. Maybe he did the only thing he felt like he could do," Zach said.

After a brief silence, Matt said, "And we did what we could do."

Matt turned slowly and leaned against the railing of the deck. They remained silent for quite some time before Matt asked, changing the subject, "Have you talked to Amanda?"

He noticed a cloud drift across Zach's eyes at the mention of his estranged daughter. "She still thinks I'm dead," Zach said before taking a long pull on his beer. "Probably won't be too happy to learn I'm alive."

"Sensitive topic. I shouldn't have raised it."

Zach stared at Matt for a moment before saying, "No, you're right. I've got to deal with it. Just so much pain for her . . . and me. I've only now started remembering . . . how much I miss her . . . and love her."

"She loves you, too, Zach. Don't sell yourself short on that one."

Zach looked at his younger brother. "Thanks. Maybe I can pull it back together somehow. Maybe Riley can help."

"That's a thought," Matt said. Riley Dwyer was Zachary's former lover. A psychiatrist in Atlanta, she had become a recluse since Zach's supposed death. It seemed Zachary's rebirth would offer new opportunities.

They fell silent again until they heard a car door shut in the driveway.

"Expecting company?" Zach asked.

Before he could answer, Colonel Jack Rampert walked into the back yard and up the steps of the deck. He was wearing his Class A Army green uniform, medals crawling over his shoulder and making him look like a Spanish dictator.

"Colonel." Matt nodded. "Beer?"

"For a smart man, you sure ask some dumb questions," Rampert replied as he twisted off the cap of the Budweiser Zach had retrieved for him. He took a quick sip and then said, "Seems that Meredith's ballsy move to steal Hellerman's hard drive paid off. We found it in the laptop of some wire-head named Jacob Olney who was killed with Meredith. The killer took Olney's PC with a bunch of Photoshop bullshit on it. Hellerman's had the attack plan and years of conspiratorial data. All these surgical actions around the United States and Central America you've been hearing about the last week or so, they've been driven by the intel we got off that hard drive."

The two brothers stared at Rampert in stunned disbelief.

"Meredith did well," Matt whispered, looking away.

"That's not why I came here, though," Rampert said, leaning against the deck rail. "Zach, I've gotten you a battlefield promotion to colonel given your basic entry date. I've also gotten you assigned to my command at Fort Bragg."

A breeze shot through the pine thicket in Matt's back yard, pushing across the batting cage net.

"You report for duty Monday."

Follow Matt and Zach Garrett in book three of the Threat Series,
HIDDEN THREAT

HIDDEN THREAT

Zachary Garrett makes a thrilling return in *Hidden Threat* with a promotion to colonel and a second chance to kill al Qaeda senior leadership. But Zachary's mission takes a deadly turn as his team plows into a fierce ambush in the Hindu Kush Mountains.

News of the esteemed colonel's death devastates the Special Forces community, yet Zachary's daughter, Amanda, is unmoved when the Army casualty assistance team appears on her doorstep. Estranged from her father, Amanda only responds to the assistance team when they mention the $500,000 life insurance payout. But there's a catch: Amanda must meet with revered psychiatrist Riley Dwyer, who has her own ties to Amanda's father.

Eager to collect her payout, Amanda reports to her first sessions with Riley and begins a mind bending journey that strips away the façade of her life. Meanwhile, new clues regarding Zachary's fate surface when his brother, Matt, and Major General Jack Rampert's team embark on a mission of revenge into forbidden Pakistan territory.

A.J. Tata's mastery of suspense keeps the reader guessing as Amanda and Matt begin a rapid-fire journey to discover the truth about Zachary in *Hidden Threat.*

Please enjoy a sample for another Variance militaristic thriller from the mind of #1 international bestseller, Steven Savile

THEN

The Testimony of Menahem Ben Jair

1

PIECES OF HATE

One garden had a serpent, the other had him.

There was a fractured beauty to it; a curious symmetry. The serpent had goaded that first betrayal with honeyed words, the forbidden fruit bitten, and the original sin on the lips of the first weak man. His own betrayal had been acted out from behind a mask of love, again on the lips, and sealed with a kiss. Both betrayals were made all the more ugly by the beauty of their surroundings. That was the agony of the garden.

Iscariot felt the weight of silver in his hand.

It was so much heavier than a few coins ought to be. But then they were more than a few coins now, weren't they? They were a life bought with silver. They were his guilt. He closed his hand around the battered leather pouch, making a fist. How much was a life worth? Really? He had thought about it a lot in the hours since the kiss. Was it the weight of the coins that bought it? The handful of iron nails driven into the wooden cross that ended it? Or the meat left to feed the carrion birds? All of these? None of them? He wanted to believe it was something more spiritual, more honest: the impact that life had on those around it, the sum of the good and the bad, deeds and thoughts.

"Take them, please," he held out the pouch for the farmer to take. "It's five times what the land's worth. More."

"I don't want your blood money, traitor," the man hawked and spat at the dirt between his feet. "Now go."

"Where can I go? I am alone."

"Anywhere away from this place. Somewhere people don't know you. If I was you, I'd go back to the temple and try to buy my soul back."

The man turned his back on him and walked away, leaving Iscariot alone in the field. "If that didn't work," he called without turning back, "I'd throw myself on God's mercy."

Iscariot followed the direction of the man's gaze to the field's single blackened tree. Lightning had struck it years ago, cleaving it down the middle. Its wooden guts were rotted through but a single hangman's branch still reached out, beckoning to him against the dusk sky.

He hurled the pouch at the mocking tree. One of the seams split as it hit the ground, scattering the coins across the parched dirt. A moment later he was on his knees, scrambling after them, tears of loss streaming down his face. Loss, not for the man he had betrayed, but for the man he had been and the man he could have been. He lay there as the sun failed, wishing the sun would sear away his flesh and char his bones but dawn came and he was still alive.

Under the anvil of the sun, he stumbled back through gates of Jerusalem, and wandered the streets for hours. His body's screams were sweated out in the heat. There was no forgiveness in the air. No one would look at him, but he couldn't bear to look at his shadow as it stretched out in front of him, so why should they want to look at him? He deserved their hate. He shielded his eyes and looked up toward the crucifixion hill. He thought he could see the shadow of the cross, black against the grass. The soldiers had taken the bodies down hours before. The only shadows up there now were ghosts.

At the temple they mocked him as he pleaded with the Pharisees to take back the silver in exchange for his confession and absolution.

"Live with what you have done, Judas, son of Kerioth. With this one deed you have ensured your legacy. Your name will live on: Judas the betrayer, Judas the coward. The money is yours, Iscariot, your burden. You cannot buy back the innocence of your soul, and it is not as though you have not killed before. Now go, the sight of you sickens us," the Pharisee said, sweeping his arm out to encompass the entire congregation gathered in prayer. He hit Iscariot's hand, scattering the silver he clutched across the stone floor. Judas fell to his knees, as though groveling at the feet of the holy man. Head down, he collected the scattered coins. The holy man kicked him away scornfully. "Take your blood money and be gone, traitor."

Iscariot struggled to his feet and stumbled toward the door.

On the road to Gethsemane he saw the familiar figure of Mary seated by the wayside. He wanted to run to her, to fall at her feet and beg for her forgiveness. She had lost so much more than the rest of them. She looked up, saw him, and smiled sadly. Her smile stopped him dead. He felt the weight of the coins in his hand. Suddenly they were as heavy as love and twice as cold. She stood and reached out for him. He had never loved her more than he did in that moment. He had gone against so much of his friend's teachings, but never more so than in coveting the woman he loved. He ran into her arms and held her, huge raking sobs shuddering through him. He couldn't cry. After all of those tears he had shed he was empty. "I am sorry. I am so sorry."

She hushed him, gentling her fingers through his hair. "They are looking for you. Matthew has whipped them up into a rage. He hates you. He always has and now he has an excuse for it. They are out of their minds with grief and loss, Judas. You can't stay here or they will kill you for what you have done. You have to go."

"There's nowhere left to go, Mary, he's seen to that. This is his revenge," he laughed bitterly at that. "I should never . . . I am sorry. It wasn't meant to end like this. All of this because, fool that I am, I couldn't help but love you."

"Our god is a jealous god," she said. She sounded utterly spent. That emptiness in her voice cut deeper than any words could have. She was crying but there was no strength to her tears. "Please, go."

"I can't," he said, and he knew that it was true. He needed to be found. He needed to feel their stones hit, he needed their anger to break his bones. He was finished with this life. The farmer was right, there was only God's mercy left to him. But what kind of mercy was that? What mercy did a suicide have with the gates to the Kingdom closed to him? Judas' mind was plagued with doubts and had been for days. His friend had known he would not be able to live with this blood on his hands, yet still he had begged for this betrayal. So perhaps this stoning was actually one final mercy?

"Please."

"Let them come. I will face them and die with what little dignity is left to me."

She wiped away the tears. "Please. If not for me, then for our son," she took his hand and placed it flat against the gentle swell of her belly.

"Our son," he repeated, falling to his knees before her. He kissed her hands and then her belly, crushing his face up against the coarse cloth of her dress. The Pharisee's words rang in his head: Judas the Betrayer. What greater betrayal could there be? He pressed the torn leather pouch into her hands. "Please, take them, for the boy, for you."

He saw the life he had lost reflected in Mary's eyes. He knew she loved him, and he knew love was not enough. He couldn't tell her how alone he felt at that moment.

She turned her back on him.

He left her, walking the long road to death. He had time to think, time to remember the promise he had made, and time to regret it. It was a walk filled with last things; he watched the sun sink down below the trees; he felt the wind in his face; he tasted the arid air on his tongue; he pulled off his robe and walked naked into the garden.

They were waiting for him.

He didn't shy away from the hurt and hatred in their eyes. He did not try to justify himself. He stood naked before them.

"You killed him," Matthew said, damning him. They were the last words Judas Iscariot heard. He held a rope in his hands. It was fashioned into a noose.

He welcomed the first stone from James as it struck his temple. He didn't flinch. He didn't feel it. Nor did he feel the second from Luke, or the third cast by John. The stones hit, one after another, each one thrown harder than the last until they drove Iscariot to his knees. All he felt was the agony of the garden. Matthew came forward with the rope and hooked it around Judas' neck.

Judas wept.

NOW

2

BURN WITH ME

It was two minutes to three when the woman walked into Trafalgar Square.

Dressed in jeans and a loose-fitting yellow tee-shirt she looked like every other summer tourist come to pay homage to Landseer's brooding lions. There was a smiley face plastered across her chest. The grin was stretched out of shape by the teardrop swell of her breasts. Only it wasn't summer. The yellow tee-shirt set her apart from the maddening crowd because everyone else was wrapped up against the spring chill with scarves and gloves woolen hats.

She stood still, a single spot of calm amid the hectic hustle of London. She uncapped the plastic bottle she held and emptied it over her head and shoulders, working the syrupy liquid in to her scalp. In less than a minute her long blonde hair was tangled and thick with grease as though it hadn't been washed in months. She smelled like the thick traffic fumes and fog of pollution that choked the city.

Pigeons landed around the feet of the man beside her as he scattered chunks of bread across the paving stones. He looked up and smiled at her. He had a gentle face. A kind smile. She wondered who loved him. Someone had to. He had the contentment of a loved man. And for a moment she pitied whoever he was about to leave behind.

Around her the tourists divided into groups: those out in search of culture headed toward the National Portrait Gallery, the thirsty ducked into the café on the corner, the royalists crossed over the road and disappeared beneath Admiralty Arch onto Whitehall, the hungry headed for Chandos Place and Covent Garden's trendy eateries and those starved of entertainment wandered up St Martin's Lane towards Leicester Square or Soho, depending upon their definition of entertainment. Businessmen in their off-the-rack suits marched in step like penguins, umbrella tips and blakeys and segs tapping out the rhythm of the day's enterprise. Red buses crawled down Cockspur Street and around the corner toward The Strand and Charring Cross. The city was alive.

A young girl in bright red duffel coat ran toward her, giggling and flapping her arms to startle the feeding birds into flight. When she was right in the middle of them the pigeons exploded upwards in a madness of feathers. The girl doubled up in laughter, her delighted shrieks chasing the pigeons up into the sky. Her enjoyment was infectious. The man rummaged in his plastic bag for another slice of white bread to tear up. The woman couldn't help but smile. She had chosen the yellow tee-shirt because it made her smile. It seemed important to her that today of all days she should smile.

She took the phone from her pocket and made the call.

"News desk," the voice on the other end was too perky for its own good. That would change in less than a minute when the screaming began.

"There is a plague coming," she said calmly. "For forty days and forty nights death shall savage the streets. Those steeped in sin shall burn. The dying begins now."

"Who is this? Who am I talking to?"

"I don't need to tell you my name. Before the day is through you will know everything there is to know about me apart from one important detail."

"And what's that?"

"Why I did it."

She ruffled the young girl's hair as she scattered another cluster of pigeons and burst into fits of giggles. The girl stopped, turned and looked up at the woman. "You smell funny."

The women reached into her pocket for her lighter. She thumbed the wheel, grating it against the flint, and touched the naked flame to her hair. She dropped the phone and stumbled forward as the fire engulfed her.

All around her the city screamed.

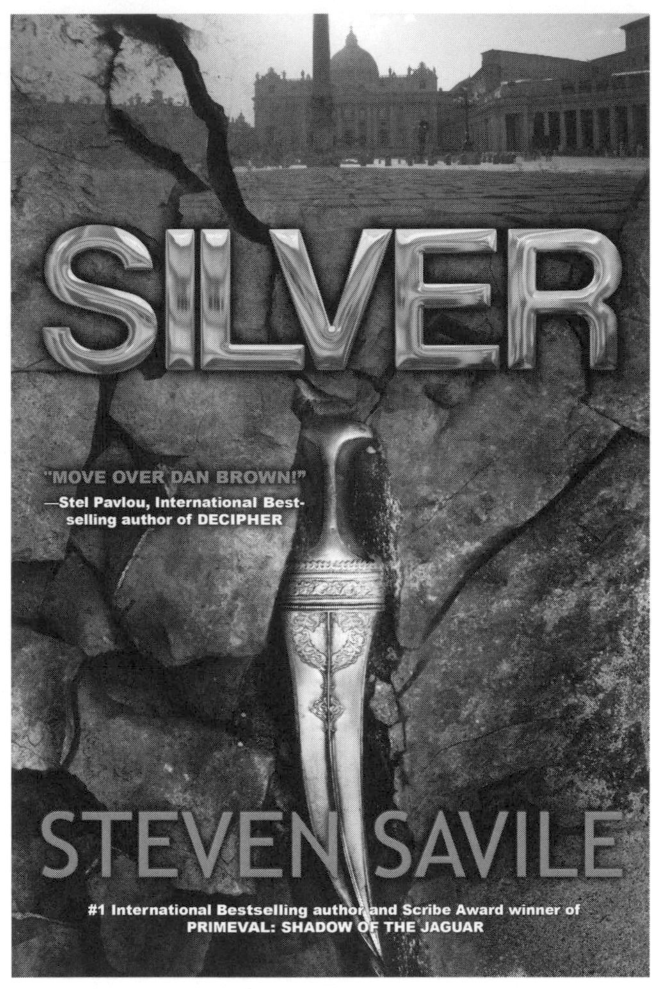

"SILVER is a wild combination of Indiana Jones, The Da Vinci Code, and The Omen. Read this book...before the world ends."
-- Kevin J Anderson, international bestselling author of THE SAGA OF SEVEN SUNS and co-author of PAUL OF DUNE

"Silver grabs you by the throat and doesn't let go. Silver is pure gold.
-- Debbie Viguie, co-author of the NY Times bestselling WICKED series

AVAILABLE JANUARY 19, 2010